I0610997

MY SOUL'S GUARDIAN

MY SOUL'S GUARDIAN

TO HEAL HER MIND, SHE HAD TO SEARCH HER SOUL

My Soul's Guardian
To heal her mind, she had to search her soul

Published by Rebel Press
Austin, TX
www.RebelPress.com

ISBN: 978-1-64339-934-8

Printed in the United States of America

DEDICATION

This book is dedicated to the men, women, and animals of our Armed Forces.

GOD BLESS AMERICA

FOREWORD

In this, her first novel, C.C. Mack distinguishes herself as a compelling and intelligent author.

The first obligation of a first-rate novelist is to tell an engaging *story*. Nothing else in the writing can replace the story. And Mack does not fail to do so. Her timing and pacing are often exquisite. She is masterful at bringing a situation to a heightened stage, holding us there until we eagerly turn to the following chapter to see what happens next to the characters. Those main characters are largely believable, three-dimensional, flesh-and-blood personages, each of which displays a gamut of appropriate emotions in reaction to mundane events, as well as those horrifying and ecstatic. The reader soon begins to care truly about these flawed, compassionate, sometimes angry and short-sighted and anguished characters, particularly Captain Caroline McKenzie, whose arduous inner journey parallels her outer one and is the backbone of the book.

It is one thing for Caroline to survive in her outer journey with the known and unknown perils that can literally explode near or under her in a war like that in Iraq, which provides the background *and* foreground for this novel's opening scenes. But for that outer journey, Caroline has at least the training, not only of a combat nurse, but also of a combatant ready to fight off the silent, furtive shapes that appear and disappear around and sometimes, unfortunately, within the complex of the combat hospital. But she is a complete novice at negotiating the inner landscape of psychic landmines compellingly laid out for her in part by the outer one.

Yet, as indicated by Mack's dedication of the book to our nation's servicemen and women, one of her purposes in this novel, in addition to composing a captivating story, is helping veterans, especially combat veterans, seek the help they need to cope with the inner devastations of war, sometimes more horrendous than the physical impairments. As a soldier returning from Vietnam back in 1970, I know how horribly difficult it was for my comrades to get past the stigma heaped on them, not only by those who could not distinguish the war from the warrior, but also by themselves, by their warrior code of stuffing the inner pain that they "should" get over by themselves. Since I had not suffered combat, I didn't think I needed any therapy, even though I was wracked by dreams for a year about being forced back to 'Nam, even though I found myself immediately crouching down at the sound of a chopper, even though I got sick to my stomach at the stench of burning garbage, and even though I was generally depressed enough to cause my then wife to worry that I might be teetering at the roof's edge of our apartment building when she came home from work. And the broken, bloodless, gouged body of a young soldier whom I had helped carry on a stretcher from a helicopter to the makeshift morgue haunted me for years. But, no, I didn't need therapy… twenty-six years later in a two-day program featuring psychodrama, among other therapeutic processes, my soul finally came home. I brought closure to myself after holding, with other participants, a funeral for that young soldier; I was profoundly startled by the enormity of my previously suppressed grief.

Such grief, quite complicated in her case, is what stalks Caroline. While she initially embodies that repressive code—despite the debilitating flashbacks that almost cost her her sanity and her job as a stateside nurse— the novel methodically traces Caroline's slow and spasmodic, two-steps-forward-one-step-back approach to her healing through therapy. With ambivalent support from her dearest friends and battling the anticipated stigma of being labelled crazy, she finally in desperation does her homework, researching the field of psychotherapeutic methods so alien to her.

Although outlining this process for readers, especially those who are skeptical soldiers or their perhaps equally doubtful loved ones, is a great service for such readers, Mack goes further by introducing what is even more alien to many—the use of hypnosis to heal the profound wounds of war. Mack has done her research in presenting the character of a wholly credible, compassionate, professional therapist, Dr. Perrin, who painstakingly introduces the intricacies of hypnotherapy to Caroline. Even though there are many induction protocols available, as a hypnotherapist myself, I could appreciate the doctor's practice choice and also his further hypnotic methods in working with Caroline's trauma. It is not long before he facilitates the beginning of the healing of her flashbacks and provides grounding exercises to recover from their debilitating effects.

But then there are other kinds of flashbacks and dreams haunting Caroline, phenomena which require Dr. Perrin to go further into territory alien to Caroline's paradigm of consciousness and identity: the arena of past lives. After ascertaining that nothing in her current life can adequately account for all of her inner sufferings, he very carefully discloses to her information about the subject, monitoring her for what Harvard psychiatrist, John Mack, calls "ontological shock," the distress that often emerges when a reliable, supposedly self-evident worldview is suddenly seen as radically incomplete or even wrong. As she absorbs what Dr. Perrin is disclosing to her, Caroline awakens to the fact that she has had at least two past lives. And these past lives, the remembrance of which is triggered by something in Caroline's current life, prove to have a major bearing on what is now going on with her, way beyond the contributions of her experience in war.

While the reality of past lives has been debated, it is difficult for someone who has actually experienced one to be very doubtful because of its vividness and power to provoke deep emotion and insight. Indeed, most of the population of the world believes in reincarnation; and America is slowly waking up to the truth that we live again and again. What also has been debated is the notion of Karma, the belief that what we do in a past life inexorably affects what we do and feel in the current incarnation. As a concept that is based on cause-and-effect, and therefore on time, Karma ably serves the purpose of bringing people to an initial awareness that their choices, whenever they are made, *do count* and help create the fabric of their lives—*we are responsible for our choices*. However, that common notion of Karma does not entirely survive the fact, as most consciousness explorers including quantum physicists believe, that ultimately there is no time; therefore, all lives—past, present and future—exist in a Spacious Present, where time-bound Karma cannot exist. So, deeds in one life, particularly a so-called past life, do not *automatically* and *inescapably* affect one's official, current life, that is, unless the official life persona *agrees, chooses*, often in a contract with others, to be so affected in order to learn more about an issue shared among a number of lives. Nevertheless, being responsible for our choices is endemic to both perspectives.

Mack's demonstrated ability to manage the presentation of Caroline's multiple and intertwining lives/personae is remarkable to observe. What is also remarkable in Mack's work is the evocation of a new paradigm of psychological/spiritual healing: the expansion of one's sense of identity. In my book, *Ending the Endless Conflict: Healing Narratives from Past-Life Regressions to the Civil War,* I present case studies of 17 individuals whom I regressed to their lives during that horrendous Conflict. In every case, whether the individual lived then or now, the psychological and spiritual pain ultimately arose from the individual's constricted, often one-dimensional sense of identity based on limiting beliefs about the self, others and the world. Healing could come only when the individual developed a sense of a more complex identity that embraced new resources enabling him or her to get out of the stuck places. Especially in the case of the individual living now, each person, by being in touch with a past-life self, expanded the sense of who he or she really is, giving each also new perspectives on others and the nature of the world.

Caroline's nursing duties hopefully restored to each injured combatant as much as possible of what he or she had been. But her adventures in consciousness gave her a new tool, one which did not merely restore what had been, but, rather, expanded the individual to embrace much more of who he or she really is. While Caroline had to deal with a major, physical alteration at the end of the novel, she was prepared for it because she had already experienced, psychologically and spiritually, what it means to transform, to enlarge one's identity.

I say to each Reader, get ready to embark on a journey that could wonderfully alter your own life!

—Joseph Mancini, Jr., Ph.D., CCHt., M.S.O.D., M.S.W.
Frederick, Maryland
August 30, 2018

CONTENTS

MY SOUL'S GUARDIAN

CHAPTER ONE

CASEVAC IRAQ

Iraq
May 2008

Watching the sky light up is an amazing display. Whether it is the fourth of July, a thunderstorm, or a celestial star burning out as it dashes across the sky, one's eyes cannot be diverted. Especially if it could be the last thing you ever see.

The spectacle tonight for my viewing: ground-to-air missiles exploding their target in the night. Immobilized by the makeshift cervical collar, I watch the bright streak directly above me arc across the darkened sky, missing its mark. This is a good thing considering I am being loaded onto another imminent target. Sounds of the Apache gunships circling above us, like vultures on the hunt, are ironically deafening. The attack helicopter is providing cover for CASEVAC—or, in civilian terms, "casualty extraction." I am one of those casualties. Contributing to the noise are snipers from my troop rendering fire shield, while under fire.

Irony abounds in this corner of hell on earth. I am in desert hell, yet I am freezing. As a registered nurse I should recognize signs of shock, but as I said, irony abounds.

My face is momentarily warmed by the downdraft of the Chinook's engines as I am loaded onto the air ambulance. The crew chief directs the medics on where to stow my body. The smell of diesel fuel, rocket fuel, adrenaline, and fear bombard my airway, which I hear is open and clear. This bit of good news comes from our battalion medic, Spencer, as he calls out a brief report on the causalities to the medics on board the extraction helicopter. The fact that my airway is open and clear is another case of irony. I've had sand and dust packed in every orifice since I deployed here seven months ago. Before exiting the helicopter that is taking me to Balad Air Base, Spencer squeezes my hand, smiles at me and says, "You're going home, Captain McKenzie."

Home—now that's irony for you. The place I couldn't wait to leave five years ago is now my dream destination. Hell, it is everyone's dream destination that is stationed in this desolate country. I close my eyes, envisioning the mountains of North Carolina, the smell and taste of Thanksgiving dinner, and the feel of my father's protective embrace. If I block everything else out, I can almost hear my mother from the kitchen, singing church hymns. The same hymns, over and over, out of tune, hummed mostly because she can't remember the words. The same hymns that forced me to wear earphones in my room. What I wouldn't give to hear my mother sing, or hum, one of those hymns right now.

I feel the vibration of the powerful twin engines before I hear them, lifting the bird ambulance into the desert sky. It lulls me to some state of sleepy consciousness, or it could be drugs the medics are pushing in my IV. Either way, my mind decides to flash scenes of my life on the inside of my closed eyelids. If these are the last moments of my life, I can look back and say, I wouldn't have changed a thing—even if I haven't had anyone truly special to share those memories with. I still would have gone to college to become a nurse. I still would have enlisted in the Army right after graduation, and I am also certain I would still be moving back to North Carolina as soon as my four-year enlistment is up—which is, ironically, only one month away. Yes, I can leave this life with no regrets. I told my friends and family how much I love them and what they mean to me before leaving the States. I made a difference in many lives as a nurse, first stateside and now as a combat nurse in Iraq. I always tried to do the right thing and show love at every opportunity. So if Karma exists—and is truly the bitch for which she is notorious—I will not come back as a dung beetle.

I smile inwardly at that thought as bright lights envelope me. I say a prayer for our troops, my family, and my friends. And since my last breath has not yet come, I begin another prayer, "God, this is Caroline again, if it is all right with you, I would like a second chance to remain in this life. Not for me, but for him. I didn't get a chance to say goodbye. I didn't tell him how much he means to me. He will never understand why I left him. Please, God, help me live so I can find him again. Amen."

CHAPTER TWO

BITCH-N-BOOZE

Asheville, North Carolina
October 2010

Caroline, glancing down at her cell phone, sees she has made it in just enough time to not be considered tardy to the "Bitch-N-Booze." This aptly-named, weekly get-together of her and her three best friends includes a lot of booze and a lot of subsequent bitching about their lives. With one last glance in the rearview mirror before exiting her vehicle, Caroline runs her fingers through her hair and checks her face. She notices the bags under her eyes, but the excitement of leaving on vacation in the morning overrides the fatigue felt from working sixty hours at the hospital over the past five days. A weekend get-away with her three best friends is what she needs right now. So why, she wonders, is a melancholy face staring back from the mirror?

Caroline walks the crowded downtown street of Asheville toward the pub. When leaving the military, she decided to try civilian life in Asheville. Where better a place to start than with her high-school chums Meredith and Kelly back in her home state of North Carolina. Caroline had kept in correspondence with Bianca, her college roommate, while Caroline traveled the globe, deployment after deployment. After Caroline's discharge from the military and subsequent move to the Blue Ridge Mountains, Bianca followed shortly after.

Her girlfriends are waiting on her to discuss the vacation agenda she has planned. The friends take turns, each picking a different weekend travel destination each season. The one who picks makes all the plans. This fall is Caroline's turn. She chose the third weekend of October in Fayetteville, West Virginia for many reasons. One, for the serenity of nature. The majestic mountains, surrounding the New River Gorge, will be painted in hues of gold, red, and orange, creating a kaleidoscope of autumn colors. Two, the third weekend is Bridge Day—a weekend festival filled with food, music, and mavericks jumping, rappelling, or zip-lining off the Western Hemisphere's longest single-arch bridge. Three, the rapids flowing wild underneath that bridge are home to whitewater rafting—something Caroline has always wanted to try.

Waiting to cross the busy, tourist-filled street, she pulls a single from her pocket and places it in a street performer's tip jar before crossing at the light. Running a mental list through her mind one more time, Caroline checks each item. Cabin has been rented for the entire weekend, copies of the trail heads they will be hiking are printed, along with itineraries for each of them. Caroline has planned activities on the hour, every hour, including observing base jumpers risk their lives on the New River Gorge Bridge. She can hear her friends now, teasing about vacationing with an Army captain. Everything in order, everything on time. No surprises, no problems. She can't understand how anyone can live in chaos. Though they live like civilians, her three friends are like the sisters she never had.

The four of them are tight as sisters, which means they have no problem voicing their opinions on each other's lives. She loves them dearly but wishes they would leave her alone about her love life, or actually, lack of one. How many times does she have to listen to, "you need a man for the cold winter nights" or "we worry about you being all alone"? Her personal favorite: "you might not be so uptight if you would get laid every once in a while."

Caroline is comically fearful of who they will try to fix her up with this month. A friend of a friend? A co-worker? Hopefully, they have run out of family members so that option should be dwindling. Caroline never saw the need to entangle her life with another's anyway, she cherishes her independence and is used to living on her own.

Caroline considers as she walks the last few steps toward the pub, *What is it about me that attracts co-dependent men who are more toxic than tantalizing? I am a beacon for narcissistic Neanderthals.* At the same time her mind conjures that thought, her melancholy mood resurfaces. A loss deep in her gut accompanies it, one she has felt often but cannot comprehend. She wonders why a man would want to be any part of her crazy, anyway. The nightmares and flashbacks, the long work hours, possible deployment, and the mood swings that sweep through her soul without warning, without explanation, are just the tip of the insanity iceberg.

Approaching the pub, she pushes these thoughts further back in her mind, as she always does, freeing her mind for the mental preparation needed for the "war with the witches" that will be declared any moment. This verbal-volley onslaught will last for the entire weekend while the four of them are together. She straightens her spine, takes a deep breath and enters Gregory's pub.

"We were starting to worry about you," Kelly whines as she steps toward Caroline to give her a hug. "You are almost a minute late." At five feet, three inches tall, Kelly is much shorter than Caroline but is still able to knock her over with her motherly embrace.

"Holy Mother of God, Kelly," Bianca barks as she tears Kelly from her strong hold, "let the poor woman sit down. Greg, pour a strong one for the Captain," Bianca orders as she looks at Caroline. "It looks like you need it."

Bianca is the no-nonsense, ball-busting type that Caroline enjoys being around. This is why they hit it off at once when they met at Duke University their freshman year.

As Greg, the pub owner, delivers her Crown and Diet Coke, Caroline notices everyone is staring at her.

"Billy Wayne Shit-balls, here it comes," she predicts, then chugs the liquid courage she held in her hand.

"Did you have another nightmare last night?" Kelly asks as she lays her hand over Caroline's.

"I just got off a twelve-hour shift, my fifth for the week. I spent every waking hour planning our trip and packing for all of us. Sorry if I do not look as refreshed as the rest of you," Caroline sarcastically apologizes while hiding her face behind the menu. "I need something on my stomach before we start drinking."

"Then take your bra off," Meredith delivers under her breath.

This starts everyone laughing, beginning the barrage of insults between them. Meredith, being extremely slim and self-admittedly jealous of Caroline's ample bosom, continues with the boob jokes. Meredith and Kelly are sisters. That sibling rivalry can go on forever with each other's flaws. Then there is Bianca Barbie-Doll, the stunner of the group. Though Caroline and Bianca are both 5'8", Bianca has model-long legs and flawless bronzed-skin to go with them. They all like to gang up and condemn her.

"Can I ask one more time why we are we going to West Virginia when we live in the fucking mountains?" Bianca's voice punctuates the last two words. "Why can't we go to a tropical beach and relax on white sand or, better yet, on tropical boys?"

"Since we are approaching our thirties, the word 'boys' is creepy. Yet surprisingly enticing all at the same time," Meredith adds while raising her glass in salute.

"I have had my fill of sand for a lifetime," Caroline reminds them.

"I am not talking about desert sand in a war zone," Bianca clarifies. "I am picturing cool, white sand, fruity drinks with umbrellas, and half-naked men around us playing Frisbee. Muscles tightening and glistening in the sun."

"You get to pick the vacation spot next time. I prefer a more 'back to nature' serenity," Caroline states.

"Fine, Pocahontas," Bianca concedes, "but can we at least have one day of relaxation worked into the triathlon you have planned for us?"

Greg delivers their food orders, breaking into the conversation. "Should I warn the authorities in West Virginia the four of you are on your way?"

"This is a low-key vacation. Just us girls mountain biking, hiking, and watching adrenaline junkies BASE jump," Caroline explains.

"I'm surprised you're not jumping," Greg comments.

"Don't give her any ideas," Meredith says as she hands her drink to Greg for a refill. "I'll enjoy the scenery from below the bridge. Not watching all 870 feet of it pass by me in a flash, along with scenes from my life."

As the plans are completed for their trip to the mountains, they are all too shit-faced to drive home. The decision is made to walk through downtown to their favorite coffee house for some much-needed sobering and live music. Stopping at the cross-walk, waiting on the light to change, the four friends discuss their next vacation in the spring. Since it is Bianca's turn to pick, sandy beaches are included. Bianca is describing the weekend cruise as they cross the street. Kelly, noticing Caroline is no longer beside her, stops in the middle of the street turning back to wait on her. Caroline hasn't left the curb and is clinging to the lamp post.

"Guys." Kelly tries to get Meredith's and Bianca's attention. "Guys!"

Bianca stops mid-sentence and turns around to see Kelly running back for Caroline. Bianca grabs Meredith's arm, pulling her back in Caroline's and Kelly's direction.

"What's wrong?" Kelly asks as she cautiously approaches Caroline.

Kelly observes the sweat breaking out on Caroline's face that is now devoid of color. Caroline stares off in the distance, her body as rigid as the post she is leaning against.

"What happened?" Meredith asks as she steps onto the curb.

"Caroline?" Bianca questionably calls her friend's name as she steps in front of Caroline as to redirect her gaze.

Caroline's eyes lock in on Bianca's, pulling her back to the present. Bianca slowly guides their bodies to the ground before Caroline passes out right in front of her.

"Caroline, what is wrong?" Kelly asks as she and Meredith sit on the curb beside them.

Meredith lifts her arm and points. The other three turn to see what Meredith is referring to but it is Bianca that voices out loud the reason for Caroline's sudden panic attack.

"Diesel fumes." Bianca explains in two simple words.

Caroline's three friends understand. The smell of the fumes from the truck on the corner must have triggered Caroline's post-traumatic stress disorder bringing back memories of the ambush in Iraq, causing an intense emotional and physical reaction.

"You are safe with us," Kelly rubs Caroline's arm. "Come back to us Sweety."

Caroline response is timid and fierce at the same time. She turns her head in each direction, looking for the enemy with wild, frightened eyes. What she sees are her three best friends staring back at her. Just as fast as the flashback hit her, it dissipates, leaving Caroline feeling like a complete idiot. She stands quickly and brushes the street from her jeans. The others follow suite, suddenly sobered by the event.

Forcing the flashback to the recesses of her mind, Caroline continues on as if the trauma of war had not crippled her only moments ago. She steps off the curb and continues on as if nothing had happened so the other three, following her lead, precede onto the coffee house without any discussion of the event. Noticing the girls eyeing one another, Caroline is picking up a weird vibe from her friends. She has a sick intuition they all have a secret they aren't sharing. They are undoubtedly trying to decide who will be the one to tell her about this "awesome guy." The man that one of them knows and who she would "really hit it off with."

After seating themselves at their favorite table in the coffee house, Caroline can't stand the suspense any longer. "You all do realize you suck at keeping things from me. Each of your faces have guilt and shame all over it, so just spit it out," Caroline urges with less confidence than she portrays.

Meredith nudges Bianca, who shoots her a dirty look.

"Caroline, you know we love you," Kelly breaks in, placing an arm around Caroline's shoulder. "We only want what is best for you."

"Stop right there! Can we please give the Caroline Dating Game a break until after vacation?" Caroline pleads.

Bianca straightens in her chair and looks across the table to Caroline. "There is someone who we think you should see but it is not a fix-up. We are worried about you. We have all talked about this and feel you need to see a professional, someone who can help you work through what we think is post-traumatic stress disorder. PTSD could be why you have the nightmares and flashbacks, why you work so much, and why none of your relationships last."

Caroline looks at her friends, each looking back at her with a concerned expression that melts her heart. Kelly and Meredith mirror one another with their heads slightly turned to one side, their foreheads crinkling with worry lines between imploring eyes. Bianca, emphasizing her concern with pouty lips with just a touch of a frown, wraps her arm around Caroline's shoulder.

They actually think I need professional psychological counseling, Caroline considers then bursts out in laughter. At first she finds this notion so absurd that she can't quit laughing. She then realizes that she alone finds this funny. No one else is sharing in the laughter. She focuses in on each of her friends.

"Listen, I understand you are concerned for me and I appreciate your concern. But come on, guys, seriously, a shrink? Get real. I am not telling a total stranger about my life for him to judge me or my choices," Caroline states, trying to calm her laughter. Then, remembering Meredith has been in counseling for years, Caroline back peddles. "I am sure some people find it helpful to have their lives dissected and sincerely believe in psychotherapy. I do not need my psyche cut open to get to the gooey center. I already know what's in there. I lived it. And besides, you know how I feel about Big Pharma."

Meredith sits back in her chair with a dreamy expression. "I love my time with my psychiatrist. It is the best hour of my week. Where else can you get a man to listen to you for a whole hour without their eyes glazing over or trying to look over your shoulder at the TV?"

"We aren't talking about your sex life, Meredith," Bianca interrupts. "We are talking about working through the horror that is Caroline's mind. And if the guy is trying to watch TV over your shoulder, then you are doing it wrong."

"The horror that is my mind," Caroline says, throwing Bianca's words back at her. "Do all of you feel this way?"

Kelly responds first, trying to de-escalate the situation. "Look, no one is saying anything is wrong with you," emphasizing "you" sympathetically. "And no one is asking you to take medication. We just want you to consider speaking to a professional about your issues."

"My issues?" Caroline mimics Kelly with emphasizing the word "my." "Out of the four of us, I am the sanest. So before you prescribe a treatment plan for me and my issues, you might want to take a look at your own lives. Now, if you will excuse me, I have last-minute items I need to pack because I am going on vacation tomorrow with my three best friends. If you see them, tell them to meet at my place at 0700 hours. I hope they show up." Caroline grabs her purse and turns toward the door.

Everyone is looking at her as she leaves the coffee house in midst of fumes. She couldn't care less what the patrons think about her tirade departure. She is, however, having a hard time wrapping her mind around what her best friends told her. Without looking, she rushes across the street, and is barely missed by an oncoming scooter that tweets his ridiculous sounding horn at her. She flips the scooter driver the bird and turns the corner towards where her car is parked.

Thinking I need a trained specialist to fix me. What do they know anyway? What makes them think they can diagnose PTSD? Caroline could have gone on for hours about their own "issues." That's the thing about being so close—they know everything about one another, good and not-so-good.

"They know me better than anyone else. How can they think I need a shrink?" Caroline says out loud as she dodges other pedestrians on the street.

What if they are right? Caroline's mind speaks back to her.

CHAPTER THREE

BENIGNLY UNBALANCED

People on the street step out of Caroline's way as she walks through downtown. She is obviously a woman on a mission and both the locals and the tourists move aside so she can pass. In her car, Caroline shifts to reverse but slams her foot on the brake, trying to relax before driving off in a fury. Until now, Caroline considered her life full of adventure. Now she is questioning not only her life choices but also her sanity and debating the difference.

What can be so wrong with me that the people who know me best think I am a hot mess? The word "crazy" has been thrown around before by them when describing her life. Caroline thought they meant "busy crazy," not "insanely crazy." Caroline loves her job as an ER nurse, which is why she works long hours and picks up extra shifts. She enjoys volunteering at the shelter. It brings her more happiness being around canines than with humans most of the time. Caroline has served her country in time of war, which gives her great pride. She has had enough excitement in war time. A benign existence now is its own reward.

Caroline considers the word "benign" that her mind used as the adjective for her life. *There is nothing wrong with benign. Benign is what you pray for if you have a tumor.* Caroline tries to think of a more descriptive meaning. Many come to mind, but benign is the most accurate at the moment. Caroline is fully aware the nightmares and occasional flashbacks are PTSD; that is textbook. She doesn't feel like it affects her life though so why see a counselor.

Some far-off thought registers in her brain as she stares at herself in the rearview mirror. At *least they didn't try to fix me up. Wait. They are not trying to fix me up. My best friends have given up on me. They not only think I am unsuitable for dating—they think I am unstable. When did I go from the eligible hot friend to the pathetic loser friend? Oh my God, I am the pathetic loser friend! How could I have not seen this before? Billy Wayne Shit-Balls, I am sitting in my car talking to myself. I am bat-shit crazy.*

Caroline continues to ponder her situation on her drive home. If she was to be honest with herself, she would admit that the nightmares and flashbacks are having severe repercussions in her life. But admitting it meant it was real and that was a reality she couldn't handle.

It wasn't until she saw the looks on all their faces that she realized how everyone else saw her. Alone, disturbed, hiding. She remembers how they looked at her, eyes wide with empathy. She knows that look from many times before—when she tells them about her nightmares or about why it didn't work out with so-and-so. It wasn't until now that she equated their empathy with pity.

Caroline calls Meredith as soon as she gets home, apologizing before Meredith can even say hello.

"I am sorry. I meant none of it. I can't deny the flashbacks concern me. Nor can I deny that I am almost afraid to go to sleep at night knowing sleep equals nightmares. I realize the dreams affect my relationships. I mean, hell, I won't even allow a man to get close enough as to warrant a sexual relationship because he might witness the terror I experience in those dreams if he sleeps over. But jeez, a shrink? You all must really think I am psychologically crippled."

"Don't you want to get to the bottom of the nightmares so they will stop? Don't you want to know the cause of all these weird dreams and feelings you have, or do you think all of that is normal?" Meredith's point hits home.

"All right. I will think about seeing someone for fuck's sake," Caroline promises, "at least to eliminate the nightmares. That would be comforting, or terrifying. I'm not sure yet. Either way, I am not making promises to stick with therapy long-term. I will hear what the therapist has to say in a consultation and then decide. Agree?"

"Agree. And remember, we are here for you. We will help you find the right type of therapy and the right therapist for you."

"There's more than one type of therapy?" Caroline asks, already wishing she wouldn't have agreed to see someone until she had researched this a little more.

"Girl, where have you been?" Meredith exclaims.

"There are hundreds of types of psychotherapy and even more variations in treatment. One type of therapy might be right for one but not right for another."

She makes Caroline promise that after vacation she will research the different therapies to find what is interesting to her. Then, once she discovers the type of therapy that is beneficial, they can whittle down the therapists in the area.

After speaking with Meredith, Caroline feels overwhelmed by the "hundreds" of possibilities Meredith described. Caroline falls into bed and covers her head with her quilt. In less than seven hours everyone will be on her doorstep ready to spend a weekend in a remote mountain cabin. Caroline will be trapped, discussing therapy options for all her crazies.

Why can't a war break out so I can be shipped out to far-off Fuckistany instead of four days with the Bitch Brood. If I don't need a psychiatrist now, I sure the hell will need one after this weekend. Caroline commiserates as she straightens her pillow and turns off the light before her mind explodes and there is nothing left to analyze.

If she knew what her mind was cooking up, she would have never went to sleep.

* * *

Whoosh!

In the desert darkness, sand and dust are flying around and through me like shrapnel. It is all I can see, except my own breath and the others' around me.

The stars are obliterated by brightly-exploded bombs. The sound of machine guns pierce my already heightened nervous system. Enemy snipers aim down on our transport vehicle. I try to join the others as they move past me, crouched low and fully loaded but I am frozen in fear. Muffled by the explosive noises, I hear someone yelling "jump!" over and over again. I look at the others. They are lining up and jumping off the back of our armored personnel truck.

"Jump! Jump!"

I can't jump. Hell, I can't even stand; my legs have no motor response. All I can do is stare upward, searching for the Apache helicopters to save us.

Suddenly, my pack is being pulled upward, hoisting me to my feet.

"Jump! Jump!"

I turn my head toward the command coming from my right side, falling sharp and loud in my ear. That is when I notice a dark form running around the side of the truck. The marine, who is pulling me to my feet, reads the alarmed expression on my face and looks in the same direction. He sees the image too. He lets go of me and swings the Maw Duce .50 caliber machine gun toward that image. I fall to my knees on the floor of the truck. Taking cover, I circle my legs with my arms. The shell casings are pinging all over the sides and back of the truck. My ears ring from the rapid fire. I close my eyes to say a prayer and it hits me. The dark image settles in my frontal cortex for recognition.

"No!" I scream, my voice echoing long and thick into the night. I leap to my feet, launching my entire body on top of the marine firing from the back of the truck.

"What the fuck, Captain?" he yells at me.

"Don't shoot. He's trying to save us."

"And you are going to get us killed! Now jump!" He grabs my pack, throwing me off the back of the truck. The landing knocks the breath from me, jarring my whole body.

Attempting to pull air into her lungs, Caroline wakes, gasping. She fights her mind to catch up to her body. She is alive. It was only a dream; a nightmare, really. The same one that she fights almost weekly. As her lungs fill with needed oxygen, she feels her heart rate slowing. She is safe in her bed though drenched in sweat. She can see the beautiful Blue Ridge Mountains through the glass of the French doors on the opposite wall. Yes, she is safe at home in Asheville. Her mind is slow to reality. Now if only her heart would also realize that it was only a dream. It feels empty and broken and, at the same time, lost in her body, without a purpose anymore.

Caroline's mind forges its way out of the darkness of this repetitive nightmare. Rationalizing her surroundings, she glances at the clock illuminating the 0600 hour. One hour before everyone arrives. Climbing slowly from bed, her body aching, Caroline walks onto her terrace for a full dose of crisp mountain air. She stretches her tightened muscles, breathing deeply. A half hour of palates and meditation is not enough to escape this sense of loss or heal her tethered soul. She forces herself to the shower while trying to convince her mind that it is just the same nightmare. The hot water from the shower feels more like tiny needles pounding on every nerve. She shuts off the water and dresses to rewarm her tensing body.

Caroline has tried to self-analyze the nightmares and the dreams, but there are too many and most of them don't even make sense to her. The nightmares of war wreak havoc in her subconscious while sleeping. The dreams, that are not military related, come in waves; snippets of indescribable visions. These dreams are rarely about anything or anyone in particular but Caroline always senses his presence. The emotions and love for him are so real in her dreams, she wants to continue living in that subconscious world just to be near him. Often, Caroline closes her eyes in an attempt to feel him with her one last time. But she always wakes with the same sense of loss and emptiness, a loneliness dwelling deep inside her. The crazy thing is, she doesn't know who he is.

Caroline descends to the kitchen, to brew a pot of coffee, aware that the nightmares are increasing in frequency. Confusion swarms her in ways she's never known. Lost in thought, she does not hear her friends enter the kitchen.

Looking upon their catatonic friend then back and forth to each other, Kelly decides to step forward to engage Caroline back to this dimension.

"Coffee ready?" Kelly's enquiry is so soft spoken that even Bianca and Meredith almost didn't hear it.

Caroline turns and finds that "look" again on her friend's faces. Realizing she had blanked out for a minute but not wanting her friends to worry, Caroline quickly opens the cabinet, obscuring her face momentarily. Shaking off the vision that had her captivated, she pulls four travel mugs from the shelf, closes the cabinet, and turns to greet her friends with a fake smile.

Bianca grabs a mug and spouts, "There better be some Baileys in the fridge."

"There better be whiskey for mine," grumbles Meredith. "Why else would we be up at this God-forsaken hour."

"I brought homemade muffins." Kelly flounces all cheery faced, holding a plate above her head like the Frisch's Big Boy.

"Dial it down a notch, Rachel Fucking Betty Ray Crocker. Not all of us are morning people," Bianca says, sliding onto the barstool at Caroline's kitchen counter, holding her cup of coffee in one hand and supporting her head with the other.

"Someone needs her favorite blueberry muffin." Kelly was never one to take a hint.

Bianca gives Kelly a scathing glance. "I will be in the back seat sleeping off this hangover. Wake me when we get there." Bianca picks up her coffee, grabs a blueberry muffin stuffing it in her mouth, and heads to the garage.

"Let's roll, bitches. There are mountain men waiting all their lives for us." Meredith throws her suitcase in the back of the SUV and calls, "Shotgun." Meredith hops up front as Caroline unpacks the back of her SUV and begins repacking it.

"Seriously, Caroline, throw the shit up in there and let's go," Bianca says. "We are going on vacation, not to war. Everything doesn't have to be properly stowed."

"I like you better when you're not awake. Go back to sleep or I will slip a sedative into your coffee." Caroline threatens.

Without opening an eye, Bianca raises her travel mug toward Caroline for her dosage.

After securing the house one last time, grabbing the most recent crime novel she is reading off the kitchen table, and ensuring she has an up-to-date insurance card and her registration in the glove box, Caroline pulls out of her garage with the Bitch Brood in tow.

CHAPTER FOUR

MOCHA MACHO

Warding off hangovers from the previous night, everyone was quiet for the first few hours of the trip. Caroline's car stereo kept her company while Meredith listened to her Ipod and Kelly read a book in the back seat beside the sleeping Bianca.

"We are stopping for gas. Anyone need a potty break?" Caroline calls to the back after crossing into West Virginia.

Everyone except for Bianca, who is still asleep, exits the vehicle. Meredith and Kelly make their way to the gas station restroom. Caroline continues singing in her head while she fills up. Gazing at the mountains full of color all around her, she smiles. She loves how the mountains burst with flame this time of year—

A voice.

Did he speak to me? She first notices the white Escalade across the pump stall, then the man beside it. Much taller than her, which is usually not the case, Caroline looks over and up into the most delicious caramel eyes. Her first thought, *They grow 'em big and fine in these hills*, is not what came out of her mouth, thank God.

"I'm sorry. Did you say something?" Caroline asks, unable to unlock the gazing hold he had on her.

"I noticed you were from Carolina. I'm from Mooresville."

The baritone voice, deep and rich as the man's skin from which it came, mesmerized Caroline's mind like a sorcerer's wheel. *Say something. Anything.*

"Asheville," Caroline blurts out just happy to have put two syllables together.

"Beautiful city. I travel there at least a dozen times a year to enjoy the Blue Ridge Mountains and the hiking trails."

Why is my mouth dry? Why can I not form a sentence? All Caroline can focus on is the blood thrumming through her ears.

"Mountains." *Come on Caroline, you know more than two syllable words. Oh God, follow that up with something quick,* her mind screams. "I love mountains. My friends and I are vacationing in Fayetteville for the weekend. Have you heard of it?"

Nodding and answering, "Yes, I have," he smiles a full-lipped, white-teeth smile of Adonis as he pulls the nozzle out from the car and places it in the pump.

Watching his forearm flex as he places the nozzle back inside the pump elicits a small shiver up Caroline's spine.. *What the Sam Hill hell is wrong with me?*

Startled by the pump kicking off in her hand, Caroline abruptly turns around, removes the nozzle, and places it in the machine. The sisters are coming out of the gas station and Caroline does not want them to see her face, which she is sure is blushing. Over her shoulder, she says an abrupt goodbye to tall, dark, and handsome, then climbs in the driver's seat.

"Have a nice vacation, Asheville," the man's warm voice penetrates Caroline through the open window.

Without glancing in his direction, Caroline answers, "You too, Mooresville." Keeping her head turned from his direction, she reaches for her seatbelt and crosses it over her trembling body, clicking it in place.

Meredith and Kelly are hardly in their seats when Caroline drops the shifter into drive and takes off.

"Where's the fire, Captain? Ass barely in seat here." Meredith snaps her seatbelt quickly.

"Peter, Paul, and Mary," Bianca snorts as she shoots up from the back seat, laughing hysterically. "I have never heard a more inept interaction between opposite sexes. Mountains, I love mountains." Bianca mimics Caroline as she falls across Kelly's lap laughing, holding her stomach. "Have you heard of it?" Bianca is sucking in air now as she continues to mock Caroline. "Oh God, you are so out of flirting practice. I have to stop or I will pee."

"You had your chance, but you preferred to eavesdrop on me so you can just sit back there and suffer," Caroline scolds.

"What are you two talking about?" Meredith asks, glaring between the two of them.

Before Bianca can say anything, Caroline taps the brake hard, propelling them all forward. Glancing in the rearview mirror, she gives Bianca a threatening look. "If you say a word, I will stop this car, climb back there, and tickle you till you piss yourself."

"Whatever, dude. It's your car," Bianca returns. "Let's change the subject. Hey, look, mountains. It's like we are at home and haven't spent three hours on the road."

The last part of the drive is like the first, mostly silent, as the girls take in the scenery of the West Virginia mountains, valleys, and streams through the car windows. They turn off Route 19 onto a dirt road just wide enough for their car. Surrounded by the mountain state foliage, thick and colorful, Caroline drives deep into the forest, following a path that runs alongside a stream. After a few miles of curvy, rutted dirt road, the trees open to an expansive park-like setting with four large cabins. Two are perched alongside the river to the right, separated by thick forest. Two more are set up on the hillside to the left. Surrounded by such dense woods, they are all practically camouflaged. Caroline reads the numbers on the parking slips outside the cabins as she continues around the curve, searching for cabin number four. Number four turns out to be the last cabin on the road, nestled deep in the trees, butting up to the steady-flowing stream.

Kelly jumps out first, snapping pictures of the woods, the cabin and the river. "It is beautiful. So secluded. I feel like a pioneer woman."

Bianca mocks Kelly. "Ah, yes, just as I remember from our history classes. Pioneer woman would jump off a wagon, take out her seven-hundred-dollar phone with built-in camera and take pictures of the Indians. Please tell me we have cell service."

"I did not sign up to go off the grid, McKenzie," Meredith gripes as she grabs her phone and holds it in the air for reception.

"Good God, do you all hear banjos playing?" Bianca asks as she cups her ear into the air. "We would have to be the last cabin on a dead-end dirt road, wouldn't we?"

"This is what a vacation is meant to be. Back to nature. No distractions. No electronics. Just the four of us roughing it in the woods," Caroline explains as she punches the code to the cabin door. The view inside, a three-story cathedral roofline with pine log ceiling and a fireplace the size of a car, leaves them breathless. They stand on the porch admiring the inside of the cabin.

"Oh yeah, this is my idea of roughing it." Meredith enters first and claims, "I get the bedroom upstairs overlooking the water."

"You can't just demand which room you get," Kelly argues with her sister.

"Uh, yeah, I can. I am in view of said room and beat the rest of you to it," Meredith proudly states as she climbs the stairs to her quarters.

"There are four bedrooms. Two upstairs and two downstairs and each share a bathroom," Caroline warns, "so pick wisely with whom you want to be sharing your toileting habits for the next three days."

Kelly makes her way to the stairs. Caroline and Bianca stay down, knowing no one besides Kelly could put up with Meredith's primping.

"Now we have a lot to do before morning so we need to get the car unpacked and read over our itinerary for the weekend."

"Aye, aye, Captain." Bianca salutes before plopping down on the couch.

"I can fix us a snack while you girls unpack the car. This is going to be so much fun," Kelly offers.

An hour later, the four of them had eaten and everything was neatly stowed away by Caroline's orders. She hands each a printed copy of the agenda for the weekend including a copy of the Gorge Guide listing all the activities for Bridge Day.

"Tonight, we are going to Adventures on the Gorge for the Taste of Bridge Day. Local vendors will have delicacies from their chefs to sample and there is live music and—"

"Is there alcohol?" Meredith cuts in. "Or am I to bring my own?"

"Yes, there is alcohol. May I finish?" Caroline continues, "Tomorrow morning at sunrise, we will hike the trails to the scenic overlook then down the gorge to the river. There we can watch the base jumpers as they land under the bridge. Many photo ops, so bring a camera. We zip-line from the top of the bridge in the afternoon. We will need to grab lunch before we zip-line."

"Do we really want possible projectiles from our GI system while propelling through the air by a cord? I will skip lunch, thank you," Meredith interjects.

"Suit yourself. The weather will be cool in the morning and then heat to the seventies in the afternoon so dress accordingly. Caroline acknowledges Kelly's raised hand.

"Will we have time for some R&R, Captain?"

"We will have a few hours to relax here at the cabin before driving into Fayetteville for dinner. After dinner, we will walk over to the Bridge Jam music festival to hear live bands. Then Sunday—"

"Oh for fuck's sake! One fun-filled marathon day at a time, please," Bianca demands, "or I might just jump naked and knackered into that hot tub and refuse to get out all weekend."

"How about I put these snacks away and we can all go for a walk," Kelly prods the others as they lay stretched out on the cabin's deck.

"Who wants to drown Caroline in that hot tub so we can just lie here all weekend drinking instead of overworking every muscle in our bodies," Bianca offers.

"We could go into town and have a few drinks bought for us," Meredith says, offering another solution.

"I am too tired for alcohol but a short walk around the cabins sounds nice." Caroline pushes off the lounger and grabs her jacket. "If you two don't come then Kelly and I will have no choice but to talk bad about you," Caroline warns.

"You can't say anything you haven't said before or I don't already know," Bianca quips as she stands, pulling her shirt over her head and grabbing the bottle floating in the ice bucket. "I am taking this wonderful bottle of champagne into the hot tub and hopefully have bubbles spread to my happy place."

"I hope you are talking about the champagne bubbles and your happy place is your mouth," Meredith says as the shucking of Bianca's pants leaves an air of ambiguity. "I'm not taking any chances. I am going with you two. I am not staying here alone with happy britches."

"No britches, just all happy," Bianca coos as she sinks naked into the bubbles.

Leaving Bianca to her bottle and bubbles and God only knows what else, the three of them head out over the crunching leaves to explore their surroundings. Spraying the sky in hues of pinks and lavenders, the sun sets behind the mountains, leaving a chilly breeze behind. The girls walk around the carved paths that pass each of the four cabins.

"We shouldn't leave Bianca alone for long," Kelly states. "Alcohol and hot tubs do not mix."

"There is no mixologist better than Bianca." Meredith lifts her head. "Do you all hear music?"

The girls pause in their stride, listening for signs of other life.

"Sounds like it's coming from that cabin up there." Kelly points to the large cabin on the hill as they pass its parking slot. Caroline looks up at the cabin with its eerie glow of lights.

"We are not alone," Meredith hauntingly states, then adds, "Hey, check out the tags on their car. They are from North Carolina too."

Caroline almost trips over herself as she recognizes the white Escalade. "No freaking way!" she exclaims as she inspects the car.

"Isn't that the same car at the gas station this morning?" Kelly asks, naïve.

"Yeah, what did we miss this morning with the 'sclade' dude?" Meredith questions Caroline.

"I made a fool of myself and do not want to run into him again, so let's go." Caroline walks back onto the path, Kelly following.

"Hold up, Captain Giddy Buns." Meredith leans on the bumper of the white Escalade. "Tell us the whole story or I will walk straight to the front door and invite him to our cabin."

"Oh good God, fine, but not here. Come on, I will tell you while we walk." Caroline, as promised, regales her embarrassing story for Meredith and Kelly while walking back to the cabin.

"Was there anyone else in the car with him?" Meredith asks, fully invested in the story.

"I didn't notice. I wanted to get back in the car and get the hell out of there. It was bad enough Bianca overheard the whole thing."

With a maternal whine, Kelly states as they reach their cabin door, "I hope Bianca is okay. We have been gone for forty-five minutes."

Meredith pushes through the door first and heads to the back deck, hollering, "Hey, Happy Britches, guess who else is here, just two cabins over?"

Bianca, head relaxing against the hot tub, opens one eye as Meredith steps on the back deck, yelling, "The gas-station dude's Escalade is parked at the bottom of the hill of that big cabin."

"Then what are we waiting for?" Bianca chuckles as she takes a sip of her champagne, sets the glass down on the side of the hot tub and steps out.

"Oh, hell to the no," Caroline commands. "We are not going over there. Can this weekend please be about us and not about us hooking up? And holy shit-balls, can you please wrap a towel around you at least?"

Caroline throws Bianca a towel and retreats to the kitchen. "I do not want to see beavers in the wild. Besides, we have to get ready to go to A Taste of Bridge Day. We leave at 1900 hours."

CHAPTER FIVE

BRIDGE DAY NIGHTMARE

"This is incredible," Kelly states as they stand in line to get tickets for their supper.

A Taste of Bridge Day Festival nestles together in a large park setting overlooking the New River Gorge. Local shops, breath-taking views, live music, and delicacies are prepared from over twenty-different vendors

"I want to try the stone pizza." Meredith walks toward the line to wait for pizza to come from the smoking hearth.

"Get me one too. I will get us some beers." Bianca heads toward the outside bar.

Caroline and Kelly walk into a shop and look at the local artistry items. Caroline buys four matching sweatshirts while Kelly browses. The four spend the evening tasting the Italian, German, and American, cuisine including visiting the wine and beer vendors repetitively. Full and slightly inebriated, they are ready to relax and watch the band. Tables are spread all around the stage but they choose one in the back that has a scenic overlook. As the band plays Southern rock, the night creeps in and so does the cool mountain air. Caroline stands to put on her new sweatshirt and locks eyes with a man seated a few tables over, closer to the stage.

"You can't be serious, God." Caroline swears as she swiftly seats herself.

"What's wrong?" Kelly asks as Bianca stands to see why Caroline is so mortified.

"He is here." Caroline whispers for some reason.

"Who?" Kelly asks, turning in her seat.

Bianca is now laughing so hard she is drawing attention to their table. "Mocha Macho is in the house!" Bianca continues laughing even though Caroline is glaring at her.

"We want to see," Kelly says as she and Meredith stand up to view the crowd. "Which one is he?"

"The one walking this way," Bianca wheezes with laughter.

Caroline looks for a quick exit but she is seated against the railing in the back. There is no avoiding this confrontation.

"Ladies, I see we meet again." Mocha Macho smiles at the other three then his caramel eyes rest solely on Caroline. "Hello, Asheville." He is standing across the table from her, which Caroline wishes she was under at the moment.

"Mooresville." Caroline nods in his direction.

Meredith stands, stepping toward him. "We haven't been properly introduced. I am Meredith, this is Kelly and Bianca, and you have already met Asheville. Her friends call her Caroline. Would you like to pull up a chair, um…?"

"Jameson. And no, as lovely as that sounds, I have friends waiting on me. I just wanted to say hello again and I hope you all enjoy Bridge Day." Jameson can tell Caroline is not interested. She hasn't made eye contact once, so he turns to head back to his table. Over his broad shoulder he says, "Enjoy the mountains, Asheville."

Kelly turns back around to face Caroline. "That's the guy from the gas station? He is as big as a tree."

"I'd like to climb to the top of that one," Meredith interjects. "I bet the view from on top is glorious."

"You all don't stand a chance." Bianca stretches her arm around Caroline. "If you didn't notice, he only had eyes for Caroline."

"By all means, Meredith, he is yours," Caroline says as she stands to put on her sweatshirt.

"I don't want your sloppy seconds. And besides, Bianca is right; he didn't take his eyes off of you. His dark-lashed, creamy soft eyes," Meredith oozes.

"He is gorgeous," Caroline says as she glances in his direction, "and there is something about those eyes. But I do not need a long-distance relationship."

"Who said anything about a relationship? Use his better God-given qualities for your own needs. Geez, Caroline, it has been a long time since you…climbed a tree," Bianca crudely rebukes.

"Besides, Mooresville is only two hours from Asheville," Kelly enthusiastically adds.

Caroline's mind drifts as they watch the band. She finds Jameson very attractive, and he is a well-mannered, educated person. Why is she making this so complicated? After the band's last set of the evening, the girls return to the cabin. Everyone readies for bed and says good night but not before Caroline barks out orders of time and place for their morning's adventures.

* * *

After the others retire to their respective rooms for the night and she is sure everyone has had time to fall asleep, Bianca pens a note, then grabs her boots and a flashlight. She walks the path to the cabin on the hill where the Escalade is parked at the bottom. Only a warm flickering glow from the cabin's burning fireplace is illuminating from inside. Bianca reaches in her pocket, pulls out the note, and places it under the windshield wiper of the Escalade and heads back to the cabin.

Bianca fixes herself a drink and walks out onto the deck, gazing into the dark woods surrounding them. She has to admit this vacation is proving to be one of the best. The mountain air is invigorating, the scenery breathtaking, and it is nice to be electronically handicapped for a few days. Bianca sips her wine as she listens to the wind blow through the tall trees. Her ears pick up a sound, probably a critter of some sort, and she cocks her head to the side. She freezes in fear. She is sure she hears someone screaming from far away. All her senses heighten in a fight-or-flight response yet she is cautious to not make any sudden movements. Bianca moves slowly backward toward the door leading inside. The muffled screaming is following her, growing hauntingly louder with each step. Bianca opens the door quietly. She hears movement from behind her. Steeling her nerves and tightening every muscle in preparation for an attack, she spins, no one is there. She tries to calm herself, rationalizing the doors are locked, but the muffled scream is accompanied now by a few grunts and gasps. Bianca swears the sound is coming from inside the cabin.

She grabs the flashlight, brandishing it over her head, ready to attack. With cautious steps, Bianca tiptoes toward the sound. She passes under the stairs that lead to her room, then realizes the sound is coming from the bedroom on the left. "Caroline!" Bianca crashes through Caroline's bedroom door, swinging the flashlight in defense, screaming like a banshee.

Startled awake, Caroline jolts up and over the side of the bed, knees crashing on the floor, taking cover behind the mattress.

"Are you okay?" Bianca calls out after she is sure no one else is in the room.

Caroline shakes her head to ensure she is awake, not sure if Bianca's shadow is part of a nightmare or horrifying reality. She reaches up and turns on the lamp on the bedside table.

"Bianca? What the fuck is the matter with you? You just scared the bejesus out of me!"

Bianca just stands there with her mouth wide open, leaving Caroline to question her own wakefulness. Bianca brings the flashlight down to her side and stumbles over her next words. "You were…thrashing… moaning…Wait, what the fuck is the matter with me?" Bianca leans on the doorframe, more composed on the outside than on the inside. "Good God, Caroline, you scared the shit out of me! What the fuck was that?"

"I had a nightmare. And by the look of you, I would say you did too. What are you doing up?" Caroline thought she saw Bianca swallow back a response before she answered her.

"Um, I couldn't sleep," Bianca lies. "I was enjoying a drink on the back deck when I heard screaming. I thought any moment someone would come running out of the woods with a machete-yielding yeti chasing after them. Are you all right?"

"I'm fine but it sure looks like you need a drink." Caroline wraps her housecoat around her and heads to the kitchen. Bianca follows in stunned silence.

"Do you think being in these woods sparked your nightmare?" Bianca asks after Caroline tells her about the nightmare.

"I wish I knew what brought these night terrors on. Then I could make them stop."

"We have only a few hours before sunrise. Do you want me to sleep with you tonight?" Bianca offers as they down the last sip from their wine glasses.

"That's okay. I am used to it by now"—Caroline notices Bianca's slump of her shoulders—"but I will come sleep with you if you are still scared."

Bianca takes her hand and leads Caroline under the stairs to her room. "Will you spoon me?"

"Now you are scaring me," Caroline says as they turn out the lights and try to get some sleep before their morning hike. Caroline stares at the ceiling for hours, thinking of climbing the tree that is planted on the hillside in cabin number one.

* * *

"What are you two fucktards back there giggling about?" Bianca demands of Kelly and Meredith as the four of them hike the trail to the overlook.

"We were just talking about why we saw you and Caroline come out of your bedroom this morning," Kelly answers.

"That explains why you two are always single," Meredith teases.

"What's your all's excuse, then?" Bianca flares back.

"Guys, look at this view." Caroline pauses on the path, halting the others in their tracks, to take in the majestic scenery of the Appalachian Mountains.

"And look how far we have to go before we are at the bottom," Bianca adds. "Can we break here for a moment?" Bianca leans against a tree perched on the edge of the precipice.

"Oh, I see an epic fail coming," Meredith declares.

The hiking descent to the water is slow but beautiful. They gaze at the mountains surrounding them and the canopy of colored leaves above them. Soon, the sound of crunching leaves underfoot is drowned out by the sound of rushing water.

"It's gorgeous!" Caroline gushes at the scene of the rapids cutting through the mountains.

"Being so close to the water, I feel my spirit rejuvenated," Kelly says as she steps out a little farther to get a better view. "Look, you can see the New River Gorge Bridge from here."

The girls strain forward and look to the right to see the monumental bridge high in the sky that connects two large mountain ranges together, wondering at the engineering marvel.

Caroline is amazed by the kayakers as they paddle their way through the rapids, over rock and whitecaps, being catapulted downstream.

"I refuse to hike back up that mountain. Caroline, this was your idea. Now find us a lift to the top or hike your soldier ass back to our cabin and get the car," Bianca demands.

"Look!" Kelly points up at the arch bridge as a base jumper throws his chute and drifts in a serpentine pattern over the river, descending to the shoreline.

The girls, invigorated by observing the parachutes open, can't wait to see them land. They hike on, reaching the target landing site a few miles from the bridge. There, buses are taking other jumpers back up the gorge to tempt fate, possibly, one last time.

"We are so on one of those buses," Meredith promises. "I will go find out who I have to blow to get a ride to the top."

"Way to go, Meredith. Take one for the team," Bianca hollers after her.

Base jumper after base jumper descend aerodynamically, some landing on the target site on shore, some in the trees. Others land in the water and are then picked up by waiting rescue boats. Caroline can't imagine the courage it takes to jump from 870 feet in the air, free-falling before tossing a piece of fabric in the air and hoping to God it unfolds as a parachute. She looks around, trying to spot Meredith, but instead finds Bianca flirting it up with a base jumper. She can always tell when Bianca has snared one. They are infatuated immediately by her looks, her confidence, her gorgeous smile, and when she wants to be, Bianca can be a brilliant conversationalist. Men hang on her every word. Bianca turns, heading back toward Caroline.

"What's his name?" Kelly asks, knowing Bianca probably has no idea.

"Derek something or another," Bianca replies. "He is from here but now lives in Virginia. I invited him and his buddies to our cookout on Sunday night."

Caroline's head snaps up. "What cookout?"

"The one we are throwing so I can get closer to Derek. Don't worry. I will handle all the details."

"For the love of God, can any of you go four whole days without a man?" Caroline pleads.

"Let's hope we never have to find out," Bianca answers.

"Got us a lift," Meredith announces, insinuating success by wiping her mouth as she joins the girls.

"You two are incredible," Caroline states. "Let's go so we can view the jumpers from up top for a while before we zip line."

Snapping back with Caroline's own words, Bianca says, "For the love of God, can you go four minutes without trying to injure us?"

CHAPTER SIX

AMBUSH ON MOORESVILLE

"Aaawww!" Bianca's screams can be heard throughout the gorge as they raft the rapids the following afternoon. Bianca could never have imagined how her words would come back to haunt her regarding being injured.

The rubber raft seems more like a rocket as it hurls through space, above the water, landing on rapidly moving water only to lift off again at the next boulder. Whitewater rafting is not for the faint of heart; it evens says that in the disclaimer they signed. Seated in the back, Bianca holds on for dear life. Kelly sits up front of the spinning vessel, loving every airborne moment. Caroline and Meredith sit in the middle on either side of the raft, adrenaline flowing as hard as the rapids. The rafting guides shout instructions as they steer through the rapids into calmer waters.

"I can't tell if I am wet from river water or if I peed myself," Meredith confesses as they climb out of the raft onto shore.

"I want to go again." Kelly claps her hands and is grinning ear to ear. "Try sitting up front the next time. You see everything up close."

"There won't be a next time"—Bianca straightens—"and besides, you looked like the dog from The Grinch cartoon sitting at the helm of the sled as it slid down the mountain. I actually think your tail was wagging a little. I need a drink and a hot tub. Please, Captain, can we go relax before the cookout tonight?"

"I can't believe we have been here forty-eight hours and you two have met enough people to throw a party." Caroline shakes her head.

"What can we say? People gravitate toward us," Bianca states.

"We charm. That's how we roll," Meredith adds.

"With enough alcohol, anyone is charming," Kelly inputs her opinion, "but I guess a nap before the party does sound good."

While shopping for groceries for the cookout, all four women are on their cell phones checking emails, Facebook, and texts. Glancing through her inbox, Caroline views the email she felt deep down was imminent. Offering to get the bread, she makes a hasty departure from the other three. Caroline looks around before opening the email, as if she was receiving a secret mission. She reads the electronic letter with reverence and trepidation before saving it to her archive file to review again after vacation. She would not mention this to her friends this weekend. It would destroy all their fun. She turns out of the aisle, turns back to get the bread she forgot, then hunts down her friends, all the while holding back the tears the email—or actual secret mission—evoked.

* * *

Back at the campsite, the hills are alive with a variety of music playing on the old hi-fi found in the cabin along with cassette tapes. People are meandering in and out of the cabin, mingling in groups, talking about where they are from and what they do for a living. It amazes Caroline how quickly information spread from one person to another about their little cookout. She couldn't have had more people show up to a party with engraved invitations. Most everyone is from out of town, staying in local cabins and in Fayetteville for Bridge Day. Caroline watches as Bianca talks with Derek, the base-jumper she met at the landing site yesterday along with…wait…*Is that the bus driver?* Caroline is amazed by her friends. She considers that if the military would use them a peace-keepers, she wouldn't have to—

Just as those ominous words cross through her mind, she spots Mocha Macho coming through the cabin door. He is accompanied by two other men, and by the sight of the female campers' jaws dropping, the three of them would not be leaving together, or alone. Before they can make eye contact, Caroline turns her back to him and swigs what is left of her rum and Diet Coke. Liquid courage is better than cowering in the corner.

"Thanks for the invite, Asheville."

Caroline puts on a false bravado, then turns to greet Jameson. Even at 5'8", she is staring straight at his chest. God, he is a tree, with thick broad branches. He even smells like the outdoors. *Pull it together, McKenzie.* Caroline wrangles her hormones.

"I believe you owe your gratitude to someone else." Caroline corrects him.

"So the note was not from you? I am hurt." As Jameson clutches his chest in demonstration, Caroline notices Bianca coming toward them.

"You aren't the only one that is going to feel pain," Caroline promises, glaring a hole through Bianca as she joins them.

"Hey, cabin number one, right?" Bianca feigns ignorance. "Glad you could make it. It seems all but one cabin on our little woodland cul-de-sac came. I invited everyone out here."

Caroline could see straight through Bianca's attempt to undermine her guilt in this little setup. She would make sure the punishment fit the crime as soon as they were alone.

"I didn't realize there were this many people staying here." Jameson seems surprised looking at the turnout.

"Most everyone here are people we have met over the past few days either at Bridge Day or in town. Only a handful are actually camping at this sight," Bianca informs them both.

Caroline, questioning her own observation skills, did not realize her three best friends were inviting everyone they met to the cookout.

"Please excuse me," Caroline requests as she shrinks away and heads for the makeshift bar on the back deck, joining Kelly. Caroline and Kelly converse with other deck-bar patrons as Caroline sips her drinks and tries to avoid Mocha Macho, which seems impossible. Every time she glances his way, there are women looking up at him, gushing. Some even bold enough to place their hand on his chest or his arm as he talks, laughing, flirting, and hair flipping. Caroline hates women who hair flip.

Meredith slides up beside Caroline on the picnic table top. "You know you could have him if you want him."

"I don't remember saying I wanted him," Caroline rebuts. "Besides, he seems busy fending off the bleach blond."

"Yeah, but he only has eyes for you. I think he wants you to save him."

Caroline takes another swig. "Damn, if she gets any closer to him she will become part of his DNA."

"His voice is so…melodic." Kelly holds out the last word.

Meredith giggles, "and such a gentleman. Damn if I couldn't corrupt him by morning."

"He sure is a panty-spritzer," Bianca crudely adds as she joins them. "He's an architect. Did he tell you that, Caroline?"

"No, he hasn't been alone for us to talk." Caroline's words come out in a snarl.

"Please tell me you will let him build something inside you. Even you can't turn that down." Meredith says, gazing at him.

Caroline, tired of their double entendre, stands to walk away. "I don't feel like standing in line."

"If you would give him one bit of attention, you would go to the front of the line. He is here for you and you are sitting on a powder keg of hormones. I so want to be you right now. Scared for Mocha Macho though. But most definitely envious of the night you could have," Bianca says.

"I will not have a night and what makes you think he is here for me?"

"Because the note left on his windshield was signed 'Asheville,'" Bianca confesses, which gains her an exasperated and even more so threatening look from Caroline.

"He hasn't taken his eyes off you all night," Meredith adds, "and neither has the blond for that matter."

"Ooh, Captain McKenzie," Bianca goads, "not afraid of the battlefield but a little female competition terrifies her."

Caroline takes another sip of liquid courage. "I am not afraid. I am just not that interested."

"Can I engage the enemy, then?" Meredith requests. "I'd like to plant my flag on him."

Caroline glances toward Jameson and the blond and hands off her drink to Meredith. "As they say in these parts, hold my beer and watch this shit." Caroline's emphasized country twang leaves them laughing as Caroline approaches her target.

"What's going on?" Kelly asks as she returns with food for them.

"We applied reverse psychology on Caroline." Kelly looks confused at Bianca's admission. "We tapped into her soldier side and she is about to deploy a hell-storm on that blond."

"Does the blond know Caroline is at DEFCON 1?" Kelly asks concernedly.

"Nope. It's an ambush," Bianca elaborates.

"Which makes this all the more entertaining." Meredith grins.

"If Caroline figures out what you two are up to, you will become public enemy number one," Kelly warns. "I actually feel sorry for you two."

"I feel sorry for Jameson. Look"—Bianca gestures toward Caroline's target—"he doesn't know what's about to hit him."

"I'm sorry to interrupt," Caroline lies. "Jameson, could you come with me for a moment? I would like you to meet someone."

"It was lovely to meet you, Trish. I hope you enjoy your weekend." Jameson removes his arm from Trish's death grip and follows Caroline toward the front door. Opening the door for her, Jameson places his hand on the small of her back, leading her to the front porch. Caroline pauses momentarily to catch her breath and let the tingles in her body subside from this unexpected touch.

"Please tell me there's no one you're wanting me to meet, and that you came to rescue me."

"The girls thought you needed rescued. I thought you were enjoying yourself."

"I would enjoy the evening much more if we could talk and get to know one another."

Caroline bit her lower lip as her pulse quickens—her mind floods with ensuing scenarios of getting to know him better.

As Caroline and Jameson walk through the woods, Caroline learns that Jameson lives on Lake Norman in Mooresville. He is thirty-four years old, has two dogs and enjoys fishing and water skiing in the summer and football and basketball all year long. He has three brothers, one of which is with him this weekend, and one sister. His parents live in Pineville outside of Charlotte. He works out of the Charlotte area and travels a lot for his job.

"You have enough information on me to fill out a small business loan, yet I know nothing of you." Jameson smiles as his gaze meets that of Caroline's. Her blue eyes search his brown to determine the intent of his interest.

"You know I live in Asheville." At Jameson's inquiring look, Caroline includes, "I work in the hospital there," she pauses, loving the attention of his gaze. Then continues, "My last name is McKenzie. I have no brothers or sisters but the friends that are with me, they are like my family. That's about it. So back to you. Who's the other person that is with you and your brother this weekend?"

"That is actually my best friend and also my foreman. If you're interested, I could hook you up." Jameson smiles as Caroline again meets his gaze, her eyes somewhat quizzical— wondering whether he is serious with that offer—hoping that he isn't.

"That won't be necessary." Caroline smiles back at him.

"So there's already someone special in your life?"

Caroline considers lying so this game they are playing can end. She decides to answer him truthfully because her hopes for the evening are stronger than her fears. Just as Caroline is about to answer him honestly— that no, she had no one special in her life—Jameson steps to the right and into a clearing, then straight on to a deck. Somehow, Jameson had circled around to his cabin on the hill without Caroline's knowledge, leading them through the woods and right where he wants her. Caroline is sure he planned it that way, leading her straight to his den of iniquity. His plans for the evening are obviously the same as hers.

"Would you like something to drink?" Jameson holds the door to his cabin open. "I make a mean cup of coffee."

Caroline's shoulder brushes his chest, his hand again maneuvering her past the threshold. Her steps pause, imagining his arms suddenly embracing her, holding her. Then her attention quickly flashes back to the present and she enters his cabin.

Just as Caroline expected, the room is immaculate, however, there are blueprints spread all across the dining room table. Jameson gathers the papers together and apologizes, "I planned on staying in tonight and working but they coaxed me out. And now I'm glad they did." Jameson gives Caroline a smile that could melt butter as he steps into the kitchen.

"Would you like a cup of coffee?"

"Yes, please."

"We can drink it on the patio deck if you would like," Jameson calls from the kitchen.

"That sounds lovely. I will take mine black," Caroline answers back as she steps out onto the scenic patio deck and takes a seat. *Oh dear Lord, what am I doing here?* Caroline, processing the ramifications, considers the pros and cons of a night of debauchery. The pros have her shifting uncomfortably in her chair. Just as she starts the cons list, Jameson opens the door carrying two aromatic cups. Caroline notes the vapor rising from the cups; the steam actually looks as if it is coming off of him. Caroline also discerns the sounds of soft jazz playing in the background as his fingers brush across hers as he hands her the steaming cup.

He leans against the railing in front of Caroline's chair, crossing one beefy leg over the other. "We have been coming here for several years for Bridge Day. It is one of my favorite weekend getaways."

"This is our first time. Where else do you like to travel?" Taking a sip, Caroline covers her face with the mug, trying not to stare eye level.

"I love going anywhere steeped in history. I am a student of architecture so I enjoy European vacations. I enjoy the outdoors more than stuffy museums though. So you know I build things for a living and that I am a nerd with a penchant for history. What about you, Caroline? What is your penchant?"

Hearing her name cross his lips, Caroline has to force her body to stay in the chair. She considers if he would be surprised to find out that her plans for the evening were the same as his. An awesome night of sex and then out the door before sunrise. *He's intelligent, worldly, gorgeous, and with the voice of Barry White and body of Shemar Moore.* Bianca enters her thoughts: *Quit overanalyzing—just have fun.* Caroline is not sure if those are Bianca's thoughts in her head or her own hormones, screaming in desire. Caroline turns to face Jamison full on, shoulders parallel to his. Her eyes search for a clue to his next move— or whether he was going to make one.

"I have many but mine are more…eclectic. I too like history but science is my main area of study. I am a Registered Nurse and work in an ER in Asheville. I am also studying languages at the local university. I always felt linguistically disabled overseas. I want to learn the various languages of the places where I have been stationed."

"You were stationed overseas?" A slow, contented smile formed on Caroline's lips as she recognized a spark of interest in Jamison's eyes—an admiration of sorts.

"Oh yeah, I am a Captain in the Army. Well, reserves now. I spent four years active duty, then moved to Asheville when I got out. But I missed the military life, so I joined the reserves."

Jameson sets his cup on the railing then crosses his arms on his chest, cocking his hip to the left. "You know, most people would start out describing themselves by saying they are a Captain in the Army." His amazement at her delayed omission is obvious in his eyes that are now piercing through Caroline's. She can feel the synaptic connection beginning to surge through her body.

She shifts again in her seat, holding back her desire for him. "What can I say? I'm eclectic."

"So, what does Captain Eclectic do for fun?"

"My friends and I travel a lot and I do volunteer work at the local animal shelter. Other than that, between work, friends, school, shelter and reservist's duties, I don't have a lot of spare time."

"You've never been married?" Jameson is holding his breath on this question.

"Weren't you paying attention? Work, friends, school, shelter and reserves. I haven't found the time it takes for a relationship. What I have found is that my military experience intimidates men. Least that's what I hope it is because if not, then they just don't find me attractive."

"I think it is sexy that I am here with GI Jane. It makes me reconsider my plans for the evening though." Now Jameson is the one shifting in his boots. "How many ways can you kill me?" He raises an eyebrow as his lips part for a soft smile.

Caroline stands and as she takes two steps toward him, she says, "Since I am GI Jane and a nurse, the possibilities are endless." She places her index finger beside her lips as if considering the ways to his demise then poses a question, "But does the number of ways matter?" Caroline steps inside his personal space and captures his gaze with hers, then softly warns, "I only need one."

His rich laughter sounds like honey pouring over gravel. Accepting the challenge, Jameson places his empty cup on the railing and confronts the Captain, toe to toe. "You are an interesting woman. What else do you like, Asheville. I mean, Captain McKenzie."

Caroline's hormones are heating her insides and taking over. Caroline contemplates her next move. *One of us has to make a move soon before his friends come back from the party or mine get worried and come looking for me.*

Caroline holds her ground, unintimidated by his size and actually throbbing at its perspective. "I love all kinds of music, sports, my favorite color is purple, my favorite flowers are tulips, and I am not much for small talk."

Jameson leans his head down, looking at her mouth. Just as they are about to touch, his eyes slowly raise to hers. Caroline meets his gaze head on and his body the rest of the way. They stare passionately at one another as their lips touch. His caramel eyes are staring a hole through her as he non-urgently deepens the kiss. Caroline, feeling her knees weaken along with the last of her resolve, she closes her eyes and leans into his body. Supporting her weight by wrapping his huge bicep arm around her lower back, Jameson pulls her even closer while his other hand slips to her neck, holding her head and mouth against his. The kiss is light and teasing at first. Jameson continues to hold her tight, his kiss becoming more intense with each passing moment. From the onslaught of Jameson's technique, Caroline's knees buckle, breaking the kiss but not the look. Keeping his gaze on her eyes, Jameson lifts Caroline into his arms and carries her to his bedroom.

CHAPTER SEVEN

MARSHALL

Caroline returned to her cabin right before sunrise and before her friends woke with their hangovers and questions. However, she did not escape the four-hour interrogation on the drive home. Not one to kiss and tell, Caroline told them all she learned of Jameson and admitted to very little after that. Soon, they were back in Asheville and life returned to normal.

"Marshall will sure be happy to see you. He's been moping around here all weekend," Francie, the director of the animal shelter, calls out to Caroline as she exits her car. "Every time a car comes up the road he goes running to see if it's you. How that dog knows your car versus all the others beats me, but he does. You might think I'm crazy, or spend too much time with these animals, but I swear, he knew it was Saturday and that you were supposed to be here. He sat by the back fence all day watching that road, getting sadder and sadder as the day went on."

"Hi, Francie." Caroline gives her a one-armed hug since she is carrying a large bag of dog food. "I missed him too. Where is he? I didn't see him in the yard when I pulled in."

"He is getting a bath this morning," Francie explains as she helps Caroline unload cleaning supplies from the back of her SUV. "I told him he had to get cleaned up before Miss Caroline got here."

As Caroline enters the shelter, the sounds of the dogs are a warm welcome. She loves volunteering at the shelter, even if she cleans out stalls most of the day. She loves her time with Marshall, a yellow lab that showed up at the shelter over a year ago as a puppy. Caroline doesn't understand why such a smart and loving dog has yet to be adopted. Francie swears that whenever strangers come around that could be interested, he shows no interest in them. He has even barked and growled at a few that wanted to take him home. Caroline has never seen that side of Marshall. She has only seen the warm, friendly Marshall. The one whose tail wags right off his butt when he sees her.

Caroline always spends an extra hour with him after she helps with the chores. They play in the yard or take a walk along the river that runs behind the shelter's property. She wishes she could take him home with her but her hectic schedule does not provide the quantity of time a dog needs. Instead, she prays every day a nice family will adopt him, one with the time to provide him the love he deserves. Until then, she will continue to visit him two or three times a week, depending on her schedule at work and reserve duties.

"There's my boy," Caroline says when Marshall enters the office area. Marshall's excitement to see her is displayed in tail wagging and shrill whines as he circles through Caroline's legs, rubbing against her. She returns his love by scratching behind his ears, his favorite spot.

"Sorry I wasn't here last Saturday but I was out of town," Caroline tries to explain to her furry companion. Marshall can't hold a grudge; he forgives her. "I missed you too, yes I did. I missed my big boy," Caroline squeaks out in a voice humans use to talk to their pets.

After Caroline and Marshall have their reunion, Caroline grabs the mop bucket and asks, "Where would you like us to start, Francie?"

"Why don't you take the dogs that are pinned in the back out to the yard? They need exercise, and besides," Francie explains, "Riley brought his boy-scout troop this weekend and they cleaned the pens out, so we are in top shape."

Caroline lets the dogs out of their pens and Marshall leads them outside to the yard. Fourteen dogs, to be exact, ranging in ages from puppies to much older dogs in a variety of types and mixtures. Caroline plays with Marshall and the new toys she brought him until they both need a rest. Together on the picnic table, while the rest of the dogs chase one other, Caroline unburdens herself from her weekend and her thoughts about seeing a psychologist. She tells Marshall of her nightmare while at the cabin. Marshall knew the Iraq story and could recite it—that is, if he weren't a dog.

She asks Marshall why that particular nightmare never changes, never reveals any new information, and why it repetitively haunts her. Caroline knows Marshall would be the type to help her analyze the nightmare, help her work through the reasoning behind it, again, if he weren't a dog. She would deny she confided in a dog for all her personal problems or questions in life. There was no one better than a dog to listen without inserting his own problems back on you. She found it cathartic to say it all out loud without fear of judgement. No matter what she said, nothing would diminish his unconditional love.

Since the weather permitted one of those warm October aberrations, Caroline stays later than normal. Marshall and Caroline bring the dogs in for their evening dinner, then she and Marshall take their walk along the Swannanoa River. The river stretches the entire property of the shelter, then curves farther into the forest for miles. Marshall and Caroline usually walk the distance of the property and then turn back, approximately three miles round trip. Today, however, they venture into the woods, crunching across fallen leaves.

Caroline makes sure they are back to the shelter before it gets dark, and says goodbye to Marshall, promising to see him in a few days. Marshall, as usual, mopes back to his pen. Caroline cries all the way home, hating to leave him behind. She works twelve-hour shifts the next three days and that is not fair to leave him alone that long. She knows all too well what it feels like to be lonely. After arriving home, she places the call that has plagued her since the weekend at the cabin.

Leaving a message on her Commander's phone, Caroline then heads upstairs for a long soak in the bath. While the hot water eases her aching muscles and clears her tangled thoughts, Caroline fantasizes about her night with Jameson. She smiles at the thought of his methodical lovemaking, neglecting not one inch of her body, then driving her over the climatic edge with a slow cadence that pounded her orgasm from deep within. An exalted breath escapes her lips as she sinks lower into the tub, knowing she will have to rewash certain areas if she continues this train of thought.

Skipping out on Jameson before he woke might not have been the appropriate action. Caroline is all too familiar with that side of herself. Similar to the reason why she will not adopt Marshall from the shelter, Caroline hates it but this is her life now and no matter how painful, she is sure she is doing the right thing. Having someone at home waiting on you would only make it that much harder to leave, and it would make it damn more difficult to die.

CHAPTER EIGHT

BLOODY FLASHBACK

"Would you like to play the zoo game with me? First, we have to dress up like animals. I will put my mask on and Sabrina will help you put your mask on." Caroline motions to the respiratory therapist to put the nebulizer mask on her two-year-old patient as she places one on herself. "Now we look like elephants at the zoo."

With a flex tube attached to the mask, Caroline walks around the ER room, trumpeting through the tube. The asthmatic toddler laughs at Caroline while Sabrina administers the bronchodilator to help him breathe.

"That could have been a war of the wills and I bet the kid would have won," Sabrina says to Caroline at the nurses' station after their patient could breathe better and was sent home.

"Thanks for your help. I doubt he would have left the mask on if he weren't an elephant."

Caroline looks up from charting and smiles back at the therapist. She loves treating children even though some of the cases are heartbreaking.

"You should see her kitty cat using an NG Tube for whiskers," Robin, the charge nurse on duty offers. Caroline has worked almost two years with Robin and the two of them have witnessed much devastation but also, a few miracles.

Caroline types out her notes, looking up when another nurse sets a vase on the desk in front of her.

"Someone has an admirer," Robin teases as she pulls up a chair beside her. "Who they from?"

"None of your business." Caroline pulls out the card to read.

"Who sent you those? They are gorgeous," Dr. Smith says as she leans in to smell the large bouquet.

"She won't tell who her admirer is," Donna says as she tries to grab the card.

"Admirer my ass," Dalynn joins in. "You don't get an arrangement like that just because someone admires you. Where in the world do you find tulips like that this time of year? Especially purple ones."

"Those are not just purple tulips. Those are post-coital purple tulips," Becky hollers out across the nurses' station.

"No way, not our Caroline. Is this guy aware he doesn't stand a chance in hell no matter how big his 'arrangement' is?" Tara, states out loud what everyone else is thinking.

Blushing, Caroline picks up the vase and heads toward the break room. "If you all are through, I'm going to lunch now." Caroline sets her flowers on the break room table and reads the card again.

Can't stop thinking of you. Call me if you ever get over your hatred for small talk. The card is signed "Mooresville" with his cell number underneath. Caroline knows this is his way of placing the ball in her court. She is now the one who will determine if this relationship will go forward. Caroline pulls out her phone, stores Jameson's phone number in her contacts and then pockets the card.

Caroline resumes her internet search of psychotherapy during her lunch break. She had spent several hours online last night after she came home from the shelter searching for answers. She researched different types including Behavioral, Cognitive, Humanistic, and Holistic. She started off taking notes on each one until the list kept growing. Then she only took notes on the ones she would even consider. Then she found a website that listed hundreds of approaches to each type of psychotherapy and tried to outline the information. After eight pages of notes, blurred eyes, and a cramped hand, Caroline put down her pen and called it a night.

As she sits in the break room researching once again, she is more confused now than before. With the failed research attempt last night, she goes a different route. *Find the therapist and let them tell me what type of therapy I need. If they can charge me $250 an hour, then by God they can figure out what a whack job I am and how to fix it.* Caroline types "psychologists in Asheville" in the search engine. By the lengthy list of psychologists, psychiatrists, and therapy groups in the Asheville area, Caroline is sure she can find at least one she can trust.

As soon as Caroline looks at the page, she sees the word "Trusting." She clicks on the link and reads the first line under the name: "Will provide a safe and trusting environment." The website reveals the psychlologist's background, training, and even testimonials. Caroline knows she should review the other links but something inside is telling her *this is the one*. As she is about to flip over to the phone icon and call the number, a picture downloads onto the website. Dr. Nikolas Perrin is staring back at her from her small screen.

His beautiful green eyes and Greek God appearance might've held her gaze a moment longer, had it not been for the current churning of emotions she was still feeling for Jameson. Caroline dials the number. A machine picks up stating the doctor is in session and to please leave a name and number and a time for him to call you back. Caroline states her name and number and asks for a call after seven p.m., if that is not too late. If so, to please call tomorrow morning.

Caroline exhales, shoulders slumping. She didn't want to leave a voice mail but it was too late. After such a buildup, the answering machine was anti-climactic. She wants to hear the voice that went with that face. Yet, she is also relieved. Caroline is still not sure if she wants to do this or not.

"Trauma Alert…Level 1…ETA five minutes. Trauma Alert…Level 1…ETA five minutes."

Caroline downs her bottle of water, throws her phone in her locker, washes her hands and runs for the trauma bays. Suiting up with personal protective wear, Caroline stands ready at the airlift bay doors, prepared for the trauma being brought in by helicopter. She hears the chopper approaching as the radio command center at the nurses' station squawks its arrival. Watching as it swings wide, levels, and lowers slowly to the tarmac outside of the ER, Caroline thinks she is ready for what is coming, but she is sadly mistaken.

* * *

My green undershirt, hardened from dirt and sweat, is sticking to me while the mortar fire is making my ears ring. RPGs are firing on the Chinooks bringing in the casualties from the field.

"Please promise to tell my mother I love her," the baby-faced marine lying

on the operating table asks of me before Jan, the nurse anesthetist, puts him under.

"You will tell her yourself," I lie with a warm smile as the anesthetist's potions take effect.

Multiple causalities are coming in from a battle fought no more than fifteen miles from our CSH Unit. This marine has lost a limb, several liters of blood, and massive quantities of flesh are burned beyond recognition all over his body. A suicide bomber had pulled straight up to the checkpoint the marines secured and detonated the bomb that took out most of the young men guarding the entrance to the old schoolhouse. Now, instead of a secure location for the corps, the old schoolhouse will be once again abandoned, possibly allowing insurgents to quester.

As my patient's heart rate plummets, mine rises. He is crashing. "I need blood over here," I scream to the orderly over the makeshift military surgical room. This baby of a man is bleeding out in front of me. My arms and hands, covered in blood, seek inside the marine's abdominal cavity, searching for any bleeders while the surgeon clamps others. So much blood, I can't stop it. Where is it coming from? It is now dripping on my shoes. So much blood.

"Caroline. Caroline."

"Lieutenant McKenzie! It is over! We can't save him."

I stand there, frozen, covered in blood, staring at this courageous mamma's boy marine. Who will tell his mother how much he loved her? Tears roll down my face, streaking the dirt under my face mask and down my neck.

"Caroline. Caroline!"

Caroline glances at the face of that marine now standing beside her, in scrubs, speaking her name. He grabs her by the shoulders and forces her to look directly at him.

"Caroline. Come on. Let's get you to break room," Chris says as he wraps his arm around Caroline's shoulder and guides her away from the trauma bay doors. "You need…Aw, hell, I have no idea what you need but whatever it is, I am sure we aren't serving it in the break room."

"We have a trauma coming in," Caroline states, catatonic-like, as Chris opens the door to the break room.

"No, we don't. The trauma arrived ten minutes ago. About the same time you left us," Chris explains while getting her a bottle of water.

Chris, another ER nurse who also serves in the Air Force Reserves, has heard of Caroline's rare flashbacks from other co-workers but has never witnessed one himself. A few minutes ago, Caroline was sweating, a pounding pulse visible in her neck, tears running down her face as she screamed for blood. Now she is white as a sheet, nursing a water bottle, and looking like she traveled through time.

"Is she okay?" Vickie asks Chris as she closes the break room door behind her. "I have called one of her friends to come and get her. They should be here soon. I will stay with her until she gets here."

"You're the boss," Chris states as he heads back to work. "Hey, Vick, does she do this often?"

"I would think once is enough," Vickie states as she cautiously approaches Caroline and sits down beside her. "How are you?"

"I'm so sorry," Caroline cries as she covers her face with her hands. "I don't know why this keeps happening. One minute I am perfectly fine, and the next I am still there, reliving every minute."

"You have nothing to be sorry about."

"Just let me splash water on my face and I will get back out there," Caroline says as she walks toward the sink.

"That won't be necessary. I reassigned your patients and have called Bianca to come get you. I want you to go home and rest."

"Really, Vickie, I will be fine." Caroline splashes. "I just need a minute."

"Caroline, hiring you is one of the best decisions I have ever made in this job. You are a highly respected and knowledgeable nurse. But you need help to deal with these flashbacks. I am worried about you. Please, I am begging you. Don't make my best decision turn out to be my worst."

Bianca arrives a few minutes later to take Caroline home. While walking to Bianca's red Mustang, Caroline says, "I feel like a suspended child being picked up at school by her mommy,"

"Playing it hot and loose with the narcotics, were you?" Bianca chides.

Caroline lays her head back on the seat rest. "I wish I was drugged right now. I don't know what happened. I was standing at the ER doors waiting for the helicopter to land with a trauma, and the next minute…I am back in Iraq, in the operating unit, watching a marine die on the table. The next thing I know, Chris is yelling my name."

"Have you had this particular flashback before?"

"Yes, but not at such a critical juncture as waiting for a trauma. What the hell is wrong with me? Why can't I get this under control?"

"Have you thought more about what we suggested? You know, therapy?" Bianca asks cautiously.

"I've done research. I even called to set up an appointment."

"Wow, that's great. Do you want to talk about it?"

"Not really, but I appreciate the ride home." Caroline turns her head to stare out the window at the passing scenery. This flashback has caused Bianca to leave her job and even worse, placed the trauma at risk by not having qualified personnel at the ready. Caroline could not forgive herself if anything happened to that patient.

Bianca settles Caroline inside her home with a blanket on the couch and a tall glass of wine in her hand, then heads back to work. Caroline's mind plays several scenarios from her seven-month tour overseas, many so debilitating to her heart that she actually aches. Others so ghastly traumatic her mind fights to keep the images locked away. Caroline is astounded to think these flashbacks will cost her the job she loves. She has to get control over this or lose everything. If there were any question about following through with therapy, her own nurse manager answered it. Caroline promised herself that she would not be Vickie's worst decision.

CHAPTER NINE

SESSION ONE – DR. NIKOLAS PERRIN

Caroline is relieved Dr. Perrin's office feels more like a friend's living room than a clinical setting. His office is on the bottom level of a three-story home, in which Caroline could only assume is his residence too. The office has a separate entrance from the main living quarters. Situated on the side of a mountain, the view from the large bay window affords breathtaking scenery of the Blue Ridge Mountains. The space is clean and tastefully decorated, in a minimalist Feng-Shui way. With the exception of a framed oath, there are no pictures on the walls. A large floor-to-ceiling ornate, wooden bookshelf covers one whole wall. The aroma in the air is unobtrusive, scented with a fresh, earthy smell. Harmonious music is playing from somewhere in the background. It too is so slight you wouldn't even notice if all your senses weren't on high alert as Caroline's are at this moment.

Seated on a chaise lounge, Caroline questions herself again why she is here. Before she can answer, Dr. Perrin enters the room and introduces himself. His picture did not do him justice. He is every bit as handsome, in a Greco-Roman way, and carries his six-foot frame with such a commanding presence. Dr. Perrin sits down in a wing-back chair askew from Caroline.

He opens a notebook and informs his new patient, "I will take notes throughout our session so do not be concerned when I am writing. Please, tell me about yourself."

Caroline cannot believe she is sitting in a shrink's office and the first thing she has to do is talk about herself. Caroline wants to go running from the room. Why did he have to call back that same evening and why did she make this appointment? She had two weeks in between his call back and her first appointment to change her mind. Between the nightmares that kept coming, the flashback at work, and Vickie's ultimatum, she is really spooked. So here she sat.

"My name is Caroline McKenzie, I am twenty-nine years old. I am a registered nurse, and a Captain in the Army. I have lived in North Carolina all my life except for my years in the Army on tours of duty. I went reservist after my four years. I have worked at the hospital in the ER ever since coming back from Iraq. Umm…never married…no children. What else do you want to know?"

"What do you do with your spare time?"

"I take a language class at the university and I volunteer at the animal shelter."

"Any time spent less… altruistically?"

Caroline flushed. "I travel frequently with friends."

"Great." Dr. Perrin continues writing. "Tell me about your formative years."

Caroline didn't like the writing, but she continued. "Raised in Winston Salem by two wonderful, working parents. Normal middle-class upbringing. Only child. I enlisted in the Army the day after I graduated from Duke and left for officer candidate training on my twenty-third birthday. I have been stationed on the east coast, west coast, and have had two tours overseas, the last being in Iraq."

Dr. Perrin sat there staring at her. This is making her feel a touch uncomfortable but the silence is what prods her on.

"I came home disillusioned of who I was and what I wanted from life. I love military life but I was sure of two things after my last tour. One: I wanted to continue nursing in the private sector and I knew where I wanted to live. Other than that, I was clueless."

"How did you know where you wanted to live?"

"My best friends from high school moved here to Asheville in our early twenties while I was at Duke. It was as good a place to start as anywhere else. In fact, it is partly because of them that I am here with you."

"How so?"

"My friends are the ones who suggested I needed help." Caroline notices the doctor writing more vigorously in his notebook.

"Ow! Bet that wasn't a pleasant conversation."

"Words were said. Feelings were hurt. Then after I survived the initial shock, they went for the Aw factor."

"The Aw factor?"

"You know. Shock and Aw! Telling me I have PTSD. Listing all the things I hate about my life and then making me feel that they were all my fault. Like I have control over what my mind mixes up while I am sleeping. Or, that it is my issues why I can't make a relationship work. They think my hours spent at work are a cover up so I do not have to be alone. Look, I don't mean to undermine your profession, but I can't imagine how talking about myself with you will help. I almost didn't show up for this appointment."

"But you came anyway. What made you change your mind?"

Silence infiltrates the room. Caroline decides at this moment it is now or never.

Caroline sits in silence for a moment longer, reflecting on her reasons for being here. "I guess…fear."

Dr. Perrin allows this time of introspection. After a long pause Caroline continues, "My flashbacks and my fears of sleeping, of any relationship, and fear of loss."

"Tell me about each of these fears." Dr. Perrin scribbles before stating, "Let's start with the fear of sleeping."

"I have nightmares a couple times a week."

"What are these nightmares about?"

"I have a reoccurring nightmare that vaguely resembles reality from when I was in Iraq. I have one reoccurring dream that makes no sense, but the gist in both is that I will die. Other dreams are random. Some I have had as long as I can remember. I do not feel immediate danger but the theme is the same. I'm going to die. Sometimes it is at the hands of another. Sometimes I feel like I want to die, like I want it to end."

Dr. Perrin immediately jots something in his notebook. Caroline wants to rip that book from his hand and throw it out the window.

"Have you ever considered harming yourself?"

"No, never." Caroline feels his gaze staring a hole through her. Then he scribbles something else.

"How about your fear of"—he glances at his notes—"relationships?"

"It's not so much the relationship part that scares me but the anticipation of how and when it will end that keeps me on guard." Caroline watches the doctor write something else and this time, he underlines it. "What did I say that you felt you had to underscore it?"

"I noted that your expectations of your relationships were an ending, instead of a beginning."

"That's not what I said."

"Isn't it?"

Caroline runs her words through her head once more. She thinks about the last few dates she has been on and realizes that even though the doc's words are not her own, they are the truth. The silence prompts Caroline to admit, "I have become used to be alone. I don't think I have ever been truly committed when dating someone. I am always expecting it to end. Again, sometimes at the hands of another and sometimes I want it to end." Caroline sits quiet and motionless as she lets that sink in, fighting back emotions she did not even know she had.

Dr. Perrin breaks the silence. "Let's continue with these fears. You stated you have a fear of loss. What type of loss?"

"That's just it. I have no idea," Caroline admits.

"Can you explain what this loss feels like?"

"Okay…Um…I feel…" Caroline's words choke into a raspy whisper, "as if a part of me is missing. Not like an arm or leg I've physically lost. Just…a feeling of emptiness I guess." Caroline wipes her eyes with her shirt sleeve and clarifies, "Like a despondency I can't explain. I have no reason to be despondent. I have a career I love, family and friends who love me. So why do I still feel like something is missing?"

Dr. Perrin hands Caroline a tissue.

Leaning forward to accept his offer of sympathy, Caroline continues, "The nightmares are why I am afraid of sleeping, but the real nightmare"—Caroline wipes the tears that are now streaming down her cheeks—"is the feeling of loss I have when I wake."

Dr. Perrin immediately writes Caroline's words. The use of pen and paper recording her deepest thoughts and fears was too much.

Caroline's emotional state is hanging by a thread at this point and she does not know how to go on. "I am sorry I have wasted your time," Caroline apologizes as she grabs her jacket and heads for the door. "I don't think this will work."

Caroline closes the door as she leaves Dr. Perrin's office. Mortified by her own actions, she sits in her car outside the doctor's office gathering her composure and considering the emotional turmoil of the last half hour. *Where did all that come from? Good God, I am unstable.* As she wipes the mascara that has blazed a path down her cheek, she is jolted out of her skin by a knock on the driver's side window.

"Have you found anything else that has worked to ease these fears?" Dr. Perrin yells through the glass.

Caroline, wishing she would have driven away immediately, rolls the window down. "Like what?"

"Like drugs or self-medication? You tell me. Have you tried anything else that has helped? If so, then Godspeed, Caroline McKenzie. If not, then I suggest we finish our session." Dr. Perrin turns and walks back toward his office. Caroline gets out of her car, closes the car door and follows him.

"Fine. But just remember, you asked for this," Caroline yells to his backside as she rushes up the sidewalk. "You better be good at what you do or you may need self-medicated."

"Oh, I am," Dr. Perrin confirms as he holds the door to his office open. Caroline steps through.

"You are what? Good at what you do? Or self-medicated?"

This makes Dr. Perrin chuckle as he directs Caroline back inside his office. She takes her seat and Dr. Perrin gets out his annoying notebook.

"How long will this take?" Caroline asks as she reseats herself on the sofa.

"How long will what take? This session or therapy as a whole?"

"Therapy."

"Therapy is based on diagnosis and what the patient is wanting to get out of therapy. I cannot determine the length of therapy at this moment but you have the option of running to your car at any time."

"During this session or therapy as a whole?" Caroline mimics his earlier question.

"Both."

"How many times a month will we meet?"

"That depends on you and what you are seeking. In the beginning, I prefer once a week. Weekly therapy will help you adjust and ease into working together. It helps me to understand your routine and integrate a treatment plan. Once we feel comfortable with one another, diagnose any outlying issues, and determine the therapy that best fits your goals, then frequency of treatment can be better determined."

"What are outlying issues?"

"Issues that your conscious self is not aware of at this time."

"You're saying I am suppressing memories in my subconscious?"

"Someone has done their homework. But no, I didn't say that. All I mean is we will examine all avenues for any issues that might try to surface."

"So what will you do to me to 'examine these avenues'?" Caroline uses air quotes around his words.

"My goal is to assist you in self-discovery, promoting healing by deeply exploring your psyche. I will do nothing to you. I will just be the facilitator. You will do the hard work. I have a few techniques I prefer for certain types of therapy which can provide valuable insights. But again, we will work together to determine the therapy that works best for both of us and most importantly, one in which you are comfortable."

"Like?"

"There is psychoanalysis, behavior and cognitive therapies, integrative or holistic therapies. Some patients use one type of therapy while others require an associative or combination of therapies. These can involve things like helping to regulate your emotions at time of stress, assisting you to restructure your cognitive thought processes, and relaxation techniques, along with dissociative awareness to help with symptoms and issues related to trauma."

"If I have PTSD, what kind of therapy would you suggest?"

"There are evidence-based therapies and techniques that have proven positive with PTSD sufferers. There are several types, and integration of these types have proven to be best practice. Revisiting the traumatic event or events, instead of suppressing them, is important in healing."

"Isn't PTSD revisiting the traumatic event over and over again? Why would I want to do that? I survived it once. I am not sure I can survive... visitation."

"There are different techniques to assist one in safely revisiting the event. Many individuals find retelling stories of the trauma and then reprocessing the memory in a new way has helped them control how the memories affect their lives."

"I hate talking about myself. What else do you got, doc?"

"Well, there is hypnotherapy. It has proven to be useful in revisiting past experiences, then realigning the negative trauma with positive results."

Caroline is shocked. "I have already lived the horror that is my life. I mean, was my life. I don't see how dredging it back up will do any good. There are things not worth remembering."

"So you feel you do not remember these incidents?"

"Oh, God no. I will never forget the horror of war."

Caroline, expecting the doctor to say something, looks up from her hands folded in her lap. Dr. Perrin is looking at her. He says nothing. Caroline, feeling uncomfortable, rethinks what she just said.

"I get it. I do remember and it is causing me continued trauma. And you think bringing all this back up, reliving what I have somehow put behind me, will help me cope more effectively?"

"I couldn't have said it better myself. Except, you haven't put it behind you. It is a part of you and it should be. I want to help make that part of you more productive in your present life. Not something you feel you must run from or repress."

"You have your work cut out for you."

"I say we both do. But first you must decide on what you are wanting out of therapy by asking yourself why you are seeking treatment." Dr. Perrin sits up to the edge of the seat. Caroline, on the other hand, slides deeper into hers.

"I will give you homework. I want you to think hard this week about what you want from therapy and make a list of your concerns and goals. I would also like you to take this journal and chronicle your daily activities. I would like you to delve deeply and consider why you are doing this activity and write that down on the right side of the page. That will lead me to a greater understanding of your character, your actions, and what motivates you."

"Is that all?" Caroline protests. "I am not that deep. I doubt I even know why I do certain things."

"That's okay too. Just write 'DK' if you truly don't know. But I bet if you examine your actions, it might help you determine your strengths and weaknesses. It may even help you with the reason for seeking therapy, even your reason for choosing me as your therapist. We all need to rationalize our actions to better understand our purpose. I do want to clarify: you have never considered harming yourself or others?"

"No, of course not. Well, not in the civilian world."

Dr. Perrin looks up from his notebook, starts to comment, then changes his mind. "Is there someone you can call if you would ever have thoughts of self-harm?"

Caroline can't believe this line of questions. "Doctor Perrin, I am not suicidal."

He scribbles another note. "The Veteran's Administration Hospital offers a suicide hotline for returning vets but you could also go to your local ER."

"I am not suicidal." Caroline sits up straighter, looking Dr. Perrin in the eyes. "I could become homicidal though if you continue with this line of questioning."

Once again, Dr. Perrin writes in his notebook. He smiles at her, which helps Caroline relax. "I am writing orders for a few tests you will need at the medical facility of your choice. You will need a complete physical with EKG, orthostatic blood pressures documented, an EEG, and a sleep study to determine any underlying sleep disorders. I would like these to be done within the next few weeks, if possible."

Dr. Perrin stands, handing her the orders.

"Is that all?" Caroline takes the orders from his hand, shoving them in her purse. After scheduling her next appointment, Caroline leaves Dr. Perrin's office with a sense of dread for her homework assignment. She isn't looking forward to all the hospital tests either. Feeling sure she knew her strengths and weaknesses, the homework would be easy enough. Why she is seeking therapy…that seems obvious too. Why she chose him for a therapist…something inside of her was telling her, he is the one.

CHAPTER TEN

GUIDELINES OF PRACTICE

Session One
November 2010

Captain Caroline McKenzie:

Caroline McKenzie is a twenty-nine-year-old, single female. Never been married. No children. Therapy suggested by concerned friends due to her friends' diagnosing traumatic stress disorder brought on by time served in Iraq as a Captain in the US Army, now reservist. Their concerns were her long hours at work, lack of lasting relationships, and flashbacks and nightmares.

Denies suicidal ideations but stated "Sometimes I feel like I want to die, like I want it to end."

Caroline, oppositional, does not feel unsatisfied with her relationships or work hours, but states the flashbacks and nightmares disrupt not only her career as an emergency room nurse but also her relationships including friends and male companions.

Flashbacks and fears of sleeping, relationships, and loss are Caroline's self-admitted, interpersonal conflicts that have led her to therapy.

Will delve deeper to understand meaning behind "real nightmare is the feeling of loss"

Caroline took much persuasion to complete entire session.

With Socratic dialogue, Caroline's own words proved helpful in self-discovery by allowing her to see hidden and new meanings within them. Time for reflection and introspection during therapy also proved helpful.

Therapy will need to include techniques to delve deeper for self-translation of these fears for proper diagnosis.

<u>Provisional Diagnoses:</u>

1) Possible Depressive Disorder: recurrent, severe, without Psychotic Features.
2) Post-Traumatic Stress Disorder: combat related: Anxiety Disorder, Not Otherwise Specified. Diagnostic criteria for PTSD: Positive history of exposure to a traumatic event—US Army Captain served in Iraq.

<u>Four symptom clusters:</u>

1. Intrusion: nightmares
2. Avoidance: fear of sleeping; fear of medical traumas at place of work
3. Negative alterations in cognitions and mood: "despondent"
4. Alterations in arousal and reactivity: sleep disturbance; over-reactive startle response. Duration, functioning, and exclusion are present.

<u>Therapeutic Plan of Care:</u>

Development of Coping Skills to reduce Anxiety and PTSD symptoms after educating on symptoms of same, cognitive behavioral therapy, as well as Psychotropic Medication recommendations for symptom management: anxiety, depression, insomnia, nightmares.

Medical needs: EKG, orthostatic blood pressures, EEG study, sleep study to determine any underlying sleep disorders.

<u>Develop Safety Plan:</u>

Included who she will contact if having thoughts of self-harm, provide emergency office number, and direction for calling local VA or going to ER if feeling unsafe.

Empower client to implement coping strategies for feelings of emptiness.

Mastering skills needed to assist with negative thought processes.

With Caroline being his last patient of the day, Dr. Perrin closes his laptop and heads for the stairs. Before turning off the light, he catches a glint of something. The sun is coming through the blinds, catching the gold flecks of the frame on the wall. Though the frame has been hanging there since he started his practice, he feels compelled to cross the room and study its contents.

GUIDELINES OF PRACTICE the header reads.

1. To keep a safe and sacred space for the client.
2. To honor the client's experience and not intrude your own agenda.
3. To abuse not the position of trust for personal gain of any kind.

The fourth one, not listed, but something he would later need to consider: To know when to refer your client to another therapist. Dr. Perrin turns off the lights and locks the door to his office. He then spends the evening trying not to think of Caroline McKenzie.

CHAPTER ELEVEN

OMISSIVE DECEPTION

After finishing her morning yoga, Caroline is having a cup of coffee at the breakfast table when her phone rings. She recognizes the number immediately. Butterflies swarm in her stomach; a smile forms on her lips. She takes a deep breath to calm her nerves and answers. Before she even says hello—

"I hear you all have a castle there in Asheville and it is the most beautiful at Christmas time." Jameson is always so upbeat, even before seven a.m.

"We do. I can't believe you have never seen The Biltmore as many times as you've been here."

"I was waiting on the right person to go with me."

"How do you ooze so much charm before daybreak?"

"It's a gift. So are you going to invite me to Asheville or not?"

"Well, since I love The Biltmore, especially at Christmas time, you're invited but only if you buy the tickets."

"You're on. How's the second weekend after Thanksgiving, or is that too short of notice?"

Caroline freezes for a moment. She has only spoken with Jameson over the phone since their night in the cabin, and now, just a few weeks away, he would be in her town. The question of where he would stay, what his expectations for the weekend were, and where this would take the relationship all flooded her mind at once.

"I hope that weekend is okay," Jameson hurries on, feeling the line going cold. "I have booked us two rooms at the Grove Park Inn."

"Jameson, that is unnecessary. You can camp out on my couch." Caroline is overwhelmed at the thoughtfulness and extravagance but still can only offer her sofa.

"I don't know if you noticed, Captain, but I am a little too tall to fit on a couch. Besides, you might be used to sleeping in foxholes but I am not. I have higher standards."

"You're comparing my couch to a foxhole? Remind me never to cook for you. I would hate for you to compare my food to K-rations."

"Another thing you should know about me…I allow no one in my kitchen," Jameson warns.

"That's probably a good thing. My cooking isn't as good as K-rations."

"So we are set for the weekend after Thanksgiving, then? I have the rooms booked for Saturday night. I could be there to take you to breakfast Saturday morning so you don't have to eat your cooking. You can pay me back by showing me around Asheville."

"You got a deal, Mooresville."

"Great. Now that that is settled. How's your week been?"

Caroline tells him she is working on Thanksgiving since her friends go to their families and her parents are on a cruise this year. She would prefer her co-workers to stay home with their children and extended families anyway since she doesn't have either one. Jameson tells her about his Turkey Day plans with his family. Caroline laughs as he regales her with Brooks' family traditions such as full-contact football with his brothers and brother-in-law. That always got them in trouble because they came in battered and bloody to the dinner table.

Over the past few weeks, he has told her stories of his upbringing, like how the three boys shared a bathroom so that his sister could have one all to herself. Or how his brother got a used car for graduation but he got stuck with the family wagon when he graduated. But Caroline knows Jameson never felt slighted; she only hears love and caring in his stories. Caroline would have loved to share her bathroom with an older sister or fight over who got the car. She has always been a little jealous of Kelly's and Meredith's connection. She had always wished for a sister. One to play dolls with her when the weather was too bad to go outside, or one to give her advice about boys or share clothes. Her parents were too academically centered to concern themselves with more children. Caroline envies Jameson's close family ties and wonders what it would be like to be a part of a large family. She has always wanted a big family and always thought she would have her own one day. But she is now realizing that that dream could be too far gone.

Caroline tells him about how Marshall had missed her and how much he loved the toys she brought him. She tells him about the supplies she took to help clean along with some dog food since the coffers are getting bare. Caroline fills Jameson in on her work (leaving out the flashback episode). She tells him about her dinner with her friends (where she hadn't mentioned she and Jameson were talking). She described her busy week (leaving out the therapy session with Dr. Perrin). But of all the things Caroline did not tell Jameson, like the details of the phone call she received yesterday, this lie by omission will be the beginning of an end to many things.

* * *

"I have homework on the first day." Caroline commiserates as she seats herself at their favorite high-top table and throws her homework down on it.

Bianca stuffs a fry in her mouth before goading Caroline. "Does he grade on a curve? Because you will probably flunk your sanity class if he doesn't."

"Here's your standard deviation." Caroline gestures with her middle finger back at Bianca.

"Or our friend Caroline could blow that bell curve if her homework is on how crazy she is." Meredith turns toward Caroline with a straight face. "Your crazy score is up there. Like way over the mean."

"I am glad my mental faculties can be a source of entertainment for you all, but can we get serious here. I don't want to go through with this." Caroline slumps over the papers.

"We will help you." Kelly picks up the papers. "It can't be that bad."

"The session wasn't bad at all. Even though I walked out and had to be coaxed back in. Dr. Perrin knows what he is talking about. He asked insightful questions that made me open up, yet he is so empathetic that you aren't scared to tell him anything. I found myself rambling on just to fill the silence. It dawned on me later that he did that on purpose. He even made me laugh at myself. But he isn't too intrusive. His voice is soft and pleasant but not in an unmanly way. Almost seductive, you know. He is charismatic and makes you feel you are talking to your best friend. I felt immediately comfortable talking to him. I felt I could trust.…What's the looks for?"

"Holy Van Halen, you're hot for teacher!" Bianca laughingly answers Caroline. "You got it bad, bad, bad."

"Can you all please not make this any more difficult than it already is?" Caroline grabs the papers back from Kelly. "I will do my own homework."

Kelly points to the lined paper on top. "What's that page?"

"I have to write everything I do this week and why I am doing it. Dr. Perrin says it will help him understand my motivations."

Bianca pantomimes writing in the air. "Saw shrink. Motivation: Need outlet for my sexual frustration."

"I am frustrated, but it is not sexually and you three are the motivation for that frustration. Maybe the doc can help me understand why I am friends with you."

"Tell us what he said about your nightmares," Kelly breaks in.

During their meal, Caroline tells them about her research and how she found Dr. Perrin. She tells them the deciding factor to seek treatment is due to the flashback she experienced during the trauma at work. She tells them about her session and the different therapies and techniques they discussed, including hypnosis.

"Oooh, sign me up. I want to be hypnotized," Meredith says. "That sounds fun."

"I don't think Dr. Perrin does it for fun," Kelly shoots her down. "Aren't you worried, though, he would have his way with you while you are under his spell?"

Bianca spews Coors over the table. "If that's what goes on then sign me up along with Meredith."

"I don't even know if that is the therapy approach he will use. Besides, I have more research on the topic as part of my homework."

"Let us help you with it," Kelly offers as she picks the papers back up and reads the questions out loud, filling in the blanks.

Besides the normal bio, demographics, medications, and medical history (including mental illness) on any medical form, the form requests any chronic diseases, phobias, relationship problems, hobbies and spiritual practices.

"This is where we come in," Kelly instructs, reading aloud the next question. "Explain your feelings for your support system at home."

"The best ever," Meredith says a little too loud as she takes the final sip of her Long Island Iced Tea. "We rock as—"

"Hey, Booz-illa," Bianca interrupts, "lower it an octave. But Meredith is right. Put down she has three of the most empathetic friends who love and support her no matter what."

"We are compassion personified," Meredith slurs, staring inside her empty glass.

"Do not write that load of crap down, Kelly." Caroline grabs the pen from her.

"Are you calling bullshit?" Bianca questions as she covers her heart with her hand.

"Damn right I am. How much empathy did you show when I broke up with your cousin Bill, or your boss, what's his name?" Caroline continues, "And how much support did I receive when I told you all of my nightmares and flashbacks. If I remember correctly, you told me I was bat-crap-crazy and needed a shrink. And compassion, ha. I begged you all to not make our weekend together in West Virginia about getting laid but did you listen?" Caroline was sorry as soon as that came out of her mouth.

"If I remember correctly"—Bianca smirks at Caroline—"only one of us got laid that weekend. Let's see, raise your hand if you climbed out of a stranger's bed and stumbled through the woods, half-dressed back to our cabin at daybreak. Come on, keep 'em up, I want to count."

"You would have had to use the Jaws of Life to get me out of his bed," Meredith adds.

"I bet the poor fucking bastard didn't even know you bolted." Bianca's head shakes in sympathy for Jameson.

"Is that why we had to pack so quickly and get the hell out of there?" Kelly asks, astonished.

"Way to go, Nancy Drew. We were wondering when you would figure that out," Bianca chastises Kelly's innocence.

"Never fucking mind." Caroline gathers up her homework and places it back in her bag.

"Have you heard from him since then?" Kelly asks.

Caroline's delay in answer leaves Meredith and Kelly with dropped jaws.

"You have, and you didn't tell us," Meredith judges. Looking at Bianca, she says, "Why don't you look as surprised as me and Kelly? You knew about this, didn't you?"

Caroline jumps in and admits, "No, I have told no one. We have been talking by phone, sometimes emails, since the first week we were back. I didn't want to tell anyone until I was sure I was interested so don't be mad at Bianca. She didn't know either."

"I sort of did," Bianca confesses.

"How?" They all say in unison.

"When I came to pick you up at work the day you had that flashback," Bianca says, "there were a dozen purple tulips in a vase in your breakroom. Who else would send or want purple tulips in October? I said nothing at the time because you were so distraught."

"Way to go, Nancy Drew." Kelly friendly slaps Bianca while throwing her own words back at her.

The girls were not to be satisfied until Caroline confessed to everything. Over many cocktails, Caroline tells them about her and Jameson's night, about the flowers, her phone call to thank him, and their ongoing internet/cell phone relationship. She does not, however, tell them he will be in Asheville next weekend. She couldn't handle the onslaught of questioning that would ensue. She already had too many questions of her own.

CHAPTER TWELVE

COYOTE FLASHBACK

"They are adorable!" Caroline says as a litter of puppies bounce all over her, licking her face and chewing on her ears. Caroline laughs as she halfheartedly tries to free herself from puppy loving.

"These mongrels were brought in this morning, all seven of them," the shelter director tells Caroline. "Oh, Lordy be, what are we gonna do? We are running out of space, food, and supplies."

"What can I do?" Caroline offers.

"Find homes for all these little ones, but for now, the dogs in the kennel need fed before they are let outside in the yard."

Caroline does as instructed, making sure all the fences are closed before letting all the dogs out, except for one. Marshall will not leave her side. She talks to him while she cleans out the kennels and fills up all the water bowls. Afterward, she grabs a leash and goes to the yard with Marshall on her heels.

"Barkley," Caroline calls for the older dog, "time for a walk."

The dog plods forward, tail wagging, knowing it is her special time. Caroline wonders if Barkley questions why she has to wear a leash but Marshall doesn't. Caroline opens the yard gate; Marshall trots ahead while Barkley sniffs at every fallen leaf cluster. Caroline loves this part of the day—taking the dogs for a walk around the shelter's property. It allows time for thoughtful reflection along with excellent exercise for her and her aging friends. Barkley, a black and white mixed breed, stops every few paces to sniff at this or that, which means Marshall is gaining ground.

"Marshall, not too close. The river current is strong. I am not fishing you out of that river if you fall in." Caroline doesn't even know why she said that. Marshall hates water.

Marshall immediately ambles back toward Caroline and Barkley. It's a shame that neither of these well-behaved dogs will probably ever be adopted. They both have been at the shelter since Caroline started and now they are like old friends. She tells them everything—her plans, her pains, and even her hopes and dreams. They never criticize or judge her; they never tell her she's crazy. Marshall suddenly sits and looks up at her. She would have tripped over him if Barkley wouldn't have pulled her to the side with the leash.

"What's up, Marshall? Is it too cold out here for you? Maybe it is time to take a break and get a drink." Caroline takes out the water bottle with the attached rubber bowl and gives each dog its turn. After their refreshment, Barkley wants to head toward the woods. Marshall, on the other hand, turns to head back to the shelter.

"Come on, Marshall, you need the exercise as much as I do," Caroline prods. "We only have a few more miles and then we will head back."

After a mile of coaxing Marshall along behind them, he sits down and refuses to go any farther. Flat-out refuses. There is no budging him. Since Marshall is the more docile of the two, Caroline has to assume something is wrong and cuts the walk short. She leads the dogs back toward the shelter, but this time, Marshall is the one hurrying everyone else.

"Slow down, Marshall. What is wrong with you today?"

Just as the three of them clear the woods and are back on the path by the river, Marshall suddenly stops, sniffs the air, and emits a low growl. This alarms Caroline since she has never heard a growl come from Marshall. Barkley growls in support and pulls on his leash, facing the same direction as Marshall. Caroline, holding steadfast to Barkley's leash, tries to get Marshall to follow her up the embankment toward the shelter while dragging Barkley behind. Marshall will not listen and ferociously barks. Barkley harmonizes with Marshall. Caroline has never seen Marshall like this, hair raised on his back, teeth gnashing as he barks. Marshall takes off back down the river path, into the woods, Barkley pulling to join him. Caroline, turning to yell for Marshall, sees what her canine companions already know is following them. A coyote is standing on the ridge, watching them.

Caroline is paralyzed in fear. Not so much for her own safety but for

Marshall's. Caroline knew of coyote presence in the Blue Ridge Mountains but she had never heard of one attacking someone. But once Marshall got to him, the coyote would have no choice but to defend herself. Caroline, not able to drag Barkley up the hill to the safety of the shelter, screams for help.

"Papa! Papa!"

Scenes flash in front of her like tuning of an old-time TV. Caroline can't trust what her mind is viewing. She is unsure if she truly just yelled that or if she only heard it in her head. Barkley, pulling on the leash, helps Caroline refocus. Her disorientation to her surroundings subsides.

She immediately looks for Marshall, who has now climbed the small incline and is running across the ridge. The coyote makes a break for the tree line and is out of sight before Marshall can get to the uninvited guest. Marshall, just short of entering the wooded area, stops and barks his warning to the creature. He then turns and heads back down the hill toward Caroline.

Barkley jumps all over Marshall when he returns to their side, like canine chest bumps and high fives. Caroline rubs Marshall's head and scratches his thick coat behind his ears. Caroline bends over and holds Marshall's face in her hands. "Thanks, Buddy. You saved us today. I promise I will listen to you from now on."

They turn up the hill toward the shelter. Caroline swears Marshall is walking with swagger.

Caroline gets home from the shelter with enough time to prepare for her class and get ready. Right before leaving for her language class, Caroline receives a text from Jameson. He acknowledges he received her email about Marshall's heroic escapades today. His text is brief, letting her know he will be out of town the rest of the week and hopes she has a great Thanksgiving. Caroline thinks the text sounds as if Jameson felt an obligatory return was needed, as opposed to him actually wanting to speak to her. She didn't even want this relationship and here she is experiencing pains of disappointment from his dismissive behavior toward her. Caroline hated irony and she hated being vulnerable.

Not feeling up to class now, she substitutes her jeans and sweater for fuzzy pajamas and climbs into bed with her homework from Dr. Perrin. When she gets to the question "significant other," Caroline *hmphs* out loud while drawing a straight line in the box. *How appropriate,* she thinks upon viewing her answer. *A flat line for significant other. It sure feels like death.* Her cynicism turns to depression so she discards her homework to the bedside floor, rolls to her side and curls her knees to her chest, forming the fetal position under the covers. A wave of loneliness crashes over her. She can feel herself going under. The faint laugh lines at the corners of her eyes become small streambeds as her tears carry her to sleep.

CHAPTER THIRTEEN

SESSION TWO – HYPNOTIC DEPTH

"Caroline. I was wondering if you would get out of your car. Please come in."

Caroline stops long enough to view the scenic landscape through the bay window, hoping this will calm her. She notices immediately the scent of the air differs from last time. It is coming from a burning joss stick on the bookshelf. Dr. Perrin does not interrupt her train of thought. She summons the courage to turn and finds him standing back, observing her. The hair on her neck rises, causing a chill to flow through her body.

Dr. Perrin breaks the spell and offers, "Would you like a beverage before we begin?"

Caroline defers, wanting only to sit down and forget that awkward moment. She walks across the open space toward the chaise lounge.

"Let's review what we discussed last week and then we will move on to your homework assignment. As I understand it, and please correct me if I'm wrong, you are seeking therapy due to what you consider to be Post-Traumatic Stress Disorder based on recurring nightmares and flashbacks. Is this correct?"

"Yes."

"I understand also that you have fears you'd like to discuss, including fear of relationships, fear of sleeping due to the nightmares, and the fear of loss that leaves you feeling despondent. Is this also correct?"

"Yes."

"Let's review your medical history."

All the prescribed tests were within normal limits. Dr. Perrin finds nothing concerning in her past that would warrant a certain type of therapy or technique, so he moves on.

"Let's discuss your homework." Dr. Perrin notices Caroline blushing. Caroline tries to not think of Bianca's comment, "hot for teacher," as she and Dr. Perrin meticulously cover each day of the week on her homework assignment. He asks her to describe her week, so Caroline goes through each day and her reasoning behind doing each activity. Other than the occasional note-taking, Dr. Perrin is immersed in what Caroline is saying. Though he is intensely watching her, she does not feel uncomfortable. She feels he is truly concerned.

When Caroline brings up going to the shelter, Dr. Perrin notices a visible change in her demeanor. Caroline becomes more animated, more relaxed, and her face takes on an ambience of happiness. Caroline describes the husky half-breeds recently dropped off at the shelter. She confides her concerns that the shelter cannot provide for all the animals.

"I had a weird episode this week at the shelter."

When asked by Dr. Perrin to describe the "episode" at the shelter, he again observes a change in her.

"A coyote was following us. I wasn't aware, but the dogs were. They tried to tell me." Caroline is looking out the bay window from her seat, staring intently. "It wasn't until Marshall took off after it that I realized it is watching us. I can't drag Barkley up the hill and I can't leave him either. I am paralyzed in fear. I yell for help."

Dr. Perrin is writing to capture her words, her emotions, and her obvious tense shift. Caroline sits quietly for a few moments before turning back to Dr. Perrin. "Marshall ran the coyote back into the woods and it was all over."

"You have never experienced this certain…'episode'?"

"No."

"What can you recall now?"

"I think I yelled the word "Papa" or I heard it in my head. I also felt fear, but I don't know why. I was in no danger. I could have made it to safety in time. I remember a vision, maybe."

"A vision?"

"Of a dog ferociously barking. But now, I can't remember if I had a vision then or if I dreamed it up later." Caroline describes the vision she had in the woods with Marshall. She explains a scene flashed in front of her eyes, but she felt a part of the scene, not like she was watching it on a screen.

Dr. Perrin remains on this line of thought. "I notice on your homework, your reasoning for volunteering at the shelter is because you love animals. I also notice your bio notes you have no pets."

"I have always had a fondness for animals. An animal doesn't care if you're a political or religious beliefs. You never have to question whether a dog loves you for your money or lack of it. An animal will love you when no one else will and that love is pure and unconditional," Caroline confesses.

"Yet you own no pets." Dr. Perrin tries to understand the importance or differentiation of the love for animals and the love for being at the shelter.

"I feel there is a void within me."

"What does this void feel like to you? Describe it for me."

"Like an abyss…One that would show up as a dark place on an x-ray." Caroline attempts to help him understand. "And when I'm at the shelter, I feel less alone, like the void can be filled."

"Is this void filled when you are around any animals or just at the shelter?"

"At the shelter I guess, because Marshall is there."

"Marshall is the yellow lab from the coyote episode?"

"Yes."

"Is Marshall up for adoption?"

"Yes. I know what you are thinking. Why don't I adopt him? My friends say the same thing but it wouldn't be fair to Marshall. I am rarely home and once a month I am gone for entire weekends with the reserve. Every time I took a vacation, I would have to board him, which I could not do to him. At the shelter, he has people who are with him all day, he gets plenty of exercise and is well cared for by the staff. What kind of life would he have with me?"

"What kind of life would you have with him?"

Dr. Perrin's hears Caroline's breath catch before answering his question. "I would come home every night to a loving companion. But I would worry all day about him. I would never feel alone. But he would be alone thirteen hours while I worked, three days a week. I would have to endure his death if I outlived him or worse, he would have to endure mine. Never understanding why I didn't return." Caroline feels the tears welling up in the corners of her eyes. "I have run this scenario through my head a thousand times. Can we please move on?"

Dr. Perrin notes the emotional change in his book and moves on as suggested. "Okay, let's run through the rest of your week."

"I met my friends out one evening."

"Are these the same friends who recommended you seek therapy?"

"Yes, it was the normal Bitch-N-Booze."

"Bitch-N-Booze?" Dr. Perrin takes that note.

"That's what we call our meetings because it's mostly what they are about—us bitching about our lives and drinking heavily to compensate."

"So did you discuss our session?"

"Yes, I tell them everything."

"And did they have an opinion?"

"Oh, God yes. They have an opinion on everything but surprisingly it was mostly positive. I don't need their approval but it is nice to be validated sometimes. And then the next two days I worked. Thankfully it was uneventful with no flashbacks and now I'm here."

Caroline purposefully leaves out her discussion with her Commander and her relationship with Jameson. She doesn't know why, other than those are two areas in her life that she is the least secure. She is not ready to open them up for discussion.

"Now that we both know why you are here, let's discuss our therapy options." Dr. Perrin sits back in his chair. "Did you do your research homework?"

"I did," Caroline proudly states.

"Well, then I am sure you have numerous questions." Dr. Perrin remains silent, allowing Caroline time to formulate her thoughts.

After several silent minutes pass, Caroline says, "Tell me more about hypnosis."

"Hypnosis is a state of mind. An altered state of consciousness, if you will. Where one can allow the conscious and subconscious a period of relaxation so that the subconscious mind can be accessed. Hypnosis allows for heightened awareness into our intuitive faculties, the part of the mind beyond that holds the key to enlightenment."

"How did you become a hypnotist?"

"I am not a hypnotist. I am a hypnotherapist. Someone who brings about therapeutic change by helping you access memories from your subconscious that the physical body has detached from your consciousness and placed there to protect you."

"Is that why people can remember all the way up to a car crash but they can't remember the actual crash? I see that a lot in the ER."

"Exactly," Dr. Perrin confirms.

"Will it make me feel strange?"

"Hypnosis, for most people, is actually a pleasant, calming, and extremely relaxing moment."

"While I am under hypnosis, what are you doing?" Kelly's worries haunt her.

"I will be your guide through your subconscious. Walking you through each step with my voice to help you to heal and reframe the traumas."

"You won't have me clucking around like a chicken?"

"No, my patients never cluck, unless that is what they want. You will always be in control and can emerge from hypnosis anytime you desire. Contrary to popular belief, you cannot be hypnotized to do anything you do not want to do. You cannot be made to reveal any deep, personal secrets. You'll be aware of the fact that you are in dialogue with me as the hypnotherapist. You are free to open your eyes at any time and you can refuse to answer any questions. You will be able to redirect the session to your own desires at any time."

"So I am in total control."

"There is a saying, 'All hypnosis is self-hypnosis.'"

"Do you plant some bad imagery in my brain so that I will cease a certain behavior or do you just swipe them from my memory?"

"I like to promote the positive. I do not want you negating your experience; I want you to cope effectively with your past traumas."

"So you're going to hypnotize me to have a positive outlook on war? Don't think it can be done, Doc."

"You're right—that can't be done. But what can happen is that you can relate your experiences positively to your present life."

"What if I can't be hypnotized?"

"Everyone goes into self-hypnosis throughout the day. Have you ever pulled in your garage at home but don't remember driving there? That is because there are many levels of hypnosis, from fully aware of what is going on around you to deeper levels of trance-like states, where actions and thoughts are totally unaware to you. While it is true some people are not able to relax their mind to the point of allowing access to the otherwise inaccessible subconscious mind, I have had very few of those cases. We will never know if this is the case until we get there. For today, I would like to work on some relaxation techniques. I would like you to start by resting comfortably on the chaise. Whatever position is comfortable for you."

Caroline twists from a seated position to lying, legs extended and arms at her side.

"We will start with progressive muscle relaxation. Bring your shoulders to your ears and tighten your muscles, holding the tension, holding, now take a deep breath. As you blow out, relax the muscles by letting the shoulders drop slowly away from your ears. We're going to do this two more times. As you are doing this, I want you to concentrate only on the tenseness of your muscles in your neck and then the relaxation of these muscles." Dr. Perrin talks her through the relaxation of her neck muscles. "Now we are going to do two more and when you exhale, I want you to blow out any thoughts from your mind. You only feel muscles tensing, then relaxation. That's right. Clear your mind with each exhale, relaxing your muscles more completely every time you breathe out."

Dr. Perrin guides Caroline from her shoulders, ultimately tensing and relaxing each major muscle group, to her toes. "Now you should recognize what it feels like when your muscles are tight versus when they are relaxed. Whenever confronted with stress, you can guide your own self through this relaxation technique."

"I feel like a gummy."

"That is your body at rest. The hypnotic trance is not much different from how you feel now. Hypnosis is just a deeper relaxed state. I would like you to practice this throughout the week, allowing your mind to focus solely on the muscles. Allow the mind to travel away from your troubles of everyday life. Focus on peace and a state of tranquility."

Draped over the chaise, Caroline asks, "You said you would guide me through the trauma. How will that work?"

"As we discussed earlier, there are different levels of hypnosis or different depths. We will discuss different traumatic experiences while you are under hypnosis. Some of these experiences will be during a light level, while others can evolve to a much deeper level. There are five levels. Level one is like tuning in the television. Blurred with occasional glimpses of clarity."

Caroline immediately thinks of her episode with Marshall.

"Level two is like watching a movie. You will view things as if they are projected on a screen. You will be somewhat detached with little physical or emotional involvement. You might even be looking down on the scene. Level three, you will be acting in the movie. You will hear sounds and possibly have some feelings but you will remain somewhat disconnected. Level four will be like living it but still aware of the present. And level five, you will be totally involved just like life itself with emotions, feelings, et cetera."

Caroline concentrates on remembering the levels but her muscles don't give a shit.

"You can experience the joy and possibly the pain that you felt at that time. Some people feel the experience but do not see it. It can be overwhelming. Don't worry; we will start slow. Sometimes the client can move between the different levels, with or without the therapist. I will take you to the lowest level of healing possible. When I bring you back out of hypnosis, you should not continue to experience the emotions. You might be slightly confused about what you are seeing or feeling during hypnosis, like people, objects, or clothing. Scenes may even flash from one to another like changing the channels. Do you have any questions?"

"Millions, but my mind is blown," Caroline admits as she raises her gelatinous muscles to a seated position.

"We are almost out of time anyway." Dr. Perrin walks to his desk and glances at his calendar. "How about we meet the Saturday after Thanksgiving?"

Caroline notes the appointment in her phone, then leaves the office, slumbering to her car, completely and utterly relaxed.

CHAPTER FOURTEEN

HYPNOSIS 101

Session Two
November 2010

Captain Caroline McKenzie:

Client provided completed requested information at beginning of session.

Reviewed her reasoning for therapy, as noted in Session One. Patient remains in agreement this session.

Review of Bio: Patient not prescribed any medications. Denies self-medicating. Denies illegal substance use. Admits to drinking one to two glasses of wine daily and occasional alcoholic beverages with friends, not alone. No significant past medical history. No mental illness in family. Not aware of any phobias. Non-practicing Christian. Hobbies include linguistics study, yoga, and travel. Client maintains Army reservist status.

Medical testing completed as per orders: No discovery, within normal limits (results attached).

Hours worked are within normal limits per week, slightly on the excessive side.

Client documents a strong support system from friends and family. Friends are supportive and honest but influence does not cross boundaries.

Verbal statements not always congruent with nonverbal cues. Client appears to be evasive at times with information or feelings she is not ready to divulge or not aware of at this time.

Discussed hypnotherapy in length.

Progressive muscle relaxation beneficial and effective this session. Suggested client to continue practice till next session, especially when under stress. Need of progressive relaxation indicated prior to hypnosis to help attune her energies.

Will discuss grounding techniques next session.

Client discusses coping techniques that include volunteering at shelter. Client is utilizing AAT (Animal-Assisted Therapy) without full awareness this is a coping strategy. Has moderate therapeutic effect. Research suggests AAT is therapeutic for trauma sufferers. Possible animal therapy during session could be explored at a later time.

Client discussed an "episode" she experienced while walking the dogs at the shelter. She described visions that flashed before her. Those visions included a dog ferociously barking, feelings of danger, and paralysis from fear. Client described the walk in past tense, shifting to present tense when retelling the "episode."

Extreme attachment bond between client and one particular shelter dog, Marshall.

If hypnotherapy technique to be considered, will discuss possible PL emergence during hypnosis. Will discuss with client at next session.

C H A P T E R   F I F T E E N

BITCH AND TEARS

"How was everyone's Thanksgiving?" Caroline asks while hugging each of her friends as they enter the pub together.

"I regret going probably as much as the Indians did," Bianca states as she strips off her coat and yells her drink order to Greg. "Next year, the bird is being stuffed with anti-depressants."

"Okay, how about you two?" Caroline asks with a touch of hope.

"Make that two, Greg." Meredith mounts the stool. "Next year, we are having Thanksgiving together. Just the four of us. I would rather spend it with loved ones than my family."

"Hey!" Kelly fights back.

"How's it going with Dr. Hottie?" Bianca asks as she slams her drink.

"Better yet, how's it going with Mooresville?" Kelly inquires.

"Both have been going fine. Jameson spent Thanksgiving with his family and we have talked a couple of times this week. Now don't go ballistic on me right now when I tell you this. He is coming here to Asheville next weekend."

"O-M-G! We should all get together," Kelly schemes.

"Is he bringing his brothers?" Meredith asks.

"One of his brothers is married. The other one is the one you blew off during the cookout at the cabin." Caroline shoots Meredith's plans down.

"Which one was he?" Meredith tries to remember.

"You know, Mocha Macho Grande." Bianca helps Meredith's recall.

"That was Jameson's brother. The tall heavy dude." Meredith slaps her forehead. "Why didn't anyone tell me?"

Bianca repeat slaps Meredith's forehead. "We did. You were too drunk as usual to listen to us."

"I believe, in fact, you said that you were too old to ride a bouncy house," Kelly adds to Meredith's embarrassment.

"Oh God, I didn't say that to him, did I?" Meredith hides her face in her folded arms on the table.

"We aren't telling," Bianca says. "We are going to make you sweat it so at Caroline's wedding, you will question the depths of your indiscretion."

"I call wedding planner," Kelly says.

"Stop. You are approaching the ballistic line. Actually, you have crossed it. And no, we all are not getting together. He is coming in next Saturday. We are staying at the Grove Park Inn Saturday night, two separate rooms, then he will leave on Sunday."

"Two rooms? Your hormones will be gnawing through the wall like termites on estrogen-laced amphetamines," Bianca foretells.

"He booked the rooms before asking if he could come. I didn't know how to tell him to cancel one," Caroline confesses.

"For fuck's sake, tell the poor man one room will be sufficient to screw his brains out. How hard is that?" Bianca has never been one to mince words.

"We need to go shopping to spruce up your…unmentionables," Kelly offers.

"I can just see Jameson's face as he undresses Caroline, right down to her army-issued undies." Meredith laughs as she acts out the moment. "Oh yeah, baby, let me slide your nurse's granny panties off those furry legs." They all fall out laughing at Caroline's lingerie expense.

"I do not always have furry legs," Caroline rebuts.

"You're right about that. They're usually pelts." Meredith pours it on.

Meredith's and Bianca's razzing, along with the recounts of being with their families the day before, has them all laughing well into the evening. Caroline has so much more to tell them. She breaks in the conversation after they have eaten, the food helping soak up some of the booze.

"I see Dr. Perrin"—Caroline emphasizes his real name while shooting Bianca a dirty look—"tomorrow. I think I will try hypnosis to help deal with the nightmares. I am hoping it will help with the flashbacks also."

Kelly takes ahold of Caroline's hand. "Are you scared? We can go with you."

"Not so much as scared as….suspicious. Maybe a little doubtful."

Caroline tells the girls everything she and Dr. Perrin discussed about hypnosis including the levels, his involvement, and the saying "all hypnosis is really self-hypnosis." Her friends are supportive, asking the right questions and actually not making fun of her at this moment. Their support means the world to her, convincing her to give it a try.

"I have one more thing I need to tell you all before we head home," Caroline announces.

"I've got a gut-fucking feeling this is going to be bad," Bianca states as she sits back down.

Kelly and Meredith throw their coats back across the chairs, mounting their seats, full attention on Caroline. By Caroline's expression, they know this is some serious shit.

"While we were in West Virginia, I received an email from my commander," Caroline starts.

Kelly is already tearing up; Meredith and Bianca, for once, are rendered speechless. The three of them have always known that Caroline could be called back up to the majors, deployed to some war zone at the drop of some politician's pen, and have begged her on numerous occasions to retire from the military. But they also know Caroline. She is a born soldier.

"I will be receiving orders soon. Orders for deployment," Caroline proceeds, "but I don't know where or when yet."

"You can't get out of it?" Kelly begs.

"I am in the military. Deployment is part of that life. Besides, I like having a purpose, a mission. I like being a part of something bigger than myself."

"Then join a sports team, for crying out loud," Meredith states while motioning for another round of drinks. "You almost got your damn-fool head shot off the last time."

"What Meredith is trying to say"—Kelly tries her hand at political correctness—"is that we are afraid something will happen to you, something worse than what happened in Iraq."

"The odds of having my convoy attacked again is extremely low. I don't even know where I am going yet. And please remember, I am part of the United States Army; we can kick some ass."

"That's what Alexander the Great thought too. And Britain. And Russia. They thought they were the fiercest team on the planet in their time. They never feared fighting the Afghanis. But then these Kush-bags just keep coming back like herpes." Bianca's voice and attitude rise to meet the challenge.

"We get you love being a soldier, Caroline. We really do, and we respect you for it," Kelly starts.

Meredith interrupts Kelly. "But can't you just work at the VA here in Asheville? That would still be serving your country."

"I will make you this promise. After my enlistment is up next year, I will not resign. I will come back home for good."

Kelly falls into Caroline's arms, sobbing. "We know you will come home to us. That's not what we're worried about."

"We are worried it will be in a box." Meredith cries along with her sister.

The foursome closed the bar down that night in booze and tears.

CHAPTER SIXTEEN

SESSION THREE –
COGNITIVE AWARENESS

Sleep had eluded Caroline after leaving the pub last night. She'd spent the night on the internet, browsing reviews of hypnotherapy, means of induction, and possible side effects. After four cups of coffee, Caroline leaves for her third appointment with Dr. Perrin. She couldn't help but correlate that this third appointment is like a third date. With social mores being as they are in this country, third dates are considered the physical challenge; chemistry versus intimacy. Caroline is comfortable with the chemistry between her and Dr. Perrin. But today, he will be touching places no man has ever gone. She will open up parts of her she has never shared with another human being. Sure, it is her mind instead of her legs, but to Caroline, that seems way more intimate.

Now standing in the foyer of Dr. Perrin's office—chewing the inside of her cheek—Caroline knocks before she loses her courage. To relax her mind, she admires the beautiful Christmas wreath hanging on his office door.

Caroline startles when Dr. Perrin answers. She laughs at herself and quickly comes up with an excuse. "I was admiring your lovely wreathe."

Dr. Perrin holds the door for her as she enters. "I bought that at the florist shop on Tunnel Road. I ordered one to be sent to a colleague and liked it so much, I had them make one for me," Dr. Perrin explains as he picks up the forsaken notebook and waits for Caroline to sit. "Would you like something to drink?"

"No, thank you."

"Then why don't we start on how your week went," Dr. Perrin directs, pen poised over paper.

Caroline begins the session by telling Dr. Perrin of her evening at the pub, where she'd informed her friends of her impending orders.

"How did they take your news?" Dr. Perrin asks, all the while writing in his book.

"We ended up in a four-way meltdown in the middle of the pub."

"That must have been alarming to the customers."

"Not the regulars. They have seen us that way many times—when Bianca's brother died, when Meredith had her heart broken by some guy. On numerous occasions, the Bitch-N-Booze has become nuclear."

"Do you know when you will be leaving?"

"Not until after the new year. Why? Do you think we are wasting our time here if I only have a few months? I was really hoping you could fix this before I left."

Dr. Perrin raises an eyebrow over his notebook. "And what are you wanting fixed?" He uses her own words.

"The nightmares, the flashbacks. I could very well be engaging an enemy soon and having a paralyzing flashback of some kind could be deadly. We sleep with our weapons strapped to our sides. I'd hate to have a nightmare and blow away my bunkmate in friendly fire."

"Caroline, this is a process, not an easy fix. Do you understand that?"

"Yes, I understand this will take time but I need this to be over, doc. I can't continue on like this."

"We should probably increase our sessions to twice a week. We can shift our focus to therapy designed to control your behavior if and when you feel a flashback coming on. I have a few more ideas but would like to get started before our time is used up talking about what we are going to do. Do you have any questions before we begin?"

Caroline shakes her head and assumes the position on the couch.

"I would like to discuss what is called grounding techniques. Grounding is a term used to describe any technique which is used to bring a person back in contact with the present moment. These techniques are essential tools to help with intrusive memories or flashbacks. These skills can help you manage feelings of intense anxiety. You can also utilize cognitive grounding skills to help you reorient yourself to place and time."

Dr. Perrin instructs Caroline through Cognitive Awareness and Sensory Awareness Grounding Exercises.

"Keeping your eyes open, look around the room. Notice your surroundings, the details, and then describe those details out loud."

Caroline begins the exercise, describing the office in vivid detail. She continues by giving a description of Dr. Perrin himself.

"And last but not least, that fucking black notebook on your lap."

"I see you are a quick learner. Well done." Dr. Perrin slips the notebook behind him. "Other sensory awareness techniques are holding a pillow, a stuffed animal, or any object that is of comfort to you, like a smooth stone. You can listen to soothing music. Focus on someone's voice or a neutral conversation. You are to utilize these tools, along with muscle relaxation, whenever you experience intense emotions or any new anxiety, high stress, or dissociative thoughts."

"Why would I have new anxiety?" Caroline questions.

Dr. Perrin is aware that what he says next could be the deciding factor. "I want you to understand, hypnosis is not without possible side effects. During the induction, the most common side effect is an increase in anxiety. You might have fear relating to loss of control. You may experience abreaction, or a sudden release of emotions, as evidenced by an excessive emotional reaction, like crying."

Dr. Perrin notes Caroline's back stiffening, her eyebrow raising over one eye, but decides to continue. "Dizziness, nausea, and cold sweats are all possible reactions to induction."

Caroline responds by shaking her head in understanding, though she does not believe any of that will happen to her. She doesn't even believe she can be hypnotized.

"Is there any more questions I can answer for you?" Dr. Perrin waits. "Are you still interested in trying hypnotherapy?" He asks since Caroline did not answer his first question.

"No. Yes. Wait." Caroline sits back up. "I have noticed recently the nightmares are much more real. I am no longer a witness to something happening. I am actually living it. It takes several seconds after I wake to even realize that I am not that person from the dream. Plus, everything is more vivid. Sounds, colors, smells."

"How about emotions? Are they also more real?"

"Actually, yes. I wake to either terror or tears, or both."

"Then you are already making progress." He continues to write.

"I am not sure that is progress and if it is, I am not sure I want that kind of progress."

"Truly experiencing the nightmares through your senses and not just as an onlooker or bystander will help bring clarity to the root of the problem. In fact, engaging the subconscious, what we will be doing with hypnosis, can bring even more clarity and cause your nightmares to be more emotionally charged. That will help find the source of the disturbance."

Caroline quips, "And once you find the disturbing force, Obi-Wan Kenobi?"

"I will not be finding the source—you will. And once you do, I will help you separate the problem or behavior and redefine or reinforce its positive purpose."

"I don't think I was this scared in Iraq." Caroline begins to lie back on the sofa but jolts back up. "Are sure you have the ability to handle this?"

Dr. Perrin, observing Caroline's obvious apprehension asks, "Are you?

"No, but let's do this thing." Caroline lies back and takes a deep breath to still her nerves.

Dr. Perrin takes her through progressive muscle relaxation first. One by one, Caroline's muscles soften systemically from Dr. Perrin's verbal commands. From head to toe, she is warm, relaxed, and calm. When he is sure Caroline is ready, the doctor lowers his voice a step and slows his breathing. He then embarks on a journey with Caroline that forever changes each of their lives.

CHAPTER SEVENTEEN

SESSION THREE – HYPNOTIC INDUCTION

"I want you to close your eyes. Take a deep breath. Let it out slowly. Take another breath in, breathing in fresh oxygen, and as you breathe out, breathe out all the tension within you. Breathe in oxygen. Let out tension. You are aware of the pain and stress leaving your body."

Dr. Perrin observes Caroline and, lowering his voice a little more, says, "The sound of my voice makes you relax comfortably in your chair. Picture a light surrounding you. Picture the color of that light. What is the color you see, Caroline?"

"A glowing lavender," Caroline calmly states.

"Feel the glowing lavender keeping you warm, keeping you safe. Feel the power from the glowing lavender providing you with energy. You feel warm, safe, and powerfully peaceful."

Dr. Perrin pauses for Caroline to assimilate the color with peace.

"With your next breath, breathe in the colorful energy. Feel the lavender enter your body, caressing every organ from the top of your head, your brain, now down through your neck and shoulders. The light is warming as it massages all your muscles in your neck. As you exhale, bad energy leaves your body, being replaced with the warm lavender-light energy. The warm lavender-light energy is spreading through your body, through your abdomen, relaxing the muscles of your back and spine. The lavender energy moves down your legs, relaxing your muscles, all the way to the tips of your toes."

He pauses for the energy to flow through Caroline. "Your eyes are getting heavy. Your facial muscles relax. Your shoulders relax. Your arms feel heavy. The lavender energy is now in every cell of your body. You are completely relaxed."

Dr. Perrin monitors Caroline's breathing for a moment. "You will hear my voice and you will remain relaxed. Now I want you to turn your thoughts inward. Picture your mind…The lavender light surrounds your mind. Follow the lavender light as it goes deeper into your mind…still deeper…deeper. Now picture your glowing lavender mind as an energy body. All you see is your lavender-light energy mind. Now picture your energy mind in front of a gate. This gate is the opening to your safe place, your happy place. You become even more relaxed as you open the gate. Walk through the gate opening. Can you describe what you are seeing?"

"It's a beautiful garden, on the banks of a lake," Caroline answers automatically, with no hesitation.

"Picture your energy body floating through your garden. Tell me about this place."

"There's a large willow tree on the shore of the lake. I am now standing underneath it."

"What do you feel?"

"The grass. It is so soft and cool."

"What else do you feel?"

"The air. It is lightly blowing off the water, keeping me cool."

"You will be able to return to this safe, happy place anytime you want. All you need to do is picture it in your mind and you will return to peace. Now let your energy guide you to a nice place in your garden—a place that is comfortable for you to sit down and relax."

Dr. Perrin waits for Caroline to find her comfort place in preparation of traveling through her mind. After several seconds, he continues with a much slower pace to his voice.

"You are a glowing lavender energy seeking wisdom and knowledge. You are fully aware of how to go deeper and deeper into your mind. Going there now as I count to five. One, going deeper and deeper. Two, feeling relaxed. Three, feeling at peace. Four, deeper and deeper into your mind. Five, your mind is now at the deepest level of relaxation."

Dr. Perrin notes the signs of trance state: attentiveness to follow command, rapid eye movement, slower and rhythmic breathing, changing of the color of her cheeks, and relaxation of her extremities.

"Remembering that you can always return to your happy place, as I count to five, you will begin viewing scenes that represent your flashback that you experienced at work. One, picture your energy light floating above that scene. Two, your mind staying relaxed, only viewing your surroundings. Three, the image is becoming more vivid. Four, you are now there, still only viewing from above, not quite feeling the emotions of the moment. Five, knowing nothing can hurt you in your energy light, describe the scene before you."

"It's the CSH unit…We are trying to save them."

"Who is 'them', Caroline?"

"All of them…All the incoming casualties."

In order to allow Caroline's subconscious to relate fully to the trauma, Dr. Perrin wants to engage all her senses.

"Using your senses, tell me what you are feeling?"

"I am physically and emotionally exhausted. My back aches from standing over the operating tables for eighteen hours straight. I am hungry and thirsty and hot. So hot."

"Using your senses, now tell me what you are hearing."

"My ears are ringing from the explosions outside…We are in a surgical operating cargo box…RPGs are trying to bring down the Chinooks that are landing outside. I hear the commander. He's yelling across the radio… He tells them we are taking on heavy fire. I hear the doctors. They are yelling at the nurses for instruments. Nurses are screaming for supplies, trying to be heard over the noise." Caroline takes a few deep breaths. "Oh God, I can hear the wails of the wounded."

Dr. Perrin notes Caroline's composure. "Continue with use of your senses. What are you smelling?"

"Smoke—something close by is on fire. Burning flesh…mixed with antiseptic…Iron smell from all the blood."

Dr. Perrin notes that Caroline exhibits signs of stress. Her brow line is tense and her neck muscles strained.

"Tell me, Caroline: where is the blood coming from?"

"It is pooling around my hands…I have to find the bleeder…The blood is so thick and warm…obscuring. The surgeon is trying to find it too. Our hands slide into each other. The blood is now up my arms and the doctor's…I see the hopelessness in his eyes. He removes his hands first from the Marine's cavity…I can't."

"Why not?"

"I can't let him die…He is only a child…A child who loves his mother."

"What do you see happening before you?"

"Carnage. Soldiers, Marines—all babies, blown apart. Controlled chaos. Orderlies run for supplies…Bodies being carried to the morgue."

"What are you doing at this time?"

"Screaming…Screaming for blood…He needs blood…No one is getting it. They are just staring at me…They're taking orders from the Major instead. He has pronounced him dead. He is already moving on to the next table."

Dr. Perrin resists the urge to ask what happens next. He waits for Caroline to play out the image.

"The orderlies are trying to take him away…I can't let them…Not till I know his name. I have to keep my promise."

"What promise?"

"To tell his mother how much he loved her." Caroline breaks into sobs at this point.

With this being Caroline's first hypnosis session, Dr. Perrin is not sure how she will cope post-hypnotically. He feels he must bring her out before she becomes too emotionally distraught, though he knows there is more work to be done.

"Caroline, I will begin to count backward from five to one. You will now listen to my voice and take these steps with me. Five, you float over the scene; peace and calm are enveloping your energy. Four, your energy light is flowing into your safe garden. Three, your body and your energy light become the same. Two, you are at peace in your garden. Your unconscious will continue to share the knowledge of this event, granting you an understanding of why the subconscious relives this event at times of stress. One, you remain in a relaxed state. Now, Caroline, open your eyes."

Caroline blinks once, then twice, slowly opening her eyes. She glances at Dr. Perrin sitting in front of her.

"Caroline," Dr. Perrin breaks her reverie. After she turns her head toward him, he asks, "How do you feel?"

"Sleepy," she says as she watches Dr. Perrin stand and reach for a tissue to give her. She realizes tears are flowing down her cheeks. She dabs the tissue to her eyes. "You were able to hypnotize me, weren't you?"

Dr. Perrin is concerned that Caroline is not remembering the event that just unfolded from her subconscious. "Can you recall what we discussed while you were under hypnosis?"

Feeling the weight of her eyelids, she closes them briefly. She can see the Marine on the table, the blood dripping on her shoes.

"I was assisting on a surgery on a Marine, Corporal Craig Michaels, but he died." She blots faster as the tears begin again.

"Have you lost a patient before or after Corporal Michaels?" Dr. Perrin is still surfing her psyche to understand the significance of the Corporal.

"Several. Before and after."

"What is your subconscious telling you now about this event?"

Caroline closes her eyes again and is silent for several minutes. The tears continue though.

"I let him down."

"Because you could not save him?"

"Yes, but also…" Caroline's tears free-flow. She reaches for another tissue to blow her nose then continues, "I didn't fulfill my promise. I never told his mother he loved her."

Caroline folds herself over her knees and sobs, rocking with guilt over never telling Corporal Michaels' mother her son's last words of his undying love for her.

For another hour, Dr. Perrin guides Caroline through the event. He discusses the harmful behaviors she has associated with this traumatic episode versus productive options to facilitate coping with loss and disappointment. He helps Caroline work through the significance of the Corporal's death, which was not about him dying or her misplaced guilt of not saving him, but rather about her not following through with his last request.

Caroline, able to talk now without bursting into tears, admits, "I haven't even tried to find his mother."

"Why is that?"

"She will ask how I know him. I will have to tell her I was the nurse on his surgery. She will hate me for not saving her son…but not as much as I do."

"Death is part of war. You cannot save them all. As a nurse, you must know this. What you are experiencing is survivor's guilt. You committed no offense by surviving. His mother will be comforted that you lived, though her son did not. What do you think Corporal Michaels would want if he could speak with you now?"

Caroline centers her thoughts on the young Marine, surprised her emotions were remaining under control. "All he asked was to tell his mother that he loved her, so I guess that is what he would want, for me to tell his mother his last thoughts were of her."

"What do you feel you need to do to comfort your conscious mind?"

"I need to find his mother," Caroline states, though not sure if tracking down the Corporal's mother years after his death will help. She fears it will bring up an old wound not only for her, but worse, for the Marine's mother.

Caroline and Dr. Perrin finish the session discussing how she'd felt during hypnosis and how she feels afterward. Dr. Perrin informs her of the potential side effects and complications of hypnosis that can occur spontaneously, such as unexpected feelings, thoughts or behaviors. Caroline sets her next appointment with Dr. Perrin before leaving his office.

Walking to her car, she thinks how easily she could be hypnotized. She doesn't remember a specific point where she'd felt she was going under. Sort of like surgery, one minute you are sniffing a mask, counting backward from a hundred, then by ninety-eight, you wake and it is all over. She likes the tranquility her body and mind are experiencing though.

Dr. Perrin opens Caroline's chart and tries to formulate his notes. Unable to stay seated, he pushes his chair back and in two long strides, is standing by the window, watching Caroline as she walks to her car. Knowing the consequences of hypnosis can not only affect the patient, but also the hypnotherapist, Dr. Perrin is having second thoughts regarding hypnotherapy with this particular patient. He has never felt this strongly connected to anyone he has hypnotized. It is not Caroline McKenzie's memories he is worried about. It is what she doesn't remember that scares him. Leaning closer to the window so he can watch her car pull onto the street, he fearfully mumbles, "What is your mind hiding from you, Captain McKenzie?" His breathy premonition on the glass fogs his view.

CHAPTER EIGHTEEN

GUARDED MEMORIES

Captain Caroline McKenzie:

Sensory and Cognitive Grounding Techniques instructed to be practiced daily to facilitate control of flashbacks.

As expected, Caroline's dreams/nightmares became more vivid, more real to her, after hypnosis.

Caroline is able to relax through progressive muscle and remained so throughout the hypnosis state.

Possible side effects of hypnosis discussed. Patient consents to move forward with hypnosis.

Guided to the flashback that she stated happened at work last month, Caroline was able to view the scene as an onlooker. Emotional involvement still relevant as evidenced by nonverbal and verbal cues including increased rate of breathing while viewing scene and emotional outbursts.

Reframing the event helped Caroline assuage the survivor's guilt: will follow up with decision to notify family.

Discussed difference in defense mechanism and coping mechanisms. Caroline utilizes defense mechanisms to cope with loss. Occurring on an unconscious level, she is unaware. Explained defense mechanisms can alter internal psychological states. Internalizing the issue and/or blaming oneself (Avoidance and Repression) can be counterproductive, leading to depression.

Discussed positive coping mechanisms that are conscious and purposeful and can aid in external solutions.

1. Support from Veteran's Administration. Emotional support from trained psychotherapist who deals solely with returning veterans.
2. Solution-Solving. Directed Caroline on path to solve issue of identifying family of lost comrade. Concerns if she does not fulfill the presumed promise, she will continue to separate herself from her memories (Dissociation) as evidenced by blocked emotions from the conscious mind, causing flashbacks (the subconscious not allowing her to move on).

Caroline acknowledges successful hypnosis but still wary of benefits. Verbally states understanding to call pager if unwarranted changes in behaviors, feelings, or thoughts ensue.

Caroline fully aware; physiologically and emotionally stable at session end.

Appointment scheduled for next week. Sessions to increase to twice a week due to possible deployment in near future.

CHAPTER NINETEEN

PANCAKES AND POWDER

Caroline, exhausted from work, still had to stop off at the mall on her way home, truly in need of new underwear. After hours in a lingerie store, Caroline is exhausted and an emotional basket case. She isn't sure if these are delayed emotions coming from her session with Dr. Perrin last weekend or if she is nervous about Jameson coming tomorrow, or a combination of the two.

Snow has fallen steadily for several hours. Asheville is expected to get six inches overnight and a few more inches are expected throughout the weekend. Caroline halfheartedly hopes the accumulation will prevent Jameson from making the two-hour trip, but since he has not called to cancel, she can only assume he will be arriving in the morning. Either way, she is in desperate need of a hot bath and a bottle of wine.

After fighting the "three weeks before Christmas" mall traffic, Caroline soaks away her frustration in the tub with a large glass of wine. She considers how much of her life she will divulge to Jameson. She figures if she tells him she sees a therapist for flashbacks and nightmares, she might as well throw in a lie about having a sexually transmitted disease. Either scenario should send him packing. After three separate phone calls from the girls, questioning her about everything from "did you buy new undies" to "you do know it is not No-shave November anymore," Caroline silences her phone before one of her friends calls back and regales her with stories of how to get her kink on. Since she had polished off an entire bottle of wine before falling asleep, Caroline considers she might need to include a drinking problem in her bio with Dr. Perrin.

Caroline wakes groggy and disillusioned the next morning but remembers no dreams or nightmares. Her head, however, is pounding from the wine the night before. Caroline's attempt to get out of bed only makes it worse.

Why did I do that to myself? I have to meet Jameson for pancakes in... Caroline glances at her phone. As she struggles to focus, she vaguely remembers silencing her phone last night. After seeing the four missed texts and two phone calls, all from Jameson, Caroline chastises herself, "I must have silenced the alarm too."

"Oh God," Caroline cries as she jumps up and heads for the bathroom with her phone. Jameson has been waiting for her for forty-five minutes at the pancake house. The first attempt to call him went straight to voicemail so she typed out a speedy text. "I am so sorry. I overslept. Please call me back."

Caroline brushes her teeth, runs a brush through her hair and is halfway dressed when her phone rings.

"I am so, so sorry," she starts without saying hello. "I had too much wine last night and I silenced my phone 'cause my stupid friends kept calling. Can you please forgive me?"

"Well, since I drove all this way in all this snow, and I was promised pancakes, I would hate to turn around and drive all the way back home without them. Besides, I need your help unloading the van."

Jameson listens as Caroline explains how she must have turned her alarm off while turning her ringer off, promising she can be there in fifteen minutes.

"Since I am already at the pancake house, why don't you give me your address and I will bring you breakfast. That way, you have time to get some caffeine in you. As I remember, you like it black, right?"

Caroline blushes. "I hate to put you out that way. I will text you my address and I will fix you breakfast to make up for all of this."

"Uh, no thanks, Captain. As I recall, your cooking, self-admitted nonetheless, is not as good as K-rations. I'm bringing breakfast."

Caroline grabs aspirin, a bottled water, and runs to finish getting ready, continuing to berate herself out loud. "It is no wonder I can't make a relationship work. The first guy that I could even consider becoming close to, I stand him up on our first date. Well, actually, second date. The first date I slept with him, then left while he was sleeping, without a note or anything. No fucking wonder I'm alone."

Twenty minutes later, Caroline motions Jameson to pull into her garage. She can't help but notice he is not driving the Escalade he had in West Virginia. He is now driving a beat-up minivan. *Oh God, he is married with kids or has kids.* Caroline tries to recall if he ever mentioned having children or ever being married. Surely that would have come up in their conversations. For the life of her, she can't even remember asking him, and what man would voluntarily provide that information?

The driver door squeaks as he exits the Detroit monstrosity, his hands full of food and a drink carrier. "Hey, Asheville, a little help over here."

Caroline is jolted out of her thoughts, hurrying over to help with the bags. She isn't sure which one smells better—the pancakes or Jameson. He is just as gorgeous as she remembers. From the Ralph Lauren ribbed sweater over a button-down shirt to the tight faded denim jeans tucked in his Timberland boots, everything about this man oozes rugged sophistication and sex.

Caroline apologizes several more times over breakfast. Jameson's nonchalant attitude toward the whole mix-up only makes him that much more desirable.

"I noticed you are driving a different vehicle." Caroline tries to be nonchalant also, stuffing her mouth full of pancake.

"About that."

Oh Lord, here it comes. Caroline's inner voice tries to brace her for the truth.

"Can we drive your car to the Inn? I do not want to show up to a five-star resort in my sister's minivan."

"Of course, but why exactly do you have your sister's minivan?" Caroline asks.

"Come on, I'll show you." Jameson takes her hand leading her back to the garage. "I hope we can deliver all this today before we go to the Inn."

Caroline cautiously looks inside the van. From floor to ceiling, front to back, the van is packed with dog food, cleaning supplies, and chew toys.

"I asked my workers to cram the van and they really came through. My sister let me use her old van since I use my car for business, too."

"Jameson." The only word she can say with the little air left inside her. He has stolen her breath. Her emotions are so raw she is having a hard time fighting back the tears. Since her mind will not form words, she throws her arms around his neck and kisses him.

"So women do go crazy for men who drive minivans," Jameson jokes after the kiss.

On the way to the shelter, Caroline tells Jameson about the new puppies and her concerns that the no-kill shelter will not be able to keep up with the supply and demands of so many new animals. She tells him how she cannot bear the thought of the shelter closing because it provides her with so much happiness and how, with Christmas around the corner, she is praying the dogs are on the top of Santa's list. Jameson's heart warms for her soft spot for animals.

"Lord Almighty, it's a miracle." Francie is delighted beyond words to see all the supplies Caroline and Jameson carry in. Marshall seems a bit excited too, as if he knows what a financial burden has been lifted off the shelter. Once the van has been emptied of its cargo, Caroline notices Marshall standing by the back gate. She yells for him to come so she can introduce Marshall to Jameson, but he continues to stare toward the woods.

"He is wanting me to take him on a walk. We go through that gate every time with Barkley and walk along the river and through the woods."

"Who is Barkley?"

"Marshall's friend. Would you like to meet her?" Jameson follows Caroline to the back where the dogs' pens are located. Barkley, wagging her tail, jumps up on the bars with excitement when she sees Caroline.

"Hi Barkley." Caroline rubs Barkley's head through the bars before unlocking the door. "Jameson, this is Miss Barkley."

Barkley jumps down from her pen and sniffs at Jameson who crouches down to fluff her fur.

"You are such a beautiful lady," Jameson shamelessly flirts.

Caroline finds Jameson's human dialogue with Barkley endearing. Obviously, so does Barkley because she prances around him then licks his offered hand before trotting over to where the leashes are hanging and pulls down her personal leash that Caroline bought.

"Not today, Barkley. I have plans. Besides, there is six inches of snow out there."

Ignoring Caroline, Barkley drops the leash at Jameson's feet then places her nose in Jameson's hand, lifting his arm to pet her.

"Wow. You have a way with dogs," Caroline observes. "Barkley, I said not today."

"We can't check in until three so we have a few hours, if you want to go for a walk." Jameson walks over to the window. "Marshall is still standing at the back gate."

Caroline leashes Barkley and together they head outside toward the gate. Marshall runs to greet them and then immediately darts back to the gate. The four of them traipse through the snow along the river path, Marshall more excited than normal—running ahead and then back, circling them, and then running from scent to scent buried in white fluff.

"Usually he walks right beside me like a bodyguard while this one pulls my arm off." That thought made Caroline realize that Barkley is not pulling on the leash. She is walking right at Jameson's side, hanging on his every command. *Bitch.*

When they return from their walk, Jameson hangs the leash back up as Caroline puts the dogs back in their pens. Saying goodbye to Marshall last, she promises she will be back sometime this week. Marshall does not seem to be as sad as he usually is when she leaves. Caroline is grateful for that. She loves working at the shelter, but leaving Marshall puts her in such a melancholy state each time that she has considered not continuing here once Marshall is adopted. She does not want to get attached to another animal. The anguish of that thought brings immediate tears to her eyes but luckily Jameson does not see. He is still at Barkley's pen, petting her and talking to her as if they had been friends for a lifetime.

C H A P T E R   T W E N T Y

THE BILTMORE

With the heavy coating of snow on the ground, The Biltmore Estate looks more like something out of a fairy tale. The road alongside the French Broad River winds through acres of forest, gardens, and manicured lawns. The entrance drive around the parklike setting is magical. Lights are flickering from the trees, shining sparkles on the fallen snow. Sunshine on white powder and Christmas lights adorn the landscape like pixie dust, illuminating each branch, each bush.

Caroline has lived in Asheville for almost two years but has never been inside the gates of this national forestry. The beauty of this nineteenth-century Châteauesque-style mansion causes Caroline to forget all about her nerves regarding spending the weekend with Jameson.

The drive up the four-mile approach road is purposely slow. Caroline and Jameson capture all the splendor of the gardens surrounding the estate. The welcoming fifty-five-foot Norway spruce takes Caroline's breath as it stands majestic on the front lawn with its 45,000 lights gleaming through the snowy branches. The sun begins its descent behind the east-facing mansion, bestowing a golden glow across the steeply pitched roof with its sixteen chimneys. The mountainous topography behind the castle blends exquisitely with the three hundred seventy-five-foot front façade of the home.

During their guided tour, Caroline and Jameson take in the opulent splendor of seventy more hand-decorated Christmas trees throughout the mansion, each more elaborate than the next. Fresh fir tree wreaths adorn doors and walls. A nostalgic yuletide scent wafts into every room, compliments of the miles of fresh garland draped throughout the house. Caroline's favorite tree is the live Fraser fir in the grandiose Banquet Hall, adorned with poinsettias, mistletoe, kissing balls, and garland. Flanked around a triple fireplace are two more trees, uniform in color, bestowing a luxurious holiday feel under the barrel-vaulted glass ceiling.

While in college, Jameson had studied about the home George Washington Vanderbilt II had built during the late 19th century. Nothing could prepare him for this Gilded-Age glamour modeled after a Loire Valley French Chateaux. It is an architectural dream and a marvel of physics with its cantilevered, counterbalanced, 102-step grand staircase that spirals up four stories.

As they check into their room, Caroline isn't so sure now if she should have had Jameson cancel the second room. It is too late to change it; besides, they are both having a great time together. Neither one can quit talking about the many splendors of the mansion and the gardens as they ready for dinner.

"Wow!" Jameson exclaims as Caroline steps out of the bathroom in her rose-gold lace cocktail gown with a slit up the leg. "You look…Wow… Amazing. How hungry are you?" Jameson kids as he admires his date for the evening.

"Very," Caroline confirms. "Plus, I spent a week's pay on this gown and someone other than you is going to see it."

Jameson steps toward her, placing one hand around her waist as the other comes from around his back, holding a blue box.

"Oh, Jameson, what did you do?"

"Just an early Christmas gift."

Caroline remains in his one arm as she lifts the lid from the box he is holding.

Against a Tiffany blue velvet roll, a diamond-faced watch sparkles back at Caroline.

"Jameson, it's lovely but I can't accept this. It's too much."

"You'll actually be doing me a favor by wearing it," Jameson says, a crooked grin forms as he places it on her wrist. "Maybe on our next date you will be on time."

Caroline smiles back at Jameson's snarky comment. The diamonds glisten as her adorned arm reaches for his face. The kiss that follows is electrifying, soft and sensual. At this point, Caroline doesn't care if she eats or not. Her back arches, moving her body closer against his.

Caroline's thoughts of perversion are interrupted by a phone ringing. Stepping out of Jameson's embrace, Caroline checks her makeup in the mirror while Jameson takes the call.

"They are ready for us downstairs, Captain McKenzie." Jameson says as he opens the door of their room. "May I get your coat for you?" Jameson asks.

"Aren't we eating downstairs in the restaurant?"

"Yes, but first, I would like to see the Christmas lights outside. It was still daylight when we came in."

Caroline, trying to hide her shock and not doing well at it, looks down at her feet. "I am in four-inch heels and an evening gown."

"That's fine." Jameson closes the door. "You can wear mine." Taking her hand, Jameson leads her down the hall.

"Do you have any idea how uncomfortable heels are?" Caroline asks as they make their way through the front lobby.

"Thanks to my fraternity days, yes I do." Jameson is undeterred and leads her through the front door, out into the twenty-degree mountain air. "Let me wrap this around you." Jameson places his coat over her shoulders as a lighted horse-drawn carriage pulls in front of them.

"Your coach, madam," an elderly gentleman says as he opens the door.

Caroline looks at Jameson with a wide open mouth. Jameson, impressed with himself for catching the Captain off-guard, grins as he takes her arm and helps her step up into the coach. The gentleman hands Jameson two blankets. Stepping into the carriage, Jameson sits beside Caroline and covers her with both blankets. He then burrows under them with her.

Caroline feels like Cinderella as they proceed through the gardens. The air is crisp and mysterious. An experience so unique she knows she will remember this for the rest of her life.

"I can't believe you did this. I love it," Caroline says.

"I heard that a horse-drawn carriage is the only way to properly arrive for dinner in a nineteenth-century castle." Jameson reaches his arm over her shoulder and pulls her closer as the night continues with mystical surprises.

Caroline curls up beside Jameson after what she can only describe as life-affirming intimacy. Their first night together at the cabin was purely about sexual gratification. Tonight took on a new realm for her—one she has never experienced before. They talk into the wee hours about their lives, family, and dreams for the future. Jameson asks her to come to Mooresville for his New Year's Eve party and adds that she can invite her friends. Caroline is sure that will also mean meeting his family. She wonders what he is leaving out of his stories, yet nothing could be as bad as her own omission. Caroline just couldn't find a way to bring up therapy or deployment, not while her legs were straddling him.

Her mind plays tricks on her while she snuggles against Jameson. *Tell him. Tell him before this goes any further.*

What was I to do? She silently answers the voice in her head. *Pull him up from his ears so I could look him in the eyes and tell him I am in therapy?'*

She knows she will have to tell him soon before an emotional attachment occurs between either of them. *Maybe tomorrow while we are taking a guided tour of the winery. Or, better yet, after we have tasted all the wine.* With a plan in place, Caroline is able to close her eyes. As they fall asleep wrapped in each other, Caroline and Jameson both know they have entered a new dimension in their relationship.

* * *

I wake to early morning chirping outside my bedroom window. I love this time of the day—birds singing, the smell of breakfast coming from the kitchen, and the sounds of the farm workers yelling commands at the plow mules outside. I snuggle further under the quilt my grandmother made for my bed, waiting until Mama comes to carry me to the kitchen table. The wash basin sits on the dresser in front of the mirror. I want so badly to walk to the dresser, pour my own water, clean myself up, and fix my own hair. But I can't. I have to wait on my mama since my legs ain't working. I lie here like a newborn fawn, unable to stand on wobbly legs, stricken with polio.

I say a silent prayer to Jesus, who stares at me from his framed picture on my wall, that soon, I will be able to feel my legs again. I want to go outside, run, climb the hills, or play with my brothers and sisters. I try moving myself but the mattress is old and some of the ropes have frayed from the frame. I sink lower into the feathers, causing my nightgown to crawl up my back, making it even more difficult for my arms to pull me up.

"Mama," *I call out to let her know I am awake.*

Mama comes and lifts me into the wheeling chair my father made, making it easier to move me around. She bathes me in the chair, brushes out my long hair then braids it, scrubs my face, and puts a line-fresh dress on me before wheeling me into the kitchen. Everyone else has already eaten and are outside either working the fields or feeding the animals. Mama tells me since it is a warm spring day, I get to sit in my chair outside for a while after breakfast. I am so excited to go outside I can hardly finish my eggs. I eat quick and wait for Mama to roll me outside where I hope to have someone to play with, if not my sisters, maybe McKinley.

Spring is my favorite time of the year. The smell of the ground plowed up for planting, the forsythias and Easter lilies blooming yellow, and the cherry blossoms bursting like white snowballs makes everything look like a fancy painting. My papa waves at me from behind Bessie, the plow mule. I wave back. He and Bessie will plow all day the fifty acres of garden soil, preparing for Mama's beans, lettuce, squash, cabbage, peppers, and tomatoes.

"There you are, McKinley," I squeal with delight as my blue tick hound jumps up, covering my clean dress with mud. "McKinley, get down. You know I will be the one in trouble when Mama finds out I got my dress dirty."

McKinley jumps down but not before coating my face with her tongue. McKinley and I play fetch and tug of war throughout the morning. Mama checks on me at lunchtime but I don't want to come inside. This is a rare warm day for spring. I lean my head back, closing my eyes from the bright sun as it warms my face.

I hear growling coming from the side of the house. I hope McKinley hasn't cornered another skunk. He stunk for weeks afterward. Papa gave him a bath with some stuff from Dr. Crowl, the vet who comes when we have a sick cow or horse. I overheard him telling Papa last week that he had to put the Farley's dog down. I didn't hear why but that must have broken poor Opal's heart. Opal and I are in the same grade at school. I cried all that day for Opal Farley.

The growling seems closer now. I try to steer my chair to turn but the wheels have sunk in the mud; it won't budge.

"McKinley," I call for him, hoping he will forget about whatever critter he's cornered and come back to me. But the growling only gets lower, louder. I look over my right shoulder. Standing about ten feet from me is a dog I ain't never seen before. He's all mangy-looking, his jaw is drooping on one side, and he's foaming at the mouth.

"Papa!" I scream so loud that it scairt the mutt but just for a minute. He stops and stares at me, then begins growling again. "Mama!" The dog is now all hunkered down, almost crawling toward me. Slobbers drip from his teeth

and his hair is standing straight up on his back.

"Papa! Papa!" I am really scairt now. My muscles in my legs don't work so good with the polio so all I have are my arms. I fly 'em about as I scream but this makes the dog begin to bark really mean like. All I can do is just sit here, paralyzed, and wait for this dog to attack me. My tears are now making my screams for help all gurgley. I am crying so hard I can hardly breathe. The dog must be scairt of my tears because he isn't getting any closer. He almost seems more afraid of me than I am of him. Then I hear McKinley.

I jerk my head to the left and see him running from the field, barking like he does when someone comes up the holler. The dog ain't afraid of me; he's afraid of McKinley.

Please let Papa be right behind him, I pray. "Papa! McKinley, no. Go get Papa!"

McKinley bolts past my chair, leaping in the air. Both dogs slam into each other. A fight breaks out that sounds like what the preacher says hell will sound like. Wailing, gnashing of teeth, screaming, and crying, but the screaming and crying are coming from me. I scream "McKinley" then "Papa" over and over while the dogs are tearing at each other's hides. Both of their furs are covered in blood but I can't tell from which dog it is coming from. Blood, saliva, and foam cover the ground as the dogs roll in the yard, intent to kill one another.

Boom! The sound stops my heart and makes my ears ring. I look up to see Papa holding his shotgun, smoke rising in the air from the blast. McKinley bolts up off the ground, scurrying under the house. The other dog doesn't get up.

Papa runs to me, picks me up and carries me inside. I try to tell him I am alright as he looks me over for any sign of being hurt.

"Please, Papa, go check on McKinley. Make sure he is okay," I plead through my tears.

"Peanut, you know I have to…"

"Papa, please," I beg, not wanting to hear what Papa is trying to tell me.

Mama runs in the house and drops at my feet, apologizing about being gone to the neighbors. I am not paying attention. I am numb all over as I watch Papa walk back outside, his shotgun slung over his shoulder.

Boom! The sound of my father's shotgun pierces my heart. I collapse into my mama's arms. My cries become wails. Mama tries to console me, explaining Papa had no choice. I do not want to hear it. How could he do that after McKinley saved me from that mean dog?

I refuse to come out of my room for dinner and remain there, alone, all night. I can see Papa in my mind, digging the hole to bury my dog, saying a few kind words, asking God to care for him. Thanking God that McKinley cared so much for me. I wonder if Opal Farley, when she hears what happened to McKinley, will cry all day for me.

My tears won't stop as Mama tries to shake the numbness from me. "It's okay. I am here. Honey, wake up."

I feel strong arms around me, attempting to console me. My chest hurts like something is squeezing the life out of it. I will never see his soft caramel-brown eyes staring up at me for a bite of my food. He will never lick my cheek in the morning to wake me. I will never have anyone that loves me as much as he did. I know Papa had no choice. McKinley would've been infected with rabies by now and it would've just been a matter of time before he went insane too. I couldn't stand to see him suffer that way. Especially since he saved my life, not caring about his own. That made me hurt more knowing he loved me as much as I loved him. He gave his life for me. My heart breaks and pours out of my eyes in sobs.

CHAPTER TWENTY-ONE

NINETEENTH CENTURY DREAM

"Caroline. Caroline. It's okay. I am here. Honey, wake up."

Jameson's words are coming through the fog that is her mind. Caroline's eyes are slow to open and are wet, as are her cheeks, neck, and ears. Jameson is leaning over her in bed, panic-stricken.

"What's wrong? Are you sick?"

Caroline is mortified at what Jameson has probably witnessed. She doesn't know what to say. Caroline sits up against the headboard, using the sheet to dry her tears-covered face.

"Please tell me what is wrong," Jameson pleads, kissing the top of her forehead.

"I had a dream, that's all," Caroline understates. She has never experienced this dream. This one is a new one for her.

Jameson pulls back. "A dream? More like a night terror. My God, honey, you were crying hysterically…screaming."

"I am sorry if I woke you." Caroline tries to downplay the nightmare by controlling her emotions.

"Do you want to tell me about it?" Jameson offers as he pulls her against him.

"No. I think I will hop in the shower and get ready for our day," Caroline says as she makes a hasty exit from the bed to the solitude of the bathroom.

Jameson feels terrible that Caroline will not open up to him. He thinks they have something special but now wonders if it is just him. He loves how excited she gets when she is around the shelter—almost childlike in her playful ways with animals. He finds her amazing in her acts of kindness toward others. She is intelligent and independent. He finds her knowledge inspiring. He likes her "GI Jane" persona proving she can take care of herself instead of the "damsel in distress" act. He has dated so many woman who were after the "big catch" with no personal interests other than finding a man. Caroline is special on her own. She is mature and he thought she'd been honest with him, until now. She is obviously hiding something. He understands some things are private and doesn't begrudge her a secret or two, but what really hurts is that it is painfully obvious she does not feel as close to him as he does to her.

Looking in the mirror, Caroline chastises herself for not emotionally handling the situation better. *Well, you handled that perfectly Men just love women who overreact.* She knows she owes him an explanation but things have been going so well. When he showed up with a van crammed with shelter supplies, her heart skipped a beat. That meant more to her than the diamond watch he gave her. He is charismatic, intelligent, and authentic. He is the first man she actually feels a deep connection with and that all started instantaneously at the gas station in West Virginia. She felt the attraction—felt it immediately. Obviously, fate did too because he ended up sharing the same camping area. For all those reasons, Caroline knows she has no choice. If this relationship is to make it past this weekend, she will have to tell him the truth. She brushes her teeth, wipes off the mascara from under her eyes and cheeks, takes a deep breath, and returns to the room to tell Jameson her dirty little secrets.

Jameson is a little surprised when she comes out still in her nighty, but the look on her face frightens the hell out of him.

"I believe I owe you an explanation," Caroline confesses. "Can we sit and talk?"

Jameson is relieved that she feels she can discuss whatever is hurting her. He has had his share of women who seem fine on the outside, then are extremely troubled on the inside. He can't imagine Caroline is that type; he has been wrong before. He pats the mattress beside him and she sits, facing straight ahead instead of toward him. Simultaneously, they both take a deep breath.

Caroline explains the dream. It is the first time she has had this particular dream, but she tells him there are many others that are repeaters. This one came with a preamble flashback. She reminds him of the story about the coyote and that she recalled yelling, or hearing in her mind, the word, Papa.

Jameson sees her choke back the tears. He wants to wrap his arms around her, take the pain away. He can see it in her eyes. He is afraid if he consoles her she will cry even harder, so he holds his position.

Caroline informs him some of her dreams come with foreshadowing flashes, like trailers before the full-blown movie. Jameson is surprised by the horror her mind can conceive. He can't wait any longer; he pulls her closer as she continues. She recounts brief snippets of other reoccurring nightmares and of some of her flashbacks.

"I don't know what causes them but the girls feel I am suffering from PTSD. They suggested I speak to a therapist. I finally agreed with them."

"Caroline, my God." Jameson drops his head to hers. "I hate that you have to go through this. Is there anything I can do to help?"

"I don't know what help I need." Caroline turns, facing him so she can see his reaction. "That is why I am seeing a psychiatrist." Caroline doesn't notice any signs of repulsion—yet.

"I do not know much about psychology. Do you mind if I ask you a few questions?" At Caroline's nod, Jameson asks, "How long has this been going on?"

"I have had weird dreams my whole life. Nothing frightening, per se, but incomprehensible. My childhood dreams never made sense to me. I knew I was the one in the dream but I didn't look like myself. Most of the nightmares and flashbacks are since I returned from Iraq." Caroline opens up about her duties overseas and some of the horrors she experienced.

"Dear Lord, baby." Jameson is more amazed by her now and holds her tighter. After a few moments of reflective silence, Jameson asks, "I am confused about one thing. What does a dog with rabies have to do with PTSD?"

"Nothing. At least that I know of. My nightmares aren't always about my time in combat. In fact, some of them aren't even in this time period. Like the one I just had."

Caroline is surprised at her composure while describing her terrors to Jameson. She feels safe, secure in the fact that he is not judging her.

"How long have you been in therapy?"

"I started seeing someone over a month ago," Caroline explains. "We haven't gotten too far yet. A lot of our time has been spent going over the reasons I have for seeking treatment, along with types of therapy or techniques."

Caroline does not feel like discussing the main technique Dr. Perrin is utilizing—hypnosis. She doesn't want to test Jameson's nonjudgmental capabilities.

"We are still in the pre-diagnosis stage."

"Pre-diagnosis? That makes it sound like you have a terminal illness."

"I am not sure you can call it an illness but it sure feels terminal to me. As I said, I have had dreams ever since I was a child."

Jameson takes her hand. "I want to help."

His compassion warms her, calming her anxiety slightly over this new dream.

"You have proven to be quite a distraction," Caroline says, folding herself into his arms. Caroline resists the urge to call Dr. Perrin and focuses on another urge. She refuses to waste another moment on her dreams when she has a life-size dream in front of her.

"A distraction? I was hoping you considered me more than a distraction, but then again, I've been called worse." Jameson leans in for a kiss and holds the gaze afterward. "I thought you said you were getting ready for our day."

"I couldn't seem to figure out how to turn on the shower." Caroline stands, pulling Jameson to his feet. "Since you are so eager to help, come help bathe me."

After Caroline and Jameson discover the finer points of a large garden tub, the rest of their day is spent in a guided tour of the winery on Biltmore estates. It might be the wine talking but Caroline is reconsidering hypnotherapy. The surreal nature of her dream has opened up new terrors that she cannot allow to take control of her mind. If her subconscious is protecting her from some form of traumas, why would she override it and possibly have to confront a horror better left locked away in the recesses of her mind. Caroline decides analysis of this nightmare would not be therapeutically healthy so there is no need for her to divulge this to Dr. Perrin.

"Earth to Caroline. Come in Captain McKenzie."

"Oh, I am so sorry Jameson. Did you say something? I think the wine has went straight to my head."

Jameson wraps his arms around her and playfully whispers into her ear, "Well, we did skip breakfast. Sounds like I am driving us to your house. Speaking of which, I better be getting on the road. The roads are going to be a mess with all this snow."

Switching cars at Caroline's house, Jameson moves his luggage from her car to his sister's minivan and then climbs behind the wheel, promising to call when he arrives home safely.

As she awaits sleep that night, Caroline smiles as she replays her weekend with Jameson. She can see herself falling for him. She wishes he hadn't been in such a hurry to leave earlier because she is actually missing him. She wonders if he misses her too.

Wait. Why didn't he want to come in? He didn't even wait to see me safely inside. He was in a sure-fire hurry to leave. Caroline felt a gripping pain in her heart, a sensation she is not used to. Jameson did text her to let her know he'd arrived home safely, which, at the time, Caroline thought was sweet. Now she wonders why he didn't call; it was just a text. That same heart-wrenching pain brought out emotions she had never dealt with before. She loved the feelings Jameson evoked inside her, all except this one; the feeling of vulnerability.

CHAPTER TWENTY-TWO

EMERGENCY FLASHBLACK

The past couple of weeks, the emergency room has been surprisingly quiet considering it is flu season. Caroline's mind, however, has been a contagious virus, infecting her whole body and others around her. Her friends have commented on everything from her short temper to her appearance. Her jump-sequence, reoccurring nightmare is almost nightly, along with flashes of various dreams tainting her days and nights. She figures her search for Corporal Michael's family has only provided fodder for that particular nightmare. Caroline's hope for a quick recovery has long gone. She now wonders if therapy can be anything less than debilitating.

She has cut back on her hours at work, only picking up eight-hour shifts instead of twelve so she can schedule more frequent therapy sessions with Dr. Perrin. For her mind, though, more therapy seems counterproductive, leaving Caroline with the emotional decision to either continue with this form of life support or pull the plug. Another painful consideration has crept into her mind over the past few days: switching doctors. She discussed this option last night with her friends at the Bitch-N-Booze, which came with mixed reviews. Bianca wants her to find another therapist but Meredith does not agree.

"It's a process that takes time." Meredith's words float in her conscious. Time is the one limitation that Caroline cannot control. Her orders were delivered certified yesterday. She is being deployed at the end of February to Afghanistan.

Splashing cold water on her face, Caroline returns to work. She is checking on Mr. Rodriquez when the charge nurse peeks her head in the room.

"I am putting a patient in room ten and it is yours."

"I'll be right there."

"Don't you worry about me, Caroline," Mr. Rodriquez states. "You can go check on your new patient. I will be fine."

"It shouldn't be long before the surgeon comes to see you. Can I get you anything?"

"No, thank you, I think I will just rest. But if you have to do something for me, you could get me a beer."

"I have already told you, no food or drink by mouth until the surgeon sees you. Besides, I polished off the last six-pack on my lunch break," Caroline jokes with Mr. Rodriquez as she leaves his room.

Caroline washes her hands and checks the doctor's orders before heading into room ten. A worried man is pacing the room while a highly sick-appearing woman is vomiting into an emesis basin over the side of her ER stretcher.

"Hello." Caroline dons her gloves, isolation gown and mask, then grabs a few towels. She runs them under cold water and hands one to her patient. "I am Caroline. I will be your nurse. Here, let me help you."

Caroline folds another damp towel and places one on the back of the patient's neck, then folds another and helps her wipe her mouth. Caroline can tell by appearance and by touch the patient has a fever.

"How long has this been going on?" Caroline asks, glancing at the chart for name and chief complaint. A quick history reveals the patient has been experiencing flu-like symptoms for a few days, and now the patient is unable to keep anything down. Caroline's suspicions of fever and dehydration are confirmed by vitals and assessment, so she rounds up the supplies to start an IV.

"Your temperature is 103.6, Mrs. Nelson."

After explaining the tests and procedures that she will be performing, Caroline starts the IV fluid to hydrate Mrs. Nelson, then tells her she will get her something for the fever.

As she enters the medicine room, the smell of antiseptic and pharmaceuticals overwhelms her senses. She suddenly feels faint and leans against the cool wall to stabilize herself. She closes her eyes for a moment to stop the room from spinning.

* * *

The room is stifling hot from the fireplace, yet I am shivering, my wet nightshirt drenched in a feverish sweat. I can feel my dog lying on the bed beside me, providing some body heat. My head feels like an iron weighted down on my pillow. I ring the bell on my bedside table. I hear the door open and footsteps walking across my bedroom.

"Why, Mrs. Van de Berg, you are fevered again," the nursemaid observes. "Let's get you in clean bed-clothing and a dry nightgown. Off the bed or I will throw you away with these sweaty sheets."

I feel my dog jump down, obeying the command of my house servant. I am lifted off my bed by strong arms, obviously by our butler. The sound of a sheet being snapped is followed by the smell of line-dried cotton.

"Mr. Van de Berg will be right upset that you are suffering again," the maid declares. "He should be home soon though with some more cinchona bark."

I am placed back on cool cotton and immediately stripped of the wet nightshirt and dressed in a dry one that smells like the sheets. The dog jumps back in bed with me and lays his head on my chest. I am immediately comforted.

Caroline feels the bile coming up her esophagus and runs for the trash can, emptying the contents of her stomach. Caroline can't explain the daydream that just flashed before her eyes as she splashes cold water on her face and rinses out her mouth. After washing her hands, she stands, looking at the medication server in the med room and trying to remember what she came to get. *Oh, Mrs. Nelson's fever. I need cinchona bark.* Caroline has no idea what cinchona bark is or why those words were even in her head.

Caroline is charting outside her patient's room after administering the ordered medications for Mrs. Nelson when she hears her name called.

"Hey, McKenzie, you got another delivery," Chris calls out across the ER.

Caroline looks to see Chris holding a large pine wreath decorated with ribbon and poinsettia flowers. She grabs the card before any else can, then carries the wreath to the breakroom where she reads the card.

Dear Ms. Grinch, it started. *You loved the wreaths and poinsettias at the Biltmore so I thought I would help you with your Christmas decorating, which I noticed you haven't started at your place.* He signed it, *The Mooresville Elf.*

Caroline loves Christmas time and enjoys driving around Asheville looking at the homes festooned with lights, wreathes, and even those wretched inflatables. She has never decorated her home because no one is ever at her house on Christmas Eve or Christmas. In fact, she volunteered to work both again just as she'd done last year. She puts up a tabletop tree in her living room a few days before the holiday and repacks it before the New Year. That is the extent of her decorations.

Caroline places the wreath on her door as soon as she gets home from work. She fixes herself a glass of wine and pulls out several boxes from the hall closet and begins decorating her little tree. Once completed, she snaps a selfie by her tabletop tree and sends it to Jameson with the tag line, "Ms. Grinch thanks you for the wreath. It made her heart grow three sizes."

Most women love this part of a relationship: the beginning. A simple phone call creating a core feeling of a thousand butterflies. The constant daydreaming of him twenty-four seven. The warm feeling that spreads through you at the mention of his name or the sound of his ringtone. Flirtatious, verbal volleys leading to exploration of mutual passions. Insinuating glances, tenuous body language. But not Caroline. She has always abhorred talking about herself. So getting to know someone in this manner is difficult for her.

Jameson and Caroline text almost daily now, nothing profound—just minute details of their day. She knows he wants more from her but she is not ready. Nonetheless, she enjoys their talks and looks forward to the next time they will see one another. They already have learned of each other's backgrounds, their professions and all that entails, hobbies, and taboos. Their discussions are becoming more and more personal, invading Caroline's safe zone. Jameson is interested in hearing about her military life, something she discusses with no one, except Dr. Perrin.

As she replaces the empty Christmas tree box back in the closet, her phone plays Jameson's ring tone.

"Your tree, Ms. Grinch, is outstanding. Now the true meaning of Christmas can come through." Jameson pokes fun at her Charlie Brown tree but Caroline finds it adorable that he can quote a line from Dr. Seuss.

After an hour conversation of Christmas pasts, Caroline expresses her nostalgia for all the Christmases she missed in the military.

"I hated being out of the country for Christmas. That is so depressing."

"What made you decide to join the military?"

"I was in college when 9/11 happened," Caroline explains. "I, like so many Americans, was ready to take up arms and destroy whoever dared to attack our nation. Part of me wanted to run to the recruiters, enlist immediately. But I was halfway through my nursing degree, so I stayed in college, but from that day on I knew I wanted to help our troops. So once I became a nurse, I made the decision to enlist. I joined the Army the day after graduation, and a few short years later had orders for Iraq."

"Why did you leave the military?"

"Even the most hard core become combat weary. So when my four-year enlistment was up, I came home. I moved to Asheville to be near friends and started my civilian nursing career. I came to miss military life, so I went reserves. You know the rest."

"Do you know how proud I am that my girlfriend serves in the military? I tell everyone," Jameson boasts. "Speaking of everyone, they are excited about meeting you."

Caroline does not understand why the word "girlfriend" makes her anxious. She feels herself shutting the floodwalls to her emotions immediately, so she changes the subject. "I will be out of town visiting my parents the next few days. I will call when I get back home."

Jameson feels her once again pulling away and wonders what he said that caused this sudden termination of their conversation. "All right, feel free to call anytime. Tell your parents I look forward to meeting them. I will pray for your safe trip."

Jameson too has a safe mode when he feels threatened, like now. He realizes she will be passing close by Charlotte on her way to Winston-Salem, but since she did not offer to stop to see him, he isn't about to beg. He does not say goodbye, talk to you soon or any other gracious salutation. If she did not want what he was offering, he respected her enough to let her go.

Caroline slams her phone on the bedside table. She is not mad at Jameson but at herself. Jameson is exactly what Caroline should want in her life. Her feelings are growing stronger; that is apparent. Everything reminds her of him. Songs, movies, even buildings. She can't pass the road signs for the Biltmore without him entering her thoughts. He has moved into her mind and, if she was honest with herself, her heart also. She is pretty sure he feels the same, though they never discuss where the relationship is going. It is for that reason alone she has to make a decision. Tell him about her orders and let him choose whether he wants to continue, or tell him nothing and give him no choice.

CHAPTER TWENTY-THREE

SESSION TEN – IRAQ ATTACK

Caroline's apprehension is palpable. Her pulse is beating so hard she can feel the vibration through the steering wheel as she drives to her appointment with Dr. Perrin. She is more fearful now of being hypnotized than she was the first time. Dreams, flashes, and nightmares are increasing in frequency, are much more cinematically creative, and seem autobiographical in nature.

Her past few sessions have been focused on techniques to control the flashbacks. But today, Dr. Perrin is planning hypnosis. However, Caroline's intent is telling Dr. Perrin of her concerns and possibly opting out of it, preferring to try another therapeutic approach to ridding her of these subconscious thoughts. She is positive he will understand once she recaps how the past few weeks of subconscious senility has superimposed itself on her life.

Dr. Perrin recognizes Caroline's level of anxiety from the moment she steps in his office. Although she is usually a good-humored person, he notices her eyes shifting anywhere around the room but toward him. She paces before finally sitting, never speaking to him, not even acknowledging his presence.

"Good afternoon, Caroline. Something on your mind?" Dr. Perrin asks.

Caroline looks up at him for the first time. "I am not sure I can continue with hypnotherapy. My…"—Caroline stammers for the right word—"condition. It is getting worse."

"Yes, we discussed that it might."

"No, you don't get it. The frequency, the vividness, and reality of it all. I came here mainly to rid myself of a certain reoccurring nightmare, the one I have had since returning from Iraq. It is the most painful and is based on actual events that happened to me. You have helped me with controlling the flashbacks from Iraq…"—Caroline considers her words carefully as to not place blame solely on Dr. Perrin for her messed up mind—"but now, I am experiencing a barrage of weird dreams and visions that are, well, quite frankly, scaring the shit out of me."

Dr. Perrin hovers his pen over the hated notebook and inquires, "Tell me about these new dreams and visions."

Rolling her eyes at the doctor's— almost too enthusiastic—inquisitive tone, she leans back on the lounger and explains, "The visions I have had since childhood are full-blown productions, now. I had a flashback, or a daydream, or something at work last week while I was treating a patient with a fever. I was in the med room getting her medication when all of a sudden I felt a heat penetrate my body. I thought I was going to pass out. Then the heat turned to a cold, clammy feeling. I had a flashback of being really sick. Then when it was over, I remembered I had come in to get a patient's med and briefly searched for cinchona bark."

The pen flew across the page as Dr. Perrin noted every word.

"I didn't even know what that was until I got home and looked it up. Cinchona bark was used to treat malaria centuries ago."

Once again, Dr. Perrin's pen takes flight across the page.

"And like the time I was with Marshall and had a brief flashback to an earlier time period. Well, that entire movie played out in a nightmare a few weeks ago. I, or some girl, was in a wheelchair being attacked by a rabid dog. Good God, what the hell is going on with me?"

Anxiety erupting, forcing Caroline from her relaxed state on the chaise, she bolts up and resumes her pacing. "I can barely handle the nightmares and flashbacks from this lifetime. I don't need new ones centuries old." Caroline walks to water cooler to wet her mouth. Caroline downs a cup of water and once again, resumes pacing the room.

Dr. Perrin rests his hand, cramping from writing Caroline's outburst. He notes she had not told him of this nightmare she had weeks ago but he doesn't question her about it. He allows silence to enter the room, not only to ensure she has spoken all she needs to but also as a calming effect.

When Caroline returns to her seat, he asks, "Do you feel safe in continuing therapy with me as your therapist?"

Caroline is taken aback by that question. It is like he can read her mind but she had already asked herself that question.

"Absolutely," she confirms.

Where the hell did that answer come from? Caroline is surprised how quickly the decision to stay with Dr. Perrin came out her mouth when her mind had wrestled with it for weeks.

"I do not want another therapist, just another type of therapy. I have all the confidence in the world in you."

"Then allow me to help you. There is more here than you can comprehend at the moment. I feel we need to work more aggressively on the nightmares you are experiencing to assist more with the PTSD. As we move forward in rectifying those issues through hypnotherapy, I am almost positive the 'time period' flashes will explain themselves, eventually. It might take work on both our parts, but I think we are onto something."

Glancing at his notes, Dr. Perrin restates Caroline's primary reason for therapy: "You said you want to 'rid yourself of a certain reoccurring nightmare,' and it has to do with something that happened in Iraq." Dr. Perrin sits his notebook to the side. "I still believe hypnosis is the best therapeutic tool for accomplishing this goal, but if you are not comfortable—

"No," Caroline interrupts, "I do not want my fears preventing us from what you consider to be the best solution. I will just have to handle this."

"If you feel you are ready, we can try to go back to Iraq today, addressing that nightmare."

Caroline's anxiety, once manifested in pacing, is now moved to the chaise lounge, working its way out in leg tremors. Dr. Perrin begins with breathing exercises to calm her, moving on to progressive muscle relaxation, allowing Caroline time to integrate peace with repose.

In his soft voice, Dr. Perrin leads Caroline through the relaxation techniques. He must repeat this process several times before Caroline visibly relaxes. He then proceeds progressively down her body, one muscle group at a time.

"Feel your whole body relaxing, warm from the inside out so that your muscles simply will not work. Now that your body is in the deepest state of relaxation, allow your mind to become just as relaxed."

Dr. Perrin observes Caroline for several breaths, monitoring for any signs of stress or tension. Once he is sure Caroline is at optimal relaxation, he begins the induction.

"I would like you to imagine a downward-leading staircase full of beautiful, warm light. You are at the top of the staircase, still relaxed, knowing what you search for is at the bottom. There are ten steps. Each step leading to a deeper level of relaxation and enlightenment. With each step, you will become more relaxed...more calm...more peaceful. Step down to the first step. You are safe and warm. You want to take the next five steps down to the knowledge your subconscious mind is hiding. Continue to slowly take those steps. As you descend, your mind becomes more relaxed, opening up to the knowledge that lies before you."

He monitors Caroline's progress from his chair. "Four steps remain to your enlightened subconscious mind. Take the next step, allowing your mind to open. Letting it happen, going deeper in trance than you ever experienced. Take the next step down. Two steps remain in front of you. With each remaining step, your trance will double, your conscious mind will connect with your subconscious, freeing knowledge. As you take the next to last step, you are approaching the trauma your mind replays for you over and over again. The trauma your subconscious is blocking, trying to keep you safe. Allow this trauma to come into the conscious mind. Take that step. With one step to go, you will remain relaxed, able to communicate the experience with me. As you take the last step down, you will discover where you are. Remaining in deep trance relaxation, yet able to speak, take the last step."

Dr. Perrin observes her reaction, then asks, "What do you notice about where you are now?"

Silence.

"It's dark. I can't see anything."

"Do you know where you are?" Dr. Perrin tries to help Caroline.

Caroline does not say anything. Dr. Perrin waits.

"I am in Iraq."

"Do you know why you are in Iraq?"

"There's a war." Caroline pauses in between. "I am here as a combat nurse."

"As you become accustomed to the darkness, ask your mind about your other senses. What do you feel?"

"The weight of my battle rattle...Sand and dust all over me...And cold." Caroline crosses her arms across her chest. "I am starting to see a mist...no, it's my breath. Everyone's breath."

"Are there others with you?"

"Yes. We are sitting in the back of a seven-ton, transport vehicle…We are stopped."

"What else do you notice about your surroundings?"

"More light. Bright flashes of repetitive lights. Movement."

Caroline stops there. Dr. Perrin allows time for Caroline to assimilate the situation in her mind. He notices Caroline is shivering.

"Caroline, you are in your energy light, safely above, only viewing the scene." Dr. Perrin waits for any observable changes in her behavior. When Caroline visibly relaxes, he continues, "As the mist clears, you are able to clearly see the scene below you. Allow yourself to become aware of your knowledge and wisdom. Do you know where are you going?" Dr. Perrin waits.

"We have not arrived at any particular destination, yet our truck has stopped."

"Using your senses, what do you hear?"

"Radio commands, everyone yelling…Barrage of small arms fire… Rapid fire of a .50 cal."

Dr. Perrin can see Caroline's eyes rapidly moving beneath her closed eyelids. Her lips are quivering in between her words yet she remains still, relaxed.

"Using your other senses, what do you smell?"

"Fear."

"Whose fear?"

"Mine and everyone else's."

"Who is everyone?"

"My battalion."

"What is causing that fear?"

"We know the highway is bomb-infested…It is extremely dangerous to travel by convoy across the barren desert of Iraq…especially in total darkness, without the benefit of headlights. We moved slowly for hours… making us highly vulnerable to enemy attack. But now we are stopped." Caroline is silent for several minutes.

"Why are you stopped?"

Caroline does not answer after several minutes, so Dr. Perrin steps back a question. "What else do you smell?"

"Diesel fuel…Gun powder…Smoke."

The doctor understands the diesel fuel could be coming from the truck she is riding in and the gunpowder smell from the guns. What he can't figure out is if the convoy is crossing the desert in darkness to avoid detection, why is everyone yelling, and where is the smoke and rapid firing coming from? He feels she has skipped an integral part of the event. He probes deeper.

"Caroline, I want to take you back. Back to before the yelling. Back to the darkness, the convoy moving across the desert. Still in darkness, what do you know is happening?"

"We were somewhere between Balad and Fallujah. We were relocating our CSH."

Caroline remains still yet her facial expressions belie her silence. Dr. Perrin can see her heartbeat in her throat. He observes her chest moving up and down with each breath, faster and faster. Caroline sits up, throwing her arms across her head.

"Caroline, what are you seeing?"

"I can't see anything anymore."

Not sure if she is still in Iraq or has come back to her safe place, Dr. Perrin asks, "Why can't you see anything?"

"I am covering my head…My eyes are closed."

"Open your eyes Caroline."

"I still can't see."

Caroline's anxiety heightening his own, Dr. Perrin sits up on the edge of his seat. "Why can't you see?"

"There is too much smoke," Caroline says, matter-of-fact.

"Where is the smoke coming from?"

"From the bomb that exploded."

CHAPTER TWENTY-FOUR

SESSION TEN – MAJOR

Dr. Perrin notes her use of past tense and writes in his notes: *memory block of the actual explosion.* He knows her subconscious has stored it away to protect her from reliving the moment when her worst fears became her reality.

"Allowing your consciousness to communicate with your subconscious mind. Tell it: All is okay to release this information. You are in a safe place to handle this information. If you feel threatened in any way, you can return to your garden." Dr. Perrin advises and waits. "You are floating above the scene. Take me through the scene, Caroline, from right before the explosion."

"We are stopped for just a second when I hear a *whoosh*." Caroline mimics the whoosh. "I know that sound…It's a rocket-propelled grenade. I am overtaken with indescribable terror from the pre-impact whoosh of the RPG…Then I hear the boom as the RPG hits its mark. The convoy we have been closely following is being ambushed by enemy troops…The lead gun truck has been hit…We cannot advance. We cannot go back… We are sitting targets."

"Then what happens, Caroline?"

"Then all hell breaks loose; noise and orders coming from every direction."

"Describe to me the scene as you are seeing it from above."

"The first explosion rocks our vehicle…Rounds begin zipping through the night air as an array of munitions rain down on us. I am crouched down covering my ears…The machine gun on the truck is deafening…We are taking sustained and heavy fire from engaging insurgents…The sound of M-16s and assault rifles increase my fear…Controlled chaos ensues. Everyone in the truck is gathering their packs and un-holstering. They are running toward the gate of the truck. My MOPP gear…equipment… it's weighing me down…I can't get up…Everyone else is duck crawling toward the tailgate of the vehicle…taking cover from enemy snipers…The enemy are aimed down on our vehicle."

Caroline is showing signs of increased agitation. Dr. Perrin realizes she is moving in and out of different levels of hypnosis. "Caroline, listen to my voice. You are floating in your energy light above the scene. You are protected and safe." Dr. Perrin waits for her composure to calm. He sees her relaxing slightly. "What happens next?"

"I hear someone yelling *jump* over and over again. But it is muffled"— Caroline turns her head slightly as if trying to hear—"by the sound of the radio squawking…by the gunfire all around us, and the popping of the blades."

"What blades?"

"From the helicopters flying over our heads. An airstrike has been called in. They are searching for movement of any enemy troops advancing toward us. I watch as the sky lights up from the explosions…Rockets and missiles are being fired from the ground… and from Cobra and Apache aircraft in the sky."

"What do you do next?"

"I look at the others. They are lining up…jumping off the back of the truck."

"Why are they jumping off the back of the truck?"

"We are trained in case of attack to disembark the vehicle…form a 360-degree perimeter around the vehicle so we can fire on any approaching enemy."

"So the others are jumping from the back of the truck. What are you doing?"

"Watching them."

"Do you not have to jump too?"

"I can't."

"You can't what?"

"I can't jump."

"Why?"

"I can't feel my legs. All I can do is stare upward, watching the air-to-ground cannon fire and rockets from the Apache helicopters."

"Why can't you feel your legs?"

"I am paralyzed."

Taking in a sharp breath, Dr. Perrin charts her words. With uncertainty as to whether her paralysis is a physical problem due to possibly being shot or if her paralysis is a mental manifestation, he proceeds with more caution. "Caroline, have you been injured?"

Silence.

"Caroline, you are in a safe place. You are only telling the event. Not reliving it. Allow your subconscious the capability of releasing this trauma for healing purposes. Are you injured?"

"No," Caroline finally says with tears forming in her eyes.

"You are viewing yourself in the back of the truck…Others are jumping from the truck. You feel paralyzed but we both know you are not. Why is your mind telling you that you can't feel your legs?"

"I have to find Major."

Dr. Perrin has no idea who "Major" is or even if that is a person, considering the acronyms the military uses. He writes the word in all caps. When he looks back up, Caroline is in a state of agitation.

He is about to redirect her or even take her out of hypnosis due to the level of anxiety she is demonstrating when she suddenly exclaims, "My pack—it's being pulled upward…I am being hoisted to my feet."

"Who is doing that?"

"The Marine in charge of protecting us. We are the only two left on the back of the truck. He is yelling for me to jump…I try to stand, but then I see something."

"What do you see?"

"I don't know…It's just a dark image running away from the truck…I fight to watch it. I can't jump. I won't be able to see him."

Caroline's tears are now dampening her shirt as she tells her trauma. "Sergeant Joe—he is pulling me to my feet; he is fighting me. Trying to get me to jump…He now sees what I see. He sees the image. He drops me. He is swinging the Maw Duce toward the desert. He is taking aim."

Dr. Perrin writes the slang word for the .50 caliber machine gun, Maw Duce, in his notes.

Caroline slightly folds her body. "I take cover…I squat down…. circling my legs with my arms. My ears are ringing from the rapid fire.

Shell casings are pinging all over the sides and back of the truck. I have to stand. I have to protect him."

Caroline is showing signs of increased anxiety. Dr. Perrin would like to bring her out but needs to find the answer to "Major." He is also concerned with bringing her out at this point with the trauma so fresh in her mind, so he proceeds.

"Protect whom?"

Caroline remains agitated yet silent.

"Caroline, who do you want to protect?"

After a few seconds, Dr. Perrin is jolted out of his seat as Caroline screams. "It's Major!"

"Caroline, take a deep breath and tell me: who is Major?"

"My friend. He is trying to save us. *Noooo*!" Caroline screams from the edge of the chaise lounge. "I leap to my feet…launching my entire body on top of the sergeant firing from the back of the truck. He has been our protector from the beginning of this shithole tour and he has always been by our side…He has even become a friend and confidant…I cannot allow Major to be shot by friendly fire."

"What does the marine in the back of the truck do?"

"He looks at me like I am insane. He is yelling at me, 'What the fuck, Lieutenant?' as he pushes me off him. But I have to protect him."

"Isn't protecting Major putting you in danger and your platoon?"

"Yes." Caroline's eyes flood with tears. "But I love him."

Dr. Perrin sees the anguish in her expressions and knows he has to bring her out soon.

"What do you say back to the sergeant?"

"I tell him it's Major…I plead as loud as I can to be heard over the gunfire and helicopters. Don't shoot! He's trying to save us."

Caroline's tears are flowing nonstop now.

"He straps his rifle and grabs me by my pack and yells back, 'And you are going to get us killed! Now jump!' I am being lifted off my feet again." Caroline startles on her chaise. "He takes me with him, off the back of the truck." Caroline exhales a hard breath. "I land on my feet but my knees give way. Oh, dear God…It's a bone-curdling jar from the weight of my gear. Sergeant Joe lands beside me…He is pushing me under the truck…I am now behind one of the tires watching the bursts of light from some of the rifles."

"Some?" Dr. Perrin has never served in the Armed Forces but figures all guns would be blazing.

"Some are out of ammunition…Some are wounded…Some are dead."

Caroline is surprisingly calm at this point, which worries the doctor more than the emotional turmoil of before. Now she is almost catatonic.

After several minutes of silence, not sure if Caroline is still in Iraq or has gone to her safe garden, he asks, "Where are you now?"

"Behind a massive tire for cover. I try to crawl under the truck to the wounded but we are pinned down."

"What are you feeling?"

"Numb…Useless…I want to treat the wounded around me. I want to run after Major. But I am too afraid to do anything."

"What happens next?"

"Another Marine rips my .9 mm from my side and places it in my hand…He is yelling something at me…But I can't hear him. I just stare at my hand. I can't fire that weapon."

"Why can't you fire your weapon?"

"It's heavy. The weight of the pistol reminds me…I am now on opposite sides of myself."

"Opposite sides?" Dr. Perrin writes this in his notebook. "What do you mean?"

"I am no longer here to save lives…I am to take one."

CHAPTER TWENTY-FIVE

SESSION TEN – REFRAMING THE TRAUMA

Caroline's hypnotic trance must come to an end. Dr. Perrin is worried that too much enlightenment could be more harmful than therapeutic. He promised her baby steps. He will keep his promise.

"Caroline. Listen to me carefully. I will now invite the subconscious mind to continue to help you find the resolution that your conscious mind seeks. As I count from ten to one, your subconscious will share with your conscious mind the deeper meaning behind the nightmare. When I get to one, you will be in your safe garden, retaining the knowledge of your subconscious."

Dr. Perrin, observing Caroline's reactions while still under hypnosis, begins. "Ten, you are floating above the scene. Your emotions are floating with you. Above the scene, only observing. Nine, take a deep breath in. As you exhale, blow the image in front of you away like blowing powder out of your hand."

Dr. Perrin watches as Caroline takes a deep breath and slowly releases it through pursed lips. He continues to guide her through the remaining eight steps. Pausing for five breath-lengths, Dr. Perrin assesses Caroline's stature for any signs of stress. "Caroline, where are you?"

"Under the willow tree."

Secure that Caroline has returned to her safe, happy place, Dr. Perrin continues with the termination of her hypnotic trance. "Now I will count backward from five. When I reach one, you will be fully awake. You will be aware of the knowledge and wisdom the subconscious is sharing with you. Five, you will remain relaxed and at peace. Four, you are opening your conscious mind to receive the knowledge and wisdom. Three, relax so your subconscious mind can release the information vital to your healing. Two, take a deep cleansing breath. And one, open your eyes."

Caroline, blinking a few times, opens her eyes. She is staring at the ceiling but then slowly turns her head, looking around the room. Recognition reaches her mind; she is with Dr. Perrin. She is surprised she feels extremely relaxed. They sit in silence, though Caroline can hear Dr. Perrin writing in his notebook.

After several minutes, he offers, "Would you like a glass of water?"

Caroline sits up on the edge of the lounger and accepts his offer. Not realizing how thirsty she is, she drinks the entire glass and places it on the table beside her.

"How do you feel?" Dr. Perrin inquires.

"Groggy. But fine."

Dr. Perrin refills her glass, allowing time for her to process the information that is possibly flooding her mind.

"Are you aware of where you went under hypnosis?"

"Yes. I was in Iraq." Caroline still is having a hard time believing that she can be hypnotized.

"Do you remember the scene you described?"

"It's the same reoccurring nightmare I have had since coming home. Except much more detailed and vivid."

"You call it a nightmare. Or is it a memory?" Dr. Perrin reaches deep inside Caroline's thoughts.

"It truly happened. We were somewhere between Balad and Fallujah just a month before my return to the States. We were relocating our surgical hospital unit to another province when we were ambushed."

"Do you think of this battle often?"

"No. Actually, I try very hard not to think about it."

"Are you sure?" Dr. Perrin calls out the subconscious mind while handing her the whole box of tissues.

Caroline sits quietly for a moment, tears forming in the corners of her eyes. She pulls out a tissue and covers her face with it. A few more minutes go by before Caroline is able to answer through heavy tears.

"I don't know," she says, shaking her head side to side, continuing to sob into the tissue as Dr. Perrin waits for the cathartic moment. "We can sit here all day but I still will not have the answers you are wanting."

"I am not wanting them, Caroline. You are."

This statement sends Caroline back into another emotional whirl and she runs to the bathroom. Ten minutes go by before Caroline emerges, emotions under control but still obviously distraught. She takes her seat across from Dr. Perrin.

Dr. Perrin asks Caroline to recall what she remembers from that time. They talk for another hour about the day her platoon was ambushed in Iraq. How she knew her life was over that day. The thoughts of military personnel showing up at her parents' house to deliver the news.

"I feel guilty that I would rather go to war than to give my parents the grandchild they long for. I feel guilty about putting my parents through such turmoil waiting for the day a black sedan pulls up in front of their house. I feel guilty that I did not respond as I am trained when we were taking heavy fire and that I am still alive and others aren't. I feel guilty that I almost got Sergeant Joe Adkins killed along with myself." Caroline blows her nose, then goes back into reflection. "Major. Oh God, Major." Caroline breaks down again, uncontrollably sobbing.

"What about Major upsets you more so than others?" Dr. Perrin wonders if Caroline recalls her profession of love for Major while under hypnosis.

"Major was my best friend over there. There was something about him."

"What happened to Major, Caroline?" Dr. Perrin has already surmised the answer by Caroline's use of past tense but he feels it important she acknowledges Major's fate, out loud.

After a few moments of deep wailing, Caroline admits, "I can't…I can't deal with this right now. I have never told anyone about Major."

"Then let's talk about your feelings of guilt. Have your parents ever stated they are disappointed in what you are doing with your life?"

"No. They tell me how proud they are that I am a nurse in the Army. They have bumper stickers on their cars that say so." A smile breaks through the tears as Caroline thinks of her parent's display of pride with bumper stickers, the American flag flying proudly from their porch and pictures of her in uniform all over the house.

"And yet you still feel guilty." It was a statement, not a question.

"I guess I think I should provide them with a normal life. Marry, have them grandchildren, et cetera. That's just not me."

"Have they ever asked you to do this?"

"No." Caroline wipes more tears away.

"So this could be your own guilt of not pursuing a different American dream?"

Uncomfortable, Caroline delivers a hateful expression and then breaks eye contact.

Dr. Perrin looks at his notes. "How about the guilt you refer to when you said 'respond how I was trained'?"

"I should have been the first off that truck when told to jump. I was closest to the back. I should have provided cover for the others as they disembarked. If I would have done what I was trained to do, others might still be alive. Sergeant Joe would not have had to risk his own life to get me off that truck."

Caroline's head drops almost to her knees as she cries, "And maybe Major wouldn't have run headlong into the enemy to draw their fire."

Beside the word "MAJOR" in his notebook, Dr. Perrin had written the phrase "loves him" and now writes "hero" in all caps.

"Do you remember why you didn't jump?" Dr. Perrin again wonders if Caroline will remember what she said under hypnosis.

Caroline sits quiet for a moment, wipes away a stray tear and, with a touch of bewilderment, states, "I couldn't feel my legs. At first, I thought I had been hit…that I was paralyzed. But as he pulled me to my feet"—Caroline sucks in air—"I see Major. He was engaging the enemy to allow us time to take cover. That was when I felt my legs back under me. I had to save him."

Caroline is astonished at the revelations that are so clearly in her mind now. Though she can't understand why she didn't feel her legs, she knows she did try to stand but couldn't. And when she did stand, she jumped on Sergeant Joe, risking her own life to save Major.

"If you would have immediately jumped, would the outcome have been any different?"

"I probably would have been shot immediately."

"What did the condition of paralysis prevent you from doing?"

"Jumping off the truck first." Caroline is not sure where he is going with this line of questioning.

"To your self-admitted instant death."

Caroline agrees by nodding.

"What did having the condition of paralysis allow you to do?"

"It allowed me time to recognize Major and keep him from being shot by one of his own. A sure death."

"In what ways was this paralysis a benefit for your life now, other than the fact that you still have one?" Dr. Perrin smiles at her.

"Well, first of all, my parents haven't been visited by the army in a black sedan and can still foster hopes of grandchildren." Caroline is able to joke.

"Then in what ways was this paralysis a detriment to your life now?"

"For one, I suffer from guilt of not providing cover for the others."

Dr. Perrin continues with this line of questioning, walking Caroline through different scenarios and how each could have affected her present-day life. This form of therapy helps Caroline to see that Dr. Perrin's questions are leading to an understanding. She'd done as she had been trained: she ultimately fought for her life and for her fellow soldiers. Dr. Perrin works with Caroline to see the positive of what happened to her without solely focusing on the negative.

Caroline refuses to speak of Major, though Dr. Perrin insists that continued repression of her feelings will only continue to harm her. But Caroline is steadfast. She knows she is not ready to discuss her relationship with Major. And she is certainly not ready to discuss the gaping hole his loss has caused.

Dr. Perrin ensures Caroline is stable and sets up another appointment at the end of the week. As she leaves the office, Caroline prays the doc will be prepared to deal with the upheaval of her subconscious. Sitting at his desk, charting his session notes, Dr. Perrin is also in prayer. He prays for clarity of what he believes to be a dual etiology.

CHAPTER TWENTY-SIX

DUAL ETIOLOGY

Session Ten
December 2010

Captain Caroline McKenzie:

Hypnotherapy determined to be best practice for dual etiology: PTSD and PLT.

(Did not reveal dual etiology at this time. Will continue to work with client on PTSD issues before advancing care to this realm.) Will discuss with client dual etiology when I feel she is more emotionally able to cope with PLT.

Utilization of spiral staircase imagery for hypnotic induction: to prepare the mind for divided consciousness, making client more responsive to external instruction.

Client able to reach level three without issue. Client intermittently had to be recalled to lower level of hypnosis; spontaneously slipping to level four and possibly level five.

Subconscious disciplined to reveal knowledge of repressed memories.

Client able to terminate hypnotherapy fully relaxed and in full control of muscle groups.

Dissociative Regression utilized—Use of dissociative hypnotic language to split awareness from the subconscious mind yet still engaging the conscious mind. This technique selected to allow client a safe distance from unpleasant emotions.

Caroline self-guided to specific trauma she experienced in Iraq as an Army Captain.

During movement of Combat Support Hospital, convoy engaged by enemy. Use of past tense describing an explosion. Client memory blocked the actual explosion, protecting her from reliving the moment and possibly the subsequent loss of a comrade as evidence by a catharsis of emotion and refusal to discuss his fate.

Secondary gains—seeking the positive and negative facet of having the condition and not having the condition.

Paralysis is not a metaphor, as first concluded. Caroline could be experiencing split memories of which she is not fully aware that could lie outside of self-awareness boundaries. Resolution could be assisted by accessing this knowledge through PLR. Will delve deeper into these memories to determine if PLR could be therapeutic in understanding behavioral patterns, health issues, relationships, and the source of her underlying feelings of loss.

Abreaction (as evidenced by uncontrollable crying) reached when describing feelings of guilt along with her feelings toward "Major." While seeking to resolve client's reasoning for paralysis, avoidance of subject was allowed at this time. Will continue to work with client; enable positive association with Major's memory.

Appointment scheduled at end of week.

Dr. Perrin's concerns for his patient leaves him restless. He is almost positive of Caroline's diagnosis. He considers that if he is right, the time remaining before her deployment will not be enough to thoroughly analyze and treat the condition. Leaning back in his desk chair, arms folded behind his head, a full awareness strikes him hard: Continuing with the present hypnotherapy could actually cause her more harm.

Staying up most of the night researching articles on PTSD and PLT, the doctor searched for any new findings on best practice. Dr. Perrin goes to bed with a heavy heart and confused mind. He realizes he is embarking on a journey with Captain McKenzie that he has never, with a patient, previously traveled.

* * *

"Without laws, chaos ensues. I am not speaking of societal laws; I am referring to universal laws: Covenants for the Greater Cause. There are twelve Karmic Laws: I advise to heed them wisely.

Karmic Laws:

1. The Great Law: What one puts into the universe will come back to one
   What I have caused in my past has affected not only my future, but hers too.

2. The Law of Creation: We are one with the universe; our intentions govern the evolution of creation
   The life I have was created by my own intentions.

3. The Law of Humility: Focus on a higher level of existence; accept what is
   I had to accept my present circumstance in order to change the future.

4. The Law of Growth: One must change themselves if one is to grow spiritually, yielding positive or negative circumstances
   The only thing I had control over was myself.

5. The Law of Responsibility: The Universal Truth— One must take responsibility for one's own life; our lives are our own doing
   To change her circumstances, I had to change my frame of mind and my surroundings.

6. The Law of Connection: Past, Present, and Future are all connected; everything in universe is connected, both large and small
   I had to put in the work if I desired a different outcome for her future.

7. The Law of Focus: Focus on spiritual values and do not allow negative thoughts or actions and expect to grow spiritually; without a selfless nature, spiritual growth is impossible
    I solely consider another as to reach my true desires.

8. The Law of Giving and Hospitality: Demonstrate what one believes is true; what we believe manifests in our actions
    My actions had to be congruent with my beliefs.

9. The Law of Here and Now: Old thoughts, behaviors, and patterns prevent one from having new ones
    I focused on our future, not our past.

10. The Law of Change: History will repeat unless one changes one's path; the present is all we have
    I made a conscious commitment to change the path of her future by being in her present.

11. The Law of Patience and Reward: All rewards require toil; true lasting joy comes from doing what is right
    My reward will only be claimed through patience and persistence.

12. The Law of Love: Significance and Inspiration— Love brings life and inspires the Whole; the best reward in life is one that leaves a lasting impression on the Whole. Karma begins and ends with love. Karma was created to propel your Soul, on a personal journey of reincarnation through the universe
    The end result for my sacrifice: her safety; her happiness.
    Our purpose can override our desires. I am living proof of that. Sort of. I chose my life's purpose, over and over again, like many other spiritual counterparts. That purpose: to protect her, for I could not before. I promised as long as I was part of this universe, I would never allow her to be alone again. I love her more than any universal law and for that, I have broken most of them.

Do you remember rule number one: cause and effect? See, karma can sometimes be filled with irony. My ironic karmic fate: To protect her life after life, I had to transform my own."

CHAPTER TWENTY-SEVEN

FOREVER HOME

After three twelve-hour shifts in a row, Caroline is just as excited to see Marshall as he is to see her. Marshall sits obediently beside Caroline as she cleans out the dog kennels. She has grown accustomed to his company and him, hers. Caroline ruffles the fur behind Marshall's ears as she cleans out Barkley's recently vacated pen.

"I know, you miss Barkley. I miss her too. We should be happy she has found her forever family. Like you and I, we will always be together forever."

Marshall knows that to be true even if Caroline isn't so sure. She always thought she would be happy for Marshall if he were to be adopted, but now she realizes she could never let that happen. She sits down on the floor to give him a much-needed belly rub and herself, much needed animal-assisted therapy.

"I found the corporals family with the help of the Marine Corps, you know, the one I told you about. It took me several days to work up the courage to call and now, I don't know why I was so terrified. She didn't blame me for letting him die but told me she was glad that her son had a compassionate nurse by his side. His mother was so appreciative that I took the time to find her and let her know her son's last words. She talked for hours about what a sweet boy he was and how proud she is of him for serving his country. This lady even thanked me for my service, though I do not feel like I deserve her thanks. I can see why corporal Michaels loved his mother. She is an amazing woman. She took my address and number and we promised one another to stay in touch. That is a promise I will keep."

Marshall sits up and tilts his head to the side, watching for a command, because he can feel Caroline's emotional state changing.

"Marshall, I have something to tell you. Well, a few things, actually."

Caroline first tells Marshall all about her sessions with Dr. Perrin.

"Remember the guy that was with me a few weeks ago? I think I am falling in love with him. I know he seems perfect on the outside and, so far, pretty perfect on the inside too, but I can't help but wonder…"

Caroline stops there, not sure of what she is wondering. Jameson has given her no reason to distrust him, no reason to second-guess his sincerity. If anything, he has been a perfect gentleman and on paper meets all the conditions that Caroline requires. He is intelligent, compassionate, romantic, funny… He has to be hiding something. A cold nose wiggles its way under her arm, reminding Caroline she is in the middle of a belly-rubbing.

Caroline continues stroking his belly. "So why do I feel that he is not the one? I love being with Jameson. I love everything about him. Why can't I shake this feeling? This feeling that there is someone else out there who I am supposed to be with."

Marshall, knowing her mood has changed, lays his head across her lap and licks her hand. This sign of emotional devotion is more than Caroline's fragile psyche can handle. Leaning into Marshall's furry neck, she weeps, purging her deepest pain. Marshall lies perfectly still, providing Caroline the release of emotion she has kept bottled for so long. She can't imagine not having Marshall to talk to; he understands her better than anyone. Caroline realizes she can never allow Marshall to go to another family.

After wiping her tears on her shirt, Caroline buries the leftover pain inside. Marshall lifts his head from Caroline's lap, and like radar to tune into her emotions, perks his ears to listen for her next command.

"Thanks for being here for me." Caroline briskly rubs Marshall's head, sucking up all the feelings she can't seem to let go of. "Now let's go get your friends. They should be adequately muddy by now."

Marshall leads Caroline to the back door, waiting as she calls the dogs in from the backyard. As Caroline expected, the wet-soaked yard from the melted snow has deposited mud all over their fur. Caroline feeds each animal before taking Marshall on his walk. Treading the muddy embankment proves tiring as Marshall leads the way past the swollen river to the woods beyond. Caroline finds a nice tree stump to rest then offers Marshall a drink from his water bottle.

"There is one more thing we need to talk about," Caroline begins. "I might be going away for a while." Tears spring into Caroline's eyes as Marshall places a muddy paw on her lap. "I am being deployed overseas. That means I will be going to Afghanistan to fight the war on terrorism. I will be gone for less than a year." Caroline leans over to take Marshall in her arms. "Now don't look so sad. I am not leaving for a few more months." Caroline hugs him and strokes his chest. "But I promise you one thing: when I get back, you are coming home with me."

Marshall looks up at her with eyes shrouded in concern. Caroline expected more excitement than what Marshall is showing. She was sure he would understand those words—"coming home with me."

"We will be each other's forever family, I promise," Caroline says with much excitement in her voice. Marshall looks up at her, turns, and then walks back up the muddy riverbank.

Caroline and Marshall return to the kennel just in time for a huge celebration. Everyone is dancing around, some are crying, but everyone is in a state of euphoria.

"Did Marshall and I miss happy hour?"

"Oh, Caroline, it's a miracle. It's a miracle, I tell you." Francie is screaming with giddiness. "I have prayed and prayed for this and God has answered my prayers. Thank you, Jesus. Hallelujah." Francie waves her hands in the air, a piece of paper clutched between her fingers.

"What has happened?" Caroline asks.

"An anonymous donor sent enough money to keep the shelter open at least another year," Francie explains between tears of joy. "Look, it was attached to this Christmas wreath that was just delivered." Francie hands Caroline a cashier's check.

The amount boggles her mind. Caroline hands back the check and examines the wreath.

"Which florist delivered this?"

"I don't know. There isn't a card and I didn't see the vehicle," Francie continues, still celebrating. "Marshall, did you hear? Your home is safe."

Caroline drops to her knees. She hugs Marshall with such love and relief that he will be cared for until she returns from Afghanistan.

"You're home for now; I haven't forgotten my promise."

Tears spill over Marshall's fur, but this time, they're not Caroline's.

* * *

Caroline leaves Asheville straight from the shelter. As she passes the Interstate 77 South exit off Interstate 40 East, she can't help but think of Jameson. It should be interesting, Jameson meeting Jack and Gloria McKenzie one day, since they know nothing about him. Caroline loves her parents but being an only child has its disadvantages. Mainly, there is not another sibling on whom to redirect their concerns. She is fortunate her parents are still young, vibrant quinquagenarians. Staring out the windshield at the endless highway, she reflects about caring for them as they grow older. She will be their only source of assistance in their old age. If she's alive. A lump forms in her throat as her chest tightens. This reflection coaxes emotions she does not want to consider, not now. *Who will take care of them if something happens to me in Afghanistan?* This thought never occurred to her in 2004 when enlisting after college. She was young and egocentric, ready to take on the world. As she gets older, the care of her parents is ever more relevant in the planning of her future. Tears begin to well in her eyes, as visons of her mother and father storm her mind.

Here she is, speculating the care her parents will need as they age, when in reality, the future holds a higher percentage of Caroline herself needing assistance than her aging parents. The culpability of her parents' golden years being replaced by nursing their wounded child brings emotions Caroline is unable to deal with at this time. When Caroline told her parents she was coming for a visit to celebrate Christmas early, since she worked Christmas Eve and Christmas Day, they were thrilled. Her mother promised to bake all her favorites and to have the tree up so she can help decorate. Caroline held those traditional images close to her heart while deployed. She longed to be home with her parents, holiday after holiday, as they passed by in Iraq. Home is never more appealing than when you are away from it. She wants to make new, lasting memories with her parents this holiday, not knowing if they will have another. Planning on telling them about her orders for Afghanistan during this visit, Caroline tries to imagine their response.

The tears threaten to flow again as she pulls into the driveway of her childhood home, a small ranch in a quiet subdivision on the outskirts of Winston-Salem. Her father has lit the bushes in red, white, and blue Christmas lights, as he has done since her graduation from boot camp—

or the actual survival of it. The American flag still proudly displayed in the front yard gives her hope this conversation will not destroy them.

Her mother answers the door, pulling her inside for a motherly hug. "Hello Mama," Caroline sighs as she wraps her arms around her mother's delicate frame.

"Hi sweetheart, oh, you feel so good!"

Caroline fights back the tears while savoring the moment. The aroma of cookies wafting from the kitchen is almost her undoing. Her mother only loosens her hold on her when her father enters the foyer.

"There's my baby girl."

She folds into her father's arms like a little girl, burying her face in his flannel shirt. He smells of cigar smoke and cookies, the scent of Christmas past. For the rest of her life, she will never smell a cigar and not think of her father. She will never eat a sugar cookie and not think of her mother, standing by the oven, apron wrapped around her, Christmas carols playing in the background. This is going to be harder than she'd thought.

"I missed you Daddy," Caroline claims as she gazes into his loving, grey eyes.

His finger touches a tear that has formed at the corner of her eye, "We are so glad you were able to come home for a few days."

Caroline thought his eyes glistened a little more than usual as he pulled her close for another hug before handing her back to her mother. Dabbing the remaining moisture from each eye and taking a deep breath, Caroline heads toward the smells of the kitchen, "How can I help with those cookies?"

Caroline and her mother cook, bake, and talk the rest of the day, never leaving the kitchen. Caroline ices the brownies as her mother describes the holiday cruise they are leaving for in a week. They had caught up on family news, neighborhood gossip, and work-related issues by the time dinner was served. Caroline never mentions Jameson, therapy, or deployment. She wants her first day home to not be infringed with questions for which she did not have answers.

Caroline crawls into her bed, the same bed in the same room she had slept in her whole childhood. As she pulls the covers over her, she waits for the sensation that had always been present in her youth—the added weight of her dog, Marshmallow, snuggling in beside her

Caroline was away at college when Marsh disappeared. The last time they were together was when she'd come home over spring break during her senior year of college to tell her parents she was enlisting in the Army. Just a few weeks later, her mother called to tell her Marshmallow was gone, ran away. Caroline would do a double-take any time she spotted a white dog, believing Marshmallow had run away to find her. Caroline grieved herself through the end of that semester, barely making it through finals.

She and Marsh had been together since she was five years old. Found at the park while on an outing with her parents, the little mongrel had approached her cautiously, rolling over on his back as little Caroline bent down to pet him.

"Please let me keep him!" she had begged.

Her parents had been apprehensive of bringing an abandoned mutt home with them, but the mutt seemed to be enamored with their daughter, only eating from her hand, staying right by her side the rest of the afternoon. After much consideration, her dad convinced her mother the fur ball could be a welcoming companion for their only child and would teach her responsibility. With her mother's final approval that day in the park, Marshmallow became a member of the McKenzie family.

Caroline remembers bathing Marsh for the first time, his clean fur puffing out after shaking the water from him. "He looks like a big marshmallow," little Caroline had announced while towel-drying her new puppy; the name stuck.

From that moment on, Caroline and Marshmallow had been inseparable. He was her best friend growing up. Her childhood would have been so lonely and those unstable years of puberty would have been much harder without him. He was her constant companion and confidant.

The events of the day have finally taken their toll on Caroline—the comfort of her daddy, the encouragement of her momma, holding back information from her parents about her orders, and now the childhood memories of Marshmallow. As she buries her face in her pillow, tears transition to sobs. Caroline allows herself a few more moments of tears before falling asleep, knowing in the morning she'd need her strength to tell her parents about her deployment orders to Afghanistan.

* * *

Dad opens the garage for me to see my birthday present, a brand-new bike without training wheels. He holds onto the seat and runs alongside. Marshmallow runs on the other side, as if balancing out my support. I don't even notice that Dad let go until I see him running past me. The handlebars start to shimmy; I can only concentrate on my dad, now two houses up the block. The harder I try to hold on, the more the bike begins to swerve. I can't take my eyes off my dad, who is now too far away to save me. I panic. I hit the pavement, scraping my knee.. Marshmallow is first to my side, licking my face then my knee. I wait for my dad to run to me, pick me up, and carry me home. He doesn't. He tells me, "Get back on." I refuse, crying for his sympathy. Marshmallow barks his disapproval of my father's plan, standing between me and the bike.

Dad sets the bike upright, again urging me onto the two-wheeled death-mobile. I make him promise to not let go. I get back on and start peddling as my dad and Marsh balance out the sides. By the end of the block, which is where my father is already standing, Daddy catches me, bike and all, and brings me to a stop. He tells me I am never allowed to cross the street; I have to stay on the sidewalk. I practiced all evening, Mom and Dad watching from the driveway as I rode past them, Marshmallow running alongside.

Caroline wakes, soothed that for once, her mind recalled a happy memory. After breakfast, Caroline tells her parents she has orders for overseas. Her mother's mouth drops open, as if to scream, but the sound never comes. It is like someone hit pause on the remote. Jack stands to embrace Caroline in his arms while his wife recovers from her shock.

Hugging her tight, he tells her how proud they are of her, and asks, "When are you leaving?"

Caroline answers, "The end of February."

Her father's gasp is not the only sound in the room. Her mother audibly chokes back tears. She envelopes Caroline in her arms. When she releases her, her mother's composure is intact. The pseudo-composure does not last long.

Gloria McKenzie asks, "Where are you going?"

"If she tells you that, Gloria, then she has to kill you." Her dad's attempt at a joke falls flat.

"Afghanistan." Caroline says with as much bravado as she can muster.

At first, Caroline thought her mother didn't hear her for she stood stiff straight like a statue for several seconds. Caroline soon realizes her mother fully heard her and understood the dangers of that part of the world. Gloria McKenzie's body convulses from restrained sobs. Jack grabs his wife's arm, supporting it by the elbow, then lowers her to a chair. Her parent's supportive façade crumbles with the word Afghanistan and together, they cry for the safety of their child.

Caroline spends the rest of the morning reassuring her mother that she will be safe, stationed on a CSH unit nowhere near the fighting. Her father does not correct his daughter as she bold-face lies to her mother. He knows as well as Caroline, there is no place safe in Afghanistan.

To try to soothe the tortured soul of a soldier's mother, Caroline decides to tell them about Jameson. As expected, her mother and father are thrilled that she has found someone with whom to share her life. Caroline tries to tell them the relationship is still new, to not get their hopes up for grandchildren yet, but this news finally stops the intermittent bursts of tears from her mother. Caroline ceases trying to downplay her relationship with Jameson; it makes her parents too happy to know she found someone.

The departure takes a little longer than expected due to her mother's precarious emotional state. Caroline had actually planned on calling Jameson and having him meet her for a late lunch at the 140/177 split. It is after 2 o'clock before Caroline gets on the road, not leaving enough time for lunch with Jameson if she is to make it back for her evening appointment with Dr. Perrin.

CHAPTER TWENTY-EIGHT

SESSION ELEVEN – GET 'EM, MAJOR

Dr. Perrin reviews his session notes in between his previous appointment and his last, with Caroline. With time running out before her deployment, he is pushed to find the answers for the breakthrough Caroline McKenzie is needing. He'd spent several hours of the past few weeks in the library and online, researching his theory. He is sure of the dual causes, but something else is nagging him. A little glitch in his mind—one which won't allow him to stop obsessing over this client or her issues.

He sets down his notes on his desk, takes off his glasses, and lets his head lull on the back of his chair. Closing his eyes, he imagines the dreams and nightmares Caroline has described while in session. In an almost state of self-hypnosis, Dr. Perrin sketches the places, the timeline, the episodes, and the people involved on the canvas of his mind. He plays Caroline's words over in his head as the images she has described act out lifetimes of events.

The doctor's eyes fly open as he sits up abruptly in his chair. "Good God. No way!" The repetition and reoccurrence is obvious to him now. "No!" He has never heard of anything like this in all his years of practice, nor during his educational training. Yet, his observations are undeniable.

He jumps to his feet, crossing the room to his bookcase, selecting and then pulling books from their honored spots. Dr. Perrin is not sure if he is trying to prove or disprove his theory. He cannot convince himself that he is right in his assessment; he would prefer to be wrong.

He has known for quite some time that telling Caroline of his secondary—or, actually, paired etiology—will upset her. But when she hears this…

Caroline's stomping feet on the mat outside breaks his concentration. He quickly sets the books he had chosen to study behind his desk as his patient enters the room. He struggles to inhale a slow, deep breath to calm himself.

Caroline smiles at Dr. Perrin, though she is still reeling from the sensitive conversations with her parents a few hours ago. She is almost frightened by what she sees. His face is set in ashen gray, like a statue, his eyes staring straight through her. He makes no attempt to speak, just continues to stare. His eyes are a darker green than usual, mesmerizing her with the inability to look away.

"Caroline, I am sorry. I was lost in thought. Please sit down."

Stilted conversation about her week and awkward glances at one another persists for the next few minutes. Caroline is already an emotional wreck and considers asking to reschedule when Dr. Perrin regains his own repose. He asks if there is anything she wants to discuss.

Caroline begins with telling the doctor about her visit with her parents, their reaction to her orders, and the emotional deluge that followed. She tells him about her dream of Marshmallow. This takes up most of her appointment time. Caroline notices Dr. Perrin seems to be taking more notes than usual and observing her a lot less. Her first conclusion is that he must be upset about something. But just as it is in nursing, no matter what is going down in your own life, you must present a strong professional front for your patient.

Caroline continues, "So shortly after losing Marshmallow, I find myself in a war zone in a foreign country for the first time, without the comforts of home. Then one day, there he was, the only semblance to my American life back home, a dog. He followed us everywhere across that fucking desert. I guess he felt safe with us, not to mention we fed him from our allotted rations, which was probably the only for sure way he knew he would get to eat."

Caroline isn't sure whether to go on; Dr. Perrin appears distracted.

"I'm sorry, Caroline," Dr. Perrin, not hearing a word she had said for several minutes and still sorting out the thoughts in his own head, apologizes and says, "Please continue."

"At first, there seemed to be confusion where the heavy fighting would take place. Our CSH unit would travel to one area in Iraq only to be told to move on to another. When we finally arrived near Balad, we set up camp. A dog wasn't allowed in the unit so he always stayed right outside the gates, watching us move about. I would feed him through the fence line, as did many others. We sort of adopted him, or he adopted us. I am not sure. Many nights we would hear him barking, just like our commander barked orders. That is how he got his name—Major."

Dr. Perrin grasps the importance of this conversation, shutting out his own thoughts. His patient is finally able to discuss the traumatic force behind her worst reoccurring nightmare.

"He barked continuously, as if his bark would protect us all. 'Get 'em, Major' could be heard across the unit, not just when he was barking. It became our platoon's motivating motto. We would call out, 'Get 'em, Major' whenever we heard explosions, or gunfire, or when we successfully pulled a young soldier out from the brink of death."

Dr. Perrin writes quickly, "Major is a dog." He does not want to miss another word.

"Then we had orders to move again. Major watched as we dissembled the whole base and packed it up. I told him what was happening, that we were on the move again. I should have known he would go with us."

Caroline's dispirited mood is choking her now, the sorrow affecting her ability to continue. She hides her face behind a tissue, trying to compose herself. Dr. Perrin is not wanting her to stop but is concerned over her emotional state.

"Caroline. Can you go on?"

Caroline shakes her head to the negative, wiping away the mournful tears of the remembrance of her time with Major, and her conscious awareness to the end of this story.

Dr. Perrin closes his notebook, leaning forward to take her hand. Touch therapy is not part of his therapeutic techniques, but her pain is so strong and endearing, flowing out of her and straight through him, he can't help himself. She glances up, viewing him through tear-laden eyes, not able to speak.

Breaking the immense tension, Dr. Perrin recaps the session, making sidebar notes in his notebook that he will later transcribe as session notes. He confirms with Caroline that being back in her family home brought on the feeling of deep loss of her family pet, Marshmallow. He checks his notes then corroborates that Marshmallow disappeared while Caroline was away at college, a few months before graduating and enlisting in the Army.

He ensures Caroline is emotionally stable to drive home and sets up their next appointment after the Christmas holiday. After Caroline leaves, Dr. Perrin updates his session notes including plan of care: Will take patient back to "Jump" sequence nightmare for recollection of significance of stray dog.

He cannot, however, write down his epiphany into Caroline's diagnosis. He can't even believe it himself. He picks up the stack of books hidden behind his desk, turns off the lights, and heads upstairs to his residence. The book's title on the top of the stack staring back at him: THE PRESENT POWER OF PAST LIVES.

* * *

Caroline calls the girls after arriving home from therapy, wishing each of them a Merry Christmas before they head home to their families. She then crawls into bed, emotionally and physically exhausted. She opens the Christmas card that came today hoping to lift her spirits. The front of the card has a picture of a Christmas tree wrapped in red, white, and blue. Her breath catches as she reads the sender's signature, Karen Michaels. She is glad she sent a holiday card a few days earlier to the corporal's mother and plans on sending one every year from now on.

She considers calling Jameson but decides against it. She will call him tomorrow, on Christmas Eve, to make sure he received her Christmas gift. She is not in the right state of mind to be uplifting and perky right now. She most definitely will not burden him with her own hysterical mind, which is biding its time, waiting for her to fall asleep.

Caroline wakes, pajamas soaked, as are the bed sheets. Placing her hand on her forehead, she feels for a temperature but her hands are too cold to be used as an effective thermometer. She pulls herself out of bed, body aching, heading for the shower to rid herself from the sweat of what she fears is a fever breaking, or she has had a nightmare she can't remember.

Glancing through the blinds, she sees the rain has not stopped. It has rained for days over the Blue Ridge Mountains, bringing flash floods due to the melting snow coupled with the rain. The rain has also prevented her from walking with Marshall. The sodden earth with its grey overcast is too depressing to think about. She closes the blind, then stops short at the mirror. She can't help but notice she looks like death warmed over. Nothing that a shower and a cup of coffee couldn't cure. She hopes she isn't coming down with something.

After the shower, Caroline dresses for her morning yoga and meditation. Stretching her aching muscles and releasing the tension, she readies her body for the transformational calming of her mind. She sits in front of the fireplace, staring into the flames as she induces a mode of consciousness, allowing her mind to acknowledge its content through meditation.

Polio has made my body weak. My breathing muscles won't work. Least that is what the doctor told mama. He said he couldn't help me. I always thought the polio would kill me but I am dying from something in my lungs. The doctor said it is a germ bug in my lungs. That's gross. I don't know how a bug got in my lungs. I close my eyes. I am too weak to stay awake. I feel like I am drowning. I can't get enough air and when I try, I cough and cough and cough. "I am sorry, Mama. I want to stay with you but I am too tired." I follow the light that is calling me. Mama is crying. She is holding onto my hand, but I want to go with him. I take my last, wet breath. I am floating, floating above my body. "Bye, Mama. He says I will see you again someday. Don't cry, I am safe. He is here with me now, guiding me. I am at peace."

I know my fever has come back. My mouth is dry; my body aches so, even the slightest movement of the mattress from my dog causes pain in all my joints. My head is full, heavy on the pillow. The blankets, nor the fire, deter the shivering from this dreadful ague. When will Michael be back? He will not be happy the maid called the doctor in his absence. But she was fearful I would die before my husband can make it back with the coveted Cinchona bark. The maid is right to be fearful; I am dying. The doctor has performed a bloodletting to rid me of the bad humors inside. It is not helping. I am so weak; my eyes are on fire underneath. I fight not to follow the light that is calling me. I want to see Michael one last time. To hold him, feel his love for me. He will be devastated. I am sorry, my darling, but I am too weak. I must go. I follow the light. I am at peace.

The shrill ring of Caroline's phone brings her out of her meditative state. As she answers, she notices her clothes are drenched in sweat again.

It is the base commander providing information of her deployment and wishing her a Merry Christmas. She confirms the date of her pre-deployment physical but barely hears a word of what the commander is relaying. She can only concentrate on the flashbacks that overtook her meditation. Polio, ague, cinchona bark are the words circling her brain as she turns on her laptop, typing the word "ague" in the search engine. Several websites on malaria appear. Caroline spends the morning researching polio and malaria and their treatments. She finds post-polio syndrome causes muscle atrophy, including a weakness of the diaphragm and chest muscles. Fluid and mucus then build up in the lungs, making it hard to take deep breaths. She studies the time period of malaria, its outbreaks and treatment, knowing already it would involve cinchona bark. Closing the lid of the laptop, she grabs the phone.

CHAPTER TWENTY-NINE

SESSION TWELVE – SUMMONING A SPIRIT

Caroline's phone call disturbs Dr. Perrin greatly, which is why he agrees to see her after work, even though it is Christmas Eve. After listening to her tell of her self-induced hypnosis during meditation, he decides he will need to inform her of his research on the subject and what he feels is the dual etiology behind her nightmares and flashbacks. When Caroline arrives, Dr. Perrin observes her emotional state, the agitation, the edge of tearfulness. He advises her of his treatment plan for the day.

"Iraq again?" Caroline questions as she paces the room. "I know why I have nightmares of Iraq. I want to know why I am dreaming of polio and the malaria.

Talking to her backside as she paces away from him, Dr. Perrin explains, "I think we need to address the issue of your emotional attachment to Major. You are repressing these memories to avoid the pain. Deep down though, you truly want to share these feelings with someone."

Caroline, still pacing the room, is not sure she wants to continue but she is equally afraid to stop now. Dr. Perrin yields to her emotional state, allowing silent lucidity to permeate the room. Several minutes go by before Caroline is able to allay her grief.

She takes a few deep breaths to calm herself, walks over to the chaise lounge, and while slowly taking her seat says, "I am putting my trust in you, Doc." Never taking her threatening eyes off Dr. Perrin, Caroline lies back on the lounger.

Dr. Perrin performs an integrated muscle relaxation, moving her rapidly through the muscle groups and then more methodically taking her to her safe place.

"As the light begins to energize you, you begin to notice the sensation of your mind housing the knowledge and wisdom that is pertinent to this issue. It is opening, opening to allow access to the subconscious."

Silent for several breaths, Dr. Perrin evaluates Caroline's hypnosis level and reactions to commands.

"I will count from one to five. When I reach five, you will be back in Iraq, at the time just prior to the explosion. You will be floating above the scene but able to use all your senses. One, your lighted energy body leaves your garden…floating upwards. Two, you are now floating over the convoy in Iraq. Floating above, you are becoming aware of the knowledge your subconscious mind has never allowed. Three, your senses are alive. Four, you will remain relaxed and at peace while listening to my voice. Five, you see the scene clearly from above."

Dr. Perrin takes notes on her level of consciousness after induction, allowing her time to assimilate. After several breaths he says, "Caroline, describe what you see."

Completely relaxed, her voice void of emotion, Caroline answers, "It is dark. I am on the back of a seven-ton transport truck moving through the desert. The lead vehicles are stirring sand in the air, making it difficult to see around us."

"Moving through the experience, experiencing all the sounds and smells to compensate for the poor visibly, what are you smelling?"

"The smell of diesel fuel…and dried sweat."

"What do you hear?"

"The truck engines…low murmurs from everyone in the back of the truck with me."

"Allow your senses to overflow, to heighten your awareness."

"I hear Major…He's barking…Not his normal bark, but the badass barking he does when he is scared." Caroline's voice increases in pace and volume. "He has followed us across the desert."

"Does anyone else hear it?"

"I look around but no one else seems to notice. Major is barking at something…or someone. He is trying to warn us."

While thinking it is amazing how this animal has followed the convoy across the desert—or, actually, followed Caroline across the desert—Dr. Perrin almost misses the signs of her anxiety intensifying.

"An RPG is fired. We are under attack!"

"What is happening Caroline?"

"The convoy stranded…Soldiers scurrying…The lead truck is on fire. I see Major. He is running around to the other side of the truck—oh God, toward the open desert."

"Why is he running away?"

"He is not running away…running toward the enemy…drawing fire away from our truck."

"Staying with Major but only following him from above, Caroline, tell me what you see."

"He is coming closer to the insurgents in the field…They are firing at us. He's going to get…Oh God, Major! He stumbles! He is rolling… rolling across the ground!" Caroline folds her body, pulling her chest to her knees and wrapping them tightly with her arms. Her head falls to her uplifted hands, catching the tears erupting from their emotional barricade.

Witnessing her self-induced deepening of her hypnotic state—then, just as abruptly, her body forming to a fetal position—Dr. Perrin wonders if this is the position she went to in the back of the truck. Possibly collapsing with emotional anguish from seeing Major gunned down, Caroline had been unable at the time to react as she had been trained to do.

With Caroline curled in a ball on the couch, uncontrollably sobbing and in a deep level of hypnosis, Dr. Perrin forces her memory.

"Caroline, you are floating above the scene. Now move away by floating higher. You are now only seeing this through a lens. You see Major shot. What do you do?"

"I collapse from the heartbreak." Caroline begins to rock back and forth, soothing her emotions like a child being rocked. She remains silent for several minutes. "I fall to my knees in the back of the truck."

"What happens next?"

"I have to see how bad Major is hurt. I can't leave him out there all alone. I try to stand on my legs."

Dr. Perrin is awestruck at the bravery of this woman—to run into the enemy's field to extract this animal. To ensure his safety and survival is an amazing amount of heroism.

"Follow the scene. Let it play out in your conscious mind. Relate to me what you see."

"Sergeant Joe is yelling for me to jump…He now grabs my pack and hurls me off the back of the truck. I hit the sandy dirt, hard. He lands beside me, pushing me behind the large tires. He takes my sidearm out of its holster and places it in my hands…He's yelling orders at me…I can't hear over the noise of explosions. Everyone is yelling…rounds are piercing the truck all around us…I try to hold the weapon in my hands but they are shaking too hard. That is when I notice my platoon engaging firepower to prevent the insurgents from overtaking our convoy. Dr. McClure is lying on the ground a few yards away…he is bleeding out. I crawl on my belly to reach him…it is too late. If I would have gotten to him sooner, maybe I could have saved him."

Dr. Perrin observes Caroline's body twitching, as if in dreamlike motion, trying to crawl to the fallen soldier. Tears are now falling, spilling down her cheeks. She does not wipe them away. Her breathing is coming in gasps, her lungs pulling in needed air, causing her chest to rise too frequently. He knows she has slipped into a deeper level of hypnosis on her own yet feels confident he can bring her back now, and she will remember.

"Caroline, I am going to count backward from five. You are to return to your safe garden on one. You will stay under hypnosis. Five, floating away from the scene, up, up, your senses less aware of what is happening below, you enter your lavender energy light. Four, your light floats above, gently blown by the wind that carries you to your garden."

Caroline's composure is returning slowly. Dr. Perrin, witnessing the tears only trickling down her cheeks now, can see her body is physically relaxing.

"Three, you can now see your garden and its many splendors from above. You descend to your happy place. Two, your lavender energy light settles inside your garden at your favorite place."

Dr. Perrin notes her tranquil repose. "One, your energy light remains with you for protection. Caroline, where are you?"

"I am sitting under the willow tree."

"Staying comfortably under the tree, we will call for the spirit of Major to come to you."

Dr. Perrin has hypnotized many clients to call out the spirits that haunt them. This is to allow them a deeper understanding regarding why their subconscious is protecting them.

"I want you to summon Major's spirit to you. Call his soul to stand before you. Let me know when he is there."

By Caroline's reaction, Dr. Perrin knows she is able to visualize Major's spirit. She is much more calm, semi-smiling, love written all over her face.

"He is here."

"Major is with you—are you sure?"

"Yes, I know him by the connection we have to one another."

"Tell him what you would like to say."

"I love you. I am so sorry," Caroline chokes out against the emotional barrage of feelings. "You are the best part of me." Caroline pauses. "Why did you do it? Why didn't you stay with me instead of run right into the enemy?"

Unable to hold back the flood of emotion she feels for this animal, Caroline drops her face downward in despair. Barely able to understand a word that is coming from her anguished heart, Dr. Perrin sets down his notebook and pen and leans forward to hear Caroline.

"He tells me he loves me, more than I can ever know, and he would die a thousand times to protect me." Caroline's heartbreak spills down her face as she says, through gut-wrenching sobs, "Please don't go, Major. My heart can't stand losing you again."

Caroline's grief and its emotional release of losing someone she loves is almost unbearable for Dr. Perrin. It is obvious to him Caroline and this dog have a special kind of connection, just as he'd thought.

Several minutes pass before Caroline's composure begins to reform, the convulsive crying relenting to weeping whimpers of sorrow. Dr. Perrin allows this time for Caroline to be with Major, observing Caroline's reactions as she confronts the nightmare that has held her captive.

Caroline takes a deep breath and continues, "He says to not be afraid; he will always be with me…It will be all right to let him go…We will see one another again."

"Is there one last thing you want to say to him before he goes?"

"Thank you. For giving my heart a chance to feel love again and for my soul a reason to live."

Dr. Perrin knows it is time to bring her out of her garden and from hypnosis, but he is curious and asks her one more question.

"Do you recognize his energy to be similar to anyone you know at this time in your life?"

With pen at paper, Dr. Perrin is prepared to prove his hypothesis. He is ready to write the name that is Major's reincarnated soul.

This question forces Caroline's emotions in a new direction, from complete agony to contemplative analysis. After several minutes, Caroline chokes out the word "Yes."

Dr. Perrin holds his pen, waiting on the breakthrough, looking down at his notebook, ready to write the forthcoming name. When Caroline doesn't respond, he looks up at her. She is staring at him. Eyes wide open.

Dr. Perrin, startled by her look, almost drops his pen as he sits back in his chair, away from her demanding gaze. His flesh crawls, causing the hair on his neck to stand. His heart races; his mouth goes dry. Caroline is no longer in a hypnotic state. Commanding his own emotions to settle, he asks, "Caroline, are you here in the present with me?"

"Yes. Um, I need a moment." Caroline sits up, leaning forward, lowering her chest over her lap. Dr. Perrin observes and notes her behavior. Caroline slowly rises, stretching her weakened post-hypnotic muscles. She walks over to the water cooler and gets a drink.

Dr. Perrin is glad she is able to get it on her own because he is not sure he can even stand at the moment. He waits for her to return to her seat and asks, "Do you remember what occurred during hypnosis?"

Caroline takes a tissue, wiping away the remnants of her abreaction, the tissue maintaining guard duty at the corners of her eyes.

"I got to see him one last time. His spirit found me." Caroline's emotions appear reconciled to the pain. Caroline dabs at her eyes. "I have tried to let go, but the two hardest memories to forget is the moment I found him and the moment he was taken from me. It is impossible to forget him. He gave me too much to remember."

Caroline fights to control the grief surfacing to her conscious mind once again.

"But then he said the strangest thing. He said he was sorry for all the pain he has caused. He only wanted to protect me. And continuing that protection might mean I will have more pain in this lifetime. What do you think he means by that?"

Dr. Perrin is not sure what the spirit of Major meant by "more pain in this lifetime." He does not like the sound of it or what it could mean for Captain McKenzie, especially if he is right and Major is actually what he suspects—a reincarnated soul.

"Caroline, I would like to discuss your feelings toward Major." Dr. Perrin rushes on before she shuts him down. "I also want to discuss with you the possibility that we are dealing with not only Post-Traumatic Stress Disorder, but another etiology, or cause, to your nightmares and flashbacks. Are you up to this?"

Caroline can't imagine anything more painful than watching Major leave her once again. If she can survive that, she can handle anything. She also knows her time is running out. She has to get answers from her subconscious soon so she nods for the doctor to continue.

"What do you remember while you were hypnotized? Caroline, I need you to confront Major's fate in Iraq so you can truly forgive yourself for his loss."

"I didn't lose him. I watched him get shot"—Caroline inhales four broken breaths to stop the quiver in her voice—"trying to save me." She clutches her chest to halt the anguish from pouring out. "I then had to leave him there, to die in that field…him never understanding why I left him."

"Could it be possible he does understand? Now that you have spoken to his spirit, do you not believe he knows there was nothing you could have done to prevent this from happening? He said he chose to be your protector. He wanted to die for you."

"Oh, dear God." The realization of the void that haunts Caroline's heart is shattering down on her. "But why me?" The words breathily wheeze from Caroline as her hands cover her face.

Not wanting to admit this to the psychologist, Caroline's inner thoughts stay private as she asks herself, *Have I actually never been happy in a relationship because I am holding out for the unconditional love I can get only from a dog?* This revelation causes Caroline to question her sanity, resulting in a sudden termination of her emotional break. She looks up at Dr. Perrin, wanting to share her feelings but afraid of his judgement.

"What is it, Caroline?"

"I know you probably think I am out of my mind holding on to feelings for a dog. I can't even imagine what you have written in that notebook. I don't know what it is about Major, but it is like he is an old soul, one that knew mine as it was forming. He loves me for who I am, flaws and all," Caroline admits. "How crazy am I?"

"You are not crazy."

Caroline looks up at the doctor, a brow raised questioning the doctor's statement.

"I judge other men's feelings for me based on the love of a dog. Sounds a little crazy to me. That kind of love does not exist within humanity."

Dr. Perrin is fully aware it is more than a dog's devotion that Caroline is seeking. He knows now is the time to present his theory. God help them both if he is wrong, or right.

CHAPTER THIRTY

SESSION TWELVE – SOUL'S FUNDAMENTAL PURPOSE

"Caroline, I would like for you to tell me again about the dreams you have had since you were a child."

"All of them?" Caroline asks, exasperated.

"Not each one individually. Is there a central theme, or setting? How have they made you feel over the years?"

Caroline doesn't know where to start. There are so many. She starts with the reason her dreams have haunted her since childhood. "In most of my dreams, I know it is me, but I don't recognize myself."

Dr. Perrin adjusts in his chair, the excitement of Caroline's journey of discovery causing an unprofessional fidgeting. He takes a deep breath, leans forward just a touch, and directs all his attention on his patient.

"It is not Caroline McKenzie." Caroline stands, pacing always seems to help clear her mind. She finds the repetitive motion of the cadence of each step soothing, like marching to the beat of a drum, allowing her mind to open. "Usually when people dream, they dream of themselves and people they know, right? But most of my dreams involve people I do not recognize. Well, I know them during the dream. Oh Jeez, this isn't making any sense." Caroline returns to the chaise and locks eyes on Dr. Perrin. "It's like I am watching a movie with supporting characters and I am the lead but another actress is playing me."

Caroline closes her eyes and pictures some of her dreams. Dr. Perrin takes this opportunity to write her confessional description in his notes, stopping when Caroline continues.

"Most of the ones I have had since childhood are simple short stories. Like a chapter out of the middle of a book. I don't know the beginning, like why or how I am there, nor the ending, what happens to her—or me, I mean. The dreams, at the time, are not disorienting. It is when I wake I realize I was in a place I have never been to, or doing something I have never done. I even speak in different languages and dialects. I don't know another language, yet I do during the dream. Is this making any sense to you?"

"I think so. Tell me more about the actress playing you in these dreams."

"During the dream, it is my story. I am living it. But when I wake, I have a blurry vision of someone else, but I know it is me."

Dr. Perrin continues with his notes, then looks at Caroline. "How do you know this?"

Caroline has no idea how to explain this to him. She considers herself lucky to be in front of a clinical therapist at this moment because she is sure she is cray-cray.

"I just feel like it happened to me."

"Okay, what about your nightmares? Are those happening to you?"

"The nightmares and flashbacks I have about Iraq, of course, those are me. They are different from the dreams. Some nightmares about Iraq are like"—Caroline tries to find the words—"fresh wounds; devastating surface wounds. Whereas the dreams that have bad endings, like the polio dream, I feel the pain deep down. Like an old wound that won't heal. Equally devastating; but a much deeper pain."

"Tell me about the pain," Dr. Perrin faintly asks.

"It's not a physical pain...though it hurts just the same." Caroline struggles for words that will convey the malady that is her mind. "Have you ever wondered how they come up with the word 'heartbreak'? Your heart doesn't physically break, yet you feel like it is." Caroline's eyes are focused on the far wall. "Your mind makes you feel the physical crushing pain in your chest."

"What caused the pain in your dream when you had polio?" Dr. Perrin asks, wanting Caroline to come to terms with the pain.

Caroline's eyes remain focused far off. "My father had to kill my dog." Her tears flow steadily now.

This statement sends Dr. Perrin's pen flying across the paper in his lap. When he looks up, he notices tears forming in Caroline's eyes. He hands Caroline a tissue, granting her time for composure and comprehension. After several minutes, Dr. Perrin guides her mind where he wants it. "How about the flashback at work regarding the cinchona bark? Was that you?"

Caroline closes her eyes to picture the scene again. "Yes, I was very sick. I was in bed with carved posters, the room decorated with a Baroque style with paneling and wallpaper, candle-burning sconces, and a large fireplace. It's weird though. I didn't see any of this, really. I just knew it looked that way. In fact, I think I was blind."

"Were you in pain then?"

"Yes. My body ached with a fever."

"Since cinchona bark hasn't been therapeutically used for centuries and polio has been eradicated in this country since the sixties, decades before you were born, I can only assume that you were not in this time period either."

"No." Going on gut-feeling alone…"when I was sick with the fever, I believe it was the 1700s. When I had polio"—Caroline can't believe she is saying it like it actually happened to her—"it was the late 1800s." Caroline looks at Dr. Perrin as he writes his notes. "Why aren't you a tad bit more shocked?"

"I find it fascinating." Dr. Perrin writes in his book.

"That's it? Fascinating? It is mortifying," Caroline corrects him.

"Caroline, I am going to need you to listen to me with an open mind. You will need to trust me and know that I have studied intensely on this subject. I have felt for a few weeks now we are dealing with more than PTSD. I believe these dreams you speak of have another cause which will require a different therapeutic approach."

At Caroline's concerned facial expression, he changes tactics. "I am talking about a therapeutic breakthrough technique. It will be similar to what we are doing now, just more progressive than traditional therapy."

"There is nothing traditional about your therapy techniques, Dr. Perrin," Caroline says with great suspicion.

"Well, then, you are really going to love this idea." Dr. Perrin sets down his notebook and looks directly at Caroline. "You have stated before that you were raised in the Christian faith, yet you were accepting of other beliefs."

"I am not so closed-minded that I assume that Christianity is the only way to Heaven. I believe all faiths are serving the same God; we just call Him something different and serve Him in different ways. I do believe that Christ is the way but I will not persecute others for believing in their own faith."

"How open-minded are you?"

"I didn't say I was open-minded," Caroline clarifies, "just not completely closed-minded."

Dr. Perrin ponders on how to begin this conversation without having her screaming and running from his office.

"I believe your subconscious has created a protective mechanism to help you cope with far-off, really far…past traumas. Your subconscious is opportunistically enabling the escape of these traumas in the form of nightmares, dreams, or flashbacks."

"Isn't that why I am here? For you to help my subconscious manage these traumas through hypnotherapy?"

"Yes, but I believe we need to redirect your therapy, still utilizing hypnosis though."

"Why?" Caroline is now even more suspicious.

Dr. Perrin leans forward in his chair, demanding her attention. "Caroline, I believe some of your traumas lie not in this lifetime. Your dreams, nightmares, and flashes could also be stemming from previous lives."

Caroline leans back, resting against the lounger, observing Dr. Perrin for several seconds. *Did I just hear him right?* Caroline had expected him to say "you need to be committed" or "you are insane" or even "get out of my office." Never once did she ever consider him saying "you have past lives." A slow grin spreads across her lips as she considers what Dr. Perrin is suggesting, and then considers which of them is the crazy one. The idea that she has had a previous life…the grin fades to nervous laughter right before Caroline bursts out laughing, wrapping her waist with her arms. Her laughter continues until the silence shrouding his side of the room is uncomfortable. She inhales the next chuckle and stands to leave his office, "You're not fucking joking!"

"Eastern cultures and most of the population of this world Caroline believe in reincarnation. It would explain the malaria dreams, the blindness, the cinchona bark, the polio dream, the feeling of paralysis, and many other snippets from nightmares you have described to me," Dr. Perrin says, inputting his rationalization before she storms from his office again. "It could explain the origin of loss, the suffering, and the pain you feel," Dr. Perrin tells her as she walks toward the door. "Caroline, it could also explain why you feel such a connection to Major."

Caroline stops before her hand reaches for the knob. She stands motionless, her back to the doctor, her heart beating a slushing percussion in her chest, reverberating into her ears. Fearing she is about to pass out, she turns around, resting her back against the door. The doctor and patient lock eyes on one another, neither sure where to go from here.

Dr. Perrin makes the first move. Walking to the water cooler, he pours two glasses, handing one to Caroline. They continue to size one another up as they finish their drinks. He reaches for her glass, setting the empty containers on the table. He stretches out his hand for her to accept what he is offering. Leading her back to the chaise lounge, he holds her hand while she sits.

Dr. Perrin picks up MaryLee Labay's book *Past Life Regression, A Guide for Practitioners* from the stack of books he has been studying and opens it to a bookmarked page.

"Let me read a passage for you." He clears his throat. "In any given life there is the consciousness and there is existence. Each is dependent on the other and without these two basic qualities a spirit would not be. Existence provides a location in space/time, and consciousness provides awareness of our existence. The continuation of existence and consciousness is the fundamental purpose of every living organism. Everything we do is based on our ability to survive, both as humans during a lifetime and as a spirit throughout eternity."

Dr. Perrin continues when Caroline offers no rebuttal, but only stunned silence. "Dysfunctional behaviors are reactions to our basic need for survival. Maladaptive behaviors can turn into habits, physically, mentally, and spiritually. To be able to survive, or continue our existence, we block our conscious of painful memories. By gaining access to the wisdom of our subconscious, we are able to heal our soul from within. It is called past life therapy."

Dr. Perrin allows Caroline time to process this information. She can't.

"So exactly how will we know if I have 'lived before'?" Caroline asks with much skepticism.

"Not if, Caroline. When. I know you have and I would like to help you travel to your past lives."

"Oh fun, a road trip." Caroline can only think of mockery at this crazy idea being presented to her.

Is the idea crazy or is he? Caroline questions inwardly as she checks all the exits from the room.

"You will re-experience your past lives through hypnosis or past life regression. It's like looking into the universe and finding your soul's journey. Through hypnosis, you can be guided to a time before this present life to uncover a previous life."

"I can't handle what has happened in this life. What makes you think I could handle another one?"

"You already are handling it. You just don't know the source of what you are trying to handle. Past Life Regression will give you a better understanding of who you are and why you do the things you do and why you feel certain ways."

"But if it is in the past—way past—exactly how is that relevant to my life now?"

"Past life therapy can offer a greater understanding of patterns of behavior, relationships, health issues, life purposes, talents, interests, and recurring challenges. Have you ever wondered why some are born with the natural penchant for music, art, or sciences? A glimpse into your previous lives can help explain your occupation, your hobbies, or relationships, or lack thereof."

Dr. Perrin noticed she sat a little taller when he said this, so he continued that train of thought. "Sometimes, the effects of a past life can be emotionally crippling. A present life relationship problem could be explained by a past life pain or heartbreak. In uncovering these issues, we can turn the negative energies to positive qualities. Without exploring these issues, past life causes of pain, phobias, or misery can perpetuate into your current life. The valuable lessons you miss out on when the past is buried in your subconscious does not allow one to grow to their fullest potential. Past life therapy can help you understand your character, your personality, and can even explain your actions or avoidance of actions. The insights that can be revealed are amazing, and I think it would be beneficial for you."

Caroline stares into his eyes, searching for any sign of mental instability. He is serious.

"So, Captain McKenzie, how much insight are you prepared to reveal? How far would you go to heal certain behaviors or problems?"

"How would I know the answer to that? I don't know where 'far' is!

Maybe not all questions have answers."

"I am just saying if you are prepared to change self-destructive thoughts or behaviors then dramatic improvements can be made in this lifetime."

That term, "self-destructive", resonates throughout Caroline's mind for a moment before she admits, "My friends say I sabotage myself in relationships. When I told them I reenlisted, Bianca told me I wanted to die and that is why I joined in the first place. So what other self-destructive behaviors are you suggesting?"

"We won't know until we get there."

"Get where? You are freaking me out! Can we just stop here and take this up next time?"

"Of course, but I need you to do some things this week."

"Billy Wayne Shit-balls. More homework?"

"I would like for you to read this." Dr. Perrine hands Caroline a book from the stack beside him.

"*The Present Power of Past Lives: The Experts Speak.*" Caroline reads the title out loud.

"Dr. Mancini's book is filled with case histories from experts in the field of past life regressions and the healing powers of past life therapy. It will also help you experience a past life regression more fully."

Dr. Perrin leaves Caroline to her thoughts. Walking to his desk, he glances at his weighted calendar, "I will call you after the first of the year to schedule." Expecting her subconscious could abruptly reveal the full scene with Major either in a flashback or a nightmare, Dr. Perrin offers, "I will be available through the holiday if you need me. Just call my cell phone."

Dr. Perrin assists Caroline in putting on her coat and opens the door to the office foyer. Caroline takes one step, notices the wreath again, and turns back around.

"I have a question."

"I am sorry. Our time is up." He smiles at Caroline.

She doesn't return the smile as she considers, "Recently, a sizable donation was made to the shelter. You wouldn't know anything about that, would you?"

"An anonymous donation?"

Caroline confirms with a nod.

"That is wonderful. I am sure you are relieved."

"You didn't answer my question."

"I was recently informed by a very astute client that not all questions have answers. Happy New Year's, Captain McKenzie."

Exiting the doctor's office, she returns his words. "Happy New Year's, Dr. Perrin."

He watches from the window as Caroline walks to her car. She turns after opening her car door, staring up at him through the window, both of them wondering if this is the last look they will ever share. As Caroline drives off, Dr. Perrin is unable to shake the suspicion that Caroline's subconscious is about to transcend this lifetime and somehow take him with her.

CHAPTER THIRTY-ONE

CONSCIOUSNESS VS. EXISTENCE

Session Twelve
December 2010

Captain Caroline McKenzie:

Emergent Session: Due to traumatic flashbacks during meditation at home.

Utilizing energy light travel to Iraq siege that produced recurrent nightmare to unblock the subconscious of the fate of beloved animal, Major.

Repressed memories, fighting against their own existence to avoid the pain, client's subconscious mind blocked what the conscious mind could not handle.

I believe viewing this animal's death at that time caused a subconscious break, allowing memories of a past life to surface to the conscious mind. Caroline reverted to a past life when she had been paralyzed and observed another pet being killed (polio dream). This causing her a pseudo-paralysis while in active combat.

Through Therapeutic healing and coping, Caroline was hypnotically directed to summon the spirit of Major. Successfully able to declare her feelings to his spirit, as he also did to her. Caroline's subconscious break with abreaction came when she stated, "I can't lose you again." This statement, along with client's belief of animal spirit stating "he will always be with me" leads me to conclude Caroline knows Major from a previous life.

Concerns for Caroline's safety due to spirit of animal stating he "chose to protect her, which will cause her more pain in this lifetime" and that they "will see one another again."

Possible reasoning for Caroline's extreme perilous choices in hobbies and reasoning behind enlistment in military and reenlistment: she is actively pursuing death to be with spirit or whoever this spirit represents in her mind.

Pain caused by polio dream, as stated by client, not by disease or dying from what is effectually diaphragmatic paralysis and possible pneumonia, but pain caused by death of her dog.

Discussion with client regarding dual diagnosis: Post-Traumatic Stress Disorder coupled with subconscious breaks of past lives. Discussed benefits of past life regression.

<u>Review of medical history and assessment for possible PLT</u>:

Captain McKenzie is not mentally ill with schizophrenia or a mental disorder.

Patient also well-grounded; not prone to fantasy.

Dr. Perrin closes Caroline's chart. Leaving his hand on the top as if on the Bible, he wonders if Captain Caroline McKenzie will ever darken his doorstep again. He looks at the calendar. Nine weeks before her deployment. He knows he has to act fast.

* * *

Have you ever questioned the very foundation of life? Your soul's purpose? What's your life worth? What cost will you spend to save the ones you love? Have you ever asked yourself, "Is there something you would die for over and over than to lose altogether?"

I am doing that, again. I have created my own existential crisis and can't figure a way out now. If it wasn't so tragic it could be an epic love story. A love that would last over time, over dimension, over celestial reaches.

I love her, like no other has ever loved her, and that love has brought extreme bliss and extreme pain. That love gave me more than just a reason to live but a reason for the extension of my soul. That love also crafted dilemmas that left either of us little choices. See, the choices we freely make in our lives change not only our own destinies, but those of others around us.

She left me, but she forgot to tell my soul how to go on without her, forcing my condemned choices. But I believe the secret in life, and death, is not in "the choices"; the secret is knowing, in the end, you wouldn't have chosen differently.

CHAPTER THIRTY-TWO

ETHERIC BLUEPRINT

The girls are meeting downtown to discuss their New Year's Eve plans. Caroline intends on bringing a little mystery to this "Bitch-N-Booze" as she waits for the others. Possibly a game of "Whodunit" of the unidentified benefactor for the shelter. She has a few unsubs in mind and wants to run it by her forensic team. Realizing she reads way too many crime novels, Caroline sees her friends enter, letting the cold in and the quiet out. Meredith and Bianca are in an acrimonious altercation about something, as usual, as they take their seats with Caroline.

Caroline glances at Kelly with the "what the fuck" look. Kelly gives the "same ole shit" shoulder shrug and eye roll.

Before Meredith and Bianca reach radioactivity level, Caroline interrupts, "I have great news."

"You figured out the second purpose of the personal massager I bought you last Christmas?" Bianca goads.

Caroline continues over the other's laughter, "The shelter received an anonymous donation to keep it open for at least another year." Caroline is almost giddy with excitement and can't wait to play her mystery game. "Who do you think could have done it? I mean, I have my suspicions—"

"Jameson," all three said in unison, talking over Caroline.

"What? No!" Caroline doubts.

"Bitch, please, he would build a new shelter if that is what you wanted," Meredith says as she motions for Greg, the bartender.

"I thought it might be my therapist. He has a wreath almost exactly like the one delivered to the shelter with the anonymous check attached to it."

"Wow. Well, then that settles it, Sherlock. Or do you think that maybe the wreaths just so happen to come from the same florist?" Bianca says as Greg delivers the drinks to the table.

"I guess, but why would Jameson do that without telling me?"

"You already slept with him so it's not to get in your pants," Meredith acknowledges, which earns her a punch in the arm from Caroline.

"Just maybe he loves you and wants to make you happy," Kelly offers sweetly.

"Loves me. We have been on, at the most, two dates."

"And you slept with him both times. You must be a spitfire between the sheets," Bianca suggests as she runs her hand up Caroline's thigh, which Caroline slaps away immediately.

"And think about it—why would your therapist do it?" Kelly asks.

"O-M-G, you schtup the shrink," Meredith teases.

"Entranced erotica. Is he taking new patients?" Bianca takes out her cell phone, pretending to make a call.

"Does he charge you for the whole hour or does he prorate? You know, in case you get off in the first fifteen minutes?" Kelly asks, this time not so sweetly.

"Stop. God Almighty, can at least one of the three of you have an unadulterated thought?" Caroline proclaims, which gets the attention of many of the bar patrons. "Change of subject, please."

As the girls talk over dinner about their week, the bond that holds them together solidifies. Caroline wants their impression of past life therapy but all the while knows it will also welcome their skepticism. Caroline forges on cautiously. "Do you all believe you have lived before?"

"Before what?" Kelly naively asks, stuffing a cheese fry in her mouth.

"No, I mean that you have previously lived in, like…another time."

"As in reincarnation?" Meredith clarifies.

"Well, yeah, I guess."

"You believe that you have lived before, like in another time and place, then died and came back in a new body?" Kelly questions Caroline but is looking more at Bianca and Meredith with a concerned look.

"I don't know what I believe yet." Caroline admits then downs the last drop of her whiskey.

"I believe it," Meredith states unequivocally.

Kelly's mouth drops open. "Our mother's crucifixes are falling off the walls right now."

"There are five basic schools of thoughts on this subject," Meredith begins her lecture. "Go the scientific route and prove it or disprove it. Believe it, relying on the same faith that's in any doctrine. You could just read it from other's experiences. Or you can experience it yourself." Meredith's knowledge on the subject leaves the other three dumbstruck. "That's right. I know shit," Meredith boasts.

"Yeah, you know shit because you read magazines all day while I work with our travel clients." Kelly passes an accusatory glare at her sister before continuing, "In this day and age, shouldn't scientists be able to prove or disprove it?" Kelly asks.

"Religions are faith-based. You either believe in it or you don't," Caroline says.

"But wouldn't you rather experience it?" Meredith asks the group.

"You got a time machine, sis?" Kelly asks.

"Dr. Perrin says to experience my past lives he will use hypnosis. It is called past life regression," Caroline informs them.

"Lives? As in plural?" Kelly is surprised. "How can your brain have memories of other lives?"

"Who says memory is the sole function of the brain?" Meredith rebuts.

"Where do you think memories come from? Your ass?" Bianca jumps in the conversation. "Then, Meredith, you better change those pants or your memories are going to be crammed together."

"Couldn't memories be more from the mind than the physical brain?" Caroline asks.

"Damn, girl, where do you keep your mind?" Bianca directs her question to Caroline.

Meredith comes to Caroline's rescue. "How about people who have had out-of-body experiences? Their physical brains don't leave their body, yet they have life memories flash before their eyes. They're able to describe what is going on as they are watching from above, like medical procedures being done on them. Or how about people who say they entered a tunnel or followed a bright light?"

"Okay, let's say that these people are telling the truth. Then the brain cannot be the stockroom of our memories," Caroline challenges, "proving that the conscious can certainly exist independently of the brain."

"Let's move past that point and assume the mind is not part of the brain," Meredith says. "Then how do memories get from one life to another life?"

The four of them, in deep consternation of Meredith's question, are oblivious to the gentleman approaching their table.

"The mind has a universal raison d'être, if you will," the gentleman says. "Much more than Western culture and Christianity attempts to explain. We are all on a universal journey together. Our etheric blueprint carries over with our soul."

They all four look at the man who joined their conversation, uninvited. Meredith; however, is the only one to look him up and down.

"With a body like that, you certainly aren't Buddha." Meredith passes a seductive glance.

"So who the fuck are you?" Bianca asks with an air of warning.

"I couldn't help but overhear your conversation from my table, ladies. I am Rajkhanna. At your service."

"What are you talking about, Raj?" Bianca sarcastically questions.

"Ooh, I just had a deja vu moment," Kelly says, rubbing her hands over the goose bumps tickling the flesh on her arms. "We were all sitting here, a man where Raj is, and Bianca asking him that exact question."

"I love deja vu moments," Meredith says while helping rub Kelly's chill from her body.

"You would," Bianca says then rolls her eyes back to Raj. "I repeat, and obviously more than once, what are you talking about, Raj?"

"The etheric blueprint. It stores all the information from past lives affecting the emotional and physical health of lives to come. It is out of this our present body is formed and how memories are carried from one life to the next. That was your question, no?"

"Doesn't your religion believe in karma?" Meredith points out, however racist it sounds.

"Ah yes, karma, where intent or actions can influence a future life. Those perceptions are grounded in spirituality. The soul can reincarnate for many reasons."

"You mean to right a wrong or complete a task?" Meredith delineates.

"To make reparation, yes. Some return to be of service or fulfill a promise," Rajkhanna explains.

"Can I just remind everyone here that we are all of the Christian faith and this conversation is probably sacrilegious?"

Meredith can't stand it when Kelly takes the sacramental high road.

"How can just talking about this be such a terrible thing, Miss Holier-Than-Thou?"

"With this theory, you are totally demolishing the whole book of Revelations, not to mention most of the Bible," Kelly says, confronting them.

"Sorry, Raj, we don't mean to ignore you or undermine your faith." Caroline looks strongly at Kelly. "I guess everyone questions the meaning of our existence in this world at some point in their lives."

"Such is our life script. Let me leave you with some cards," Rajkhanna removes four business cards from his wallet. Laying his cards on the table, he offers, "I have a shop downtown if any of you are interested in discussing this further at a later time, but I must go for now. Ladies, it has been a pleasure talking with you." Just as fast as he'd entered the conversation, Rajkhanna walks away and out of their present lives.

"Did anyone else find it coincidentally strange that Raj just so happened to be here with the answers we were seeking plus Kelly has this deja vu moment?" Meredith asks.

"I find it a coincidence. That's all." Bianca says with a warning look toward Meredith.

"The Bible does state you have to be born again," Meredith quotes.

"That means spiritually, not physically, you nefarious ninny," Kelly corrects her sister.

"Does it, nymph? Did God tell you that personally?" Meredith questions her translation.

"Christianity acknowledges that we have a soul which continues after death," Caroline professes, "but where does it go before Heaven, or Hell? The Bible says it is eternal. It has to go somewhere after it transverses the realm after death."

"I know what you mean," Meredith philosophizes. "There has to be more to life than death or more to the universe than life, death, repeat."

"I read somewhere that researchers are trying to prove past lives with children because time has not faded their memories yet," Bianca says.

"Or alcohol." Meredith slams the last bit of vodka in her glass.

"Children are able to provide details of places, then the researchers verify it," Bianca elaborates. "And not just places, but vocabulary, clothing, and customs too."

"I read a story one time where this little girl was in a coma for some reason—I don't remember—but when she woke up, she could play the piano like a concert pianist…Never had taken a lesson in her life," Meredith says with a mystic undertone.

"You read that article to me," Kelly says, "and the story included one about the little girl in England who was able to draw a castle that is in Budapest, yet she has never been there but swears she lived there before."

"While I was researching past life regression, I found an article where someone envisioned the grave of the person they were before, hundreds of years ago," Caroline hauntingly adds, "and sure enough, the grave is there with that person's name on it."

Meredith's eyes grow big. "Ooooh, schpooky."

"It could be a complete hoax. He had already seen the grave and made it all up or it was a memory from a film or book." Kelly's skepticism shines since she is the only one not inebriated.

"The proper terminology for that is 'cryptomnesia,'" Meredith advises.

"How do you know that, you big weirdo?" Bianca is actually impressed.

Kelly pays the tab and herds the lushes to the car before a fight breaks out between Meredith and Bianca. "Can we just finish this tonight by saying there are many things that we cannot explain?"

"Like déjà vu," Bianca speaks up, then pours herself into Kelly's backseat.

That is the last word in the car for the night. Meredith and Bianca are passed out in the back seat as Kelly drives Caroline home. Caroline stares out the passenger-side glass, contemplating her believe system, or lack of it.

As Caroline steps out of the car at her house, she turns back and asks, "Kell, do you think I should try this past life regression? What if it's all a bunch of hooey?"

"If it is, then you won't regress. What did you lose?"

Caroline shakes her heavy head at Kelly's profound words considering her devout faith, later realizing Kelly's faith did not leave room for questions. She admired that about her friend. Leaning against the inside doorjamb, Caroline asks herself, "What if it's real? What if I have lived previous lives? Then all I could lose is my sanity."

CHAPTER THIRTY-THREE

MOORESVILLE

Caroline isn't sure about spending the whole weekend in Mooresville, which is Jameson's Christmas wish, but here she is, driving east, bags packed. Caroline will be spending the entire New Year's weekend with Jameson, so she drives her own car to his New Year's Eve party. Driving alone also gives her time to reflect on her sessions with Dr. Perrin. Much of her therapy has been centered on her ability to control the flashbacks at will. Though the fear of a flashback haunts her daily, Dr. Perrin's instructions on grounding techniques, meditation, and muscle relaxation have proven to decrease the depths her subconscious can take her. Together, she and Dr. Perrin have explored the nightmares and her dreams she has had since childhood. Caroline is not happy with the frequency of the nightmares, which are presenting themselves almost nightly, and plans on telling him so at her next appointment. Caroline is fearful therapy will not be able to stop the nightmares as she had hoped, but she has to admit she wouldn't be doing what she is doing right now if something wasn't working.

She is excited to see where he lives with his three kids, as he calls them. She sent each of them dog toys for Christmas, along with a case of the wine Jameson loved from their Biltmore wine tasting. He told her during one of their many telephone calls that he got another dog, his third, and that she was fitting in well with his family of pets. Jameson also claims that a cat frequents his house for food and some attention but never stays. Caroline envies the cat. If she could figure a way to only commit to food, fun, and the occasional "attention," she would not be obsessing over when and how she would tell him about her deployment. "Damn lucky cat," she thinks as she pulls onto the exit toward Lake Norman.

Caroline takes in the gorgeous water and country atmosphere. Mooresville had developed substantially since her last time by here. She usually follows I40 on to Winston-Salem, then heads south to reach Fort Bragg for reservist duty, so she rarely has reasons to travel past Mooresville. The pines grow tall along the lakeside, waving a serene welcome as they blow in the wind.

As the two cars wind through the homes nestled on the banks of the lake, Caroline is astonished at the opulent lifestyle on this lakefront. The homes are large-scale with acreage. She continues to eye the beautiful lake scenery until her GPS notifies her: "Destination is on your right." She glances at the architectural marvel that sits on at least two acres, butting up to the shoreline on a secluded private road.

Of course, Caroline thinks as she parks in the driveway, Bianca pulling in behind her. She stares at his home, picturing him planning, designing, and building each room. She notices the rock that he had quarried from Carolina stone, the glass that reaches three stories high at the front façade, the cedar on top that blends with the scenery. But what Caroline loves most is the landscaping. Pine trees on the far sides of the lawn leading to the woods envelope the home and grounds like a protective fortress.

The commotion outside the driver's window brings her out of her reverie. Meredith is banging on her window while Kelly is jumping up and down behind her like a Jack Russell terrier. "Can you believe this shit?" Meredith exclaims as she motions with her arm the expanse of the estate. "You have hit pay dirt."

"Keep your voice down. Geez, he probably has cameras watching us right now," Caroline warns as she steps out of her vehicle. "They are probably all over the house too, so no funny business." Caroline scolds them as if they are children in church, reminding them to be on their Sunday-best behavior.

Though it is winter, there are plenty of evergreen trees and bushes in an array of greens that provide an earthy setting for the fifty yards of lawn frontage from the road. As they walk the driveway made of large-scale, cemented, stone pavers that correlate with the stone on the outside of the house, barking commences and Caroline realizes Jameson is at the door, letting the dogs out to greet them. First a black lab reaches them with the enthusiasm of a puppy, yet Caroline already knows the lab is five years old. Next comes a mixed breed, a little more ferocious sounding, but tail wagging all the same. Caroline feels she already knows Jameson's children because he has talked of them often.

"Girls, I would like you to meet Lucy." Caroline rubs the head of the retriever. "And this is Abraham"—she scratches behind the German-shepherd-slash-collie mix's ears.

The four of them love on both dogs and vice versa. Caroline picks up a flash of black and white streaking toward her and turns in time to receive the third dog, who Jameson has recently added to his home.

"Barkley!" Caroline collapses to her knees on the driveway in an amalgam of emotion. She never thought she would see Barkley again, not since she was adopted from the shelter. Jameson never mentioned he was the one who adopted her, but at this point, Caroline didn't care. Barkley has a forever home—one where she can come and see Barkley anytime she wants. That thought brings Caroline a spontaneous flood of raw emotions. If she destroys this relationship like she's done all the others, she will never seeing Barkley again.

"Don't be mad." Jameson steps out on the driveway. "I wanted it to be a surprise. Dogs, inside! Come on in." Jameson takes Caroline's hand, leading her up the winding walkway.

Meredith, Bianca, and Kelly follow command, as do the dogs, and all eight of them walk inside. Jameson explains, as he takes the girls on a tour, how he felt he and Barkley had this connection from the moment he met her at the shelter. So when he left Caroline's house that day, he drove straight to the shelter and adopted her.

"You were probably wondering why I didn't come in or why I went home so early, but I had to make it to the shelter before it closed. You weren't mad, were you?"

"I didn't notice," Caroline lies. She can't be mad at Jameson now that she sees how happy Barkley is with Lucy and Abraham.

The four of them dress for the evening in the room off the main level, the one Jameson designates for guests. He offers the room to Bianca, Meredith, and Kelly for the entire weekend but they decline. They do not want to impinge on Caroline's three day ecstasy adventure. Other guests start arriving around nine p.m., as per the invitation—mostly friends from around the lake, a few co-workers and business colleagues. Jameson's family, however, came an hour early to meet his girlfriend.

As a large, boisterous crowd enters the house, Jameson takes Caroline's hand and pulls her away from her friends sitting at the bar in Jameson's billiard room.

"I want you to meet my family." Hand in hand, they cross the threshold of the foyer.

"Mom, this is my girlfriend, Caroline McKenzie. Caroline, my mother, Kimberly Brooks."

"It's a pleasure to meet you," Caroline says as she offers her hand, trying not to show her surprise by his description of her.

"Put that thang away and come here for a real family hug," Mrs. Brooks says as she slaps away Caroline's hand and pulls her into a warm, loving embrace.

"And this is my father, David Brooks. My sister, Jacqueline and her husband, Mark; My brother Jared and his wife, Holly; and, of course, you remember my brother Jacob from the cookout at the cabin."

Caroline smiles, shaking hands and getting hugs. Caroline is overwhelmed at the vastness of Jameson's family, all in front of her at once.

"Coats go in closet. Who wants a drink?" Jameson offers and after a show of hands, heads toward the bar.

"Caroline. Help us take these dishes into the kitchen," Jameson's mother tells more than asks as she lifts serving trays from the men's arms and distributes them between Caroline, Holly, and Jacqueline. Caroline doesn't get a chance to plead for help from Jameson. He is already making his way to the bar with the guys.

Jameson introduces his father, brothers, and brother-in-law to Bianca, Meredith, and Kelly, who have been drinking expensive wine for hours now. Jameson sees Caroline out of the corner of his eye being led by his mother to the kitchen, arm in arm, chatting her up. He smiles at her expense.

"So I hear you all work together?" Meredith asks the Brooks men.

"Some of us work; others, well, who knows," Jameson ribs Jared. "Jared here is the Chief Executive Officer of our firm. You can call him 'Meeting Majesty'."

"I prefer Your Highness." Jared bows.

"He sends us a memo every so often so we know he still works there," Jameson fires back.

"And what is it you do for the firm?" Kelly asks Jacob.

"Why don't you save that question for some night you have trouble sleeping?" Jared receives a snarl from Jacob for his continued slam of his profession.

"I am the Chief Financial Officer," Jacob says demurely.

"And your sister?"

"She runs the office and us." Jacob admits. They all agree Jacqueline is the boss.

"So what is Jameson?" Bianca asks anyone.

"The Chief Operating Officer," Jacob answers.

"The only one who actually works in the field and keeps our projects on time," Jameson clarifies.

"Oh yes, Jameson finds it important to always have a budget to ignore." Jacob demystifies Jameson's exaggeration of his importance.

"Did you hear the one about the interesting accountant?" Jared asks, and after everyone shakes their heads, he concludes, "Because there isn't one."

"Accounting might be the most boring occupation in the world to some, but if it weren't for me, you people would be homeless," Jacob informs them all.

"Boys," Jameson's father scolds, "You have three beautiful women sitting here and you are fighting amongst yourselves. I am sorry, ladies. We tried to raise them right. Jameson Bastian, hadn't you better be checking on your woman? Your mother is probably devouring the carcass by now."

Jameson makes a beeline for the kitchen, noticing as he enters that Caroline looks like a gazelle trapped by a pride of lions.

"Mother, why don't you go and stop the fight between dumb and dumber out there. Holly, you might want to reign Jared in a little. He is once again abusing the baby," Jameson says, referring to Jared, the oldest of the three, picking on Jacob, the youngest.

"I told those two no fighting tonight. We wanted to make a good impression for Caroline, not have her running from this family like—"

"A gazelle." Jameson finishes her thought.

"Caroline, I hope we have more time together before you return to Asheville. Come on, you two. Let's give these love birds some alone time," Kimberly Brooks suggests as she and Jacqueline and Holly retreat from the kitchen.

"Oh Lord, you look like I need a drink," Jameson says as he wraps his arms around her and laughs.

"They know everything about me, Jameson, and what they didn't know they had no problem asking," Caroline says as she steps out of his embrace and grabs a water bottle from the refrigerator, taking a healthy drink. The surprising references to her being part of Jameson's life forever are frightening her more than being shot at in war. At least in war, you can run for cover or you have a weapon to fire back in defense. Caroline has no response to these insinuations from his family. She isn't sure if they are saying things that Jameson would not approve of or if he had placed these ideas in their heads.

"I have told them all about you. What did they ask that they didn't already know?" Jameson asks as he swipes her water bottle.

"How many children I wanted to have?" Caroline delivers the line as Jameson takes a drink, causing him to choke on the cold liquid.

After Jameson finishes coughing the water from his lungs he apologizes. "You're kidding. Oh God, I am sorry."

"What exactly did you tell them?"

Jameson pulls Caroline against him, wrapping one arm around her waist and one behind her head. Jameson lowers his head to her lips and mouths, "They know you are important to me," then kisses Caroline softly. The kiss deepens, weakening Caroline's knees. She wishes there wasn't a full house of guests at the moment so she can explore where this kiss might lead. Unfortunately, she will never find out.

CHAPTER THIRTY-FOUR

RELATIONSHIP SABOTAGE

The house is full by eleven p.m. Caroline and her friends are meeting some very interesting people and a lot of single men. Meredith and Bianca are eating up the attention; however, Kelly has not left her barstool all night. And neither has Jacob. The two talk for hours as everyone else mingles around the house, some playing pool while others are singing around the piano or playing basketball in the indoor court Jameson has set up in one of the three attached garages.

Caroline takes the opportunity to snatch a drink from the bar. Rounding up Meredith and Bianca, Caroline drags them with her to meet up with Kelly.

"Did you see that dude? You just pulled me away from my future betrothed," Meredith spats as she and Bianca follow Caroline to the bar.

"I am not interested in your latest conquest. I am freaking out here." Caroline pours herself whiskey and downs the shot.

"Jacob, would you excuse us for a moment?" Kelly bats her lashes and off Jacob goes to join his brothers. "Did you have a flashback?" Kelly asks.

"No, more like a flash-forward." Caroline pours another round. "His family is all up in my business, asking how many kids I want and how I will redecorate this place. I feel like we are already married. Who the hell does that?"

"Loving family members who are showing acceptance of Jameson's decision. Ones who are trying to make you feel like part of the family," Kelly says, always with the positive spin.

"The bitches," Meredith sarcastically offers, then slams her umpteenth shot of the night.

"I have known him less than three months."

"I have only known…shit, Bianca, what was his name?"

"Hunter, you big harlot."

"Right, I have only known Hunter for three minutes and I can hear harps playing."

"You're not hearing harps. That's your vagina crying," Bianca corrects her. "Caroline, you are blowing this way out of proportion. Can you just relax and take this one day at a time? If you feel this is going too fast, just talk to him. Tell him you want to move slower. Or are you going to sabotage this relationship too? Personally, I would be all over that. He has shown you nothing but respect and caring, he is gorgeous, has money, some equally gorgeous friends, and his family is lovely."

"They truly are," Kelly agrees. "Jacob is as nice as can be."

Meredith, Bianca, and Caroline all turn to stare at Kelly.

"What did I say?" Kelly asks, feeling the pressure.

"Is Kelly getting her groove back?" Bianca goads. Kelly blushes.

"We can have a double wedding by the lake. I can be Kelly's maid of honor and Bianca can be Caroline's." Meredith and Bianca clink glasses to her master plan.

"Thank you. You two have been so helpful talking me off the ledge. Only thing you did was put Kelly up there with me." Caroline departs the three in a huff, making her way outside for fresh air.

"So, tell us more about this Jacob," Meredith says, refilling their glasses while allowing Caroline to go off alone in a snit.

Caroline regrets not grabbing her coat as soon as she hits the cold breeze coming off the lake. The air is so crisp, burning her lungs yet filling them with much needed oxygen to help clear her head.

"Put this on."

Caroline jumps back as Jameson wraps his coat around her shoulders.

"Why are you outside all alone? Are you not enjoying yourself? Did my family say something else to you?" Jameson asks.

"I hope I didn't make you worry. I just needed some fresh air. I am sorry you felt you had to come find me."

"Oh, I didn't. I was on my way out to set up the show. Just waiting on Mark."

"The show?"

"It is almost midnight. You better go in and get warmed up because in ten minutes I am coming to take you to our front row seats."

Mark, joining them on the deck, cuts the kiss short that Jameson landed heavy and heated on Caroline's mouth. Jameson comes in the back patio doors a few minutes later and asks everyone to come outside. As Caroline makes her way toward the door, she wonders why Mark would be doing a show outside in the middle of winter.

Jameson takes her hand, then leads her in the opposite direction of everyone else. "I have a special place for the two of us."

He leads her up the staircase to a large loft room, the only one on the second level. Caroline is enchanted when he opens the twelve-foot French doors into his bedroom. One whole wall is the large foyer window that extends from the ground floor to the top of the ceiling. Across from the large window, the loft overlooks the downstairs family room guarded by a solid glass railing.

"Jameson, it is breathtaking up here."

Farther through the library/sitting area is Jameson's massive bed and en suite. He leads her into the bedroom area, through a set of glass doors, and out onto the balcony overlooking the back lawn and lake. Three tall patio heaters are warming the night air of the outdoor living space. Champagne is chilling in a stainless steel ice bucket on the table positioned between two large loungers draped with blankets.

"You have thought of everything." Caroline looks over the balcony to the lawn full of guests. I feel like a queen."

Caroline raises her hand, waving the pageant wave. Jameson pours the champagne and pats the cushion beside him. He hands her a glass, then wraps her in a fluffy blanket. The blanket smells of Jameson and she wonders if he did that on purpose.

"But how are we to see the show from here?"

Whoosh! Whoosh! Whoosh! Boom!

The sky lights up in a multitude of fairy lights drifting immediately back to earth. Caroline screams and falls to her knees, spilling champagne while taking cover. She begins to belly crawl to safety when she feels herself being lifted in the air and carried inside. Jameson lays Caroline on the bed and goes back to close the door and pull the blinds.

"God, I am sorry, Caroline. I thought I told you Mark sets off fireworks at midnight each year." Jameson takes a quaking Caroline in his arms and rocks back and forth. "I am so stupid. I didn't realize…Oh, God, I am so sorry." He continues to hold her, rocking, waiting for Caroline to say something.

"It's okay. I am fine," Caroline lies as she uses the calming techniques Dr. Perrin has taught her.

"Caroline, where are you?" Caroline can hear Bianca yelling from downstairs.

"She's up here," Jameson answers.

Bianca, followed by Meredith and Kelly, run up the stairs and into the bedroom. "Are you okay?" Bianca grabs Caroline, displacing Jameson's arms.

"Yes. I had a brief moment but it was gone as fast as it came. I just did what Dr. Perrin said to do and it worked. I was able to calm myself before entering the twilight zone."

Caroline and her friends are pleased at her ability to fend off a full-blown flashback. Jameson, however, is sitting on the end of the bed, not quite comprehending the breakthrough Caroline just experienced. But Bianca makes sure he understands all too well how bad he just screwed up. Kelly replaces Bianca's compassionate arms while Bianca stands over Jameson.

"Have you lost your ever-fucking mind? You know she has PTSD and you decided it would be entertaining to have a bomb parade. Dick-wad!"

"I am truly sorry, sweetheart, for upsetting you." Jameson looks at Caroline and back to Bianca. "I thought she knew we were putting off fireworks." Jameson reaches for Caroline, yet she stays in Kelly's embrace.

"Does this look like someone in the know?" Meredith motions to Caroline, who is still shaking in Kelly's arms.

"What can I do, Caroline?" Jameson's remorse level is not quite high enough for Bianca but she can tell he is concerned so she backs off. "I will run down to the lake and have Mark to stop," he offers.

Jameson jumps up but Caroline stops him. "I will be fine, Jameson. Don't ruin everyone's fun on my account. In fact, girls, if you want to see the rest of the show, there is champagne, blankets and heaters through the balcony doors."

Bianca starts to refuse the offer but Caroline insists. "In fact, Jameson, can you open the blinds? I would like to see the firework display but I think I will stay here, on the bed."

The girls close the door behind them and Jameson opens the blinds. He curls up beside Caroline, and together, from the bed, they watch as the last of the fireworks shoot into the night air, explode, and float colorfully back to earth.

* * *

Caroline convinces the girls to spend the night and leave in the morning. She still isn't sure if she is staying the whole weekend and wants someone to ride back with her if she does decide to leave.

Jameson lets the dogs run the yard as the sun comes up, hoping to blow off their extra energy from being locked up all evening. He can't believe he was so stupid not to consider her past. First the nightmare at the Biltmore and now this. Caroline is the first woman he has met in a long time that he actually can see himself with long-term. He loves their long talks, her passion for her work and the world, and appreciates her independence. He is sure she is the one for him; he's not so sure she feels the same. He hopes this weekend will answer that question. Heading back into the kitchen, Jameson begins breakfast for his overnight guests.

"Can I help?" Kelly flits in like a bluebird in spring.

"Please tell me there is coffee." Bianca flounces in like a vulture on a caffeine hunt.

"Where's Meredith?" Jameson asks, rightfully concerned since she passed out cold on the couch around four a.m.

"I woke her. She is probably puking her guts out in one of your many bathrooms." Bianca takes a swig of the hot coffee Jameson pours for her. "At least, you better hope she is in a bathroom."

"I'll go check on her. She's my sister."

After Kelly leaves the room, Jameson offers sarcastically, "Can the dick-wad fix you some breakfast?"

"Sorry, I shouldn't have called you that. I am just really protective of my friends and can't stand the thought of one of them being hurt. We have less than two months before she is deployed to Afghanistan and she still is experiencing flashbacks and nightmares. I actually think her PTSD is getting worse with therapy instead of better"—Bianca chokes back her tears—"which means it is my fault she is being sent back to that hellhole worse off than before." Bianca wipes her tears with a napkin and looks up at Jameson. "I'm the one who told her she needed therapy. Why are looking at me that way?"

Jameson walks away from Bianca like a man on a mission, leaving her perplexed at what just transpired. He takes the stairs two at a time with Bianca hot on his heels. Bursting into his own bedroom, he is stopped short at the sight of Caroline blow-drying her hair. Such a simple act, an everyday occurrence in most households, but not his. He could get used to seeing her every morning getting ready for her day. Then he remembers why he is so mad.

Walking to the outlet, Jameson yanks the dryer's cord from the wall. "We need to talk," Jameson scorches Caroline with a fierce look. Not taking his eyes off Caroline, Jameson commands, "Bianca, get out."

"Jameson, Bianca didn't mean it last night—"

"This has nothing to do with last night or anything else in the past." Jameson removes the hair dryer from Caroline's hands, dropping it to the floor. "It has to do with our future." Caroline is stunned by the emotion in Jameson's voice as he takes her hands in his. His eyes soften from anger to hurt. "When were you going to tell me you had orders to go to war?"

Caroline glances at Bianca's retreating backside before making eye contact with Jameson. "This weekend. I thought about telling you when we were at the Biltmore—"

"You have had orders since November?" Jameson drops her hands, running his own through his hair as he walks away, into the bedroom. "Am I just a game you decided to play until you went off to be GI Jane?"

Caroline's spine stiffens at the tasteless use of his pet name for her. She squares her shoulders for the ensuing battle and follows him into the bedroom. "Jameson, I know you are upset, but please, try not to say anything you can't take back."

Jameson turns to confront her face to face. "Then why don't you start talking for once."

Caroline had never had a lover's quarrel in her life. She didn't know how to respond or even where to start. Her silence was gasoline poured on fire, fueling Jameson's anger.

"I received an email while we were in West Virginia—"

"So you have known the whole time we have been dating that you were leaving for Afghanistan yet you didn't see the need in telling me." Jameson turns his back on her and walks to look out the window. Caroline crosses the room, wanting to hold him, to fix this, and tell him how sorry she is.

"Damn it Caroline." Jameson says with his back still turned, "I can't believe while I am falling in love with you, you were lying to me the whole time."

Jameson's declaration stops her in her tracks. It has finally happened. A man is telling her he loves her for the first time and she actually feels the same way toward him. This should be one of the happiest moments in their lives yet she is standing within feet of him, trembling in fear, unable to cope with the feelings threatening her conscious. He said, falling in love, not fell. It might not be too late to save him from the horror of watching someone you love be shipped off to war. She will not ask him to wait on her, or worse, lose her all together. She will fix this now.

Swallowing the apology in her throat, she stands in the middle of the room, places her hands on her hips, and tells him how much she loves him, the only way she knows how.

"I don't owe you or anyone else an explanation about my life or my choices."

Jameson shoulders flip him around in a fury. Standing in front of him is a woman he has never seen before. Arrogant, vicious, and cruel.

"And furthermore, I have a commitment to serve my country. I never made such a commitment to you."

"Then what are we doing here? What is this?" Jameson implores, hands flailing in air."

"You knew I was in the military the first night we met. If you didn't want to date someone who could be shipped off to war then you had ample opportunity to turn away."

"I don't have an issue with your orders to go to war. I have an issue with you lying to me!"

"I didn't lie." Caroline grabs her suitcase and begins throwing in her belongings, including her heart. "I was planning on telling you when the time was right."

"When was that gonna be? While you were over international waters?"

Zipping up her suitcase and throwing it over her shoulder, Caroline crosses Jameson's bedroom, bent on escaping before her emotions break loose.

Jameson reaches out, grabbing the strap of the luggage, "Are you really just going to leave without another word."

Swallowing hard then sucking in a courageous gulp of air, Caroline says over her departing shoulder, "Goodbye Jameson."

CHAPTER THIRTY-FIVE

MARSHALL'S SPIRIT

Caroline stares out the kitchen window as she unpacks the groceries she picked up after work. Her scrubs, cold and wet as the outdoors, drape heavily on her vanishing frame but less so than her mood. It has been a week since she and Jameson ended their relationship. The pain she feels for withholding the truth about her deployment isn't half as bad as having to walk away, unable to divulge her true feelings for him. Several times she has started to dial his number but stops before pressing the call button, for she knows, deep down, she saved Jameson from worse pain of losing her in war. The remorse envelopes her; the sadness cripples her to the point she is experiencing difficulty just going through her normal routine. Caroline knows she must eat, but her stomach is tied in knots, not allowing anything to stay down long, so she quits trying.

Her day to day life is unbearable, even going to work is an arduous task, finding it excruciating to comfort others while her world is falling apart. From extreme exhaustion, Caroline's body crashes and burns for a few hours at a time before her mind awakens her to this misery. To beat everything else, Caroline is suffering her first cold of the season. This is why she went to the store after work, to get cough medicine. Nurses being the worst patients, she does not read the recommended dosage, she tips the bottle up and drinks it until she is afraid it will come back up. Wrapping a blanket over her body and head, Caroline passes out on the couch, her heart crying itself to sleep. Awakening in the middle of the night, she stumbles into the kitchen to find her phone to call Dr. Perrin, thinking that, after all, isn't heartbreak something shrinks are able to help with. Her screen lights up with several messages and texts. One from her mother, one from her father, one from the shelter, and seven more from her friends. She knows they are concerned for her but she can't handle hearing his name, let alone talking about the pain dwelling inside her. She leaves the ringer off, deciding on a hot bath instead of calling the doc. Trading her phone for a bottle of wine, the one Jameson bought her at the Biltmore—the one she was saving for their first anniversary—she heads up the stairs.

Flushed from the hot bath and the wine, Caroline slips into her favorite soft pajamas, lights a fire downstairs, and turns on her computer. Caroline checks the forecast first, since Mother Nature decided the Blue Ridge Mountains needed a deluge of precipitation and cold weather over the past week, although She didn't make it cold enough to snow. Caroline reads that by the morning there is to be a break in the gloomy weather— the rain moving out, crisp mountain winter air moving in. She thought the bright sunshine pictorial on the weather app would lighten her spirits, but such is life and heartache; not even the glowing orb can brighten her mood. She is still numb to the bone, not by weathering the storms outside but by weathering the ones continuously squalling in her heart and mind over Jameson.

Typing in the search engine, Caroline researches past life regression and reincarnation. Hours later, her eyes burning from the bright screen, she closes her laptop. She stands to stretch her aching back muscles from hunching over a computer screen for…

"Two hours," Caroline exclaims out loud as she checks the clock on the mantel. She can't imagine it has been a couple of hours since she sat down to research past life regression and reincarnation but admits to herself that she found the topics interesting and wanted to continue looking into past life therapy. It dawns on her that her last flashback was at Jameson's fireworks display and she hasn't had one nightmare this week. Caroline accounts this to her lack of sleep, sure she hasn't relaxed deep enough for REM.

Since it is now almost three in the morning, it is too late to call anyone and she is sure she will catch hell for not returning phone calls sooner. The flash of headlights pulling into her driveway catches her eye as she passes the kitchen window. Stopping, she watches as the driver door opens and the interior car light illuminates the driver's and passenger's faces.

"Bianca and Meredith?"

Caroline is almost plowed down as she opens the back door for their entrance. She starts to laugh at their pajama-clad, rain-soaked attire when she notices the horror-stricken faces of her two best friends.

"Is something wrong with Kelly?" Caroline guesses since Kelly is obviously absent. "I'll get my coat and purse…Is she in the hospital?" Caroline calls out as she fumbles with the arms of her coat, uncoordinated movements preventing her arm from going in the sleeve as she hurries back into the kitchen. With one look at Bianca, then Meredith, she stops short. Her shoulders slump, causing her coat to drop to the floor in a heap from lack of substantial body support.

Bianca takes Caroline's arm, leads her to the breakfast nook table, and positions her in front of one of the chairs. "Sweety, we need you to sit down. There has been an accident."

Caroline doesn't remember the rest of the conversation. All she can remember is the blood thrumming through her ears, a blackness taking over her vision as she spirals into a tunnel of despair, collapsing to the floor, much in the way her coat had, without bodily support.

*　*　*

Standing on the sodden ground of the animal shelter the next afternoon, the sun shining on the freshly unearthed gravesite, Caroline is supported by her three best friends, the shelter's volunteers, and her parents. Her father stomps a shepherd's hook deep into the earth so Caroline can hang Marshall's favorite toys from the curved, double arms above his terrestrial tomb.

Francie wails as she places a stone on the grave and then walks back to the shelter, but not before embracing Caroline in a friendly, supportive embrace. Caroline stands rigid from shock, not returning the act of empathy. The volunteers follow Francie, leaving Caroline, her parents, and her friends alone. They too try to walk away, making it a few yards before stopping to wait on Caroline, who stands stoic over Marshall's last resting place.

With a whispered voice, Caroline's mother asks her friends to clarify what happened. Bianca informs Caroline's parents of Marshall's bizarre accident: his escape from the shelter while a volunteer scrubbed his kennel to the subsequent finding of his body less than a mile downstream. Marshall had obviously gotten too close to the swollen riverbanks and drowned. The shelter had called Caroline several times as soon as Marshall was noticed missing and had made more call attempts after he was found. Past midnight, when Caroline had still not answered her phone, Francie had called Bianca, Bianca called Meredith and Kelly, and they all continued to call Caroline for several hours while out searching for Marshall in the rain.

Once Marshall's body was found by a shelter volunteer, Bianca and Meredith had decided to go to Caroline's house to inform her instead of the shelter calling again. They knew the impact this would have on Caroline and were worried how she would be able to cope—first the breakup with Jameson, and now Marshall.

Bianca approaches slowly, wrapping a sisterly arm over Caroline's shoulder, turning her away from the grave and walking her to the car. At home, Caroline is placed on the couch in front of the fireplace with a warm brandy and a blanket covering her lap. Her mother's attempts to feed her are subverted by Caroline's catatonic refusal, and her friends' struggles to enlighten her mood are even less fruitful.

Caroline cannot understand how this had happened. Marshall hated the water. He would never go near the river on their walks, staying close on their well-worn path on the upper embankment, never venturing down the slope toward the water.

"Marshall was different from the rest. When I looked into his eyes, it was like he knew me. Like he knew my inner thoughts and my feelings." Caroline inhales sharply, then exhales slowly through pursed lips, trying to control her emotions. "He knew my heart."

The four friends sit together and cry over Marshall's bizarre death. Minutes pass as they share Caroline's bereavement before Bianca's single six-word statement ends their mourning period.

"He was like an old soul."

Caroline's reaction to Bianca's words shatters the grief-stricken moment. Caroline sits up, throws off the blanket, hurdles over Bianca, Meredith, and Kelly, who are wrapped up with her, and runs for her phone. Her scream frightens her friends, who make it to the kitchen in time to see Caroline hurl her phone across the room.

"Fucking voice mail," Caroline says through gritted teeth.

"Who are we calling this late at night?" Bianca asks, concerned.

"Dr. Perrin. He can help me talk to Marshall," Caroline says as she gathers her coat and keys.

"Caroline, you cannot drive in the state you are in," Kelly enforces.

"What do you mean he can help you talk to Marshall? And put the keys down; you aren't going anywhere like this." Bianca steps toward Caroline, ready to take her down if she has to but also knowing she would get her ass handed to her in the process.

"He helped me talk to Major's spirit…"

While Caroline went on and on about talking to the spirit of a dead dog from Iraq, Meredith's and Kelly's worries for their friend's mental stability grow stronger. Bianca, on the other hand, is just plain pissed.

"Caroline, tell me his address and I will personally go speak with him. I will even bring him back here if he is home, but I do not want you out driving right now."

"I don't think he makes house calls," Caroline advises.

Bianca taps the address into her phone, puts on her coat, and says before closing the door behind her, "He will make an exception. I promise."

CHAPTER THIRTY-SIX

HOUSE CALL

Bianca bangs on the doctor's front door to his residence, not his office, until her knuckles ache. The porch light forewarns of someone's approach, so Bianca steps back a few paces, placing her hand on the railing to calm her nerves.

Obviously wrestled out of bed, Dr. Nikolas Perrin answers the door, finger-combing his thick black hair from his eyes. Expecting it to be one of his patients possibly having some form of a psychotic break, he is stunned to see a woman he does not know, grasping his railing as if she wanted to rip it out of the concrete. Not just any woman; the most beautiful woman he has ever seen.

Straightening his back and squaring his shoulders, Dr. Perrin asks, "Can I help you, miss?"

With the winter's cold pouring in the doorway, causing his bare chest to pucker, Dr. Perrin is shamefully aware of his half-naked body. This woman's eyes, glaring at him, shooting darts at his exposed neck, is not helping.

Bianca, who not ten seconds ago was planning on ripping the psychiatrist a new one for putting crazy notions in Caroline's head, has lost all train of thought at the sight of her victim. Caroline had said he was nice-looking but not that he was a Greek God.

"Miss?"

Shaking off the hormonal release, Bianca folds her arms across her chest, which she subsequently juts forward, and introduces herself in true

Bianca fashion. "Who the fuck do you think you are—some voodoo witch doctor? My friend Caroline is at home, emotionally distraught over the death of her dog, and thinks you can contact him from the great beyond. Listen to me, you licensed, loathsome slime-ball. You are going to—"

Bianca's barrage is cut short as Dr. Perrin turns and runs up the inside stairs, hollering as he goes, "I'll get dressed and we will head over to Caroline's." He disappears behind a door at the top of the stairs.

Stepping inside, shutting the cold out, Bianca warns under her breath, "Damn right we will."

She notices the well-kept three-story home has a masculine, almost mystic feel to it. Little electric pulses ascend her vertebrae, causing her to shiver when the sensation reaches her neck. No female touches are apparent to the place. *Has Caroline ever mentioned if he is married?*

Within minutes, Dr. Perrin is descending the stairs. "You drive. Your car will be warm," he states as he grabs his coat from the closet by the door.

Bianca informs Dr. Perrin of Marshall's death, Caroline's catatonic state at the memorial, and her outburst about talking to Marshall's spirit.

"I do not appreciate you filling her head with this bullshit. You are supposed to be helping her deal with her wartime traumas, but instead you are misguiding her, relying on her emotional battle scars to milk her out of more money. Well, you are going to come clean tonight and tell her the truth," Bianca commands.

"And what is the truth?" Dr. Perrin asks.

"That you are a fraud. That you made her think she was talking to some spirit and that you can't really help her talk to Marshall. Then you will apologize for hurting her. We will then try to pick up the pieces of her shattered psyche before she is deployed to that fucking hellhole."

"And if I refuse your most gracious offer?"

Bianca slams the brakes, sending Dr. Perrin forward as far as the seatbelt will allow.

"First of all, you do not have the option to refuse. Second, I will have your license revoked and your name trashed in this community."

"And third?" Dr. Perrin requests with a raised brow and crooked smirk.

Bianca floors the gas, her Mustang fishtailing on the icy pavement. "Third, your ass is walking home."

Neither speak the rest of the way to Caroline's. Walking up the driveway, Bianca reminds Dr. Perrin of his objectives. "Fraud, apology. That is why you are here."

"Then I walk home, got it." Dr. Perrin smiles as he holds the screen door open for his hostile, but very intriguing, chauffeur.

Caroline demands her three friends stay in the kitchen while she and Dr. Perrin go into the living room. Dr. Perrin and Bianca lock eyes, hers displaying a warning glare, his lifting at the sides as his smile reaches up to meet the hazel orbs. Bianca fights the urge to smack that smirk from his face.

"What the hell was that look for?" Kelly asks Bianca. "He is goading you. He obviously doesn't know what he's asking for."

"Oh, I think he knows exactly what he is asking for," Meredith comments. "Why didn't I offer to go get him? Maybe he would look at me that way."

"What way?" Bianca asks, already knowing where Meredith's mind is going.

"You had to feel the vibe coming from him."

"I woke him from a dead sleep, cussed him out, called him names, threatened his license, and kidnapped him. The only vibe coming from him is contempt."

"Hell, that's better than some of your other first dates," Meredith teases.

"Oh, it's your meet-cute. One you can tell your grandchildren about some day," Kelly adds.

"I cannot tell small children what I said to him. Trust me."

In the living room, Caroline begs Dr. Perrin to take her to her garden to speak with Marshall's spirit. "Do you think Major knew Marshall was going to die and that is what he meant by 'pains in this lifetime'? And if he did, why didn't he warn me so I could protect Marshall?"

Dr. Perrin observes a most distraught Caroline, unable to cope with such a loss. He attempts to calm her with muscle relaxation, but once Caroline figures out he is not inducing hypnosis, her agitation returns. He explains that is not how soul regression works. Caroline wants to try anyway.

"I believe you will get to speak with Marshall again one day, just not today. The next few sessions, Caroline, will have critical discoveries that will progress your therapy to a new realm of enlightenment. I need you to be fully aware of the possibility that when we identify the root of the problem, there could be more pain. But with exploration comes the real work."

The more Dr. Perrin refuses hypnosis, the harder she pleads, as if her tears were deafening his words. He attempts to steer her to the real reason for her hysterical break by asking her questions about Marshall. She fondly remembers the adorable puppy who had showed up at the shelter not long after she moved to Asheville. She tells Dr. Perrin how Barkley and Marshall made friends instantly. The thought of Barkley breaks her heart all over again. Caroline cannot contain the bittersweet agony of knowing Barkley is safe but she will no longer be a part of her life. Dr. Perrin picks up immediately on the transference. It is not Barkley she will miss, but Jameson, so he asks her what happened with the relationship. For hours, Dr. Perrin listens as Caroline tells him her reasoning behind breaking it off with Jameson. Though this also caused Caroline much emotional pain, she was at least off the subject of trying to find and talk with Marshall's soul.

The dawn sparkling through the window surprised them both. Time had lapsed while treating Caroline's broken heart, but Dr. Perrin had scheduled appointments this morning and had to end their impromptu, night session.

Dr. Perrin isn't sure how to tell his client his suspicion without affecting the planned therapy, so he omits certain information. He wants Caroline to understand the deepest core of the problem. After she connects the idea of past lives with certain traumas, he feels they will be able to focus more on the causes of her reoccurring dreams and nightmares instead of them side-stepping the real issue. Questioning his ethics and his deceit to his client, Dr. Perrin determines this is best for this patient.

"I have to go now. I have other clients coming soon. I will see you tomorrow evening, right?" He reaches in his pocket where his phone should be but is not. "I left my phone at home. May I use yours to call a cab?"

"Bianca dragged you out of bed and drove you here; she can drive you home."

"That is not necessary." Dr. Perrin declines the offer a little too abruptly. "She scares me."

Dr. Perrin leaves through the front door as the taxi pulls in Caroline's drive, avoiding the kitchen and its inhabitants. After breakfast, Kelly, Bianca, and Meredith leave so Caroline can get some sleep. Bianca wanted to stay just in case Caroline had a nightmare but Caroline persuaded her to go, explaining she hadn't had a nightmare in weeks. Bianca need not worry; Caroline sleeps most of the day without one remembered nightmare. When she wakes, she reads several more articles on past life therapy. She has made real progress in controlling her flashbacks, able to prevent most of them from turning her mind into a LSD trip. Her nightmares continue but with less frequency of occurrence. So why, Caroline considers, would she risk a journey into her subconscious, dredging up memories from the past, the far past possibly. As the sun sets over the Blue Ridge Mountains, Caroline makes up her mind. The bottom line; the fact that she has had these weird dreams her whole life and has had nightmares from hell that haunt her still, Caroline decides to follow her doctor's advice.

* * *

Caroline picks up on Dr. Perrin's apprehension as she enters his office the next evening. She wants to run from the room. Instead, she takes several drinks from her water bottle, screws on the lid, takes a few deep breaths, and assumes her position on the chaise, albeit stretched out and tense.

"Do you have any questions before we start?" Dr. Perrin confirms with his patient.

Caroline shakes her head. The doctor begins with muscle relaxation, and after several minutes, Dr. Perrin proceeds with the hypnotic trance, beginning from her safe garden. He monitors her ability to follow command. As he feels Caroline is in a sufficient meditative state, he begins with the trance induction.

"I want you to take a walk with me, through your garden. As we walk, you feel excess weighted stress and pressure leaving your body with each cleansing breath. As we move along the path, you are coming closer to the garden gate. The garden gate is to past lives you have experienced before. Caroline, when you walk through the gate, you will go back to a previous life that is a source of your dreams. Do you want to try?"

"Yes," Caroline answers in a soft, drowsy voice, reaffirming to Dr. Perrin her trance state. He finds himself holding his breath. He exhales, relaxes his own muscles, and continues.

"You walk up to the gate. This is the gate to happy memories. You are calm, warm, and relaxed as you witness a joyful time in this past life." Dr. Perrin monitors Caroline's reaction.

"As I count to five, you will slowly open the beautiful gate. Going to a memory of that time when you feel good and joyful. You will be able to tell me about these happy times as you experience them.

"One, pushing the gate with your hand, slowly. Two, you are opening the gate to the past. Three, the gate is widening as your subconscious is restoring these happy memories to your consciousness. Four, back in time in that life to only memories when you were happy. Five, walk through the gate. Describe what you are seeing, Caroline."

"Trees," Caroline calmly states.

"Are you alone?"

"I am…but I feel others around me."

"What are you doing at this moment?"

"Hiding."

This statement concerns Dr. Perrin. Did she not listen to his command to go to a happy memory? He has seen this happen before. The subconscious has its own agenda and only brings forth memories that need dealt with or sometimes will not allow the patient to discover these memories at all for their own protection. He has to have a clearer image of what is happening and from whom she is hiding.

"I will count backward from three. When I get to one you will know your location and the date of this scene. Three, two, one," Dr. Perrin counts quickly. "Where are you?"

"In the woods."

"Are you still hiding?"

"Yes. They are searching for me."

Dr. Perrin does not observe any signs of stress. Caroline is actually smiling.

"What are you feeling?"

"Excited."

Dr. Perrin is relieved that she is not scared but is still apprehensive about leaving her under. "Caroline, listen to me carefully: let the scene play out until you are in a safe place."

"Oh, I am in a safe place…they will never find me here."

"Who is searching for you?"

"Opal's brother, Tyler. He is 'it.' He has already found Opal and my cousin, Allen. He won't find me. I am hiding in a hollowed-out tree."

Dr. Perrin realizes she is playing the child's game of hide and seek. This must be a happy memory for her. He notes her voice is that of a small child.

"Tyler's yelling for me…telling me it's getting dark. I have to come out of hiding…I know it is a trick. He says he is going to get McKinley if I don't come out right now." Caroline snickers.

"What is making you laugh?

"Tyler is a sore loser. He can't stand it…he can't find me…he's getting my dog Mckinley to do it for him…cheater…McKinley finds me. Sniffed me out of all those trees…such a smart dog."

Dr. Perrin, working on a hunch, asks, "Tell me about your dog." He watches Caroline's face light up and smile.

"He's a mutt…followed me home one day…we have been best friends ever since. I named him after our new president. Papa didn't want me to keep him but McKinley eventually won his heart. McKinley walks me to the schoolhouse every morning…he is always waiting for me when I get out. I thought he stayed there all day…Mama says he comes home and goes back for me. How he knows to tell time I will never understand. I love him as much as he loves me. I am so glad he chose me to follow home."

Dr. Perrin is awestruck at the animated child in front of him. Caroline has the same soft Carolina drawl to her voice as the one from her polio dream, higher, louder, and with a country twang. She is even speaking quickly and nonstop like an excited child. He also notes she is referring to the same dog of that same dream.

"It's a good thang…it's getting dark."

"Do you know your name and how old you are?"

"Catherine…I am six years old."

"Do you know the date?"

"It is May…1897."

Dr. Perrin inwardly smiles. His patient is experiencing her first past life regression.

CHAPTER THIRTY-SEVEN

SESSION THIRTEEN – REMOVING THE VEIL

Dr. Perrin is recording this session but he also is taking notes on his own reactions and his assessment of the patient that is not apparent by voice only. He charts how he only had her remember joyful times so that she does not experience post-regression traumatic memories so soon in her regression therapy.

"Caroline, listen to my voice. I will begin to count backward from five. When I reach five you will return to your safe garden, floating away from that life but retaining all the happy memories from this past life. Five… Four…Three…You are floating back to your garden. Two…One. You are in your safe garden, in front of the gate again. It is still open—open to the past. As I count to five, we will slowly walk through the beautiful gate again. This time…going to a happy memory in another past life. A past life your subconscious has allowed to escape in the form of a flashback. I want you to go to the life where you are in need of cinchona bark. You will be able to tell me about these happy times as you experience them.

Dr. Perrin reaches five, assesses for any signs of distress, and then asks, "Caroline, do you know where you are?"

"I am in England." Caroline's voice assumes a British accent with an aristocratic air.

"Do you know who you are?"

"Nicolette Hamilton."

"Do you know what year it is?" Dr. Perrin waits with pen in hand. "1697."

"Using your senses, what do you observe around you?"

Caroline does not answer immediately. Dr. Perrin considers she may either be coming out of her trance or she may be floating to a deeper level of hypnosis. Observing no signs of stress, he waits for her to answer.

"Beautiful flowers. I am in a lovely flower garden…behind a large estate home. It is a warm sunny day…Everyone is dressed so elegantly. I can hear music beginning to play."

"What are you doing at this time?"

Caroline remains quiet, searching her subconscious mind for the answers. Dr. Perrin observes tears forming in Caroline's eyes as she exclaims, "Oh, I am to be married. It is my wedding day."

Dr. Perrin rapidly writes her every word as Caroline describes her wedding with little prompting from him.

"We have waited for this day for so long…it's finally here." Caroline pauses for several breaths, tears flowing, gliding softly over her cheeks and past her smiling lips.

"Caroline, listen to my voice. I will again count backward from five. When I reach one, you will be back in your safe garden. Five, your subconscious is allowing these memories to briefly remain in your present-life conscious to recall at will. Four, your lavender energy light is traveling, floating from this past life to the present. Three, you are floating over your garden, feeling calm and peaceful, relaxed. Two, you slowly float down to your willow tree by the shore in your safe garden, still remembering your regression memories. One, still relaxed, you are in this present life. Open your eyes."

Caroline does as she is advised, opening her eyes to her present life. Dr. Perrin notes her relaxed posture, her overall calm demeanor.

"Was that me?" Caroline asks after several minutes of silent introspection.

"Did you feel it was you?"

"Yes. First, I was a little girl playing in the woods. Then I was getting married. But I wasn't the same person. I was…" Caroline closes her eyes to reflect on the liberated subconscious scenes. "A little girl in the 1800s, but I was a grown woman in the 1600s." Caroline opens her eyes and stares at Dr. Perrin, imploring answers that are not forthcoming from the doctor. "Were those dreams from previous lives or did I just make that up in my head?"

"I am more interested in what you think they were."

Caroline rolls her eyes at the psychological foreplay and answers, "It's like I am remembering something that happened to me yesterday, not centuries ago. It is phenomenally genuine…yet it isn't me…but I feel the emotion inside as if it is happening to me. So is this real or not?"

"Proving or disproving the reality of your subconscious is not the goal for this type of therapy. The goal is self-knowledge and healing."

Caroline calmly eases herself up to the side of the chaise lounge, more calmly than she feels inside, and looks him dead in the eye. "You would not have suggested past life therapy if you didn't believe we have lived previous lives, so knock it off with the screwball shrink-talk and tell me what this is about. I leave for a war-torn country in a few weeks where my mental faculties will be tested hourly. I do not need this bullshit in my life right now so start talking, doc."

Caroline's perception of psychology doesn't surprise him. She is a highly intelligent woman whom, at this moment, not only is right in her analysis of him, but deserves the best outcome therapy can offer. He would usually not assist in clients' fitting the pieces of the puzzle together in such an intrusive manner, but time was running out for Captain Caroline McKenzie.

"The little girl, playing in the woods, from the 1800s," Dr. Perrin says, beginning his analytical exegesis of her nightmares and flashbacks, "is the same girl who is paralyzed with polio later in life, correct? The dog who finds her in the woods, McKinley, he is the same one that saves her from the rabid dog when she is in the wheelchair?"

"Yes." Caroline can see the visions in her mind without being under hypnosis.

"And is the woman who is getting married…this is the same woman from the 1600s, who is later sick with a fever and in need of cinchona bark?"

"Y-yes," Caroline answers a little more cautiously, not sure of where Dr. Perrin is heading.

"Past life therapy is to look beyond the veil of actual events that have left permanent tattoos on our souls and determine how these past traumas affect our present-day life." Dr. Perrin leans forward in his chair, looking directly into Caroline's eyes. "When our past traumas are deeply anchored with emotion, the subconscious removes those memories to the unconscious to protect us from the pain. Then the unconscious, to ensure you never feel that pain again, provides you with instinctual—or unconscious, impulsive reactions—to certain situations. For example, the startle reflex. It is instinctual; you are born with it."

Dr. Perrin gives Caroline a few seconds to process this information, then continues, "You were paralyzed when the little girl with polio, Catherine, was attacked by a rabid dog. If you hadn't been, your evolutionary mechanism for flight would have made you run from fear. The dog would have pursued instantly; you would have been killed before McKinley could have gotten there to save you. Then, you were tormented with the knowledge that your father had to kill McKinley. You were paralyzed, literally, with polio, unable to get to McKinley to keep your father from killing him, which kept you from watching him be put down. So when you came under attack in Iraq, your subconscious tried to protect you by making you believe you couldn't move. You felt paralyzed due to a subconscious, protective-guided paralysis. This is why you could not move when the sergeant was yelling for you to jump. This paralysis also kept you from witnessing Major being shot and gave you an excuse for not running after him to protect him from a certain death."

"Oh my God." Caroline's pulse and breathing quicken. The acknowledgement of her past trauma bleeding into her present life is more than she can handle, but the doctor is not finished.

"In your past life as Nicolette Hamilton, you were in love, deliriously happy. You became ill with fever and died, leaving him prematurely. Again, your subconscious has blocked the pain and the guilt of leaving the man you love and causing him to go on without you. You have subconsciously built instinctual defense mechanisms to guard against the development of any strong feelings toward another, effectually destroying any relationship. If my suspicions are correct, you withheld the information of your deployment from Jameson, knowing he would find out, ensuring the demise of the relationship before you fell in love with him or him with you, or before you had to leave the relationship prematurely for Afghanistan. Am I right, Caroline?" Dr. Perrin probes, requiring her to address and accept the dysfunctional behaviors carried over from her past lives.

Caroline focuses on Dr. Perrin's question. With a hitch in her voice as new emotions begin to choke her with the truth, she spews, "Not entirely. I am already in love with Jameson. And I am not protecting him from leaving him prematurely for Afghanistan. I am protecting him from me leaving this life prematurely by being killed in war, because I know he loves me too."

The spoken knowledge of her love for Jameson doubles her over. Caroline wraps her arms around her waist, trying to crush the pain in her chest and abdomen. This impassioned sentiment inspires a catharsis of emotion, erupting from deep inside her.

Dr. Perrin cannot help himself. His own emotions enmesh with Caroline's as his arms envelope her convulsing frame. Caroline's body melts into his, her head supported on his chest as she confronts the grief her subconscious has held tight for almost half a millennium.

It has taken most of Caroline's session to digest all the information Dr. Perrin has introduced to her conscious mind and the rest of it to regain her composure. Now with heightened anxiety from her raw emotional state, Caroline paces the office while Dr. Perrin further explains past life therapy.

"So you are saying you want me to relive traumas from previous lives so that I can get to the root cause of why my mind is a hot, effed-up mess."

"Do you remember how skeptical you were about hypnotherapy at first? You no longer experience the nightmares from your attack in Iraq, or the flashback to the CSH trying to save that young marine. How is his family, by the way?"

"I got a Christmas card from his mother. She is doing much better knowing he was not in any pain before he died and that his thoughts were of her and his family…Okay, I see your point."

"Oh, I am not done. The flashback you had when you tried to treat a fever with cinchona bark—you said your research showed it treated malaria, right? Nicolette lived in England in 1698. There was no cure for malaria back then. If that was the cause of Nicolette's fevers, the only treatment back then was cinchona bark, a source of quinine used as a muscle relaxant to stop the shivering brought on by malarial fevers. Do you see now? Your nightmares, your flashbacks, and your meditation dreams are actual spontaneous past life regressions from your previous lives."

Caroline abruptly faces Dr. Perrin, her eyes locking on his while she takes a moment to catch her breath. "Regressions? They're not just dreams? You're telling me I am traveling into the past on my own. Why… Why would I do that?"

"Because you have unresolved traumas that are being triggered by something in this present life."

"Like what?"

"I will safely regress you to each of these time periods so we can find out."

"Do we want to know that answer?"

Dr. Perrin is sure he knows the trigger. He isn't so sure if his patient can handle the answer.

CHAPTER THIRTY-EIGHT

A SOUL'S JOURNEY

Session Thirteen: Recorded
January 2011

Captain Caroline McKenzie:

Trance induction with guided imagery of garden gate metaphor.
First Past Life Regression: Patient regressed successfully to 1897.
Patient appears to be of school age who was in a state of play.
Speech, language, and observable behaviors indicative of child age.
Patient recalls her name is Catherine.
Second Regression: Patient is in England in 1698.
Name: Nicolette Hamilton.
Speech and language appear to be of British descent, woman of marrying age.
Joyful specificity: Her wedding day.
Post Regression Phase: Patient emphatic for assistance connecting past lives to current issues.

It is my belief patient is suffering from traumas in past lives which need to be reframed for full resolution of nightmare and flashbacks, which I believe are actual spontaneous self-regressions. Possible trigger during this lifetime causing spontaneous regressions to past lives.

Next appointment scheduled two days from now. Patient will undergo

PLR to traumatic events in each of those time periods.

Dr. Perrin closes his notebook but remains at his desk, mind wandering. He'd wanted to ask Caroline about Bianca's relationship status but decided against it. It would be less than ethical to date a patient's best friend but he hasn't been able to think of anything else since she threatened his practice and his life. To keep his mind off Bianca and focus on Caroline, Dr. Perrin heads upstairs to his study where he has several articles and books he feels will help him explain the trigger phenomenon Caroline is experiencing. He is positive of his supposition on the triggering force behind Caroline's nightmares but is hoping the journal articles and books can disprove his theory. If he is correct, Caroline's heart and whole world could be on a trajectory of pain and disillusionment that he is sure all the therapy in the world cannot fix.

"Please let me be wrong," he pleads to the theoretical gods as he reads the title of the first article: *Afterlife, a Soul's Journey.*

* * *

"You reap what you sow" is not necessarily true nor entirely false; however, it is the theoretical basis of reincarnation. An infinite rebirthing of the soul into different bodies is built on the foundational laws of karma. Karma is the judicial system to which reincarnation must obey. I have lived by those laws; I have died by those laws; I have been less than honorable when breaking those laws.

Our physical forms are the vessels in which we travel in this world as we search for ultimate self-actualization through love. Before entering those vessels, we must choose the life lesson which needs learned or the egregious act deserving of reparation, committed in a previous life. The choice is not to be taken lightly for it is a sacred promise to the universe of your soul's eternal search for integrity, morality, compassion, and love. So you can see why souls must return as often as necessary, since not too many get it right the first time.

The vows we make in one lifetime cross over to the next until the vow is fulfilled or the lesson is learned. Not until one reaches true enlightenment—nirvana— will a soul be released from its ethereal vows. Once ordained with true enlightenment, a physical form is no longer needed. Such is the cycle of souls.

My soul has made the trip several times. It has been a journey I have been lucky enough to travel, yet unlucky enough to need to. Less than stellar choices from previous lives can keep you on this cosmic carousel, as can unfulfilled promises. What you are slated to learn from these bad choices or the urgency of which you are needed to return determines the time spent between lives. Let's just say I haven't had a whole lot of time in the afterlife. I incarnate almost immediately because I made a promise to protect her, but more importantly, she needs me.

CHAPTER THIRTY-NINE

FRIENDSHIP THERAPY

"I need you." Caroline texted her friends. *"Can we please meet at my house instead of the bar? I do not feel like going out tonight."*

Bianca responds first with an empathic *of course*, followed by Kelly's *see you at your place*, then Meredith's *is this BYOB?*

Lying by the fireplace in Caroline's living room, the four discuss Caroline's past life regression session for hours. Marguerites and munchies almost completely polished off, Meredith stands to stretch her legs.

"I have always believed in reincarnation. I have never had a dream or nightmare suggesting of its proof, but I believe it," Meredith admits as she stumbles toward the kitchen with the empty pitcher.

"How can we both have been raised in the same house, by the same parents, and have completely different viewpoints on life and religion?" Kelly calls out to her sister, then addresses the other two. "I am equally assured that I have never had a previous life."

Meredith returns with a full pitcher and begins pouring. "Of course you haven't, sweetie." Meredith mockingly fluffs her sister's hair. "You are brand new."

"I can't believe you have never told any of us about these past life dreams," Bianca says as she holds up her glass for a refill. "So, when you dream, you feel you are in a previous time?"

"Not always. They have been just dreams, or visions. I never thought that much about them. I assumed everyone had them. Once I started therapy with Dr. Perrin, the visions became more vivid, more emotional, more like a memory than a dream."

The immediate sympathetic reaction from her friends opens the dam of emotions Caroline had been fighting all evening.

"What does the doctor say you should do?" Kelly asks as she strokes Caroline's hair.

"He says it is going to get worse before it gets better. He plans on regressing me tomorrow, but this time it won't be to just happy memories. He wants my unconscious to reveal the pain that I am transporting from one life to the next."

"Is he out of his fucking mind? How the hell is that going to help?"

Caroline is startled by Bianca's dramatic reaction. "Don't you get it? You all have been right all along. I sabotage myself. Not only in life but in relationships too." Caroline tries to suck back the tears to no avail. "I destroyed the best thing that ever happened to me because I am too afraid to feel the pain that comes with leaving someone behind."

Caroline experiences the emotional break she has been denying herself over the loss of Jameson. Wrapped in the loving arms of her friends, Caroline admits to the destructive behaviors that destroyed her and Jameson's relationship.

"Any time I try to picture us 'happily ever after,' I resort right back to the pain I feel when a relationship ends. I actually thought when I told him about my deployment, he would tell me he was proud of me and would be waiting for me when I got home. I even envisioned our reunion at the airport when I landed back in the States. Wives holding signs, husbands waving miniature American flags, kids with balloons, waiting on their mom or dad to rush off the plane. I pictured Jameson on the tarmac, in a patriotic-colored shirt, holding flowers, searching for me as I exit the door. Then he spots me and opens his arms wide as I launch myself into them. He hugs me so tight I can barely breathe and tells me how much he missed me…how much he loves me. We kiss, never taking our eyes off each other." Caroline's tears flow with anguish from dreams that will never be.

"That sounds so romantic." Bianca covers her heart with her hand. "Puke. And nothing like you," Bianca challenges, then pauses, looking into Caroline's eyes and shouting, "Venus and Adonis, you're in love!" Caroline cries harder, making Bianca feel badly about her outspoken revelation.

"What does it matter? I am leaving in a few weeks. Why would I start anything now? It is best for the both of us that it ended. And if I am able to come back, maybe then I can offer him something more than a long-distance relationship with someone who might not ever be whole again."

The four best friends cling together, supporting each other by discussing their own fears of relationships and their plans for the future. Kelly tells them about Jameson's brother Jacob and the possibility of something between them. Meredith brings up her and Kelly's mother, who is showing possible signs of early onset dementia, and describes the ramifications this will have on their lives. Bianca, however, remains silent. She is still seething from the idea of Dr. Perrin regressing Caroline so close to her deployment date and considers what she can do to prevent it. She has until tomorrow afternoon to figure out a way to stop Dr. Perrin from harming Caroline, even if that means she has to harm him instead.

It is well past two in the morning when Bianca finds herself, once again, on Dr. Perrin's front step. Bianca is working up her courage to confront the doctor when the door opens without even the first knock.

"I heard your Mustang coming up the drive," Dr. Perrin says as he steps out on the porch and locks the door with his key, ready to be driven to Caroline's. "What happened? How is she?"

Bianca is confused for a moment but remembers quickly her reason for being here. "Nothing happened and Caroline is fine, for now. That is not why I came."

Dr. Perrin takes a step toward Bianca to look closer into her eyes and seductively says, "You don't seem like the type of woman to make booty-calls, so why are you here?"

Bianca swallows the last bit of saliva from her suddenly dry mouth. "You can holster the charm, cowboy. This isn't my first showdown. What in hypnotic hell are you thinking? Taking Caroline back to some time or place to dredge up painful memories. Do you know what that could do to her?"

Seeing the fire radiating from her coal-dark irises sends a warm feeling through him. Dr. Perrin smiles at Bianca, not in the least intimidated by her threatening glare. A mistake he will only make once.

"Remove that smirk from your face, Dr. Perrin, or God so help me…" Bianca fairly warns.

Lost by the female inferno in front of him, Dr. Perrin fails to heed her warning and smiles. "Call me Nikolas."

"Fine, Nikolas. Have it your way." Bianca's frozen hand heats the side of his face, effectively removing the smirk.

The shock of being slapped across the face produces a sort of taunting laugh from the doctor, not what Bianca was expecting. As she raises her hand again to ensure he understands, she is gripped tightly by her upper arms and pulled against his chest. The spark between their bodies, as their eyes glare at one another, is combustible. He forcefully releases Bianca, pushing her slightly away, and turns away from her.

As Dr. Perrin unlocks the door, Bianca steels her nerves for the next round. "If you think for one moment you are hiding inside your castle of psychoses, think again, *Nikolas.*"

Dr. Nikolas Perrin opens the door to his home, steps aside, and offers, "Would you like to continue this inside where it is warm?"

CHAPTER FORTY

SESSION FOURTEEN – SPIRITUAL REALMS

"Let me point out, we cannot, by choice, remember anything in our subconscious without some technique or trigger. That is just how the subconscious works," Dr. Perrin informs Caroline as they prepare for her Past Life Regression. "I would like to discover what is triggering your subconscious to reveal pieces of itself. But most importantly, I want you to be able to reframe any dysfunctional behaviors or feelings associated to this trigger. That is called closure. We will continue through step progression of hypnosis so you may go deeper to experience these emotions. To reframe the trauma, you must confront the trigger, or the painful memory. Do you have any questions?"

"Will I see myself die? Will I feel the pain of dying?"

"You could possibly watch yourself die, yes, but why do you think death is painful? Death could be the most enjoyable part of life. Death is the only path for a soul to reach peace. It is where your soul resides."

"You might not want to ever council suicide patients. I don't think you would be too successful," Caroline states as she lies on the lounger.

"On the contrary. When I explain that taking one's own life will stunt the next life and will further its karmic effects along the evolutionary process for many lives to come, many patients prefer to find alternate ways of coping."

Once Caroline is comfortably reclining, Dr. Perrin asks, "Are you ready?"

Caroline is never less ready for anything in her life and that included being shipped to a war zone at the age of twenty-four. But she had survived that, so she nodded in agreement and closed her eyes.

"Turning your attention to the space of your own being. Nothing else around you except the support of the chaise on your body, holding you, allowing you to let go any muscle tension. Knowing you are held softly, yet surely, you can focus on relaxing all your muscles. Your head is heavy against the chaise, becoming heavier as your eyelids close and become difficult to open. The muscles of the jaw and neck droop, allowing your shoulders to fall away from your body, no longer needed to hold your head. Your arms grow heavy, like boulders pulled by gravity. Your hands relax, all the way to the tips of your fingers." Dr. Perrin lowers his voice an octave and slows his own breathing to conform to hers.

"Shifting your focus to your body, your chest is light, oxygen flowing throughout your cells. Your lungs are two balloons floating freely, full of oxygen. Your heart slows. You feel your spine as it turns into a warm, wet noodle, releasing the tension from your neck all the way to your bottom. Your legs, no longer needed for support, become as heavy as your arms. Your feet fall to the side, no longer supported by bone. All your muscles are relaxed as warm oxygen soothes your insides."

Dr. Perrin joins his energy with Caroline's for the exploration of her subconscious. Dr. Perrin and Caroline begin the journey into Caroline's mind through past life regression.

"Caroline, direct your warm, glowing energy light from inside you to only your mind. Your mind is the only part left of you. It is alone, unattached from your body, floating weightless. It is now only a lavender glowing orb, your energy light, floating away from your body, further up, further. No longer part of your present body. It is one with the universe, floating through space, with the lucidity of peace. The transparent lavender glowing orb is now floating through the clouds. There are several clouds through which the orb floats. Can you see the clouds?"

"Yes."

"Direct your orb with your mind, as it is one in the same, to enter the cloud from a previous life. The life where you were Catherine. Do you know which cloud is that lifetime?"

"Yes, I am here."

"I will now count from one to five. You are to follow my direction with each number.

Dr. Perrin opens his eyes as he reaches five to observe his patient. "Catherine, can you feel me as your energy guide?"

"Yes, sir," Caroline, as Catherine, answers with a childlike voice.

"What year is it?"

"1899."

"Tell me what you are feeling."

"I am sad."

"Why are you sad?"

"My mama is crying…'cause I am dying. My spirit guide is waiting for me in the light."

"What does your spirit guide look like?"

"Warmth and light…peace...love."

"Do you know your spirit guide?"

"Yes, he is always with me…guiding me. Protecting me."

"Do you know him by a particular name?"

"I know him by many names."

"Catherine, what name reminds you most of your spirit guide?"

"Michael."

Dr. Perrin's eyes widen, his mind searching. He does not remember her ever talking about a Michael. Maybe his presupposition has been wrong all along.

"Who is Michael to you?"

"Someone I once knew…in a previous life."

Dr. Perrin quickly jots this new information down in his notes, not so much for documentation purposes but to wrap his head around the fact he has been wrong. He was sure Caroline had a soul protector, another soul who follows her, life after life, keeping her safe. And he was sure he knew who it was.

How could I have been so wrong? Dr. Perrin questions.

"Catherine, I am going to count backward from five. I need you to follow my instructions with each step and retain all memories in your conscious mind."

After taking her through the first four steps, Dr. Perrin prompts, "One, open the unconscious mind to a previous life when you met Michael, your spirit guide. Share this wisdom with your conscious mind. Catherine, enter the cloud to that life." Dr. Perrin takes several calming breaths, providing Caroline time to travel, then asks, "Do you know where you are?"

"I am in bed in my home," Caroline, as Nicolette, answers with a British accent.

"What is your name?"

"Nicolette Van de Berg."

Recognizing the change of her last name from Hamilton to Van de Berg, Dr. Perrin assumes that is her married name.

"Is Michael with you now?"

"No."

Dr. Perrin is at a loss. He is thinking about bringing her out of hypnosis, not because of her distress, as usual, but because of his own. Then Nicolette speaks without a prompt. "I am so very tired. May I follow the light?"

"What light do you see?"

"The light of peace. I know my suffering will be over soon."

"Nicolette, are you wanting to die?"

"No, I want to live, if only to feel Michael one more time…I do not want to take this resentment with me…My body is ravaged with fever…I am shaking violently…The doctor has tried everything, including purging my bad humors, but without the cinchona bark, my body is burning from within. I am so very tired. I cannot wait for Michael much longer."

"Who is Michael to you?"

"He is my husband," Caroline says, smiling and confirming Dr. Perrin's suspicion.

"Where is Michael now?"

"He has went out to procure cinchona bark for my fever…I do not know how far he had to travel or when he will return…The bark is extremely rare, especially with the outbreak of the ague…He has been gone for several days. I am too weak to stay. The light is calling me."

Dr. Perrin understands that by letting Nicolette go, he may not discover the information needed to confirm his diagnosis today. He is running out of time. He believes there is a soul following Caroline. Without finding who that soul is, he will not be able to help Caroline reframe her past; he will not be able to stop the nightmares and flashbacks altogether. He will be sending the captain to war with past traumas haunting her. He is afraid her mind will not survive the real enemy—her own subconscious. He still needs to clarify one more thing. "When did Michael become your spirit guide?"

"I met Michael in 1695 in England. I didn't meet my spirit guide until my soul had been in limbo for several years. That is when I was reunited with Michael's soul."

"Michael died several years after you?" Dr. Perrin asks, surprised at the coincidence.

"Michael didn't know how to go on without me, so he joined me."

"You may enter the light, Nicolette," Dr. Perrin suggests, freeing her from the pain of that world. He watches as Caroline's body relaxes, every muscle becoming limp. "I am going to count backward from five. You will remain as your energy light inside your safe garden. Five, four, three, two, one. Caroline, do you know where you are?"

"I am under my willow tree by the lake in my garden."

"Do you remember regressing to two former past lives?"

"Yes."

"We are going to discuss these past lives and how they relate to your nightmares and flashbacks, focusing on the source, or trigger, that is provoking these subconscious hauntings. Is that all right with you?"

"Yes."

"When Catherine died, you told your mother to not cry, that you were safe and he was there waiting on you. Who is he?"

"My spirit guide. He is always waiting for me when my soul enters. That is how I know I need to follow the light."

"Have you had more previous lives than the two we just viewed?"

"Yes."

"And your spirit guide was there then, waiting for you?"

"Yes."

"Is it the same spirit guide each time?"

"Yes."

Dr. Perrin notes the smile that forms on Caroline's face and then watches it disappear with his next question.

"Caroline, tell me about Nicolette's feelings of resentment."

"He left me…so many times."

"Who left you?"

"Michael. He says it is the expected life of a diplomat for the Crown and I knew this when I married him. I believe he doesn't want to be with me…I love him so much but hate him for leaving me alone, only servants with whom to talk. If I did not have Maggie, my poodle, I would go crazy.

As much as he says he loves me, he still leaves me to do the king's bidding. I do not know if I will ever forgive him for a lifetime of loneliness. I would have preferred the life of a single lady-turned-spinster than married and alone. He knew I was dying yet he left me, again. He could have sent a servant for the Cinchona, but he went instead. It is only fitting—I have spent my life alone…now I will die alone."

Dr. Perrin recognizes Caroline is slipping in and out of characters from her past. He sees the tears forming in Caroline's eyes. He sees the anguish on her face. This loneliness pains her deeply, even though it is centuries old. He writes *rather be single than married and alone* and then denotes it with a star.

"Caroline, I would like you to remain as your energy light in your garden. Together, we will summon your spirit guide. We will ask for a higher understanding of your resentment and forgiveness for harboring the toxic emotion. We will ask for guidance in all matters relating to this present life. We will ask for clarity in resolving your nightmares and flashbacks. Most importantly, we will ask for a stronger connection, a fuller relationship, with your spirit guide from this day forward. Are you ready to begin?"

"Yes. I am ready."

"Repeat after me. I now invite with all the love, peace, and wisdom of the universe"—Dr. Perrin pauses for Caroline to repeat his words—"my spirit guide to come to me, in this garden."

Caroline repeats as directed. Dr. Perrin is aware of a new energy presence. He cannot see anything, but he feels the vibration change in the energy surrounding him and Caroline.

"Is he with you now, Caroline?"

"Yes, he is here. He says he can feel you too."

Dr. Perrin didn't need Caroline's translation from her spirit guide. In his mind, he heard her spirit guide say those words to him. He channels his own energy vibration back to Caroline's guide. "Caroline, tell him why you have called him here."

"I need your help resolving my unconscious mind of the traumas from the past that are affecting my present life. My subconscious needs your help in letting go past resentments. I need to know the significance of the nightmares that continually haunt me. I need your help in finding answers to what my subconscious is protecting from me. But most of all, I need and want to know you on a deeper, metaphysical level. Can you help me?"

"I love you. I will do anything for you. You know that."

Both Caroline and Dr. Perrin feel his words. Dr. Perrin wasn't sure if the soul would allow him to be part of their ethereal realm. The fact that he has means he must trust him to help Caroline.

"I can't seem to let go of the resentment I have toward you for leaving me alone. For not being there when I was dying. I know you love me. You killed yourself to be with me as my spirit guide. So why do I continue to feel this way?"

"Because you have every right to feel that way. I did leave you when you needed me most but it was because I loved you so much. I could not stand another moment watching you suffer from the malarial disease, so I chose to retrieve the medicine you needed. I felt helpless sitting by your bedside. I could not bear your pain; it was too much for my heart to take. I am sorry for that. I should have been a stronger person for you. That is why my soul made the promise to protect you for as long as you needed me. I will never leave you again. Know, I will find a way to always be with you, in every realm your soul travels."

"You don't have to do that. You have suffered enough. But I do have one favor to ask. Can you help me understand the nightmares that plague my present life?"

"Those too are my fault. My promise to protect you has placed our souls in continuous contact. Your subconscious protects your conscious mind from remembering traumas you would otherwise be unable to handle. My presence in your conscious world is threatening that defense mechanism by provoking memories of which you are not consciously aware. When the subconscious is triggered, it gives you only the amount of information you can handle at one time. When I chose the vessel-form of protection to keep you safe, I was not aware it would continue to prompt your past memories in subsequent lives. I never knew I was causing you stress or any kind of pain. I was only trying to provide you with fearless protection and devotion."

"I don't want to lose you again. At least we have the time between our earthly assignments to be together. Do not risk that. Death is not something I fear because I know you are waiting on the other side."

"I do not want to cause you anymore pain in this lifetime or any other. I love you."

Caroline's emotions are erupting.. Choked with tears, Caroline cries, "I love you too."

Dr. Perrin feels the release of energy from the spirit guide, a detachment of vitality between the three of them.

Dr. Perrin observes and notes Caroline's reaction and level of hypnosis. Now, he is sure the triggering force behind Caroline's subconscious divulgence is as he expected. He knows who Michael is in her present life. He has to decide on the right time to tell her and it has to be soon. He would have asked the spirit guide to confirm his suspicion but does not want Caroline to hear the answer. He will just have to find another way to prove his theory.

"Caroline." Dr. Perrin regains her attention. "I want you to focus your mind on peaceful meditation while in your energy light. Concentrate on retaining the information your spirit guide provided. Breathe in fresh air around you; breathe out any stress or pain you may feel. Take two more cleansing breaths. As I count backwards from five, you will release the resentment you have held for centuries knowing Michael loves you, knowing he gave his life to be with you and has found a way to continually be by your side. I will now count backward from five. At one, you will be awake in this present life with all the knowledge from your spirit guide."

He takes her through the countdown steps, instructing her to find forgiveness for Michael's transgressions and to replace the resentment with feelings of love and enlightenment. At the count of one, Caroline is slow to open her eyes...but when she does, Dr. Perrin questions the efficacy of the hypnosis. Her eyes are wide with alarm, her breathing labored. He takes several minutes in muscle relaxation, calming Caroline until she is no longer showing signs of stress.

"Caroline. What do you remember?"

"I remember entering my garden...then leaving it," Caroline says in a monotone voice.

"What else do you remember?"

Caroline is silent. She stands and looks directly at the doctor, then turns to leave.

"Caroline. I think you should stay so we can discuss your session. I am not sure it is safe for you to leave at this time." Dr. Perrin remains seated so as to not alarm her.

Caroline smiles, yet her body language is catatonic. "I will call to make my next appointment. I must go."

CHAPTER FORTY-ONE

TIMELINE

Captain Caroline McKenzie:

Patient consents for PLR.

Patient experiences two deaths from two separate lives.

Patient states, "Rather be single than married and alone." This statement coincides with Caroline's reactions to relationships.

Together, therapist and patient summoned Caroline's spirit guide. To assist with reframing and resolution, a higher understanding of her resentment, forgiveness, and guidance in this life with nightmares were requested from her spirit guide.

Spirit guide confirms he is Michael, first time hearing this name in our sessions..

Spirit Guide confesses his part in her nightmares and flashbacks as the triggering force by remaining in her life in some "vessel form" (which form his soul follows hers could not be verified though I have my suspicions).

Patient states she is not afraid of death, knowing he is waiting on other side for her. This action coincides with Caroline's extreme behavioral risk-taking.

My theory of a soul following her life after life presumably correct.

Unable to discuss with patient after de-hypnosis. Patient states she doesn't remember anything besides entering and leaving her safe place.

It is this therapist's belief Caroline does remember, her conscious mind retaining the knowledge of several past lives; however, her mind cannot process this information at this time.

Dr. Perrin's mind would not allow him to decompress after Caroline's session, even after his immediate review of the recorded session and obsessive charting, outlining each facet of her care. If his theory of a soul following her is correct, as he presumes, then why is Caroline not able to distinguish this person in her present life by soul recognition? Or does she truly know who this person is but cannot cope with the ramifications this soul could have on her present life?

These questions and more haunt Dr. Perrin all evening. Researching the malarial outbreak in England in the late 1690s, Dr. Perrin comes across a map and timeline depicting the spread of the disease. Studying the timeline closely, Dr. Perrin is suddenly able to picture in his mind Caroline's lives on the linear graphic tool. This just might be the answer they need to help Caroline and himself comprehend the critical milestones of Caroline's lives.

Dr. Perrin tapes several sheets of paper side by side along one wall of his office. Reviewing all his session notes, he charts Caroline's lives that he is aware of, beginning with Nicolette. When he is finished, the chart is a display of events in each of her lives in chronological order. Standing back, observing her soul's lifetime as a whole. Reviewing again exactly what her spirit guide said, the phrase "fearless protection and devotion" rattles through his head like a pinball, electrifying synapses until he is sure he knows who the trigger is in Caroline's life. Now he has to tell Caroline.

* * *

I fell in love with Nicolette the moment I met her. It felt like meeting a stranger that I had known since the beginning of time. We both knew our souls were destined to meet. When that happens, nothing on this earth or in any dimension can prevent it.

Nicolette and I were far greater than the sum of our separate selves. We were married that following summer,

Mr. and Mrs. Michael Van de Berg.

We mistook her symptoms at first, the vomiting and the fatigue, believing instead she was with child. Then the chills came. The doctors diagnosed her with the ague. Her symptoms flared about every four days. She would cry out in pain from the muscle aches caused by the shaking chills. Nicolette violently shook until the fever broke. Each reoccurrence weakened my beautiful Nicolette and a host of doctors told me she would not survive. The only treatment, not for the illness but for the shaking symptoms, was the bark from the cinchona tree. This is not a native tree to England and had to be shipped from foreign land. I traveled for days to reach the ship carrying the bark for the recent outbreak of the illness in England. The demand of the bark drove the price up phenomenally.

I didn't possess the bravery she had—never did. She had the courage of a lion, the heart of a dog, and the soul of a warrior. What she ever saw in me I will never know. But, God, we loved each other fiercely. She is my life, my whole world. She is my one true love. So I owe her mine.

The desolation Nicolette's death caused…well, there are no words. I couldn't go on without her, so I took my own life. My soul searched for her soul for years. I begged to be joined with the other half of mine. My spirit guide entered my meditation and asked what I truly wanted.

"When you quit thinking of yourself and only for her, offering her unconditional love, your soul will be given the opportunity of repentance and will be granted its destiny."

I promised to protect and care for her. My soul transmigrated into an earthly form and I was able to find her, life after life. I was able to protect her and love her unconditionally as no man could.

CHAPTER FORTY-TWO

FOREVER HAUNTING PAIN

"Surprise!"

Caroline gasps at the sight of her friends and coworkers all in one room as she enters Greg's bar. "Wow, I so did not expect this"—Caroline turns her snarly grin to her three best friends who are cowering by the bar—"especially considering I specifically said, 'no surprise party.'"

"Everyone at work was asking about a going-away party for you, so who was I to tell them no?" Bianca replied, her caution of Caroline's wrath evident in her approach to hug her.

"Bitch, please," Meredith hollers out. "They didn't come for you. They came for the free alcohol."

"Cheers," Chris salutes, raising his glass and downing the liquid.

Caroline's heart wrenches at the thought of leaving Chris and her other coworkers behind. Yesterday was her last shift at the hospital and now she has three days to pack before leaving Asheville for Fayetteville. Her orders state for her to be at Womack Army Medical Center on Fort Bragg for her physical on Saturday morning. She will then have two days of training and debriefing on the base. On Tuesday, just one week away, she deploys to somewhere in Afghanistan for nine months. She is not sure where she will be stationed, but right now, that does not matter. She is home in North Carolina with all the people she loves most. Well, almost all of them.

Caroline scans the room, her heart seeking relief from the pain, but he is not here. She wonders if Jameson wasn't invited, or if he was, did he choose not to come. Caroline suppresses the liquid agony threatening to erupt, her grief causing waves of nausea each time she thinks of him. She wants to drown with each wave, never to feel this sorrow again. But instead, she fights on, as any good soldier would do when confronted with utter devastation. She places a deceiving smile on her face and greets each guest.

"Let's get you a drink," Meredith suggests as she leads Caroline to the bar. Everyone wants to show their appreciation for her service or give the captain a farewell hug. Despite Meredith's attempts of redirection, pulling her away from clingy talkers, it still takes a while to get to the bar. Meredith orders the two of them a drink as Caroline hugs Greg, the owner, over the polished mahogany wood.

"Where's Jacob?" Meredith asks Kelly, who shoots a wide-eyed gaze back at her sister.

"Kelly, it's okay. I am happy for you." Caroline lays a hand on Kelly's arm for reassurance. "Just because it didn't work out for Jameson and I doesn't mean you have to avoid his brother. You should have invited him."

"I did, but Jameson told him he couldn't come."

"What?" Caroline unintentionally grips Kelly's arm.

"Jameson thought it would be too weird if Jacob came and he didn't. Plus, he didn't think you wanted him here." Kelly extracts her arm from Caroline's grip before saying, "He thought it would be too hard on you."

"Oh, did he? Does he think I am so pathetic that I would just curl up in the fetal position after losing him?" Caroline's firm stance is impressive but the quiver in her voice as she said "losing him" was less convincing.

"Well," Kelly reminds her, "you sort'a actually did."

Grabbing her drink, Caroline pushes her way to the exit, stepping outside for a breath of fresh, frigid mountain air.

Caroline had wanted a quiet evening at home to process everything Dr. Perrin had explained to her. The past two weeks of sessions had not included past life regression. In fact, Dr. Perrin hadn't hypnotized her at all. They reviewed her coping mechanisms in case a flashback or nightmare emerged. They discussed the heartache she felt over Marshall's death. But most of her last six sessions had been about Jameson and the continued pain that goes on and on without him. Caroline had never been in love, never had her heart broken, before Jameson, so she has no experience in piecing one back together. Now when she wakes crying, she can't say it is just a nightmare. This agony is her reality.

Before meeting Jameson, she was afraid to fall asleep. Now, she's afraid she'll fall apart. It has been over six weeks since she last spoke to Jameson at the New Year's Eve party. She can't believe how bad it still hurts. Never knowing what could have been between them will haunt her forever.

"If you truly are in my mind to protect me from pain," Caroline thinks out loud, hoping her subconscious can hear her sarcasm, "then you suck at your job. My heart is being ripped apart. What do I have to do to forget this pain?"

"Are you all right?"

Caroline, not wanting to appear crazy to everyone on the street, lifts her cell phone to her face as if she is talking to someone other than herself. She notices a text from Dr. Perrin: "I need to discuss something with you. Something that could help you understand why you have the nightmares and flashbacks. I was going to wait until you returned home but the more I think about it, I believe knowing the trigger for these memories could be therapeutic while you are away. May I drop by tomorrow after my last appointment?"

Caroline thinks of all the errands she has for tomorrow, but she can tell something is bothering Dr. Perrin. Plus, she is interested to hear about this "trigger" he keeps bringing up, so she texts her agreement to meet with him. Of course, this was before her common sense was drowned in alcohol and her emotions were floating like unsecured bobbers on the waves of a perfect storm.

"Why did you let her drink that much?" Kelly reprimands her sister and Bianca while holding Caroline's hair out of the toilet.

Kelly had driven Caroline home after her party with Meredith along for the ride, who was also in no shape to drive herself. Nikolas drove Bianca home since she lived on the opposite side of town. While making them eat to soak up the alcohol and then pouring coffee into them, Kelly scolds them for acting like college freshman with recently-handed freedom who don't know how to handle it.

Meredith suggests, "We need to stay the night with Caroline. I am worried about her drunk-text threshold."

Kelly looks up at Meredith with a "what the fuck are you talking about" look.

"You know, how some medications lower a body's seizure threshold… Well, alcohol lowers the drunk-text threshold."

Kelly hadn't known there was a label for it—the drunk-text threshold—but she has to admit she had texted an ex while drunk, so she agrees to stay. Taking care of Caroline is not a problem; getting her phone away from her proves to be a little more difficult. While getting pajamas for the three of them, Caroline hides in her closet and texts Jameson.

Meredith handles damage control with Jameson when he calls Caroline back over the texts she had sent. Telling him Caroline was not fully aware that she had sent them, Meredith suggests he forget about the texts. At first, Jameson demanded to talk to Caroline, even threatening to drive to Asheville. But Meredith promises she will have Caroline call him in the morning if she truly and soberly felt the words confided in the drunk texts.

After the contents of Caroline's stomach is emptied plus some, the three end up on the couch, cozy under some blankets.

"This is so stupid. We only dated two and a half months. We were over before we had a chance to begin," Caroline cries, collapsing into Kelly's waiting arms, her words trembling out of her. "When will this pain go away?"

Kelly, holding tight to stop Caroline's shaking grief, tries to bandage her wounds as only a best friend can, with love and honesty. "How long you know someone is not what counts. What counts is how he made you feel. Temporary doesn't convince your heart it is any less real."

"He made you breathless from the moment you met him. This is going to take some time. And truthfully, not all the pain will fully go away," Meredith bluntly states, which garners her a dirty look from her sister. "Well, it doesn't. Some pain stays with you forever."

"You are not helping," Kelly says.

Meredith climbs off the couch, grumbling, "Fine, I'm getting a beer. Anyone want anything while I'm up?"

"Tissues, please."

"What Miss Sensitivity is getting at," Kelly says, explaining love lost, "is that you will always remember the color of his eyes from the first time he looked deeply into yours. You will replay the sound of his laughter the first time you made him laugh. You will miss him sometimes…constantly, at first, then occasionally, then from time to time when a memory is sparked. You will have times when the pain feels unbearable, like now, but that pain is heartbreak, covered with regret, wrapped in loneliness, and boxed up tight in fear and insecurity. As time passes, the layers peel away like an onion."

"Yeah, and no matter how many layers are shred"—Meredith returns with her brutal honesty—"you are always left with the stinky, burn-your-eyes, make-you-cry core called heartbreak."

Caroline sobs for several minutes in Kelly's arms before pulling away to blow her nose.

"I need to hear the truth. I need to face this. I destroyed the best relationship I have ever had. I broke my own heart. If I could just talk to him…" Caroline stops mid-sentence, taking her phone from her back pocket.

"No." Meredith grabs Caroline's cellphone from her. "You are leaving in two days. You ended the relationship because you did not want to go to war and have him worried about you the whole time. Let him have some closure."

"When will I get closure?" Caroline asks.

Meredith looks Caroline directly in her red, swollen eyes and explains, "Not until you quit fantasizing about what might have been and accept that for now, you must let it go. For God's sake, your life depends on it right now."

Kelly finally figures out why her sister is being so brutal with Caroline's emotions. Meredith does not want to see Caroline go off to a war zone thinking of Jameson. All her faculties will be required to just stay alive. Heartbreak can make one not care whether they live or die, and they both wanted her to fight to come back home to them.

Caroline wakes the next morning with a horrendous headache throbbing from temple to tonsils. The last thing she remembers is Kelly tucking her into bed, then her and Meredith squeezing in on each side. Neither are in bed with her now; they must have already left. Caroline fumbles for her phone on the bedside table, then strains to see the time.

"Billy Wayne Shit-balls, it's after noon." Caroline curses as she heads for the shower. Dr. Perrin said his last appointment was at two so he should be here a little after three. Caroline wanted to clean her house today, dump all the old food from the refrigerator, and take any canned or nonperishables to the homeless shelter. Wiping the steam from the mirror, she assesses the damage.

"There is not enough makeup on the East Coast," Caroline says to the merciless mirror, her swollen, mottled face mimicking the words back at her.

Caroline hurries her errands and pulls into her garage as Dr. Perrin is pulling up the drive.

"I am sorry I have nothing to offer you to drink besides water," Caroline apologizes as Dr. Perrin enters the kitchen.

"Water is fine." He takes a seat at the kitchen table as he considers how to start this conversation.

"You mentioned a trigger." Caroline joins him at the table. "It must be one hell of a sustaining trigger since I have had these dreams all my life."

Dr. Perrin removes a piece of paper from his pocket, unfolds it, and slides it across the table in front of Caroline. Caroline glances at the paper first, then lowers her head for a better look. Her eyes widen as the expression on her face turns to shock. Caroline slowly stands, mesmerized, knocking her chair backward as she steps away from the table and away from Dr. Perrin.

Caroline, straining each word, says, "You…you cannot be serious. I am beginning to wonder which of us needs their mind altered."

Dr. Perrin knows by her reaction she understands the three timelines he has drafted on the paper. The first is Caroline's present life, Catherine's life on the second, and Nicolette's on the third. Interwoven within Caroline's timeline is the fateful entrance of Marshmallow, Major, and Marshall. Catherine's timeline similarly depicts the same fateful occurrence of McKinley. Though Nicolette's timeline from 1697 does not demonstrate how or when her poodle entered her life, he is still written in the timeline at Nicolette's death.

"Caroline, do you understand the significance of your pets in these timelines?"

Caroline stands three feet from the table, all the while staring at the paper, not uttering a word of acknowledgement to Dr. Perrin.

"Please, Caroline, sit down so I can explain."

Her reaction to the timeline convinces Dr. Perrin he is on the right track. Somewhere, deep in her subconscious core, guarded for her protection, she knows. He stands, takes her by the hand, and leads her back to the table. He holds out the chair as Caroline sits, not sure if she is even aware of her physical movement. He remains standing, pulling the paper into view.

"I want to begin with Nicolette. She is the one I am least sure of, the one I believe could have been the beginning to all of this. In all your lives, there is a significant bond with a dog, except in Nicolette's. You have mentioned the poodle staying by your side while you were ill, but never did you portray a reciprocal devotion as you have to the others. In Catherine's life, McKinley showed up the summer before she was diagnosed with polio, at age six. Catherine died, of what we can assume was pneumonia or paralytic polio, months after your—I mean, Catherine's—father had to put McKinley down."

Dr. Perrin is choosing his words carefully. He does not want to say "shot" or "killed," afraid it will shock Caroline's system.

"The next life you remember is this one, your present life as Caroline McKenzie." Dr. Perrin points to the top timeline, far left. "Once again, a dog, Marshmallow, finds you around the age of six. He is with you until you go to college. He disappears inexplicably right before you enter the military. Enter Major. He is with you in Iraq, dies heroically, then you are sent home."

Dr. Perrin glances down at Caroline. She seems to be following his direction, at least with her eyes if not with her mind.

"Shortly after you arrive home from Iraq, Marshall shows up at the shelter where you volunteer. He also leaves this earth by inexplicable means, once you had orders to deploy to Afghanistan. Do you see what I am getting at? In each life, Catherine's and Caroline's, when you are in danger, a dog enters your life, protecting you from harm."

Dr. Perrin knows this is where it is going to get real for Caroline. This is where her mind will decide to acknowledge the truth, no matter how painful. He doesn't have long to wait.

"Get out," Caroline calmly says.

"I know this is hard to believe, Caroline. But with what we know about reincarnation, a soul is able to choose its earthly form as long as it is following the Karmic Laws. I believe someone has chosen to follow you, life after life, for your own protection. That is what your spirit guide told you. It does not mean this person is following you in human form though. I believe the dogs in your life are the triggers to your nightmares and dreams because they represent another time and another place your soul has lived. I believe your spirit guide transmigrates into the form of a dog to protect you."

Dr. Perrin waits for any form of response from Caroline to signal she understands what he is telling her. He, however, is not prepared for her violent reaction.

Caroline stands toe to toe with Dr. Perrin. With a wild look in her eye, Caroline says through gritted teeth, "I said, get out!" Caroline plants her fists on his chest and shoves. "Don't you ever contact me again, do you understand? You need help, Dr. Perrin. You are out of your God-damn mind." Caroline's last words to Dr. Perrin spew venom as her voice crescendos. "Now get the fuck out of my life."

Dr. Perrin opens his mouth to try to calm Caroline but reconsiders as she steps toward him with a face full of rage. He turns away from Caroline and does not look back until he reaches his car. Hoping she will come after him, he waits by his car for several minutes. She doesn't come. Dr. Perrin forces himself to leave Captain Caroline McKenzie, the patient that has altered his own belief system. As he drives home, he considers calling Bianca to explain and to send her to check on Caroline, but he can't. That is a violation of patient confidentiality, and right now, he does not want to give Caroline McKenzie any legitimate cause to have his license revoked.

Even if Caroline believes him, her subconscious would never allow her full disclosure. It would guard against the truth. Because if Caroline agrees with his theory, then she would have to realize her destiny in Afghanistan is already predetermined.

CHAPTER FORTY-THREE

AFGHANISTAN

Caroline sits in her tent, writing a letter home about her miraculous finding.

Hi Bestees,

Since this is not my first rodeo, I acclimated quickly to my new base in the Helmond Province in Afghanistan. I share a tent with two other nurses, who work the night shift. Some days the boredom wants to kill you as much as the Taliban. I am thankful for the boredom though. This means the Taliban are not fighting, probably due to winter climate, and our troops are not coming in as mass casualties. Then other days, we can have five to six traumas brought to us at once. There is no rhyme or reason behind what you can expect in this part of the world.

My first few weeks were spent in training, learning procedure and protocol of the Combat Support Hospital. I work in the Emergency Room, which is actually a tent on the outside yet a fully stocked and staffed ER on the inside. The CSH is equipped with a pharmacy, lab, and radiology department as well as five operating suites. A complete yet portable hospital that can be assembled in less than eighteen hours anywhere it is needed. CSH units are used mostly for stabilization purposes. Patients are triaged and supportive surgeries are performed. If a patient requires intensive, long-term care, he or she is airlifted to Kandahar Air Base. That is where I was hoping to serve, but no such luck.

Being stationed in a mobile combat support hospital is not without its own dangers. The compound has posted guards around the perimeter, but let's face facts: its God-damn Afghani desert surrounding us. We, even as military personnel, are not allowed past the wire fence line. All extra-curricular activities must be performed within the small perimeter.

Today, the start of my third week in Afghanistan is a typical beginning. I prepare for my day, first with the quarter-mile trek to the latrine, which is nothing more than an open pit behind canvass. We have been promised a higher level of creature comforts, but for now we must endure the primitive living conditions. I then exercise by running for an hour or so to stay in shape followed by meditation before going to the ER.

February in Afghanistan is about the same temperature as Asheville. Temperatures around forty or fifty through the day and twenties at night. My breath comes out in vapor form, the cold air making it difficult to take a deep breath. My heart is racing; my breathing is labored. I slow my pace under the dark of predawn. I pinch my side to relieve the side stitch under my ribcage. I bend at the waist, pinching deeper, trying to catch my breath when I catch a glimpse of something running behind the tents. My heart quickens again, my breath ceases altogether. I am too afraid to run. I am too afraid to make even the slightest movement. The possibility of enemy infiltration into the compound is always present, a threat every service personnel monitors while outside.

I gauge the distance between me and the closest tent, one hundred yards away at the most. My heartbeat is pounding out of my ears. I wonder if whatever is waiting for me can hear my heart pulsing through my veins. I refuse to stand here another moment paralyzed in fear. The holster strapped to my side audibly clicks open as I remove my sidearm. I prepare to bolt for the tent a football field away, finger on the trigger, when I see movement, low to the ground, again. He darts behind the same tent I was heading for—the supply tent. I aim my issued .9mm toward the tent and haul ass, sand kicking up in my wake. I look for anyone else around as I run for cover. I see no one, not even the mystery man. Fear is building as I get closer to the tent. Has the enemy entered our supply tent or is he waiting, watching me run toward him? Ten yards left to the side of the tent. Eight…five…I am counting down the distance at a full sprint.

I double over with pain in my side as I try to press my back to the tent. Catching my breath, I hear no movement from inside the tent. I smell nothing unusual. The darkness allows only shadowy images, but I see none. With all my senses heightened, I duck under the first rope tie-down and stop, locked and loaded, waiting on an ambush to come around the corner of the tent. Nothing. I take the next step in the same direction, toward the corner of the tent, where I saw the apparition take cover. Does he know I am here? Is he as afraid as I am?

I hear movement first, the sound of sand and gravel being disturbed. I hold my position, making him come to me. The sound is low and to the ground, slight movements, the enemy possibly foraging for lout. I wait. The disturbance of the gravel and the shifting of the sand is grating on my every nerve as it advances toward me. My body is preparing for attack, the hormonal cascade initiating hyperarousal within my body. As he turns the corner of the tent, my dilated pupils take focus as my weapon takes aim at its little body, its little furry body.

It's a dog: a pup, really. An orphaned canine. At first I think my mind is playing tricks on me. I gasp out loud, scaring him. He lowers down, all fours tucked under him, head down, his ears pinned back. I look around to see if anyone is watching. Strays are not allowed on base and are to be disposed of immediately due to disease. His eyes widen as we both realize my sidearm is still aimed down on him. He rolls over, exposing his belly, his tail wagging, brushing sand and dirt puffs from underneath him.

I can't help myself. I holster the .9mm and squat to rub his offered belly. He whines a soft sigh of relief as I further scratch behind his ears and along his spine to above his tail, which is wagging now to beat the band. He hops around with excitement, nipping at my fingers as he licks them. I pick him up, holding him in my arms as he tries to bombard my face with puppy kisses. For the first time in the three weeks that I have been stationed here, I laugh.

Adopting a pet while on duty overseas is strictly prohibited. I tell him that as I set him back on the ground. I continue to repeat that to him, as much for my benefit as his, as the pup follows me back to my quarters. I explain to him he is not allowed here. I tell him he needs to find another home as he lies down in the sand outside my tent.

I list all the reasons in my head why I cannot keep this pup with me as I prepare for my shift in the CSH. I am decisively convinced in the matter as I grab a K-ration breakfast and head to work. His warm eyes meet mine as he leaps at me as I exit my tent. I stay strong. I forcefully tell him to go away, then we split my breakfast bar. I remind him he has to stay hidden as he follows me to the CSH unit for morning duty.

I am relieved—okay, a little disheartened—when he is not waiting on me when my shift is over. As I walk toward the latrine area, my eyes dart around, not for the enemy but for my puppy, the one I know I can't keep. At the next tent over, I see his miniature body roll out from under the canvas tent that is puddling on the ground. I point out that life on a military base in the middle of the desert is not suitable for a dog as he follows me back to my quarters. He would have to stay out of the way, hidden from others, and that was no life to lead. I explained this to him as we shared my dinner. But puppies do not listen any more than toddlers.

As I bathe him that evening with my allotted bottled water, we come to an understanding. I cannot keep him as my pet nor can he stay here on base. He lifts his paw up to me in acceptance; we shake on it. Then we decide on his name, Max. Because I know he will be a maximum pain in my ass.

* * *

Over the next seven months, the pup grows to be a shorthaired, oversized crossbreed between possibly some form of a terrier and a Great Dane. By the end of Caroline's deployment, Max's back, while he stands on all fours, comes to Caroline's hip. If he stands on his hind legs, he is taller than most anyone he comes in contact with, which is everyone on the base. It is impossible to hide a dog the size of Max. He has also grown to be loved by every person on the base, even the commander.

He'd slept outside Caroline's tent from the first night and never left her side. Wherever she goes, so does a 175 pound dog. Caroline is no longer frightened to be outside, away from others, since Max stays on alert. He runs with her every morning around the compound, never complaining about the heat. He shares her meager food allotments, never begging for more, taking only what is offered. Caroline had requested dog treats and toys from home and, of course, her parents and friends oblige.

Mail-call delivers a large box to Caroline the first part of September. Being so close to her birthday, she is sure it will be stuffed full of presents from her three best friends. She is half right. It is loaded to the top, not of presents for her but of dog snacks, dog food, chew toys, and a collar with a dangling silver tag shaped like a paw. It reads "Max" on one side and "Captain Caroline McKenzie" on the other. Caroline and Max empty the contents. When the bottom of the box does not offer a card, Caroline flips the box top back over to see its postmarked location: "Charlotte."

Max senses something is wrong immediately. One minute Caroline is happy, displaying all the new toys for him, and the next she crouches down then falls to her bottom, staring at the package as if it had a bomb inside. Max immediately goes on alert, sniffing the package for any scent of an explosive since Caroline abruptly sat beside it.

She has allowed Max to be included in the everyday reinforcement training with the K-9 war dogs and their trainers while she is working in the CSH unit. Max gets valuable training and exercise instead of waiting outside the ER for Caroline to finish her shift. The trainers release Max a few minutes before her shift ends so Max can escort Caroline safely back to her tent. Even though he misses Caroline while she is working, Max enjoys his time with the trainers and the bomb-sniffing war dogs.

Max does not understand Caroline's reaction to the box. He does not smell any form of explosive, so he doesn't know why she sat down hard beside it all of a sudden. That is what the war dogs are trained to do if they smell an explosive—to sit down beside it.

He nuzzles under her arm that is wrapped around her legs, lifting it so she can pet him. Max lays his head on her lap, enjoying the scratches to the top of his head until he feels the first drop of water. He looks up at Caroline to find the drops are coming from her. His ears lay back, his eyes softening as he licks her tears away. This only makes her do it more, so he sits back and waits for her to tell him what to do.

Caroline climbs into her bed, the pillow now catching her tears. The bond between them enables Max to feel her emotions, much like reading her mind. He does it by scent, using his nose as a crystal ball. It breaks his heart to feel her pain, so Max decides to do the one thing that always makes her happy. He jumps on the barrack cot beside her and lays his head across her chest. And waits. The physical pressure generates a hormonal response within her human body, effectually reducing anxiety and fear. It will only be a matter of time before she falls asleep. It feels like forever until Max feels her muscles relax throughout her body. He knows she is asleep so he closes his eyes too, continuing to lay in the cramped cot, his head resting over her heart.

Caroline wakes to a reverberating sound in her chest that buries itself silent into her bones. She smiles as she realizes the sound is Max snoring peacefully. She lays her hand on his head, stroking his soft fur as she remembers why she is in bed in the first place. The box…from Jameson. One of the most beneficial, character-building attributes to being in a war zone is the deep appreciation you gain for faith, family, and friends. Caroline has only one month left before returning stateside and when she does, she wants Jameson to be there waiting for her. She wants the dream reunion no matter how corny it sounds. No more allowing her fears from her past lives to stand in the way of what she wants in this life, and what she wants is a lifetime with Jameson.

Swinging her legs off her cot and uprooting Max from his slumber, Caroline pulls out a notebook and pen. Staying up the rest of the night to make sure she writes from the heart and not her messed-up mind, Caroline inscribes the emotions she has been holding since New Year's. As soon as she signs the bottom with love, she addresses the envelope to Jameson Bastian Brooks and heads for the makeshift post office.

Max knows something is about to happen. He can feel Caroline's excitement. He jumps from the cot and heads out with her into the predawn hours. Shaking with anticipation, his ears perked and tail wagging a happy beat, Max trots alongside Caroline. With his nose enamored by the smell of Caroline's happiness, he almost misses it—the scent he has been trained to pick up by the handlers of the war dogs. He raises his head then lowers it. He is positive now. There is an explosive close by.

He stops immediately and sits, just like his buddies do for their trainers when they sniff out a device. Even though he will not have the actual title or prestige, Max has been trained in war dog tactics. However, Captain Caroline McKenzie has not. She is not trained as a war dog handler, therefore missing the cues Max is demonstrating. He barks at her yet she continues, not noticing he has stopped. His bark is the last sound Caroline hears before the IED blows her off her feet.

Sirens scream across the base, alerting all personnel of a possible attack. Soldiers scurry to their posts, medical personnel hurry to the surgical units, and all are in extreme terror. With no one sure if there are more devices, the war dogs and their handlers are called out to secure the area first. This takes several minutes for the area to be deemed safe for rescue maneuvers.

The "golden hour," the optimal amount of time to get a wounded soldier off the battlefield to increase the odds of survival, is ticking down. Twenty-two minutes have passed from the point of the explosion to the first medic reaching Caroline, who had been blown over twenty-five feet back from the point of origin. Normally, the medic would have moved on to the next wounded after the quick "blood sweep" assessment of Caroline's injuries. His attention needed to be placed on those who had a possible chance of survival. But the sight of Max lying injured across the captain—blood and debris soaking into his coat, his eyes pleading for help—broke the medic's heart into a thousand pieces. He drops to his knees, pushes Max to the side, and triages Captain McKenzie.

CHAPTER FORTY-FOUR

MAX

I try to stand. I can't seem to get my legs underneath me. Something has happened. My mind remembers the explosion simultaneous with my body registering the pain. One of my legs must be broken from the explosion. What went wrong? I knew the bomb was close. I alerted Caroline just as I have been trained to do by the war dog handlers. I try to stand again, to flee from the possibility of other dangers, but the pain brings me down once more. I look around for help but the smoke, sand, and dust storm from the explosion muddy the air. Relying on my other senses, especially smell—but again, that too is altered from the smoke—I search for Caroline.

My ears perk up when I hear someone call out for all personnel to report to the CSH. Someone other than me is hurt. Someone needs immediate medical attention. That is when it all comes flooding back to me. Caroline! I rotate 180 degrees, sliding my belly across the sand. At first, the debris in the air limits my ability to find her. That is when the true panic sets in. Raising my head, I engage my most powerful weapon. Searching the area, scanning the air, I find her less than twenty-five yards from me, smoke smoldering off her clothes. My mind screams out of anguish as my

*body reacts. Crawling, dragging my broken leg behind
me, I reach Caroline, I heave my body on top of hers.
I try to wake her. I beg for her to come back to me. My
mouth is too dry. I am not sure she can feel me caring
for her wounds the best I can. I yell for help, the sound
coming out of my smoke-filled throat as a weak bark.
So I do the only thing I know to bring her back to me:
I lay my head on her heart.*

*When help does arrive, they push me to the side
so they can administer care in their own human way.
People are moving in every direction, aiding those who
suffered the blast. It seems Caroline has taken the brunt
of the blow force. All I can do is watch as the medics
wrap Caroline, preparing her removal from the scene.
I want to go to her, make her feel my love.*

*Several men lift her in their arms, carrying her to
the CSH unit. I watch as this well-oiled machine of
human character protect and serve one another. I crawl
the best I can, following the soldiers who have Caroline.*

* * *

Caroline is laid on a gurney as Corporal Kevin Jordan reports his assessment of Captain McKenzie's injuries.

"Massive blood loss. No breath sounds distinguishable on left. Diminished on right side. Pulse weak. Heart rate in forties and falling. Agonal respirations. Pupils pinpoint and nonreactive. Both legs shattered from the blast and at least one arm broken."

"Secure an airway, get her in the back, and let's get her opened," Dr. Mozaffari directs while wheeling Caroline into surgery, where uniform, controlled chaos ensues.

* * *

*I stay outside the CSH unit all day and all night.
Kevin sat with me most of the afternoon, informing me
of Caroline's condition. He even treated my wounds by
cleaning the debris and blood from my fur, repairing my*

ear, which must have been torn from flying shrapnel, and bracing my broken right hind leg. Angie, Caroline's tent-mate, tries to get me to eat but I can't. She promises to take care of me until Caroline comes back for me but I already know that will never happen. She tells me Caroline will be moved to another hospital for intensive care soon.

As the sun rises over the desert, I hear the chinooks coming for the wounded. I clumsily stand, hoping to catch a glimpse of Caroline as they carry her to the waiting helicopter. Gurney after gurney is carried to the landing site but no Caroline yet. Jeff, the sergeant in charge of the war dogs, bends down beside me and explains he will be taking me back to the kennels at the training center. He clasps a leash to my new collar Caroline had just given me the night before. I like Jeff but I am not budging until I see Caroline and he knows that.

"Bring her out," Jeff called.

The door opens to the CSH unit. A large machine comes out first, then the gurney with Caroline's body on it. She is attached to the machine by a tube in her mouth. Her head is wrapped in white gauze, her body draped, tubes and bags hanging all around her. I try to get closer but Jeff holds the leash tight. He tells me they are taking care of her and I will be staying with him until she gets better. Then the gurney stops.

Jeff leads me over to Caroline so I can see her. She doesn't smell the same to me but I know it is her. I nuzzle under Caroline's arm to lift it so she can scratch my head. But her fingers don't move. Her arm has something hard and white wrapped around it. Jeff pulls on the leash, forcing me to step back as the medics carry Caroline to the waiting helicopter.

The sound of the engines preparing for liftoff sends piercing pain through my ears to the center of my brain. I stifle the urge to cover my head from the pain so I can watch Caroline's rescuers take her away from me. I lie in the sand, tears flowing, as the sound of her possible salvation fades over the desert. I know I will never see her again in this lifetime so I beg for the sweet release of death. I do not want to go on without her. I have let her down again. I was not able to protect her. So I close my eyes, picturing her, waiting for death to take me to the spiritual realm.

$$* * *$$

It has been over a month since Caroline was taken away from me. I lie in the shade, watching as the war-dogs train, still unable to reconcile why Caroline smelled different to me. Had her soul already left the body? Is her soul searching for me now? I must find a way to get to her. I must pass over to be waiting on Caroline when she enters the spiritual realm. The fact that I am still here could only mean one thing. Her spiritual guide is not needed yet. My existence is proof of her survival.

CHAPTER FORTY-FIVE

STAGES OF GRIEF

Caroline, still groggy from the anesthesia, wakes from her eighth surgery in three weeks. Her first two surgeries, in her own CSH unit in Afghanistan, were for stabilization purposes. Major arterial bleeds had to be repaired, bones had to be stabilized, and debris had to be removed from her abdominal cavity, all four extremities, and her eyes. Burr holes had to be drilled to relieve the pressure off her brain from the traumatic head wound.

Upon arrival at the Craig Joint Theatre Hospital on Bagram Airbase in Afghanistan, four more surgeries were performed—two for urgent life-saving measures—before Caroline had ever woken from her coma.

Caroline was transported for intensive care treatment to Landstuhl, the US Hospital on Ramstein Air Base in Germany on September eleventh, her thirtieth birthday. On October seventh, after two more surgeries, Caroline, for the first time, opens her eyes to see her parents sitting by her bedside. Her mother's head is bowed over their intertwined hands, her father, on his knees beside her mother, leading the prayer. Tears flood her eyes, streaming down her temples, being soaked up by the bandage wrapping her head.

What hell have I put them through? Caroline thinks. Then the obvious question: *what hell have I been through?* The tears and accompanied drainage to the back of her throat make her want to swallow. She tries but her throat hurts. It feels swollen and closed off. Caroline panics, suddenly aware she is unable to breathe. Alarm bells frighten her, closing off her airway even tighter. She fights to take a breath but something is blocking her airway.

Her father is off his knees, yelling out the door; her mother is crying as she leans over her, trying to tell her something. Caroline can only hear the loud noise coming from the bedside machine as she fights for a single breath. As fast as the nurse enters the room, Caroline feels her mind swim within its bandaged frame.

Captain McKenzie wakes once again a few hours later from the forced sedation by the nurse to prevent Caroline from extubating herself. She does not see her parents. Instead, standing around her bedside is a team of medical personnel. The blood thrums through her head as she tries to listen to the woman leaning over the bed, speaking to her. She is telling her something about pulling a tube, telling her not to fight, to breathe easy.

Caroline moves only her eyes as she looks at the others around her bed. She realizes what is being said to her. The doctor is saying she is to be extubated. They are pulling the tube that is helping her breathe. She needs to relax and the tube will be removed from her throat. She will then be able to breathe on her own.

After removing the breathing tube, Caroline's first words—actually, mimed—to her parents come with tears. "I'm sorry," she tries to say.

Her mother and father collapse at the bedside, praising the Lord for bringing their daughter back to them. The nurse and physician move closer to the bed as her parents step back. The nurse takes her hand; the doctor takes a seat by the bed. The next half hour of Caroline's life is a blur as the physician informs her of where she is and the journey that brought her to the hospital in Germany. She explains the multiple surgeries and the injuries her body has endured over the past weeks. It is now that Caroline learns the extent of the explosion, which she does not remember, and the disfigurement the blast caused.

Her mind processes the grief in stages—the first stage being denial, allowing her conscious mind to pace the feelings of loss. Caroline questions the words the doctor is saying to her: "Burns. Holes drilled in your head. Your leg…amputated." Her mind tunes the doctor out as she consciously tries to feel both of her legs. Her eyes follow her concentration, looking down on the blankets covering her lower extremities. She tries to lift the right leg, then the left, without success for either one. Her muscles are too weak from being in a coma for so many weeks. She understands this, being a nurse. What she can't understand is if her left leg has been amputated, why can she still feel it beneath the covers?

As the doctor stands to leave, stating she will give her time to process the information, the nurse informs her speech therapy, occupational therapy, and physical therapy will be coming in to work with her soon. Caroline confirms with a nod, her throat still too swollen to speak. She will prove they are all wrong. Caroline, exhausted from the prognostic discussion and possibly pharmacologically chilled from pain meds, falls into a deep sleep.

Caroline's dream begins back in Afghanistan, her mind walking her through the last morning on the base. Her excitement to send Jameson's letter and how it felt to finally confess her love for him, albeit in written form, passes through her stored memory bank. Her dream-state remembrance of love then turns violent, swirling brief, hallucinogenic images past her sleeping conscious mind, then retreating. Caroline startles awake, disoriented, drenched in sweat, and hysterical.

"Max!" Caroline's raspy voice calls out. Though barely audible, the anguished tone behind the name brings her visitor quickly to her bedside.

"Caroline. I am here. It is okay. You are fine," Kelly's voice soothes as Caroline's eyes stare wildly back at her. "We are all here. You are going to be okay." Kelly grips her hand with her own.

Caroline is not worried about herself. She wants to know about Max. She tries to squeeze Kelly's hand back to make her understand the urgency of what her damaged vocal cords are trying to say. "Max?"

"There is a letter for you"—Kelly pauses as she reaches for the stack of mail on the table—"from Sergeant Jeff Nogard. Shall I read it to you?"

Caroline nods, expectant grief gathering in the corners of her eyes, spilling down her face. Kelly begins, "Dear Captain McKenzie. Do not worry. Max is alive and well. Everyone on the base is taking turns caring for him. He misses you terribly though."

The hollow part of Caroline's chest cries out, in part due to relief to find Max is okay and partly due to the misguided misery Max must be feeling, not knowing what happened to her or why she abandoned him.

Kelly takes Caroline in her arms, careful of the tubes and lines coming out of her.

"He's okay. He is safe on the base. Jeff goes on to say he told Max that you were getting better."

Kelly does not tell Caroline that another letter from the sergeant, postmarked last week, explained the CSH unit would be debunking by November first and Max would not be allowed to travel with them. And just in case it doesn't work out as they hope, Kelly does not tell Caroline the plans that were set in motion from day one after the explosion. She allows Caroline to fall asleep, comforted by the fact that Max is alive and being taken care of.

* * *

The following month after Caroline woke from her coma, physical therapy has been Caroline's way of dealing with the next phase of grief: anger. The anchoring strength of anger offers her a ballast for the nothingness she feels from her loss. Caroline represses the multitude of emotions bombarding her mind so she doesn't have to think about the loss of her career. Her military career is over and working as a nurse is hard enough with two legs, making it impossible to go back to the hospital. She doesn't even know who she is anymore. Losing a limb impacts every aspect of her life. Physically, she must learn to walk with crutches now until a prosthesis can be fitted to the stump that used to be her left leg. She can't imagine her life without the adventurous side of her. The altered physical appearance makes her feel less whole to the point she can't look at the residual limb. And as bad as she hates to admit it, she feels less of a woman. But first, Caroline has to retrain all her muscles from being in a coma for weeks. Some muscles are just weak, but others seem to have totally forgotten their purpose in her body.

"Come on, Kommandant," Meredith jokingly speaks broken German with a harsh accent, "give us vier more leg lifts."

Caroline, lying on her back on a mat, tries to kick the hand Meredith holds up, four more times, while Bianca and Kelly bounce on the exercise balls shouting encouragements from across the room. After leg lifts, the four of them pass the medicine balls back and forth, strengthening Caroline's muscles but weakening her resolve to remain their friend.

"Bloody hell, Duchess, you are as weak as a kitten," Bianca tries out her British accent recently required on her layover at Heathrow Airport.

"Can we please speak American English?" Caroline begs, having had enough of her friend's slanderous attempts at a foreign language. She laughs as they tell her stories of their travel adventures across "the pond" while they work her muscles harder than the physical therapist ever dreamed of doing.

Emotionally, Caroline is doing what a soldier is trained to do: persevering through the adversity confronting her. Transferring all her emotions into anger, she pushes herself through the pain and bitterness, past exhaustion. If Caroline only had herself to consider, she might not be a woman on the verge, but that is not the case. The guilt she feels over her friends' and family's torment over wondering if she would survive brings her to tears each time she looks at one of them. Knowing they all had put their own lives on hold to be there for her is heartwarming, but she worries about her friends' financial stability as well as her own.

Her parents had already left Germany, returning home to take care of personal business. Before leaving, they explained to Caroline their decision to sell the home in Winston-Salem. They had to return to sign the paperwork. Caroline can't believe how fast life can change. So she works harder to get better quicker, to be transferred to the States sooner. Then she can start working on finding Max.

The mental aspect is the most challenging. Caroline questions every decision she has ever made in her life. But as she looks around the room at her friends, who are now horse-playing on the physical therapy equipment, she knows there is no use in bargaining. She wouldn't have changed a thing. One small past alteration or choice might have resulted in a life without her three best friends. To help her cope, Caroline bottles up all the frustration of how her life is changing and funnels that grief into anger.

She refuses to let others see her as weak, but sometimes while mourning the loss of her life as she knew it, the weakness flows from her eyes. She cries herself to sleep every night. This is the only time she is not on constant watch. The doctors and therapists warned her parents and friends of the depression that is bound to surface. The sadness, the regret, the fear of helplessness, and the vulnerability will take over, so Caroline is never left completely alone. However, the real yet subtler part of depression is not visible to anyone but Caroline. The most private part is bidding her old life goodbye.

Trying to suppress the heartache from the most profound loss in her life, Caroline hides her face in the hospital pillow, sobbing uncontrollably. She doesn't want to live a life without Jameson, nor can she see one with him. She would never burden his life with her handicap. Caroline remembers the letter she wrote to him right before the explosion, asking him to meet her at Fort Bragg upon her return home. She pictures herself running into his arms which wrap around her, lifting her off the ground for her welcome-home kiss. The thought of never feeling his love again is more than Caroline can bear.

Her emotional descent into anguish wakes Bianca, who is on duty tonight, sleeping on a cot in Caroline's hospital room.

"Caroline, it's just a nightmare," Bianca yells as she runs to the bedside. "Wake up. It is only a dream."

Caroline chokes on her tears as she takes in a shuddering breath. "I am not dreaming. I am awake and the nightmare is real this time."

Bianca crawls into bed with her, holding Caroline's trembling body tight. "We are going to get through this together, so talk to me."

Bianca's attempt at comforting words only propels Caroline into convulsions. She tries to tell Bianca what she has not told anyone except Max—"I love him. I miss him so much"—but the words come out as fragmented pieces spewed from her broken heart.

"Oh, honey. I know you love him. And if he is alive, we will find him."

Caroline's entire body freezes as Bianca's words penetrate: *if he is alive?*

"You always have had a soft spot in your heart for animals. I am surprised you didn't become a veterinarian."

Of course, Bianca thinks that Caroline is talking about Max. Embarrassed at her outburst, Caroline decides to continue the deception.

"He was my only semblance of humanity while in that hellhole. I miss him and I know he misses me too. I can feel it. I have to find him." Caroline talks for hours about Max and how he helped her keep her sanity while in that God-forsaken country.

"Oh God, Bianca. I am so sorry. I haven't even asked you what is going on in your life. Are you and Dr. Perrin still seeing each other?"

"Yes, we are and we have you to thank," Bianca pokes. "If you weren't such a lunatic, I would have never met him."

Caroline bites the arm wrapped around her. Bianca jerks her arm away, laughing as she gets up, then helps Caroline reposition in the bed. After covering her back up and fluffing her pillows, Bianca pours them both a glass of water and pulls a chair closer to the bed.

"It is almost daylight. Meredith and Kelly will be here any minute for the day shift. I will be back this afternoon though to talk with the doctors about your transfer stateside to Walter Reed hospital."

The door opens slowly and quietly while Meredith and Kelly slink in with cups of coffee in their hands.

"Hey, you're up already," Kelly says, bright as the morning sun. "We have coffee."

"Thanks be to Jesus," Bianca says and grabs one from Meredith as she leans over to kiss Caroline on the forehead.

"Whoa, girlfriend. You really need a bath and a good hair scrubbing. Does this hospital come with a spa?" Meredith scrunches up her nose at her bedridden friend.

"No, princess, hospitals are for saving your ass, not kissing it," Bianca preaches.

"Hell, there's a Starbucks, so why not a spa?"

"It is up to us to get Captain Crazy here to the shower today, so when I come back, I will bring some toiletries from the hotel," Bianca offers as she stands to leave.

"Well, I think you look beautiful," Kelly says as she kisses Caroline's cheek, "but a nice bath wouldn't hurt."

"Bring some makeup with you too," Meredith says as she pinches Caroline's cheek. "Let's see if we can dial down the crazy a notch with a little coloring."

Caroline slaps Meredith's hand away from her face as she asks, "Bianca, can you stay for just a few more minutes? There is something I need to tell you all."

Caroline's three best friends pull chairs to her bedside to listen as she tells them about her therapy sessions with Dr. Perrin. When Caroline tells them about the trigger Dr. Perrin believes to be the source of her nightmares, dreams, and flashbacks—her dogs—all three faces turn to fearful apprehension.

* * *

I am now with Caroline as we walk the trail along the river behind the animal shelter in Asheville. We are so happy together. It's a shame we had to die. I can only assume Caroline has left this world since I am now floating upward, though I do not remember how I died. The only reason I would be returning now to the celestial sphere is to be present as Caroline's spirit guide when she arrives.

I feel myself floating higher and higher, my mind replaying our many lives. My sluggish soul, heavy with grief I guess, has not crossed over as easily as before. In fact, nothing is the same as before. I have always remembered how I died. Too much time has passed between consciousness and the celestial realm, and I can still feel my earthly body. It is not my soul that is sluggish; it is my body. My head is spinning as I descend from the heavens, pressure building between my ears. I smell…well, I shouldn't smell or feel anything, yet I do. I try to open my eyes. They are too heavy.

I must have been dreaming but it felt as if I had left my body. Though slow to arouse, I can now see around me. I am in a small bar cage inside a much larger metal one that feels like it is falling from the sky. About the time I convince myself that can't be happening, the larger cage hits something, bounces twice, and is rolling to a stop. I prepare myself for an impact that never comes.

Then I see it—the light many souls speak of after death. The brightness, causing me to shut my eyes, is not comforting or peaceful. A silhouette form enters the light as the smell of fuel floods my nostrils. Speaking calm words as he approaches—yet I can smell his fear—he opens the cage slowly. He leads me off the large metal tube, into the cold, and straight to another man waiting by a car.

This man then offers his hand for me to sniff. He doesn't have to worry about me biting him; I am muzzled. His scent carries the smell of several different dogs, like Jeff, the war-dog handler. I haven't yet decided to trust him. Then he demands the removal of the muzzle.

"It is customary to muzzle all animals after they are drugged to handle the flight. I suggest you leave it on until the drugs are out of his system."

"Remove the muzzle," *the stranger says.*

For some reason, this stranger trusts me and I smell no fear coming from him, which is odd considering my size. He rubs my head like we are old friends. We might not have ever met in this life but I know him. I have heard many stories about him. This is the man who has replaced me; the man who is living the life I can only dream of; the man who loves her as much as I do; the man who will take me to Caroline.

CHAPTER FORTY-SIX

REUNION OF SOULS

Caroline can't believe just a year ago, the four of them were in a cabin in West Virginia, throwing a party for dozens of people they had never met. It was also the trip where she met Jameson. She has not asked about him since her accident. The pain is too raw to speak his name. Her friends must understand this, for they have not mentioned him either. Caroline considers calling Jameson when she returns home but as the stark reality of her condition hits her, she chokes back the tears that form knowing she will never be a whole woman again. She would never want to saddle Jameson with her own disability.

Meredith has finished drying Caroline's hair and Bianca is helping her apply a little makeup. Kelly is pacing back and forth to the hospital room's door, overly chatty, even for her. Caroline knows her friends are up to something. Since it is her last day before flying to Walter Reed in the States, Caroline guesses her friends are planning a party. She doesn't want to ruin the surprise so she plays clueless, though she really doesn't feel like a party.

Caroline is grateful for her friends and parents. They have stayed by her side through all of this and have cheered her on as she regained her strength and abilities. Caroline's grief over her injuries and loss, including the loss of Max and Jameson, is so ultimately personal that she feels alone in her pain. But she can't imagine going through this without her friends and family.

Caroline needed a few more weeks of rehabilitation in the States, where she would be fitted for her prosthetic in Maryland at Walter Reed before being able to return to Asheville. Her heart's anguish gripped her again as she thought of going back to Asheville without Marshall being there. She had promised him a "forever home" when she returned from Afghanistan, but now she has no one. Not Marshall, not Max, not Jameson.

The depression hits her again, the grief hanging on, acceptance nowhere in sight. Caroline can't imagine what it will take to ever accept what had happened to her, or to forget about Jameson and move on. She makes the decision right there and then: as soon as she had her leg, she would go back to Afghanistan, though this time as a civilian. She would find Max and keep her promise to Marshall to have a "forever family."

Caroline is lost in thought and misses the flurry of activity in her room and the commotion outside in the hall. What she first notices is her three best friends, standing together by the window and acting very suspicious—Bianca and Meredith sporting goofy grins and Kelly with tears quietly streaming down her face. Caroline starts to ask *what the fuck* when she hears the door to her hospital room open. Her head turns to the opposite wall as the nurse walks in, holding the door open.

"Captain McKenzie, you have a visitor."

"Thank you, Jaime. They can come in."

"I don't think we have a choice," the nurse admits as she takes cover behind the door.

Before Caroline can see who it is, she hears the tapping on the tile floor. The sound of claws pawing for traction against the slippery surface, gaining in pace and volume as the pair crash through the small hospital room door.

Jameson's arm jerks forward, as if ripped from the shoulder, his feet pulled out from under him, as the Great Dane mix hears Caroline's voice for the first time in several months. Dragging Jameson behind him, Max makes it to the side of the bed before Jameson can stop him.

"Max!" Caroline's arms open wide, which Max takes to mean to jump up on the bed, so he does. Caroline throws her arms around him, burying her face in his neck. Her heart implodes inside her chest, weeks of devastating grief fragmenting into tiny pieces that pour from her eyes. The scene has the same effect on everyone else. Bianca, Meredith, and Kelly are holding one another, bawling their eyes out. Nurses, doctors, and therapists, who have heard story after story about Max, are all watching from the doorway as Captain McKenzie is reunited with her wartime companion. Even Max is crying in a howling, wistful way as he licks away each of Caroline's tears.

"God, I missed you, buddy," Caroline says through the barrage of doggy-loving. "It's okay. I am fine. We survived, together. I will never leave you again."

Max gives Caroline one more lap up the side of her face and jumps off the bed to sit at Jameson's feet. He looks at Caroline, then up to Jameson, then back at Caroline, and back up to Jameson.

Caroline can't breathe, let alone speak. Her heart is in her throat. Her emotions, teetering between extreme euphoria and unimaginable amazement, leave her speechless and motionless.

The last time Jameson saw Caroline, she was in a coma with tubes everywhere, fighting for her life. Now, in front of him, sits a warrior. The most beautiful warrior he could ever dream of and one who has stolen his breath, and his heart. Jameson has spent the last few months, preparing himself for two scenarios. The first scenario, not even fathomable, was what if Caroline does not survive. He knew he would still find Max and bring him home though the dog would be a constant reminder to the love Jameson lost. The second scenario involved crews working to make his house accessible for Caroline. He knew he was bringing Max home and prayed daily that Captain McKenzie would agree to come home with him also. Jameson knew Caroline would find it difficult to feel whole with him but he was not taking no for an answer. Jameson had thought of everything except what he would say to Caroline. He feels the small push on the back of his knee, then a forceful shove on the back of his thigh. Jameson looks down to see Max staring up at him. Jameson finally gets the hint. He walks to Caroline's bedside, drops on one knee, and, taking her hand in his, kisses it ever so softly. The curling of her fingers around his is his undoing. Pent-up fear, frustration, and remorse escapes his eyes as he presses his lips harder into the palm of her hand.

Caroline runs her fingers through his hair, not able to keep her hands off him another moment. She slides her hand down his temples to his cheek as he looks up at her. They both stare at one another. Caroline's lips form a soft smile as Max walks to her bedside and licks their linked hands, breaking the spell between them.

"Thank you for finding Max. How can I ever repay you?"

"You can marry me and give me, Barkley, Lucy, Abraham, and Max a forever home with a forever family."

The romanticism of the moment is too much for Kelly. Her wails can be heard down the halls of the hospital. Bianca and Meredith pull Kelly tightly to them, stifling her sobs that killed the intimate moment.

"We are a package deal," Caroline bargains with Jameson.

Jameson sits on the side of the bed, taking Caroline in his arms. "Fine with me. Barkley will love having Max to play with. Besides, what's one more dog when you already have three?"

"I'm not talking about Max." Caroline motions her head toward her three friends. "I am talking about them."

Jameson wearily looks at the three sobbing friends and reconsiders. "You drive a hard bargain, Captain McKenzie. Max, do we have a deal?"

Max jumps up on the bed, stretching out between Caroline and Jameson, rolling onto his back for some tummy rubbing. Caroline scrambles with her arms for the sheet as Max's movement strips her of the blanket covering her absent limb. Jameson gently grasps her wrists, holding her eyes within his. Caroline can see what she had only seen before from her canine companions, unconditional love. The loss of her leg did not cause her to feel less of a woman with Jameson. He made her feel whole. He made her feel enough.

Caroline, Jameson, and Max spend the evening alone in the small hospital room. Wrapped in each other's arms, Jameson relates the events of the weeks following the explosion, the ones Caroline does not remember.

"Your parents were notified first then they called Bianca. Your friends knew," Jameson swallows his next words—if you survive—"the first thing you would want to know was how Max was doing. They also figured you would move hell or high water to get back to Afghanistan to find him. So they elicited my help in finding Max and bringing him to the States while they helped in your recovery."

After the shock of hearing about Caroline's critical condition, Jameson wanted to leave immediately for Afghanistan. Her parents explained to him that she would not be allowed visitors until she was stable enough to be moved to Landstuhl in Germany. Since waiting would be hell for him, Kelly, Meredith, and Bianca gave him an outlet for his remorse and desolation: finding Max.

Jameson started with the military, calling Fort Bragg, which was his first rejection. The multiple rejections mounted as each higher-ranking officer explained the military does not condone adoption of animals by personnel on duty in a foreign country. As much as Jameson hated the overwhelming dismissals, he understood the premise, but he was not to be deterred. After weeks of rejection, Jameson had decided to find Max on his own.

Researching how he could possibly go to Afghanistan himself to track down Max, he stumbled upon Nowzad's website. Nowzad, an organization that rescues animals from various parts of the world, helps reunite these animals with their forever friend. Their website described the lifeline these animals provided to the military personnel while away from home, being as much as a salvation to them as they are to the animal. These animals allowed soldiers and marines a respite from war and moments of peace, home, and love. Not finding Max wasn't an option, so Jameson contacted Nowzad.

When Jameson received the call of Caroline's transfer to Germany, he couldn't get there fast enough. He sat by Caroline's bedside, willing her to come back to him. Due to his work, Jameson had to return home after ten days at Ramstein, but only to wrap up a project and continue the search for Max. After the call from Bianca, informing Jameson Caroline was awake, Jameson handed over all the business to his family and provided no return date. He had planned Max's reunion with Caroline from the moment Nowzad informed him they had Max in their custody, just a few weeks prior. He wired all the money for Max's immunizations, his care, and his flight to Germany. With Nowzad's help, he worked out the logistics of flying a dog into another country. He convinced the hospital administration to allow the visitation and planned it all with Caroline's friends. When Nowzad notified him yesterday that Max could travel to Germany, he arranged the receipt of Max at the airport and even his and Max's flights back to the States.

"I am so sorry to hear about Marshall." Jameson held her tighter, trying to hold her heart from falling to pieces. Caroline had so much to tell Jameson, like the discovery of her past lives and the belief that her dead husband's soul from the 17th century is inside a dog…well, she doesn't want to ruin a tender moment with something he might find a little crazy, so she asks him something she has wanted to know for almost a year.

"Did you send the sizable donation with the Christmas wreath last year to the shelter?

"It wasn't me, but I wish I would have thought of it. You would surely have fallen head over heels for me then."

"Jameson? Starting a marriage off in a lie is not healthy." Caroline silently scorns her own self, once again, she is withholding information from the man who loves her.

"I promise, I had nothing to do with it. But if it means you will marry me sooner, I will take full responsibility." Jameson's smile touches Caroline's then turns into a passionate kiss.

Caroline recovers from having her world rocked from Jameson's lips and asks, "If you didn't make the donation, who do you think did? He or she had to be someone with a large amount of discretionary income."

"It could have been one person?" Jameson considers out loud. "Or," he gestures to the picture on Caroline's bedside table of herself and her three best friends, "could be several people who pooled their money together."

Caroline had never thought of her friends being responsible for keeping the shelter open. She recalls telling them about the donation while at the bar one evening. A tear surfaces, then glides down her face as she remembers the three of them quickly, and simultaneously, shouting out Jameson's name as the likely suspect, as if rehearsed.

As visiting hours come to a close, Caroline asks Jameson to call her parents in North Carolina to inform them about Max, his proposal, and her flight information for the following day.

Reaching her arm up, Caroline says, "Hand me your phone and I will type in the number."

Jameson explains he has the number because he has been in constant contact with them since their three worlds came crashing down in September. "Since we aren't keeping secrets, I have something else to tell you." Jameson stands and walks to the end of the bed, just in case Caroline does not appreciate his announcement. Max feels the tension in the room and jumps up to lie beside Caroline, laying his head on her chest. "You know the lot beside my house?" He continues after Caroline nods her head, apprehensively. "Well, I bought it and I am building a small house there."

Caroline understands why he would buy the lot beside his house; to keep anyone else from building on it, possibly obscuring his view of the lake. What she can't understand is why he would build a small house on it. Who does he know that needs a small...Caroline's mind flashes to her parents telling her they had sold their home.

"You are so cute when your mind solves a puzzle," Jameson says, hoping to butter her up so she won't be mad. "Once your parents knew

I was proposing as soon as you woke—and they seemed to believe you would say yes—they asked me about real estate in Mooresville. They want to be closer to their future grandchildren. How could I say no to that?" Jameson asks warily. "I have been meaning to purchase the lot next door anyway, and with your parents that close, we will have babysitters anytime we want."

Caroline smiles up at the man who has made all her dreams come true. "You do realize that you will also have in-laws anytime you don't want." Caroline flips his words back to him. "My parents can be somewhat smothering at times."

Jameson walks to the head of the bed, leans down to kiss her and whispers a warning against her soft lips, "You haven't seen smothering parents yet."

Jameson steps into the hall to call Jack and Gloria McKenzie, leaving Caroline alone with the snoring hound dog. She kisses Max on the top of his head and runs her nails behind his ears for a loving scratch.

"I am sorry I almost got us killed. I realize now you were trying to tell me there was a bomb. Oh God, Max, I almost lost you again." Caroline questions her use of the word "again," then she remembers Dr. Perrin's trigger theory. She lifts Max's face to hers, staring into the windows of his soul, and promises, "Michael, I will never leave you. I would die for you before I let anything separate us again." Caroline thinks she sees flashes of their lives in his eyes but she is definitely sure she hears his response.

"You would die for me; but I have lived for you."

EPILOGUE

Imagine your soul as a large, deep lake: the water still; the surface as shiny as glass. Standing on the shore, you are able to see deep down through the clear, dark water into its life-filled depths. The wind picks up; leaves and debris swirl around you before floating to the lake's surface, causing little ripples. With more leaves come more ripples. The heavier the debris, the larger and more obscuring the ripples become. You are no longer able to see your true soul.

You can't do anything about the leaves and debris. They are the karma that followed you from your previous life. You do, however, have control over the wind, which blows from your thoughts and your actions. You have choices and these choices will determine how the winds of karma will blow. No matter how many leaves or how much debris, if the winds remain calm, the past will remain on the outer perimeter of the lake. The lake's surface remains visible. Allow ego and evil to whip up a windstorm, and your soul becomes layered with past transgressions, the lake's bottom obscured from your view.

Karmic winds are silenced by inner peace, which is found by non-tainted thoughts and actions. Those that are not from your ego, selfish desires, or evil ways. Inner peace can be achieved and goes hand in hand with unconditional love for the universe and its inhabitants. With clear water, the light of your inner soul, the core of your being, can shine through to the surface.

You are given many opportunities, several lives, to filter the amount of debris threatening to clutter your lake. This is the path to enlightenment. I allowed my own selfish fears to contaminate the lake of my soul by leaving Nicolette alone to die. This choice altered the sacred path of my soul. I had to choose the best way to regain my footing on the road to nirvana. My choice: to live for someone else. Their happiness, their security, their needs and desires would be my reason for living. I would survive on unconditional love for another. But how?

First I made a vow to protect Nicolette throughout her lives. She would never again die alone. But I knew the limitations of man and its ego-based, selfish nature. So I chose the only form that could live solely for another, a worldly vessel of unconditional love, a dog. I knew I would never experience her love the same as when I was Michael, a man who could love a woman. I knew I would always be, and nothing more, her pet. What I didn't know was how much she would love me anyway.

It hasn't been easy—protecting her, I mean— especially when she was a child. Lord, the things I had to do to keep her from fatally injuring herself, like the time I fell in the pool. A curly-headed five-year-old Caroline was heading straight for the neighbor's pool. I sprinted across that yard, barking so someone would come outside. I dove my body between hers and the edge, knocking her away from the water but falling in myself. Her mother picks that time to come outside and yells at me for being in the neighbor's pool. I got a demonstrative "Bad Dog" and was forced to stay outside to dry off. Or how about the time I accidentally bit Caroline's six-year-old hand while extricating a pair of scissors during an episode of "scissor sprint."

Then there was that one time I had to lock my jaw around a horse's hind leg to keep the beast from kicking Catherine. The damn thing punted me across the barn, plus I got whipped by Catherine's dad for biting the horse's leg.

Oh, and the time Caroline learned to ride a bike. I stayed between her and the road, barking whenever she got too close to it. I even sacrificed my body, forcing her off the bike when she unsteadily veered toward the street. She would then yell at me, telling me I wouldn't be allowed to go with her anymore if I didn't quit barking and knocking her over. Like I had a choice. Then came the day she was crossing the road. She didn't see the car careening down the street, nor did the car see her. I ran right in front of the car, making him swerve in a direction away from Caroline. How we both didn't die that day, God only knows. And, of course, there was that time I had to save Catherine from the insane, rabid dog. It cost me my life, but it was either me or her. I didn't get to save Catherine from polio, the illness that took her life, but I was there, waiting on the other side so she would not feel scared or alone.

Many times, while waiting in my celestial soul, I thought of incarnating into a male form to be part of Nicolette's, sorry, Caroline's earthly world. She has so much love to give. That is why she grieves so. All the bottled-up grief, resting in her hollow chest, is love with no place to go. I have lost my chance to be with her that way. She is in love with someone else. Someone who loves her as much as I do. Someone who will take care of her. Now I am the one who grieves, my last act of love for Caroline.

ACKNOWLEDGEMENTS

The writing of this book, or any liberty we as Americans possess, would not have been possible without the vigilant protection of the United States Armed Forces. For your service to our country, I am eternally grateful. I hope my words will be a constant reminder to all Americans of your sacrifice and dedication, and what is the ultimate cost for our freedom.

This book is the byproduct from years of bereavement over the heartbreaking loss of a special soul. I know we will be together again in our next life. Until then, I will remember our time fondly for you gave me too much to forget.

This book required years of research on military life, the Iraq and Afghanistan Wars, psychology, and on the practice of hypnotherapy and past life regression. Without the following amazing authors guiding my hand, I could not have completed this book:

To Chantelle Taylor for her novel, *Battleworn – The Memoir of a Combat Medic in Afghanistan*. And to Cdr. Cheryl Lynn Ruff with Cdr. K. Sue Roper, thank you for your service and your literary work, *Ruff's War – A Navy Nurse On The Frontline In Iraq*. For her own valor and grace in telling such a moving story, a special thanks to Gayle Tzemach Lemmon for *Ashley's War*.

To Mary Elizabeth Raines for *The Laughing Cherub Guide To Past Life Regression*. And to Judy Hall for her help from her book on *Past Life Therapy*. To Jo Ana Starr, PhD, for her book on *Quantum Hypnosis Scripts*. And offering a gracious hand, Mary Lee LaBay and her books, *Past Life*

Regression—A Guide for Practitioners and *Hypnotherapy—A Client-Centered Approach*. Thank you Mary Lee for the encouragement and for talking me through the labyrinth of my mind.

A special acknowledgement to Dr. Joseph Mancini for his endless research and devotion to healing through past life regression and for giving me the courage to one day, take me my own journey to my past lives.

My most profound thanks for the lessons in psychology and the free, non-biased, often brutal, but filled with love, counseling services for my entire life. You are my soul's mate, I love you Vickie.

My life would not be as wonderfully colorful without the special friendships that have been part of this life's journey for over four decades, Rona Hatten Greene (for being CC's biggest fan and for all the beautiful sunrises) and Jamie Ferguson Curnutte (for the laughter, the road-trips, the love, and for our future duets).

I would like to express my deepest appreciation for the military guidance from Sgt. Joe Adkins, Sgt. Spencer Jett, Senior Flight Examiner Loadmaster Mark Campbell, and Captain Chris Woods.

The best part of writing this book is all the wonderful people I have met on this journey. I would like to thank them for providing me with love and moral, emotional, physical, spiritual, and technical support. Without them, I would not have been able to complete this book: Casey Bond (fairy tale author extraordinaire), Peggy Grigowski (my princess and co-conspirator), Jan Walters (my mentor and who I want to be when I grow up), Catherine Martin (the wild spirit I wish I was), Craig Wainwright (the British Titan), Greg Newson (for making me feel like an author and wanting to have my babies), Matt Stickler (the computer genius), Nicky T (for all the sage advice and encouragement for CC), and Marshall (for your Christ-centered guiding light and for the many poetic dances). I love you all.

They say a picture is worth a thousand words. It truly is when Thor Moreno with Fearless Cinema transforms an author's book and vision into cinematic excellence. Thank you Thor and Annette Duffy for creating a trailer that made my dreams come to life on screen. Thanks to the wonderful actors and actresses that breathed life into my characters: Stephanie Schneider, Klay Williams, Edward Corpus, Haley Wilson, Maddie Sell, Clare Long, Brandon Ulrich, Donald Thatcher, and Kari Leigh Bienert.

For her artistry in making an old woman presentable on paperback, a great amount of credit goes to my book-cover photographer, Bridgette Seitz of Elegant Exposure in Barboursville, WV.

It has been a pleasure working with Ken Dunn, Michael Kopp, Delaney Nelson, and Leslie Garcia at Rebel Press and GoRead.com.

The love of good friends and colleagues is the foundation of this story and I am blessed to have their support in my life. The characters in this book are an amalgam of the friendships that have entered my life and I hope you all know how much you mean to me.

An author needs at least three things: A good story, the commitment to complete it, and a great editor to fix it. Ashely E. Schwartz, who took my chaotic words and polished them so that you could actually make sense of my heart's work, is the best in the business.

Of course, authors love to describe settings that are as beautiful and vibrant as their characters. A shout out to the citizens of Asheville, North Carolina, Mooresville, N.C., and Fayetteville, WV. Land so naturally abundant with beautiful serenity, I could not imagine more perfect settings for my novel.

Thanks to you, the reader, for having enough faith in my story to take the time to accompany this author through her pain of losing someone she loved dearly. This novel has been a labor of love and the remedy for a shattered heart. I wish all your dreams are pleasant journeys of soulful healing.

How do you thank your parents for all that they have done for you? I love you so much for making me feel so special and giving me the inner courage to be me, and loving me anyway. God bless you for contributing to the fulfillment of many of my dreams for this life.

To my family for the lifelong lessons of love and faith that you have bestowed within me and upon me, you will always have my undying love. Without you, my life's story would not have been so rich and colorful. Special thanks to Pam and Buddy Smith for the seclusion my mind needed to complete this work.

A special kind of love and appreciation to my children who have been my greatest labor of love. Holly Caroline and Craig Allen, I hope you know you are my world. Jared, so glad you are part of our family and thanks for giving us our most special gift. Abilene Claire, Mamaw's special angel and God's answered prayers, you are my soul. And to my dog Abrham, I have never felt so loved. You are the message within my words.

With a soulful, heartfelt praise for the man who is the hero of my own life story. He is my protector, my closest friend, and who has truly taught me the meaning of unconditional love, my husband Mike. You are a dream come true.

CC Mack writes heart-wrenching, cross-genre, romance fiction. Her debut novel, *My Soul's Guardian,* a suspense-filled metaphysical novel, was born out of love lost. CC's other novels, in various stages of production, include inspirational and historical romance fictions that honestly embrace societal issues of their time and always incorporate elements of her love for animals.

As a professional author, CC finds joy in her dual careers: one as a registered nurse, caring for her pediatric patients, and two as an author, writing novels and poetry inspired from her heart. But her greatest joys in life are her perfect granddaughter and her children (one girl, one boy, and one dog). Her post-graduate studies include child development and honing her craft as a novelist. She is a self-proclaimed history and science nerd and loves reading books on those topics along with books from her favorite writers (you know who you are) and novels that take her breath.

CC strives to live life to the fullest which includes all outdoor activities such as hiking, watersports such as swimming and kayaking, traveling, and hanging out with friends (you know who you are).

Born in the Appalachian Mountains of West Virginia, CC Mack resides there with her lifelong love and best friend, her husband Mike, and the one who loves her unconditionally, her dog Abrham.

Follow her at ccmack.com

www.ingramcontent.com/pod-product-compliance
Lightning Source LLC
Chambersburg PA
CBHW070628100726
47907CB00007B/1898